11/03

D1396752

RED
zone

RED zone

A NOVEL BASED ON A TRUE STORY

ALAN MCTEER

GreyCore Press

McTeer, Alan.
   Red zone : a novel based on a true story / Alan
McTeer
   p. cm
   LCCN 2003105234
   ISBN 0-9671851-9-X

   1. Drug traffic—Fiction. 2. Aviation—Fiction.
3. South America—Fiction 4. Adventure stories.
I. Title.

PS3613.C5885R44 2003   813'.6
                                 QBI33-1396

*I would like to thank my publisher, Joan Schweighardt,
for her confidence in this story, and for all the hours
of hard work that have made this book possible.
Without her there would be nothing. Thank you Joan.*

EA$Y MONEY

May 28, 1990, Homestead Airport, South Florida

The airplane is a 1977 twin engine Cessna 421-C, large enough to hold seven or eight people comfortably, and, with her pressurized cabin, capable of cruising at 250 mph at 25,000 feet. I've completed enough of the preflight preparations to know she's in beautiful condition, in spite of her years. I'm standing on the wing, working Rain-X into the windshield and making small talk with the old man, when my copilot and interpreter pulls up in a gray Honda. I flew with Mario once before. He's a young Cuban raised in Miami, a bodybuilder and a karate expert. A pretty boy. Also arrogant. I acknowledge him and his driver, José, with a nod and am turning back to the windshield and the old man when I notice that there are passengers in the car. While they struggle to get out with their fat Naugahyde suitcases, Mario walks up to the wing. He's wearing a loud, flowery dress shirt and pleated pants that bag outward and then taper at the cuff. He looks like he might be going to a Miami disco. "Are we ready? These people are in a panic to go," he says, and he turns on his heel before I can answer.

I stare at the two well-dressed Colombians as they shove their suitcases through the airplane's door and then follow Mario back to the car for more. Their second load consists of cartons and Kmart shopping bags. I notice shoeboxes, toys, and corn chips protruding from some of the bags as they load them. "The deal was to deliver the airplane, not passengers," I say to the old man.

The old man's eyebrows and shoulders lift, but his expression is merely amused. "My friend," he exclaims, "what's the problem? You have lots of seats! Two more people won't make any difference. And anyway, they know the Customs agents at Cartagena. You won't have any problem."

I jump off the wing and land in front of him, bending so that we're face to face. Out of the corner of my eye I see the Colombians going by again with more bags, paper and plastic, and Mario behind them with the cooler. "How do I know what they're carrying?"

The old man's eyes twinkle behind his thick glasses. "I can't say no," he explains. "They represent the owners of the plane."

I turn aside to consider. My gaze falls on José, who is bending over the Honda's trunk, pulling the remaining parcels forward. The old man gave me $7,000 ten days ago, on the day this flight was originally scheduled to run. I've already spent most of it; my sense of obligation rises up in me like an aftertaste. The remaining $3,000 is to be given to me in Panama, our destination after picking up the owners' pilot in Cartagena. I'm counting on this final payment, but I understand how things go. Still, $7,000 is not bad for a day's work. The question is, is it enough to justify transporting guns or drug money?

"We're dead if we get a ramp check," I explain.

The old man waves his arm in the air as if to sweep away my objections. "Dalé, dalé, dalé," he says.

The Colombians, who have finished loading, join Mario behind me. All three are talking at once. "Dalé, dalé, dalé," I hear.

I don't like being rushed, especially during a preflight check on an airplane I've never flown before. But I feel confident that this plane will do another ten hours, the decisive criterion for any plane I intend to fly. "Get in," I tell them, and I begin going over the preparations in my head, trying to work out whether I've completed them all. "Dalé, dalé, dalé," the Colombians cry from the cabin. Go, go, go, the Latin response to delay regardless of its cause. I toss the Windex, the Rain-X, and the rags into the paper bag in which I've already placed my passport case. I feel ready, but it's hard to be sure because of the chaos. I pick up the bag and step into the airplane. The rags give off a nasty alcohol odor. Normally I'd stuff the bag into the nose compartment, along with my flight bag, but since I'm eager to let these Colombians know how pissed off I am, I pitch it into the cabin instead. I look up from the thwack it makes into their faces. They gape back at me resentfully, their possessions towering around them, crowding the cabin.

I join Mario in the cockpit and climb into the left seat, buckle myself in, and sweep my eyes over the dash. The layout is as pretty as any I've seen. The sight of it brings me some comfort, a sense of security. Mario is waving the checklist. As soon as he sees he has my attention, he begins to read off the engine start procedures. I begin to carry them out. The Colombians, who are watching the routine, exclaim behind us. "Let's go! Go, go!" and some other things besides. I try to shut them out. I start the left engine, check the oil pressure, the temperature, and start the right engine. All goes well; we are idling very nicely, all gauges in the green.

Outside the old man and José are standing side by side with their arms folded. Manolo, who is short and plump, looks like a cartoon character next to the tall, thin Cuban. Taxiing to the runway, I check the systems. I'm beginning to feel more confident. When I release the brakes and apply full power, the Colombians quiet down. We lift off smoothly, energetically. I'm 38 now, but the satisfaction of a smooth takeoff in a powerful airplane is no less than it was when I was 12, an air cadet, and just beginning my flight instruction in British Columbia, Canada.

After takeoff, I immediately raise the landing gear and build airspeed—a big safety factor in an aircraft as heavy as this one. At 500 feet I reduce the power from 100 percent to 90 percent, from full power to climb power. At 1,000 feet I reduce the power again to 75 percent, easing the fuel flow so as not to burn any more than is necessary. Then I level off and tell Mario to take over.

The cloud base is 200 feet above us, solid and extensive. My plan is to hold this altitude until we've passed it. The TV weather forecast earlier said the break should come somewhere near the Bahamas. Then we'll be able to climb into smoother air and relax on autopilot. In the meantime, Mario is doing fine, staying aligned on the required track. Nevertheless, I keep an eye on him, checking him each time he wanders off by a degree or two until he gets us back on course. He looks at me defiantly each time, but he makes the effort anyway.

The sky ahead of us is gray and receding into blackness, as if we are approaching the mouth of a tunnel. Above Key Marathon I turn on the weather radar and am surprised to see the size of the flashing red patches on the screen. The storm will be worse than the weather report indicated. We have the option of turning back at this point, but once we've left U.S. airspace, readmission is no longer legal for an aircraft that hasn't filed a flight plan.

The downpour begins and is almost immediately torrential. I glance at Mario. His face is tight, but I can't tell whether it's because he's scared or pissed off. "Do you want to turn back?" I ask. I have to shout over the noise of the pounding rain. I'm testing him, taunting him, almost hoping he will say yes. But he gives me a quick look and goes back to work.

The Rain-X is working fine; the water beads and flies off. I feel proud for having thought to apply it. But the pounding of the rain intensifies and my pride dwindles somewhat as I realize that the state of the windshield won't matter much if the deluge is sufficient to cause engine failure. The engines do have a limit, but who knows what it is. We reach for our life jackets and work our way into them. Mario tells the Colombians where to look for theirs, but they only stare back at him. I consider the Colombians, the bags, cartons, and suitcases piled up to the ceiling, the 300 gallons of gas we're carrying in the wings, the scant 1,000 feet between us and the black sea below. The survival raft is at the back of the cabin, buried beyond the Colombians and their fortress of acquisitions. I try to imagine getting to it with our heavy aircraft in an accelerated descent. Impossible.

The blackness turns gray as suddenly as it began, and we find ourselves breaking out into scattered conditions. Mario and I look at each other. The Colombians begin to chat, their cigarette smoke filling the cabin. I check my map and heading and am pleased to see that we're still on course, cruising along between the Bahamas and Cuba.

Once, on a similar flight, I dared to take the obvious shortcut and fly over Cuba without permission. "Everyone does it," I'd been told; typical bullshit. Less than five minutes into Cuban airspace, flying at about 8,000 feet, I found myself with two MiG-21s on either side, wing to wing—no, make that wing over wing—as if we were three old buddies out practicing formation flying. The suddenness of their appearance and the caliber of their formation-flying skills were as impressive as they were alarming. The pilot in the MiG on my right signaled for me to turn left and get the hell out of his airspace. But my copilot, a crazy Jamaican, signaled back to him that we meant to continue. There was a lot of signaling after that, maybe a full minute's worth. Then all at once the MiGs rolled off us and fell out of sight. The Jamaican showed me his teeth. "No problem, man," he said. I shrugged, unhappy with the situation, when one of the MiGs soared up in front of us, his afterburner glowing red. His exhaust hit us like a train. We reeled and spun, inverted. "No problem, man!" I shouted back at the Jamaican as I righted the airplane. Then I turned around and headed back toward the Bahamas, the quickest route out of Cuban airspace. I applied full power and lowered the nose to attain the maximum airspeed of approximately 250 mph. But the two guys in the MiGs had no intention of letting our little party break up so early. They turned away only to come back again from below, cutting in front of us at three or four times our speed. Then, turning steeply on their sides, they pulled around and disappeared. When they materialized again, they were coming from above, moving like bullets, putting on a real show. There was nothing for me to do but keep my heading and hope they were having too much fun to remember to shoot us down once we were over water.

Climbing through 1,400 feet I notice a problem. The de-ice boots, the rubber tubes on the leading edge of the wings (in which air is pumped to break up snow and ice) are inflated. Mario checks his side. Same thing. I can see where the force of the rain has torn away some of the patches sealing holes in the boots. Now the forward motion of the airplane is forcing air into them, swelling them to their maximum size. It will cost us airspeed, and speed is range. During the long climb to 25,000 feet, I estimate the maximum penalty to be a half hour added to our flying time; we will still have plenty of reserve.

Three hours and ten minutes into our flight we see Haiti. With most of her trees consumed for firewood, she looks like an abandoned barge adrift in the sea. Small thunderheads are building around her, but we're well above them, gliding through a bright blue sky. By dinnertime these rolling clouds will join together to create one monster cloud that might top 60,000 feet, filled with rain, something you don't want to mess with. But the only cloud we're likely to encounter now is the one the Colombians are generating in the cabin with their cigarettes.

The next leg of our journey will take us over 500 miles of water. I check the systems to make sure we're ready for it. Oil pressure, engine temperature, cylinder head temperature, and exhaust gas temperature all look good. I adjust our heading to compensate for the Caribbean's reliable crosswind and enter the new heading into the autopilot. Seeing everything is under control, Mario goes back into the cabin to make some sandwiches. I can hear him chatting with our passengers. I can't make out all they're saying, but it sounds cheerful enough. We take our lunch at 25,000 feet over the Caribbean—nice, very nice.

With the storm and some distance behind us, it seems senseless to continue to be angry with Mario and the Colombians, and I feel myself let it go.

One hour and 40 minutes later I sight land and realize right away that I've made a navigational error. The crosswind I calculated for just wasn't there. The Guajira isn't the best part of South America to be in. Right underneath its name on the map is "ZONA ROJO" or "RED ZONE," and there are 200 miles of restricted air space all around it. We're only 40 miles or so away from the edge of the restricted area. I mumble my favorite response to a bad situation and turn the command for the autopilot 30 degrees to the right. Still, after so many miles of water, I can't help but be relieved to know that land is nearby. To compensate for needling Mario earlier, I explain my mistake.

But the Colombians have seen land too now, and like two impatient kids in the backseat of a car, they start up again, wanting to know how much longer. Mario calculates and tells them about an hour and a half. Ten minutes go by and they ask again. I'm wondering how many times they'll ask in all when I notice the cigarette smoke in the cabin smells less like Marlboros and more like some chemical vapor. I'm in the process of checking the electrical load meter to see if there are any extreme readings when Mario's hand slams down on my shoulder. "Fire!" he cries.

I turn in time to see my paper bag going up, its blue flame dancing from side to side as if with so much to choose from it can't decide what to envelop next. Beyond the flame I see the faces of the Colombians staring back at me. They grin and shrug their shoulders like clowns waiting for some reaction to their stunt. My passport and maps are in that bag. I jerk my head to indicate the lower part of Mario's seat. "Under there," I tell him. "Get out the extinguisher and put out the fire, and tell them no more cigarettes."

While Mario is fumbling under the seat, I rifle through my recollections for some indication that I checked for the fire extinguisher earlier. But except for the voices, the dalé, dalé, dalé during my pre-flight check, I come up blank. I feel a wrenching in my gut. When Mario resurfaces, he articulates what I already know. "The holder is empty!" he cries. "It's not there! Is there another extinguisher in the plane?"

"Not that I know of." My answer disgusts me.

The cabin is rapidly filling with smoke. I force myself to think, to concentrate. How can I put out this fire? If I depressurize the cabin at this altitude, the fire can't possibly burn. I look down to check the oxygen gauge on my emergency bottle and put on the mask. I push the depressurization toggle to the off position. The switch, which was probably never used before, breaks off in my hand. Determined to depressurize the cabin nevertheless, I reach down on my left and find the pressurization dump valve lever, which is mechanically connected to a plug in the rear of the aircraft. When pulled it will open a large hole in the rear of the airplane. Like a skeptical chess player, I try to think out the sequence of events: if I pull the dumps, the pressure will fall from 7,000 feet cabin altitude to our cruising altitude of 25,000 feet. But the pressurization can't be turned off because the switch is broken. The pressurization system will try to compensate by supplying the maximum amount of air; it will blow through the cabin with tremendous force creating a powerful wind current. I think of the other negative effects of rapidly depressurizing the cabin—ruptured eardrums, bleeding eyes. This is not a great option.

I remove my hand from the dump valve and prepare for an emergency descent. I pull the power back to idle, put down the landing gear and lower the flaps to the maximum, to create drag, and point her nose toward the sea. I yell at Mario to go back and try to put out the fire. He leaps out of his seat, but with the plane in a near vertical dive, it's all he can do to stay upright. I watch the rapid reverse spinning of the altimeter. We are falling at 6,000 to 7,000 feet per minute.

When we begin to level out, I glance back and see Mario and the Colombians through the veil of smoke. Mario is pulling bags toward him, trying to put out the fire one bag at a time. The Colombians are flapping about like beached fish, fanning the flames with their jackets, making things worse.

Passing through 1,000 feet, I raise the landing gear and flaps, then call Mario forward. He appears almost immediately. "You're not going to get it out, are you?" I shout.

"No. It's getting worse," he shouts back at me, his green eyes sinking behind the tears welling up in them from the smoke.

"We're going to put her down in the water," I shout.

He stays close, waiting to receive his orders, but at about 100 feet, it becomes clear that the seas are too high. I glance at Mario. I can see he's terrified. "What are we going to do?" he screams.

"We've got to get to land," I shout. Since I know I can't make it to Cartagena, I turn south toward the Guajira of the Colombian peninsula. Meanwhile the smoke is getting worse and it smells far more toxic. My eyes are stinging. I cover one, and when the one I'm using becomes useless, I cover that one and use the other. It hardly seems to matter for all that I can see anyway with the windshield fogging up.

The Guajira's many desert runways are used almost exclusively for drug activity. Landing on any one of them without the owner's permission is the equivalent to landing in ten-foot seas. And while it may sound like a contradiction, there's also a heavy military presence there.

I continue down the coast to what I take to be Venezuela and hope I can make it to Maracaibo. But after a couple of minutes of choking and with visibility steadily decreasing, I realize we won't get that far. I begin looking for a field large enough to land in. The smoke impedes my peripheral vision and I can see little more than what's just below— and nothing below appears to resemble a field of any dimension. For four or five minutes we continue on in this way, with the fire still burning, the smoke increasing, the Colombians on the floor by the vents choking and crying out in Spanish, and Mario continually shouting, "Land it! Land it now!" I look at the side vent window on the airplane. How badly I want to open it, but I know the increased airflow will only ignite what isn't burning already. I don't know how much longer I'll be able to fly the airplane before the fire gets so hot that it melts through the tail and I lose control.

We are on the south side of the Guajira peninsula, not far from the beach. I tell Mario to strap himself into one of the cabin seats and prepare for a rough landing. He's about to carry out my order when I put out my hand to halt him. "Don't let me burn," I tell him emphatically. "Do your best to get me out of here." When I was a student the owner of the company where I rented my airplanes crashed his plane on take-off and burned to death. I had my share of nightmares about it. I feel a knot tightening in my stomach. Mario clamps his fingers around my wrist, a gesture I take to mean he intends to comply with my request.

I turn the large Cessna into the wind and drop the flaps and landing gear, readying it for what could be a rough landing. What I can see through the smoke appears to be a small field. It looks less than promising, but it'll have to do. I reduce the speed as much as possible. The beeping of the stall indicator confirms that we're almost to the point where the plane will fall out of the sky. When the indicator begins to buzz, I apply just enough power to keep it flying. With the smoke thick on the windshield, visibility and depth perception are nearly zero. I move the control column back and forth, trying to feel my way onto the field, maintaining just enough airspeed to keep her aloft until the last possible second.

The wheels touch down smoothly. The earth feels incredibly solid beneath us. I lock the brakes and pull the column back as far as I can to get the weight off the nose wheel. Otherwise any hole or soft spot in the grass will knock it off. In front of me I see what appears to have once been a road. A slight elevation in the field sends us into the air again. When we touch down on the other side, I jam on the brakes once more. Still, the speed of our deceleration seems out of proportion to the size of the field as I viewed it from above. I pull the mixtures back to fuel cutoff, shutting the engines down, and prepare myself mentally for the impact of a crash.

The tires finally dig into the surface, and after what seems like a long time, we jolt to a stop. I can only see a few feet ahead of me, and what I am seeing is a hill, small but steep faced. That we have stopped just short of it seems like a miracle. I shout to Mario, "Open the emergency door!" But when I look, I see that he's already in motion, tearing the seat out of his way.

The emergency door rips out easily in his powerful hands. Crying, "Come on, Alan, get out!" he throws the door aside and leaps out of the hole. I'm right behind him. Gasping and choking, the Colombians hurl themselves through the hole to the ground right behind us.

I suck as much of the warm humid air into my lungs as possible. It's hard not to be exhilarated. "Holy shit! I'm alive," I shout at the top of my voice.

My laughter borders on hysteria. Mario's does too. "What a landing!" he shouts between coughs. "What a landing you made!"

One of the Colombians stumbles to his feet, goes around behind the craft and pops open the door. With the air rushing in through the emergency exit, the fire gets the oxygen it needs and shoots out at once. Undaunted, the Colombian reaches in and begins pulling things out. Some of them are still burning. The light stuff is tumbled away by the wind with sparks flying everywhere. The other Colombian joins the first. Cartons topple and break open. I see a blur of toys, clothes, and price tags. "What now?" I hear Mario ask.

He's not laughing now; I'm not either. I nod. "We have a problem."

I look away from the burning plane and spot some young Indians about 70 yards off, stretching their necks to see what's happened. The Colombians, who have finally come to their senses and stopped trying to rescue their possessions, see them too. They pull out handguns. But as the Indians don't come any closer, they turn their aggression on Mario and me. I understand enough of what they're saying to know that they're very unhappy to have landed in Venezuela. "Whose fault is that?" I shout.

"You landed here," they shout back at me. They gesture toward our surroundings, their guns still in hand.

"Yes, because the airplane is on fire! Do you remember how the fire started?"

Mario translates their unbelievable response. They merely tossed a match; they were using my paper bag as an ashtray. They don't see how such an innocent act could result in our landing in Venezuela. When we reach Colombia, someone will have to pay.

Well, it isn't going to be me. My passport is gone, and Mario says his is too. The Colombians have their paperwork intact. Going to Colombia without papers in the company of two angry Colombians showing guns is not even an option. It's dusk now, not dark enough to reveal the city lights that I'm hoping will indicate Maracaibo. But I point in the direction I expect to find them and tell Mario we can make it there by morning, get ourselves a couple of passports at the British Embassy and be out of the country in two or three days. Piece of cake.

"How much money do you have?" Mario asks. "Because I don't have any."

I'm carrying $1,800 in hundreds and maybe $200 in small bills. "I've got enough to get us on an airplane out of here," I assure him.

He stares at me. Then he turns to look at the Colombians, who are engaged in a dispute of their own. "Mario," I say, "what's the alternative? We could stay here and wait for the Venezuelan police. But they'll ask us questions we won't be able to answer."

He's still uncertain. I tell him some of the warnings I've had from other pilots who had the misfortune to encounter Venezuelan police. The Colombians, in the meantime, are gathering up their belongings, preparing for the trek to Colombia. It occurs to me that they're lucky to have salvaged no more than they're capable of carrying.

Mario makes his decision, finally; I can see it register on his face. Then he shields his face from the flames that are still pouring out of the airplane and goes around to the front of the plane and retrieves our flight bags from the nose compartment. "Let's do it, man," he says, and he turns toward the beach.

PUERTO LIMÓN

The heat is nearly unbearable. The sand is soft, and though the dunes aren't all that high, they are numerous. The wind continues to blow, pelting us with sand. I note the full moon suspended over the water and the gleam it casts on the crests of the waves, but our measured pace and general dissatisfaction with the way things have gone make it impossible for me to value it for anything more than its light.

We've covered about five miles when we see two silhouettes waist deep in the waves, bending and pulling at cages or nets. Nearby them on the beach are two wheelbarrows. My position is this: we have abandoned the airplane. We know nothing about it. We don't want anyone to associate us with it. I explain this to Mario. His one-shoulder shrug indicates that he's not much interested in my position. But when I veer off to put some distance between us and the fishermen, he's right behind me.

We round a point and see some lights. They're intense, but too close together to be those of the city. We move in their direction for another five miles or so, until we're near enough to see a facility with lots of cars parked in front of it, encircled with a high fence. Thinking that it might be a military compound, we leave the beach at once and move inland, making our way, more or less, in the direction of the diffused light that I believe is Maracaibo. We find paths. We go through a small village. But even though we're moving forward, the distance between us and the glow seems to stay the same. "Why are we doing this?" Mario asks. "Why didn't we go to Colombia?" His tone is reproachful.

"Look, Mario," I reply. "You made your decision back at the airplane. If you feel you want to turn back now, go ahead. I'm going to Maracaibo. I'll get some papers and be out of here in a couple of days.

You do what you want."

The terrain is desert-like, scrubby, sandy, and full of rolling hills. We're weary and our feet burn. We're both in good physical condition, so we continue to trudge along without the need to rest. When we do stop, it's only to share some of the water I've carried from home in my bag. It's only one quart, and since I don't know how long we'll have to make it last, I take offense when I see Mario gulping from the bottle. I try to explain that we're in the desert, that even if we come across water, drinking it will probably make us sick. Mario nods and rolls his eyes as if I'm a drill sergeant trying to make things tough on him for no good reason. He continues to gulp.

We pass goats and sheep, and, unbelievably, combinations of the two. Dogs come running out of the bushes and we throw rocks at them to keep them at bay. Later we encounter more dogs, but as there are no rocks, we fake it. The dogs respond just the same. We hear a clamor in the distance, but when we turn on the flashlight, we see that it's only wild mules, eight or ten of them. We encounter more as we go along. They seem to be everywhere. Sometimes a group walks right across our path and scares the shit out of us. Another time whipping sounds startle us, but when we investigate, we find that these are only the shredded remains of plastic trash bags caught in the bushes and flapping like flags in the wind.

Occasionally, we hear a rattling coming from the high grass surrounding us. Each time I stop, Mario sighs irritably. "All right," I say to him, losing patience. "You want to keep walking? Go ahead. See what happens. If you give these snakes enough time to pick up your heat signal, they'll know that you're too big to eat and leave us alone. But if you don't, they may strike. Do you think it's worth the chance?"

The moon descends, but there are plenty of stars to give off light, and the scrubby trees seem to give off an illumination of their own. Some of the paths we take cross through small farms. We're on one of them, walking behind the farmer's adobe house, when a pig darts out of the brush. "It's a wild pig!" Mario screams. He leaps to my side. "Wild pig, man, it's a wild pig!"

The pig, which is as startled as Mario, is also no less shrill. He gets away from us as fast as he can. I jump back into the bushes and pull Mario down beside me. Then I look back to see if there's any movement from inside the little house. One light bulb is burning at its center, exposing bare walls. I'm about to get up when I remember the blisters on my feet. I open my bag and feel for extra socks and put them on over the pair that I'm already wearing. Mario sees what I'm doing and does the same. "It wasn't a wild pig," I tell him. Of course he already knows that by now, but I feel compelled to remind him just the same. "It was the farmer's pig. Now let's get the hell out of here before the farmer decides we're trying to steal his bloody pig and comes out shooting."

We bicker less after this, but only because it's too much of an effort. We're dragging our legs now, walking like two old men under the weight of a heavy load. The heat hasn't let up. It's 3:00 a.m. and still about 85 degrees Fahrenheit. If not for the 25 mph winds, we might have reached the point of exhaustion long ago. When we come to a deserted shack on the side of the dirt road we've been traveling on, we look at each other and nod. We have to rest. But for all that we exert ourselves weeding through the trash that surrounds the shack, we can find nothing to break open the lock. Lying down on the ground on the leeward side we punch our bags into pillows. It's less than comfortable. To aid my effort to actually fall asleep, I begin to think about the events that led me to working with Manolo, the old man. These are events that I think of often in the middle of the night. Often, they carry over into my dreams.

I met Manolo through a man called Raul Hernandez, an ex-drug smuggler who decided to go straight rather than wait around for the

DEA to catch up with him. Or at least that was what he told me. I liked the guy; I admired his willingness to part ways with the bad guys and the big bucks to pursue another vocation entirely. One night he came to my house and explained the form he thought his new vocation might take. "The tariff on airplanes in places like Colombia and Venezuela is very high, as much as 400 percent," he said. "So if a pilot orders an airplane that costs $100,000, he's got an additional $400,000 to pay in taxes. But, should his plane be destroyed, which happens all the time down there, he still owns the registration. So here's the deal. He gets in touch with me and tells me to find an identical airplane, or as near as possible, to the one that was destroyed. I get someone who knows all about airplanes to locate one, buy it for cash, and fly it down to a place in Miami where it can be repainted with the South American registration numbers from the destroyed airplane. We tack on our percentage to the original price and this pilot flies it down. Now the South American owner has a new airplane to replace the old one, and he saved himself a hell of a lot of money. And my pilot and I have made us a nice little profit in a short amount of time. What do you say? Do you want to be my pilot?"

I'd had my own little problems with the DEA earlier. People ask pilots for all kinds of favors. I accommodated a friend who wanted supplies transported to a remote island in the Bahamas in my Aero Commander 680 F. It turned out that these people were involved in a minor smuggling operation and I arrived at exactly the wrong time. The DEA had infiltrated their group some months before and when the bust came down of course I was arrested along with the rest of them, guilty by association. Not only was I busted, but my airplane was confiscated.

In the following months my lack of involvement became obvious to the DEA. Not having money for a big-name lawyer separated me from the rest of the group, for starters. The DEA agent, a man called

Justin Kane, made a deal with my lawyer to hold off on any charges if I made an effort to put myself in a situation where I might be able to infiltrate one of the South American smuggling factions that was bringing coke into the U.S. This deal didn't sit well with me at all. I was innocent and now I was being asked to put my life in danger to avoid an expensive court hearing that would only prove something that everyone already knew—that I was innocent. But I told Kane I'd try because, really, what choice did I have?

Ferrying airplanes for Hernandez seemed just the thing to keep me in the loop enough to satisfy my commitment to Kane. I didn't think it likely that I would really find myself in a situation of any complexity, but it would look like I was trying and that was as far as I wanted this to go. In the meantime, I might make myself enough money to purchase an airplane to replace the one I'd lost to the U.S. government. Then I could retire into obscurity, into the workaday world where I had been a pilot flying freight throughout the Caribbean—a labor of love from which I had wandered. But as it turned out, Hernandez didn't have the contacts in South America to provide us with any work. So he hooked up with a middleman, the old man, Manolo, who would put together our first deal.

Manolo, who has a residence in Venezuela as well as one in Miami, knew someone who needed a 421 Cessna. I found one for sale in Nebraska for $72,000. Manolo and Hernandez and I flew up to Lincoln on an airliner to have a look. We were shocked. The airplane was beautiful. The engines, which I'd been told over the phone had some time on them, looked like new and ran perfectly. The airplane should have sold for about $140,000. We bought it on the spot and flew it directly to the paint shop to have the American numbers removed and replaced with Venezuelan ones. When it was ready, Manolo told me to fly it down to Venezuela.

Hernandez asked me to wait a few days before coming back, to stay with the airplane until I received confirmation that Manolo had given him the $100,000 that was our profit.

I got the confirmation and returned on a commercial airliner. As soon as I was home, I phoned Hernandez's beeper number to find out when I could pick up my share of the money, 50 grand. He called me back a few minutes later. "Something terrible happened," he exclaimed. "I have to see you right away."

Rather than ask on the phone, I took down the address of his new apartment in South Miami and drove right over from my home in Fort Lauderdale. When I arrived, he told me he'd moved because his previous apartment had been robbed. He said he'd put our money, the $100,000, into the wall in his bedroom closet and that someone had broken into his apartment and found the hiding spot and robbed us. "That's an incredible story," I said "Do you really expect me to believe this? How stupid do you think I am?"

"No, no, no," he countered. "You're my friend, my brother. I swear to you, I was robbed."

It didn't matter whether I believed him or not; I was still out a lot of money. Everybody in the neighborhood knew about Raul's past and that he was still a con man who usually had a lot of cash around him, so it was very possible that someone did rob him.

Not willing to start a war over this, I decided to give him the benefit of the doubt. I actually started to believe that the money had been stolen and there was nothing I could do but forget it. But in the weeks that followed, whenever I repeated the story to any of our mutual acquaintances, their response was a gush of laughter. "That's Raul Hernandez," they all said. "He played you for a fool. That's why he had to get out of the smuggling business. He crossed too many of his friends. He doesn't have any left who would trust him." What an idiot I was to trust this man with my money!

A lot of good this information did me. I was still out my money.

The more I thought about it, the more pissed off I got. In the beginning I couldn't sleep at night. But after a while, thinking about what happened actually began to put me to sleep. There were no more details to add to the story, nothing new to punch around in my head. The sheer repetition of the few facts I had became my sedative. The only good part was that I no longer worked for Hernandez. It should have ended there. But I still didn't have the money to buy the airplane to replace my impounded Aero Commander.

The DEA agent was still convinced that I might get a job offer in South America if I stuck with it long enough. So when Manolo got in touch with me and asked me to ferry planes for him, I agreed. The money he was prepared to pay was nowhere near what Hernandez had promised, but at least he could pay. And we got along fine. On the one trip I did for him he didn't try to cross me in any way.

I begin to dream, and in my dream I'm still walking and wondering how I can be dreaming when I feel myself awake. I'm just slipping into a deeper place when I feel something crawling on my back. I leap into the air screaming and slapping at my back with both hands. Mario opens his eyes and is immediately on his feet, screaming too. For 30 seconds we shriek and jump like two crazies. When we look at each other, we begin to laugh. I sweep my hand over my back one last time. Nothing there. We laugh harder. Mario says, "Hey, let's get the hell out of here."

It's 4:00 a.m. now. As we walk, I gaze toward the east, waiting for the first indication that the sun is on the rise, thinking this new day will find us setting our course for home. We hear a truck coming behind us and dive off the long straight road we've been walking on to hide in the bushes. It takes forever for the truck to finally pass. And then we see that it's only a peasant farmer driving slowly in an old, beat-up Toyota pickup.

We begin to walk again, finally closing in on the glow. But when the light that I've been waiting for appears on the horizon, it becomes apparent that the town ahead of us is far too small to be Maracaibo. It's nothing but another village, somewhat larger than the others. In the distance we see men sitting in the shadows of their porches in their underwear. I begin to feel exposed, unprotected. I find myself looking and listening for helicopters or military vehicles. My feeling of vulnerability increases when I glance at Mario. I'd forgotten about his disco outfit. It seemed ridiculous enough in the airplane, but here, at 4:30 in the morning, in some small city in Venezuela where the peasants are sitting around in their underwear, it looks downright dangerous.

I suggest to Mario that he should change his clothes as soon as possible. He looks down at his shirt and then up at me as if at last I have truly insulted him. But before he can comment we see our first policeman, and he's coming our way. We lower our heads, allowing our hats to cover our faces, and we walk past him. I whisper to Mario, "If anyone speaks to us, you do the talking. If there's any problem, bribe them. We have U.S. dollars. Anything goes wrong, anything at all, offer money."

We pass more peasants, some walking with mules. They don't pay any more attention to us than the policeman did. Now that I've spent the night walking, I can easily understand why the peasants are up so early. Already the heat is intensifying. In a few hours it will be prohibitive. I'm hoping we'll reach Maracaibo before that.

The houses we pass, adobe and straw shacks, are right on the road. As we get farther into the city, there are some sand-brick houses with tin roofs. These give way to shops, and then, at the center of the city, a plaza. There are taxis here, but there are also some soldiers. We pass the first few without incident and I begin to relax. Two drunks advance from an alley and say something to Mario that I can't make out. When I ask him what they said, he answers, "Nothing, nothing." He is staring ahead, testy again.

Some miles out of the village we see a sign for Maracaibo, but without any numbers to indicate its distance. A taxi goes by and I try to wave the driver down. He has no passengers, but still he doesn't stop for us. Another taxi goes by and the same thing happens. When we spot another peasant, I tell Mario to ask him what's going on. The peasant explains that passengers are picked up only in the village, in the plaza.

This is not a satisfying response. While I'm trying to decide what to do about it, a truck goes by, full of soldiers heading for the village. Though they stare at us indifferently, I feel a sense of panic rising up in me, mingling with the fatigue. This is not a safe place. We have to get to Maracaibo. I look at Mario. His weariness shows in his face. Beyond him I see more peasants, leaning against a fence, talking casually, their eyes fixed in our direction. They don't look unfriendly. I suggest to Mario that we go over and see if we can get more information from them.

They're very friendly, very eager to talk to two gringo strangers, but they give us the same bad news; we will have to go back to the village to get a cab. Something occurs to me and I tell Mario to ask, very casually, if there are any roadblocks between here and Maracaibo. Mario talks to them for a minute .

"Did you ask them?" I persist. I know enough Spanish to know that he hasn't fully explained my question. But Mario ignores me. The spokesman says something to him that I don't get. "You have to translate for me. I need to know what's going on," I say. He gives me his one-shoulder shrug. "Mario, ask if there are roadblocks."

Now he obliges me, but grudgingly. "No," he says. "There aren't any roadblocks."

"Do you know what I mean by roadblocks?" I continue to probe him. "They're not the same as the roadblocks we have at home. There are those too of course, but I'm talking about the permanent roadblocks where they stop all the cars and buses. Is that what you asked about?"

"Yeah, yeah, yeah," is the only response I can get from him. He turns back to the peasants to ask them if they know how far it is to Maracaibo. They don't. They think it may be about one hour by car. That's all they can tell us.

On the way back to the village, Mario changes into a plain white T-shirt. With his flashy pants, he still looks questionable, but not as bad as before. A liquor store is just opening. I spent some time in Bolivia a few years ago and I know that South American liquor stores are generally eager to exchange U.S. dollars for the local currency—in this case, Bolivars. Before entering, I give Mario some money and remind him again that he should do the talking. I ask him to listen carefully to their dialect and try to speak as they do and find out the best way to Maracaibo. I ask him to pick up a few beers for me and whatever he wants for himself and to exchange as much money as he can.

We're lucky. Mario is able to exchange $20 for beer and soda and some Bolivars. "What did he say was the best way to get to Maracaibo?" I ask when we're outside again.

Mario shrugs and admits he forgot to ask. I send him in again. He returns in a moment, chuckling. There's a bus coming up the road, and he cocks his head to indicate it. "The bus is the best way, Alan," he says, "and here it comes."

This is the most enthusiasm Mario has shown in some time. It's clear that he wants to get on this bus. But as I turn again to look at it, I'm not so sure it's the best idea. I feel I need to collect my thoughts before jumping onto the colorful machine that's slowing down before us. "I think we need to check things out," I say. "Let's not move so fast. Let's make sure there are no problems."

"There's no problem. I asked the guy in the liquor store. It's okay!" Mario insists.

The bus stops. Mario looks at me anxiously. It's dalé, dalé, dalé, all over again. "It's not that easy, Mario," I say. "This could be a bad idea."

The door opens and already the driver is looking down at us as if we're holding him up. Beyond him I glimpse legs, sprawled legs that make me think that the riders they belong to must be content and enjoying the ride. A new wave of fatigue washes over me. I climb onto the bus like a man in a dream, and while Mario pays the driver, I look for a place to sit. But the seats are all taken—every last one. It seems like a cruel trick. We stand on the stairs as the bus takes off, staring at the other passengers. "Better than walking," Mario says. I look at him. He's smiling.

Once we leave the village, the bus begins to whip down the road at 70 mph. The faster the better. I want nothing more than to reach Maracaibo. The road is straight and parallel to the beach. We pass more trash bag pennants clinging to the shrubs, and now with the light, I note that some are blue, a color I didn't know they came in. They dwindle when the brush does. Then we begin to see peasants working the salt ponds.

"What's that?" Mario asks. He's never seen a salt pond before. I explain that when the tide goes out, some water is left behind. When the water evaporates, the salt is left. The peasants gather the salt to sell. I point out the hills of white salt. Some are four feet high. They glisten in the sun like small glaciers.

We're discussing our situation when the bus begins to slow down. I look ahead and see a sign for Puerto Limón. Beyond it I see the bridge itself, and at the end of the bridge, between two small concrete buildings, the roadblock.

My body stiffens. My thoughts collide and tumble over one another. We creep over the bridge and come to a full stop. The driver opens the door and Mario and I step out. We linger by the bus and let the other passengers file past us. "We've got to play it cool," I whisper.

Mario is staring ahead with his eyes wide open. I know he's frightened—we both are—but it makes me nervous to see how blatantly his face reflects his fear. "I think we should split up," I add. "You don't know me, and I don't know you. Anything happens, we're tourists and we lost our papers. They were stolen."

He nods. We separate and merge with the crowd. Afraid to focus on any one thing or person in particular, I sweep my eyes over everything. I see swamp below, barbed wire, concrete, rifles, military people, Customs people, and Immigration people… This doesn't look good. I notice the young woman walking just ahead of me. She's carrying a small child. I catch up with her, hoping it will look like we're together. "What a nice baby!" I say in my best Spanish. I make myself smile.

She acknowledges my compliment and goes on to say more, but I hear a whistle, and, mindlessly, I look away from her to see a soldier motioning to me. He's sitting, looking bored, fat and lazy. I cock my head toward the woman's words and pretend I haven't noticed him. But the Indian walking behind me decides to help me out. "Hey, Mister," he says. "The guard wants to talk to you. He wants you to go over to him."

As if on cue, the people walking near me disperse. The soldier lumbers to his feet. He has so many layers of fat that his stomach looks like a stairway leading to his chin. "Where are your papers?" he asks. When I hesitate, he adds, "I want to see them, now."

"They're in my bag," I answer.

A smile appears in the folds of his face. "Only a gringo would be stupid enough to leave his papers with his bag," he says softly, through his teeth.

"I'll get them; they're on the bus," I assure him, and I turn towards the bus.

The driver sees me coming and hands me my bag. My heart is racing. I look left and right and see only the swamp and the barbed wire.

This is the perfect place for a roadblock; there's nowhere to escape. I feel utterly doomed. "Show me your papers," the guard says again when I return to him.

I open my bag. I don't have to try very hard to look agitated. "They're gone," I cry. "They were in my passport case. Someone's stolen my passport case!"

"Where are you coming from?"

"Colombia," I lie.

The Immigration people are watching. When the soldier jerks his head towards them, they rise in unison, like separate parts of the same body. While the soldier explains the situation, I turn to them, probing their faces for some sign of sympathy. "Someone must have taken my papers," I explain. "I had them when I came into Venezuela this morning from Colombia on the other bus."

They raise their eyebrows and cock their heads. A few grin. I can see that there are no takers among them. I look aside, trying to decide what to do next, and see Mario approaching. I can hardly believe it! What a fool! He could have gotten through. With his white T-shirt and his Latin looks, no one would have bothered him. I feel angry with him for being such a fool. I also feel an overwhelming tenderness. "What's going on? Can I help?" he asks.

The Immigration people swing their faces in his direction. "Who are you? Where are your papers?" one asks.

Mario goes back to the bus, gets his bag, opens it and exclaims. No papers! His must have been stolen too. His expression is convincing. It's as if he's reconsidered and decided that this is all a joke. I'm impressed and appalled simultaneously. But the Immigration people don't share his sense of humor. They usher us into the smaller of the two concrete buildings and put us into handcuffs. Our charge is Indocumentato, without documents.

The room is tiny, maybe twelve by five. There's a desk, a few chairs, one door, some windows high up, and a water cooler in one corner. The heat is stifling. Our clothes are wet with perspiration. We stink. We're nearly senseless with fatigue and confusion. The Venezuelans question us. We stick to our story. We're tourists. We've come into Venezuela from Colombia. Our papers have been stolen.

They go through our pockets and find our wallets. They remove our identification and our money—or, in my case, all of my money except for the $400 I have hidden away in my wallet's secret compartment. "Alan Richards," one of the officers reads. I nod. They return our wallets to us and place our IDs in a folder. They leave the folder on the desk and go out.

I go to the desk and retrieve my ID. Then I go to the water cooler and get a drink. Mario stares at the folder as if he'd like to get his ID back too, but then he glances at the closed door and changes his mind. He has a drink instead. We sit for a while. Then we get more water. A man comes in, straight and tall in his blue uniform. There is an urgency about his gestures that makes me think he must be the boss of the Immigration people, or the DAS, as they are called. "You're from the airplane," he states as he looms over us.

"What airplane?" I ask innocently, over the surge of blood pounding in my ears. "We don't know anything about an airplane. We came here by bus."

"Don't play with me, Gringo," he advises, emphasizing each word. "If you admit you're from the airplane, I might be able to help you…to make things easier for you. But to do this, you must tell me right now that you're from the plane. Do you have any idea how much trouble you're in?"

"But we don't know anything about any airplane," I answer quickly. "We had our passports stolen when we were on the bus, that's all. I'm Canadian. I'd like you to contact the British Embassy; I'm registered with them. It's important that they learn that I'm here without papers. They'll pay for this information." I hope this makes him think that there's money involved.

He snorts a disgusted laugh and walks out. Another man comes in. He's black, tall, and thin. His brown uniform is impeccable, the creases in his pants as rigid as the scowl on his face. Pure military. He looks us over and nods slowly. It's clear to me immediately that he wants us, that he's hungry for our hides. And I know I'm right when the Immigration people come in behind him and explain that we are their prisoners. An argument ensues. I can't tell if it's that their Spanish has speeded up or my ability to understand has slowed down, but I don't get much of it. I take advantage of the commotion to go over our story again with Mario. We're tourists. We met in Colombia and got on the bus together. Someone stole our papers.

The group takes their argument outside the door and a DAS agent we haven't seen before comes in, smiling. "Do you need some water?" he asks pleasantly. We both say yes and watch while he goes to the cooler and gets it for us. While we drink, he asks for our names and addresses. He has our money. He counts it out, has us sign a receipt for it, and returns it to us. I tell him he can have it back again if he gets us to Maracaibo. His smile vanishes for a moment so that I guess he's considering. Then his smile returns and he tells us that we'll be better off if we admit we're from the airplane.

"We're not," we answer together—cute, considering the circumstances.

He throws his hands out. "You had your chance," he warns us. "I have no choice but to turn you over to the Guardia Nacional."

Mario's eyes enlarge. His natural arrogance is giving way again. "And what will happen to us then?" he asks in the voice of a ten-year-old.

"Nothing much," the agent says. "They'll take you out to the airplane and fingerprint you. If your prints match the ones in the plane, they'll charge you."

Mario's lips quiver. "So then, when they don't find our prints they'll let us go," he explains to me in English.

I nod. When we left, the plane was burning good. I doubt they'll find any prints. The DAS agent talks to us a little longer, imparting hints as to how we should handle ourselves with the Guardia Nacional. When he leaves, Mario and I discuss our options and decide we're still better off sticking to our story. As if the repetition will make it true, we repeat it over to each other again. In fact, I'm so tired and confused that I'm on the verge of believing it myself. But then the door flies open and the pistols and rifles I see send me plummeting right back to reality.

"Quien es el piloto? Quien es el piloto?" the men shout. Who's the pilot? Before we can formulate a response, they begin to strike us with their pistols. I try to block the blows to my head with my cuffed hands, but most hit home anyway. My head responds with thumps, throbs, and shrieks. I can hardly think. For a moment I don't know where I am.

"Who's the pilot?" Mario screams. "We came by bus. We didn't come by plane!" The DAS agent, the smiler, appears behind the thugs from the Guardia Nacional. "You didn't say this was going to happen," Mario charges. "You said they would take our fingerprints and check us out. They're saying we're guilty!"

Mario's insolence gets him a few more blows on the head. The smiler screams, "You can't do that here!" The Guardia Nacional scream back at him. The guy nearest to me screams, "Who's the pilot?" again, and when I open my mouth to answer, I am hit again too. We're all screaming. When I see the blood trickling down the side of Mario's head, I become aware of the dripping sensation on my own scalp and scream louder. "You can't do this! Stop! What the hell are you people doing?" I shout in English.

Someone grabs my shoulders and pulls me to my feet. Someone else punches me in the face. I feel my wallet being yanked from my pocket and then they punch me again. My wallet is returned. I'm lifted, shoved, thrown, airborne. I land on my knees outdoors and glimpse a pickup truck. I'm pulled to the wall of the building and pushed up against it. When I catch my breath, I find there's a rifle under my chin. I avert my head and see Mario in a comparable position. "Explain to them," I groan.

He opens his mouth to oblige me, but his words are met with a fist. The Guardia Nacional colonel—Salinas, I hear the others calling him—shouts an order. The rifles retreat. Mario and I are lifted again and thrown headfirst into the back of the truck. Five Guardia Nacional climb in, stepping over us as carelessly as if we were bags of grain, and settle themselves, one at each corner and one in the center. They are still shouting, still demanding answers. "I don't understand," I stammer back at them. "I don't understand what you're saying!"

In fact, I don't. My knowledge of Spanish is only passable under the best of circumstances. Too much is happening too fast now. I'm scared and I ache all over. Their words are shadows compared to my pain; I find it impossible to differentiate between them. But my ignorance serves me well. For all that I am hit with something, a shovel or a piece of steel piping, each time I voice it, Mario, who does understand and who is, therefore, questioned more intently, is hit harder and more often. Or maybe they hit him more because they can, because their shovels and pipes bounce back from his chest and arms like sticks on rocks.

As we move along, the Guardia Nacional tire of using their shovels on us; apparently they realize that they'll never get in a really good swing in such cramped quarters. They pick up our bags instead and dump our belongings out in the truck bed. They find our extra T-shirts and wrap them around their fists. Now, with their improvised gloves, they go at us again. We twist our bodies and block their punches as best we can, but it doesn't do much good. One of them, seeing how well Mario takes his punches, opts for an alternative strategy. Using both feet, he kicks Mario hard in the chest, a very professional shot. I cringe, thinking that Mario's ribs must be broken, and hold my breath waiting to hear him cry out. But he doesn't. A second of silence passes, and then he breathes out from his mouth. It sounds like a gust of wind.

It doesn't take very long at all for us to reach the field where the airplane is. We drive right up to it. It seems to me that much time has passed since we abandoned the plane...weeks, months. There are soldiers all around, maybe 50 of them, all with rifles and other combat gear. There are also some men in plain clothes. Salinas, the colonel, gets out from the front of the truck to confer with these plainclothes men. Then he gives an order and the soldiers get into their trucks and retreat. We are left alone with Salinas and the nasty-looking men in plain clothes.

I've never seen such mean-looking men before. Their faces are distinct, but the meanness is so prevalent in all of them that it seems to blur their features. They drag me out of the truck. They jump in on Mario, uncuff his hands, and cuff them again behind him so that now he is completely defenseless. As I am being dragged away, I see one of them hitting Mario with a steel pipe while another kicks him in the chest. Amazingly, Mario makes no response. He keeps his eyes averted as if he doesn't care to know what's coming next. "Please! Enough! Leave him alone," I scream. "I'll tell you whatever you need to know. Please leave him alone."

The meanest of these boys is about five feet nine inches, 220 pounds. He has a black mustache and is very Mexican looking. "You are in no position to negotiate or make demands," he growls. Then he pounds me. I'm pushed and kicked by the others for several seconds, and then I find myself at Salinas's feet, near the airplane's wing. The man by Salinas's side is skinny, older, gray, but just as mean looking as the others. He accuses me of flying drugs *into* Venezuela. In the midst of all this misery, the accusation seems comical. I can't help myself; I laugh. "Who flies drugs *into* Venezuela?" I ask. "Nobody flies drugs into Venezuela!" They hit me, two or three punches, not hard, but enough to let me know I've responded incorrectly. As they pull me to my feet again, I notice a gas can on the ground, and then Mario being dragged over to the door of the airplane. One of the nasty boys grabs hold of his hair and pulls his head back. Another hits him with his pistol. "Talk, Gringo! Talk!" These are a few of the words I can understand.

Mario doesn't talk. I can't tell if it's because the beating has left him senseless or if his natural arrogance is at work again. Salinas calls out an order to get Mario ready. The old guy explains to me that Mario and I will have until the count of five to admit we're from the airplane. At five, if we haven't talked, they'll blow Mario's brains out. And after that it won't matter what I say. When I look away from him, I see the pistol being cocked at the back of Mario's head, a 9mm.

Salinas, who's also looking at Mario, tilts his head as if considering something. "Turn him," he tells his men. "Turn him so the brains go into the field and not onto the airplane steps. We will still have to carry the bodies in before we burn it and I don't want to get blood on my shoes."

As I jerk my head toward the gas can, Mario cries out, "Kill me! Go ahead and kill me!"

I begin to scream insanely. "Call the DEA, the FBI, call the Canadian government. They'll tell you who we are."

"You're not in Canada now," the old guy yells back. "You're not in the United States. This is our country. We do things our way here." He punches me hard, sending me to the ground. I look around for others, for the soldiers, for help, but there's no one in sight. No one is going to save us. No one is ever going to know. I don't even realize that Salinas is counting until I hear him say "four."

"Wait!" I shout, and I pull myself to my feet. I try to look at Mario, to see how he's doing, but I can't manage to turn my head that far. The silence is awful, unbearable. I have never felt such a silence before. "I'll tell you whatever you want to know," I say clearly, slowly. "What do you want to know?"

Salinas steps forward. "You're from this airplane, aren't you?"

"Yes," I answer, and someone hits me in the face with a pistol. With my eyes closed against the smarting, I begin to sink again. I hit the ground with a thud but feel myself sinking further. I want to keep going, all the way down to oblivion. I feel like the power to do so is just within my reach, but someone kicks me hard in the back and then I feel myself rising back up into the pain. "We had to land," I stammer. "The airplane was on fire. You can see that we had to land. We had no choice."

"Where did the other two go?" Salinas asks.

I recall the Indians who witnessed our landing. "To Colombia," I mumble.

"You came to buy drugs, didn't you?" Salinas yells.

"No…," I begin. But it must be the wrong answer because I'm hit in the head, grabbed, pulled along the ground, dragged towards Mario, and pulled to my feet again, forced to look at him, at the gun pointing at his head.

"You came to buy drugs," Salinas yells again, but now it is more a statement than a question.

"We didn't come to buy drugs," I explain. "First you wanted me to say we came to deliver drugs. Now you're telling me we came to buy them."

I wait to be struck. It doesn't matter anymore. One more punch or pistol whipping won't make much difference. I wait, but it doesn't come.

Salinas says, "You came to buy drugs, didn't you?"

I shake my head, sorry that I can't accommodate him. "No," I say.

He turns to the old guy. "Start counting."

"Okay. Enough," I say quickly. "You want me to say I came to buy drugs? Okay, then I came to buy drugs."

There's a silence, as if the thugs are waiting to see whether I'll try to retract my words. Then Salinas smiles. He's gotten what he wanted without having to desecrate the airplane with blood and brains. Beyond him I see the gun receding from the back of Mario's head. Then Mario is dragged forward, away from the airplane's door. They speak to him, rapidly, using phrases too complicated for me to fully understand. But I get enough to know that they're telling him that now that they have our confession, it cannot be altered. If we try to change it, we're dead. As long as we're held within the prison system, they will have easy access to us. Mario nods. He's in complete agreement.

Mario and I are brought to the door of the airplane. I find myself peering in. Although it's well charred, it still appears to be structurally sound. The old guy enters, begins to grope around in the debris. "Where's the money?" he asks.

I want to laugh, but my face hurts too much. They must know there isn't any money in the airplane. Anything that wasn't bolted down is gone now, and some of what was too. The Indians again.

Mario is saying to Salinas, "It's a game of cat and mouse you play here." Salinas smiles and tips his head as if he is pleased that Mario should notice. "Only problem is, we're the mice," Mario adds. "We're not your enemies. We want to cooperate with you."

"How much money do you have?" Salinas asks.

"You've taken all our money," Mario answers.

Salinas's smile falls off at once. His hand rises and he delivers a quick blow to the side of Mario's head. "We haven't touched your money," he shouts. "Look in your pockets. If you've lost your money, that's your fault." Then he smiles again.

Mario and I nod eagerly. It's clear enough: if we lost our money, it's our fault.

The old guy comes out of the airplane and asks us some more questions, simple things like, "Where did you bury the money?"

I try to explain to him once and for all. "This isn't a smuggling airplane. They use Navajos, Senecas, and Turboprops for flying drugs," I say. "The Cessna 421 is definitely not a drug plane. It can't carry that kind of weight."

We hear a car and look up. Military people get out, majors, generals, colonels, who knows? They walk around the airplane looking at everything, saying little. More and more plainclothes men arrive on the scene. The field is beginning to look like a parking lot. Some of the men have cameras. Others have questions for our captors. "Yes, I got their confession," Salinas brags. He turns to the old guy. "They admitted they're from the plane," he says.

"Yeah," the old guy confirms. "They're drug smugglers. They admitted everything."

The soldiers return and form a perimeter around the airplane. We're on display for a while—the drug smugglers. Then a truck with more soldiers arrives and we're put into it. These guys are all very young, all carrying 7.62 mm rifles. Some have side arms and full combat gear. I recall the truck full of soldiers that passed us earlier, before the bus and the roadblock. They could be the very same guys.

We drive away with our new friends, out of the field, through the villages, back over Puerto Limón, and past the roadblock. Nobody punches us. Nobody questions us. It takes us only about 15 minutes in all to arrive at a military base. We're ushered into an air-conditioned room featuring a color TV and left alone. We sit on chairs and stare at the television. We have nothing to say to each other.

THE FIRST SIX DAYS

In the late afternoon we're taken to the commander's office and asked if there's anyone we would like to talk to. Mario answers right away. He'd like to contact the U.S. Consul in Maracaibo. I'd like to talk to my fiancée, Jenny, to let her know I'm okay. But as I don't know how many people "anyone" implies, I ask to be put in touch with the British Consul, the Canadian Ambassador, or the local DEA representative. Any one of them will do. My objective is to make sure someone in a position of authority knows I'm here. This way the Guardia Nacional can't say later I never existed.

We're taken back to our room, and while we wait for word that our calls can be put through, we eat rice and meat, both dry, on dirty plates with dirty utensils. Very appetizing, but as we haven't had solid food since the sandwiches on the airplane, we manage to get it all down. A sergeant comes in, a tall skinny guy. "Is there anyone I can phone for you?" he asks in a clandestine manner that suggests this is between him and us.

"I'd like to call Manolo," Mario says. "He's my uncle." He gives the man Manolo's Miami phone number. I can hardly believe my ears. Mario hardly knows Manolo, and since the man has a residence in Venezuela, I'm sure it's not a good idea to involve him. But there isn't a lot I can say to Mario with the sergeant standing there.

Later we're brought back to the commander's office. There's an attractive woman there with long black hair. She tells us she is the fis-cal, a word I don't understand. I can tell by Mario's glazed expression he doesn't understand either. She asks a few questions and I try to answer them, but when she sees how poor my Spanish is, she grows inpatient and conducts the first part of her interview with Mario. When I ask him what's being said, he tells me, "I think she's here to represent us, to make sure our civil rights aren't violated."

I forgive her immediately and lower my head so she can tally up my cuts and bruises. I pull up my shirt and show her the ones on my chest. Mario does the same. I look from his chest to mine and realize that I appear to be more badly beaten. He actually looks pretty good. No swelling, nothing.

"How did you come to Venezuela?" she asks.

We lower our shirts, eager to tell her. But just then Salinas marches in. "We came to buy drugs," we say in unison like robots. "We weren't able to purchase them, so we abandoned the airplane." She writes it all down.

"And the fire?" she asks, lifting one brow.

We started the fire, I tell her.

Mario looks at me. Then he turns back to her and nods his confirmation. She furrows her thick, black brows. I can see our story makes no sense to her. She's right. It's a bad story and she knows it. "But why did you land in that field?" she asks.

"To buy drugs," Mario says.

She shakes her head. "You didn't land there to buy drugs."

We ramble on, handing her more bullshit, keeping an eye on Salinas. A good man; he sees we're having trouble and comes right to our aid. We didn't come to that field to buy drugs, he explains to all of us. We came to a different spot, but our contact wasn't there, so we flew to the spot where they found the airplane. We thank him for his assistance. He's pleased to have been of help.

We're back in our room wondering what will happen next when Mario begins to think he may have made a mistake. Now he thinks fiscal may mean prosecuting attorney. Before I can bawl him out, we're dragged out again. We return to the office and are told by Salinas that our calls can now be put through.

Salinas dials the U.S. Consul first. But before he hands Mario the phone, he explains to the representative there that we're confessed drug smugglers. When Mario gets on the line, he's told by the Americans that because of his Cuban status they won't be able to assist him. We look at each other. We can't believe they're so easily duped, that they would buy Salinas's story without question. "Were there any drugs found, any money?" they might have had the decency to ask. Apparently the small details aren't of interest to them.

Salinas calls the British Consul next, and after putting in a good word for me, he hands over the phone. The man on the other end, Harry Reading, doesn't comment on the Salinas prologue. Instead he tells me he's heard all about the airplane and asks how the fire started. I tell him I was on my way to Cartagena when someone in the airplane mistook a paper bag for an ashtray. Harry laughs. "Then you were a long way off course," he tells me. He promises to investigate and see what he can do to help me out. Before we hang up, I give him Jenny's number. I ask him to call her right away and let her know I'm alive and well.

The door opens and a tall, chunky, German-looking woman struts in with a clean-shaven, thin captain who has a tape recorder in hand. Salinas begins to explain that the woman, Hilda, is the local DEA representative. But Hilda, who is too impatient to wait for him to make a proper introduction, cuts him off with a wave of her hand. "You've been here before," she declares. "This isn't the first time you've come to buy drugs. We know you've been here before."

Mario and I look at each other with astonishment. What an incredible thing for her to say! We're in no condition to assimilate all these additions to our story. This is not exactly what we were expecting from the DEA. "What are you saying?" I exclaim. "You haven't even heard our story and you're accusing us of smuggling here before?"

She ignores my interruption and begins to read us our rights. Then she breaks off in mid-sentence and whines, "You know your rights."

She continues to badger us with her fantastic accusations. I turn to Mario. I can see by the earnestness in his expression that he's waiting to get a word in. Salinas is still standing over us, but as this interview is being conducted in English, he doesn't have much to say. I shake my head. "Don't bother," I tell Mario. "She's not going to help."

When Hilda calms down, she asks for our names. We give them to her: Alan Richards and Mario Alyeo Rodriguez. Then she shifts in her chair in a way that makes me think our interview is ending. I'm determined to keep her here. I don't want the DEA representative walking away believing we're drug smugglers. "Bad things are happening," I say in a tone I hope won't alert Salinas to my intent. "Very bad things. We're told to say things that aren't true."

"You mean your confession isn't true?" she asks sarcastically.

"Not for a minute," I tell her. "Why would anyone come to Venezuela to buy drugs? Besides, what would you say if you had a gun to your head?"

She laughs. "You didn't come to Venezuela to buy drugs," she explains to me. "You were on your way to Colombia when the airplane caught on fire. We know the whole story."

"In that case, why don't you tell me what the story is and I'll agree to it. That way we can save everybody a lot of time," I say. "Your story is so stupid it's hard to believe. Why would I fly over Venezuela to get to Colombia? Was I lost? When you decide on what story we're going with, let me know. I'll memorize it."

"I feel sorry for you, Mr. Richards," she responds. "The last people who landed in Venezuela without permission spent two years going through the process before they finally got a judge to order their release. This is how the Venezuelan system works. You won't get out quickly. It's not like the United States. There's no bail. You stay in prison until you're acquitted or convicted. Do you know what's really funny? If you were in the United States, this case wouldn't even be prosecuted, but here, it's a big deal."

"But we haven't been charged with anything yet!"

"We'll see about that tomorrow," she replies. "Tomorrow morning we're all going out to the airplane. We'll get some prints. Then we'll know for sure that you two are from the plane."

Back in our room Mario and I discuss the situation. We're so tired and confused that when one of us makes a point, the other takes a long time to comment on it, and the conversation quickly becomes annoying. We agree that we should tell Hilda our original story. We're tourists. Someone stole our papers. We don't know anything about an airplane. Mario reminds me that the Guardia Nacional just might kill us if they learn we've changed our tune. "Yeah," I mumble, "that could happen." Then I run out of steam and fall asleep.

We have boiled eggs, bread and sweet black coffee for breakfast. After last night's dinner, it seems like a feast. Then we're brought to Hilda and the two captains, the intelligence people who will be gathering evidence. One of them is the skinny guy with the recorder who was with her last night. There are introductions all around and then Hilda and company depart for their helicopter while Mario and I are escorted to a large army truck.

We meet again in the field and try some small talk while the wind waves the grass back and forth. Mario and I are careful not to say anything that might associate us with the aircraft. Salinas arrives. He tells the intelligence people to go into the craft and check for fingerprints. When he moves to follow them, I say to Hilda, "What happens if our prints aren't in the airplane?"

"They will be," she replies without looking at me. "They'll be in the airplane all right." Her mind is made up.

With our personal guards right behind us, Mario and I wander toward the airplane door to see how the captains are doing. Just inside the door, I notice a melted yellow container. I pick it up and chuckle.

It's the container that once held the Rain-X. I stroll back to Hilda's side. I'm tempted to tell her about my friend the DEA agent back in Miami. But of course our affiliation has always been strictly between him, me, and my lawyer. I've never even met Justin Kane. All our communication has been over the telephone. Besides, I can see by the way she's standing that Hilda wouldn't believe me anyway. I get to thinking that maybe I can mellow her out by asking her something about herself. "Where are you from?" I say.

Without looking at me, she tells me she was born in Mexico. She must be about 45 or 46. It occurs to me that her father was probably one of the Nazis who escaped to Latin America after the war. When the intelligence people finish their work, Hilda asks in Spanish, "Did you find any prints?"

"Between the smoke damage and the Indians," the skinny captain answers, "we can't get anything."

"I'm only guessing, but I'll bet you didn't want us to hear that," I say lightly with a smile, trying to add some humor to the situation. Mario grins at me. Then he turns to show Hilda his grin. But she only glances at him and looks back at the airplane, unruffled by this glitch.

We hear a helicopter and we all look up at once. It's a Bell 206, and coming our way. When it lands, two Venezuelan Air Force pilots get out. They salute Salinas and the others and walk past us with their chests out and their heads held high. Hotshots! Hotshot pilots. We watch as they hook up the Cessna to a truck and tow it back to the part of the field where we first touched down. I assume they're planning to fly the plane to Maracaibo. I figure there must be around 60 gallons of gas left, enough fuel for the trip, yet nice and light for the short take-off. With help from the wind blowing at a constant 30 to 40 knots on her nose, they shouldn't have a problem.

The pilots order their small crew to clean the airplane inside and out, especially the windshield. Then they start the engines, and after a brief warm up, they taxi it around the field. They are revving the engines like kids at a drag race experimenting with a new car, playing roughly with these delicate motors. I can't help but think of the damage they're doing. They put the flaps down and apply full power for takeoff. I can't believe my eyes! They are fully 90 degrees, maybe 100 degrees crosswind in 30 knot winds gusting to 40! These guys are the biggest morons on the planet. Every pilot in the world knows you must take off into the wind when it's blowing this hard. The maximum allowable limit for a crosswind takeoff in this airplane is 17 knots. Right now between eight and ten grand is all that's needed to repair the damage from the fire. There's no reason to destroy her. I feel like shouting it. I don't, but I mutter something about the crosswind and how this isn't going to work. I can't help myself. Hilda glances at me. The pilots get the airplane up to 70, 75 mph ground speed. The left wing lifts. The right wing digs into the soft sand gracefully, pivoting the airplane sideways, lifting all three wheels into the air. She touches down completely sideways; the landing gear digs in and snaps off like dried twigs. She bounces up soaring sideways for at least 80 feet without her landing gear, which is still tumbling through the air, rotating leisurely like a football in a slow motion replay. Then she's down again. The propellers are still turning when the plane pounds to earth for the third time. The tremendous thrust of the propellers working at full speed pitches the plane back into the air again, at least six or seven feet. Finally the morons manage to pull the power off. When she touches down once more, it's her last; she skids along on the grass kicking up a cloud of dust. We stare in disbelief while it settles, our eyes wide and our mouths open. Then, as if the starter of a race has finally said "go" we all begin to run the 200 or so yards between us and the disaster.

The damage is incredible. The force of the propellers hitting the ground at full power has twisted the engines off their mounts, which are now just a twisted mess of aluminum. The propellers are bent back and chewed up good. Both wings are dented and twisted way past the possibility of repair. Even the fuselage going to the tail is bent with an upward curl. The pilot part of me, which right now accounts for a large percent, feels miserable about this. I feel as if I just witnessed an attack on a friend, as if I have just betrayed one by standing by. The other half of me is amused, especially when the pilots kick open the door and stroll out of the plane as though nothing has happened. One of them says to Salinas with an amazing measure of confidence, "Don't worry. We'll send some mechanics to fix it. We should be able to take it out of here tomorrow."

I look away from the pilots, astounded at what I've just heard, and into Hilda's light-colored eyes. They are flaming with excitement and anger. "I suppose I'll be blamed for this too, right, Hilda?" I ask, almost laughing.

She's still staring after the two pilots. "You won't be blamed for this," she says impatiently. Then she smiles, shrewdly. "But there's something you should know. They're taking you to Caracas tomorrow, to see if they can identify you."

I stare at the ground and try to cut through my bewilderment with logic. I can't think why any people in Caracas would be having a problem with my identity. I tell myself that Justin Kane has learned that I'm here and is trying to help me, that maybe Jenny informed the lawyer about my situation…and that he would definitely contact Kane.

Later that evening we're informed that under Venezuelan law a prisoner cannot be kept at a military base very long. How long is very long? No one seems to know. Nevertheless, the decision is made and Mario and I are taken to the local prison and put into a cell with five or six drunks. As the drunks are really drunk, our arrival has no effect on them, but the guards are very distracted indeed. We're the big drug people in their minds, and they anticipate an onslaught of other big drug people coming to rescue us. They really believe this. If they bothered to ask us, maybe we would tell them that they have nothing to fear, that there is no one coming to rescue us, that, unfortunately, we really don't have any connections. But they press their concerns on one another and don't speak to us at all.

We're just getting to know the drunks a little when a guard comes and takes us to the maximum security cell. Here it's hot, stifling, without any windows, vents, or mattresses. There are the bars and the guard beyond them, and that's it. Or so we think at first. The light dims and we see there are also cockroaches, good-sized roaches. They come out through the cracks in the walls to begin a game of tag. Then the rats come out from the holes at the bottom of the cracks, and they want to play too; they want to be IT. So does Mario. He removes his shoe and sits down in the middle of the cell. He swats at the roaches as they run from the rats. Some of the roaches he hits fly up and hit me. I'm so tired and puzzled about this identity thing that I resist the urge to join in the game. "Got him," I hear Mario exclaim, and when I open my eyes, I see him lifting one of the rats by its tail. He flings it into a corner. He goes easy on the roaches but he really lays into the rats. Even with my eyes closed I can tell the difference. When the guard comes to wake us up early the next morning, there are six dead rats in the corner, maybe 50 dead roaches distributed evenly around the cell, and Mario, asleep in the center of the cell with his shoe in his hand.

We do some paperwork at the prison and then return with our buddies from the Guardia Nacional to the military base. Hilda is there to meet us with her two friends from intelligence. They cuff me and get me ready for the trip to Caracas. Mario looks disappointed, as if he's going to miss something by staying behind.

We board a helicopter to Maracaibo, an Aerospatiale 350, a beautiful little machine. We lift off the pad, climb to about 900 feet, and fly along the coast. I finally get to see Maracaibo from the air, a big flat city on the northwest tip of the Bay of Maracaibo. In the distance I can see the oilrigs that give Venezuela its wealth. We land on a pad owned by the Guardia Nacional. A beautiful, clean landing. There are soldiers surrounding us when we get out, but only one has a gun drawn. We enter the terminal and proceed to a lounge area. Hilda and her intelligence friends ask the helicopter pilot, who is also a Guardia Nacional captain, to keep an eye on me while they purchase our tickets for the flight to Caracas.

I ask this pilot some questions about the 350. He responds by asking me if I would like to have a tour of the helicopter maintenance facility. "Sure," I say. As we are leaving the lounge area, one of the soldiers starts up. But the pilot, who is unarmed, puts his palm in his face. "Relax," he tells him. "It's okay. I've got him." And we walk on by.

"So you're the pilot from the airplane?" the captain pilot says.

"Yes," I answer.

"Do you fly helicopters too?" Yes again. "Have you ever flown in combat?"

I lift my shirt with my cuffed hands and show him a portion of the scar that runs from my rib cage to my pelvis. "I was shot down twice in Vietnam," I tell him. "This scar is the result of the second crash." Actually, the scar is the product of the operation that kept me out of Vietnam. But it's an impressive scar nonetheless. He asks if I want to see the officers' barracks. "Sure," I say again. I've got nothing else to do.

We enter the dining room. There are some officers eating there. One is with a woman, probably his wife. The pilot brings me over and introduces me. "This is the pilot from the airplane," he brags. The officer rises and reaches for one of my cuffed hands as if he's very pleased to meet me. I have to laugh to myself. Only in South America!

My buddy and I finish our tour and return to the lounge area. But Hilda still hasn't returned, so we stroll back to the maintenance facility and continue our conversation about airplanes and combat flying. I can tell he really likes me. He changes the subject and asks if I've been charged yet. I tell him I haven't, that Salinas took my confession to the general, but I'm pretty sure it won't stick.

"You entered Venezuelan airspace without permission," he reminds me regretfully.

"So what?" I say. "How long can they hold me for that?"

He shakes his head and stretches the corners of his lower lip toward his chin. "They can hold you for investigation for as long as they want. Some people who aren't charged with anything stay two, three years."

"Come on. You're kidding me."

But his lip contorts further, revealing his lower teeth, and I can see he is downright sorry for me. "How bad are the jails?" I ask.

"Not good, my friend. The prisoners fight over food, clothing. Two, three a day get killed. They have knives." He extends his left arm and taps its crook with the fingers of his right hand. "Knives this long," he tells me.

I stare at the place where he's still tapping. The length he's indicating brings a picture of a sword to mind, not a knife. "It can't be that bad," I say. "How's that possible?"

"The jails are full. Five thousand prisoners in a facility meant for 500."

"How can this be true?" I know I'm being redundant, but I can't seem to check myself.

"That's just the way it is," he says. "I feel sorry for you, my friend. I feel real sorry."

I know that what I'm about to ask him is taking a big chance, but I feel as if we have bonded as pilots, that I can trust him to some extent. "But can't I just pay some people? Isn't that how it works down here? You pay the right people and they get you out?"

He tilts his head from side to side. "Sometimes, sometimes it's possible to pay. The problem is, your case is too big. You're in the newspaper. Look."

He leads me over to a corner, to a cluttered metal desk. Sitting on top of the clutter is a newspaper, and sure enough, there I am on the front page standing near the nose of the airplane. "And there's another problem," he explains while I am still drinking in this one. "Now the airplane is in pieces."

I look at him and laugh. He nods as if to encourage me toward the part that is implied. It's easy enough, once I make the effort. "They took the airplane, confiscated the airplane, crashed the airplane. A violation of international aviation laws—unless they can justify it with a good story, and I'm sure they'll have one."

The two captains show up with an armed guard, and it's clear even before they speak that they're astounded to find the pilot conversing so casually with me. They spend a moment discussing the situation with my new friend. But since he's a captain too, they don't get very far. To bolster himself, one of the captains tells the young guard to shoot me if I try to run while they escort me back to the main terminal building. We catch up with Hilda. She has our tickets and is ready to go. But my little chat with the pilot has left my throat dry. I ask her if there's any chance of getting something to drink. "What would you like?" she asks.

"A beer," I tell her. "I could really use a beer."

"No way," she says. "We'll find you a soda."

I'm pre-boarded into a DC-9. I sit in the back beside one of the captains and watch the unshackled passengers board. They are a combination of poor people, business people, and vacationers. I spot an American couple among them. They look disgusted with each other. They sit close enough for me to hear that they are arguing about their botched-up vacation. I want to tell them they should be happy; things can get a lot worse.

We take off and before long have reached cruising altitude. We're served a snack and juice. The captains, after a short debate, decide that I'm harmless and remove my handcuffs so that I can eat. When the captain at my side gets up, Hilda takes his place. She has some questions for me. Who do I work for? What's my mission? She wants to know everything.

After all my helicopter pilot friend told me, I'm afraid I won't get another chance to tell anyone the truth. So even though I know better, I tell Hilda. I didn't come to buy drugs. I just came to deliver a plane. There is a man in Miami, a DEA agent, who might be willing to vouch for me. I give her his name. "Will you help me?" I ask bluntly.

"Can you help me?" she says, incensed. "Obviously you and the people you work for are involved with drugs!"

"No, Hilda," I sing. "It's not obvious. I just ferry airplanes. I take them from point A to point B. What happens after that is none of my affair, none of my business, and that's the truth."

She lectures me. Her reasoning goes like this: I'm a pilot; I know some Spanish; I know South America; so therefore I must be involved with drugs. A very logical woman. She warns me that the computer link-up in Caracas will confirm all this. "Then I guess we'll have to wait until Caracas," I say so as not to have to listen to her anymore.

We land clean and smooth. It occurs to me that with all my problems, it's ludicrous that I should take note of the landing. But I can't help myself. We come to a nice easy stop on a very long runway not far from the sea and taxi to the terminal. Then we—Hilda, the captains, the guard, and I—sit back and watch the other passengers exit. When they've all gone, we disembark.

At the gate we're met by soldiers with machine guns. They escort us to the waiting area in the terminal. When the car arrives, they escort us back out. I get into the back seat of a Chevy Chevelle and sit between the two captains. Nice and cozy. Hilda sits in the front with the driver.

We head south, take a turn, pay a toll, and begin to climb. Eventually we enter a tunnel. The tunnel is long and exhaust fumes hang within like a fixed fog. We come out of the tunnel and head uphill again for a long time. Then we enter a second, even longer tunnel. When we come out of this one, we're in the city of Caracas, the capital of Venezuela.

It's evening by now and Caracas is all lit up and looks enormous. It fills the valley and spreads up onto the sides of the mountains surrounding it. The military compound is located on the mountainside. It too is huge. We stop at the gate and the driver shows his ID. When we reach our destination, two guards with machine guns step forward to open the door and help me out of the car. They push me up against a wall. Hilda and the captains tell the guards to watch me while they go in and announce our arrival. When I turn to look after them, one of the guards jams his gun into my ribs. "Don't turn around," he demands.

"They told you to watch me!" I shout back in my rotten Spanish. "They didn't tell you to stick your gun into me." A discussion ensues in which they refer to me as a smart-ass gringo. I'm having the same discussion with myself and reach the same conclusion. I keep my mouth shut after that.

Five minutes later another guard appears and gives the first two an order. They take me into the building, down a flight of stairs, and into a long hall in the basement. At the end of the hall is a door. One of them opens it. Another pushes me in.

The room is small, concrete. There's a table, a couple of chairs, and an indentation, a gully along the floor that makes me think it's a drainage system—but for what? The gully leads off into a corner, and sure enough, there's a drain there. They push me into the opposite corner and tell me to sit. Two of the guards leave. The other stands at the door with his machine gun aimed at me.

For 15 minutes I stare at this young guard and his machine gun. His eyes flutter. I can tell I'm making him nervous. A colonel comes in. He's very tall, maybe 6'11", with sideburns, but bald on top. "Mr. Richards," he says, "we have a problem. We've learned that you've been operating in our country for quite a while."

I open my mouth to respond, but he tells me we'll continue our interview tomorrow, which is fine by me. He and the guard uncuff me and make me lie down face up on the table. Then they cuff each of my limbs to the table's legs, so I'm spread out. The colonel leaves. Every hour and a half another guard comes by to make sure my guard isn't dozing. But he does doze; we both do. And each time I awaken, I marvel that I'm able to sleep in this position and with this new complication on my mind.

Early in the morning, maybe four a.m., my bladder awakens me. In turn, I awaken the guard. "Can I go to the bathroom?" I ask.

"No," he says grumpily.

"I have to go pretty badly," I insist.

"Go in your pants," he says.

"I don't think the colonel would like that. I have an interview with him in a few hours," I remind him.

"The interview will take place here. You won't be leaving this room no more. You might as well do what you have to do here because you won't be leaving this room."

I assume I've misunderstood. "What do you mean by 'no more'?" I ask.

His teeth flash. "What are you, a stupid gringo? Don't you understand what's happening here?"

"No, I don't," I tell him. "I've done nothing."

"You're from the airplane. They've brought you here to talk. In this room, you will talk. In this room, everyone talks."

My state of mind is such that it's possible for me to ignore my bladder for some time. But after a couple of hours, it begins competing in earnest for my attention. For the first time since childhood, I wet my pants. I'm very angry. Nothing that's been done to me since I arrived in Venezuela angers me as much as this.

I sleep again, on and off, until another young soldier comes in and announces that it's breakfast time. The two uncuff me and hand me a plate of scrambled eggs and bread. Would a man about to be tortured receive such a breakfast? I ask myself. I decide that the guard was only putting me on, punishing me for awakening him with my bladder problems, or maybe for staring at him earlier. I half realize that I'm deceiving myself, but I'm not ready to come to terms with the alternative.

I finish my meal and am cuffed to the table again. I doze for a while longer. Late in the morning two captains come in, and before I can even get a good look at them, the black one walks up to me and slaps me across the face a few times. "Your name is Gonzalo," he shouts.

"What?"

"Your name is Gonzalo. Alfonso Gonzalo."

I bark in astonishment. "Are you crazy? Do I look like a Gonzalo?"

He lowers his voice to lend his words more gravity. "Your name is Gonzalo. I know you. You've been smuggling here before. We've met before."

"We've met in Venezuela?"

"You know it. You must admit it. Otherwise it will be very painful for you."

I stare into his unflinching eyes hoping that he'll take note of the integrity in mine, and maybe the color too.

"I am not Gonzalo. I don't know you. I've never met you before."

I see his fist coming up, and I turn my head to take it on one cheek. But he notices and adjusts his swing. I feel the force as he makes contact. My mouth fills with blood. I feel around with my tongue and discover I've lost a tooth. The next punch breaks a crown. "Don't be smart," he tells me. "You are Gonzalo."

I look to the other captain for help. "What can I say?" I ask him. "I don't know Gonzalo. I have never been to Venezuela on drug business in my life."

The black man slaps me again with an open hand. The other guy looks on without any expression. There is one big difference between these guys and Salinas and his boys. Salinas didn't really believe the things he wanted us to say. These boys do. They believe I'm Gonzalo. I have no doubt about it.

The captains leave. I breathe deeply and try to relax. About a half an hour later two different men enter the room. One is a white man with an Afro-style haircut. The other is dark, Latin. They're both slim. Neither looks particularly mean. The one with the Afro puts his face close to mine and says in broken English, "You must tell us the truth. If you don't, you will be made to suffer beyond anything you have ever known."

I stare at him. The threat doesn't sound half as bad in English as it did in Spanish. I begin to think that maybe I can trust this one. "I'm not Gonzalo," I confide.

He turns, mumbles something to the lieutenant, and in response the lieutenant quickly leaves the room. When he returns, he is carrying two sizeable black boxes, one of which is clearly a tape recorder. He places them both beside me on the table. I turn my head to look. The second black box is larger than the first. It has some electrical outlets and two rods on long wires. It looks a little like a battery charger. "What's that?" I ask the one with the Afro.

"Just something to make sure we don't overload the electricity coming out of the walls," he answers.

I look at the walls. I don't know what he's talking about. "What do you mean?"

He picks up his gadget, holds it high enough for me to see. Then he plugs it in and touches the two rod ends together. There's a flash, and not the kind you get from a 12-volt battery. It's more like a lightning bolt.

The captain and I stare at each other. There is not one grain of compassion in his eyes. I wonder how I failed to notice this before. He is all mean, all evil; I can see that now. He has never done a good deed in his entire life. He brings his black box around to the end of the table and touches one rod to my left foot, one to my handcuffs, holds them there for a split second, just enough to show me how it works. The surge of electricity is incredible. "Are you going to cooperate with us?" he asks.

My foot is still quivering. I lift my head to try and get a look at it. "Yes," I say. "I will definitely tell you anything you want."

"I want to know the names of the people you worked with when you were here working under the name Gonzalo," he says slowly, as if I might have some trouble getting it all.

I lift my face a little, try to let him see that I would gladly give him all the names if only that were possible. But as it isn't, I come back to the same response. "I've never used the name Gonzalo. I'm not Gonzalo."

This time he hits my right foot and my handcuffs. The electricity shoots through my body. I bounce, thrashing about like a fish. But something else follows: semi-consciousness. Everything is black. I'm stunned, lost, coasting in neutral. I'm alone in some dark place with a pain that is nameless.

When I return, I see the frizzy-haired captain in front of me. But I don't know who he is. I don't even know who I am. "Why are you here?" I ask.

One side of his mouth swings upward, a half-smile. "Are you ready?" he asks. "Do you know where you are?"

Things are starting to come back to me. The answer is there, on the tip of my tongue, but I have to concentrate for a while before I can verbalize it. "I'm in Caracas, Venezuela."

He nods, satisfied. "Now tell me about Gonzalo. Tell me who you worked with in Venezuela."

"I don't know Gonzalo," I mumble.

He zaps me again, immediately, this time on both legs, from one leg to the other. My muscles contract. I feel myself racing toward death. It seems an agreeable destination, but I fall just short of it. The pain, the terrible sensation, continues, and I can't tell whether the electrodes are still on me or not. I hear voices speaking in Spanish, but I can't discern a word. I don't want to. Then the voices give way to silence.

Time passes. Maybe two hours. I'm so happy to be alone, cherishing my memory as it gradually returns to me.

Her features are a blur at first, but I make an effort and bring Jenny's face into focus. Such a lovely woman; such a lovely face. Dark thick hair; pale skin; quiet eyes, a serene expression like that of a saint. I see her smile. Then I see her turn slowly toward her violin. She seems always to be turning toward her violin. How many times I have wanted to accuse her of caring more about it than me. But when I look at the thing, something about its size and shape tells me that the accusation would sound ridiculous. A grown man... A piece of wood.

In my vision, she is playing, her head high and turned, her chin on the chin rest, her white neck beautiful, like the music.

The guy with the Afro returns with the black guy from earlier. They come right up to me, punch me in the chest and stomach. "You are Gonzalo," the white one says. "Your name is Alfonso Gonzalo. You must confess. When you stop lying, we'll stop, not before."

It has taken me a long time, almost all the time they were gone, to wade through the confusion and identify myself. I am not about to give it up so easily. "Hey pal," I begin. I try to shout it, but it doesn't come off like that. I'm not even sure what language I'm speaking. "You do anything you want to me. But I still don't know Gonzalo. I am not Gonzalo."

The black captain steps up, straight-faced, and puts one electrode to my foot and the other to my groin. The pain is incredible, unbearable. There are no words for it. It's pain and something more than pain. Electricity. He removes the electrodes quickly and slaps me hard on the side of the head. When he yells, "Admit that you're Gonzalo," I hear him with only one ear.

"I don't know any Gonzalo," I croak. He hits me again, immediately, my leg and my groin. Only this time he holds the electrodes there longer. I feel myself jerking about on the hard surface of the table. I begin to gag. At first I don't know why I should be gagging, but then I realize that my tongue is in my throat. I can hear myself gagging, choking, groaning, but at the same time another part of me is rushing away from the realization that these inhuman sounds are emanating from me. I feel certain that these are the last sounds I'll ever hear. My hands are cuffed. My feet are cuffed. There is nothing I can do to get my tongue out of my throat. I'm willing to die, to get it over with. Then a feeling comes into my body; a grayness that turns to a bright light creeps up into me. I can't see any part of my body—I can't see anything—but I know my body is giving way to this light. The brightness is my friend, my ally. It enters peacefully, bringing me peace. Suddenly there is something else—black lines on my hands. I'm mystified. I wish I could sit up and take a look. I have no doubt that they're visible. They progress at varying rates up my arms like the thick lines on a bar graph. I can see them without looking. I can hear the captains talking. They seem to be very far away, maybe out in the hall. They must be out in the hall because their voices remain casual; they're not exclaiming over this strange phenomenon, these black bar graph lines spreading through my body, overtaking the light.

I awaken to the words, "This man can't take any more electricity." Initially, they don't mean much to me. I'm more interested in figuring out what's different about the way my body feels. Then it comes to me, I'm still on the table, but on my stomach instead of my back. I open my eyes and see the legs of the two guards who are standing against the wall. When I turn my head, I see a captain, one I haven't met before, and a doctor with a stethoscope dangling from his neck. The doctor is talking to the captain, and since my shirt is off, I assume I've been examined. When the doctor says again, "You can't do this to him anymore," I realize that he's speaking about me, and I perk my functional ear for the captain's response.

"But we need to get information from him," the captain says. I note that he's young, soft-spoken.

"No more electrical current," the doctor insists.

No more electrical current. Their conversation continues, but I am content to drift away on these words.

I'm not aware that the captain and the doctor have left until the guards step forward to turn me over and I see that there are no others in the room. They cuff me to the table again. I sleep, awaken, sleep, awaken. I dream of black lines and a black room, shadows, violin music, a white neck and skin as smooth as marble.

I hear a click and open my eyes. The two captains, the black one and the one with the Afro, are back again with their black boxes. The click was the tape recorder. It's running. "Are you going to tell us that you're Gonzalo?" the one with the Afro asks.

I close my eyes and mumble, "Yes, I'm Gonzalo. I admit it. I've been working in Venezuela with drugs with another man. Whatever he says, I did it. Just leave me alone."

When I don't hear any response, I dare to open my eyes. I catch the two fools smiling at each other. They've broken me. They're so pleased. They pick up their boxes and leave the room.

Later the young captain comes in, the one who was with the doctor. He smiles. "Look, you help us and we'll help you," he says. "Tell me who Manolo is."

"Manolo," I mumble. It has familiar ring. Then I place him.

As far as I know, Manolo buys airplanes in the U.S., then sells them down here. I've had plenty of conversations with the old man. I know how he lives. I would be willing to swear that he isn't involved with drugs. I'm not about to say anything incriminating about Manolo, but I don't want to deny knowing him either. "I know Manolo," I say. "He lives in Venezuela, near Caracas. Or in Caracas. I don't know."

The captain leaves. Later he returns with the other two. The black captain walks over and slaps me hard across the face to make sure I'm still with it. The one with the Afro comes in for a few quick punches. "Why did you say you were Gonzalo?" he yells.

I laugh. How can I do otherwise? "Why the hell do you think? I'll tell you whatever you want me to tell you. You're just too stupid to figure it out!"

His thin lips tremble with disgust. The black captain takes something out of his pocket and shoves it into my face. "This is Gonzalo!" he screams.

I bring my eyes into focus and see a mean-looking man staring back at me from the snap shot the black captain is holding. He looks nothing like me. The two mean captains stomp out of the room making sure I know I've really let them down. The young one, the nice one, asks, "Were you bringing drugs into Venezuela?"

"If you want me to say yes, then yes. If you want me to say no, then no. You just tell me what you want," I tell him.

He lowers his face toward mine. "I want the truth," he says in his soft voice.

An emotion stirs in me, a tenderness for this young man who would ask me for the truth without a box in his hand. But I resist the urge to be taken in by it. "If you want the truth," I say, "then why does everyone tell me that I'll be killed if I tell the truth?"

"The truth," he whispers.

He's too nice. I can't help myself. I begin to tell him the truth. "I ferried down the plane," I say. "There was a fire." His dark eyes flood with empathy. I go on to tell him the long version, about the Colombians and how they were using the bag with the windshield cleaners and the rags and my passport as an ashtray. I tell him all about Rain-X, what a great product it is, how it has an alcohol base, how alcohol burns with a very clean flame, how the two moron Colombians probably didn't even see this beautiful, clean flame until it was too late.

"I'll try to help you," he says.

I feel like weeping. "How?"

"I'll try to get you to the United States."

"Good," I say. "Do what you can."

I sleep for a long time. In the morning the nice captain comes in and asks if he can get me anything. I tell him I need a shower. He tells me he can make that happen. I love him like I love my mother.

My guards uncuff me and slide me off the table. My legs are stiff. I can hardly walk. They lead me up to the Guardia Nacional's living quarters and provide me with a towel that's in shreds. The water is cold and there's no soap. I don't want to disturb the scabs on my head, so I don't rinse my hair as thoroughly as I'd like. The shower is a treat nonetheless.

I must be smiling when I come out wrapped only in the shredded towel, because the guard who's waiting to cuff me takes one look at me and begins to snarl. On the way down the stairs, he butts me in the shoulder with his rifle. Tough guy. Butts a handcuffed man who can barely walk, knocks me down the stairs just because I'm nice and clean from the shower. "Man, you are tough," I tell him.

I get up on the table all by myself and go to sleep again. I sleep all day, all night. When I awaken in the morning, my clothes are returned to me, washed and pressed; I take this to be a very good sign.

The guard tells me that I'm to get ready to return to Maracaibo. This is great news. I never want to be in Caracas again. Hilda shows up with her partner from the DEA, a skinny guy who bluntly states that there's no record of my being a confidential informant. They look to me for a response. I laugh. Thank you, Justin Kane. I don't owe shit to the DEA now, not to the impatient Hilda or her skinny friend who were conveniently absent when the electrodes let loose on my groin.

Hilda changes the subject and tells me she wants to hear my story again. "I came down to buy drugs," I tell her, "and they told me if I didn't stick to that story, I'd be killed. Don't you get it?"

She throws up her hands in disgust. "Al," she says, "the general wants to see you. He's a very nice man." I can't think how she learned that I hate being called Al. "What happens after that," she continues, "is out of my hands. The DEA can't help you." She hesitates, looking for my reaction to this distressing news. When I don't give her one, she says, "Venezuela is a sovereign country. This doesn't involve us. You broke Venezuela's laws, not American ones." I say my goodbyes, tell her I'm truly sorry I won't be seeing her around anymore.

Later I'm taken up to see the general. Hilda was right; he is a nice guy. A skinny, balding guy with glasses, and a pleasant smile. Easy-going. The frizzy-haired captain is with him, acting as interpreter. The general has three questions for me, that's it. Who stole my money at the border crossing where I was first arrested? Who have I worked with in Venezuela? And what does Manolo look like?

The first question is too stupid to answer. Who cares who stole my money? I'm not certain myself. And even if I did know, I wouldn't say. I have enough enemies already. "I don't know," I tell the general. The second question is easier. "I've worked with no one in Venezuela," I answer in Spanish so as to exclude the guy with the Afro.

"And what about Manolo?" the general reiterates. "Is he balding? Round face? Glasses? Pot belly? Short?"

I stare at him for a moment, thinking, but before I can decide how to respond, I'm told to leave the room.

I go outside and stand with the guards for about an hour. The two captains who originally escorted me to the airplane turn up and politely escort me to a waiting car. We drive through the tunnel, down the big hill, through the second tunnel, and arrive at the airport. On the airplane I ask them, "Did I say something to piss off the general? What will happen to me now?"

"Do you have any idea how much trouble you've caused the general? Now you go to jail," the tall one answers slowly.

"For what? I haven't been charged with anything."

"You're to be held for investigation…and these things in Venezuela can take a very long time."

"How long?"

"Two, three, four years. Who knows?"

I sit back and take in the view from the window. The other captain asks me if I want a cigarette. I'm not a smoker, but what the hell. "Light the sucker up," I say.

The cigarette makes me dizzy. I begin to feel like I might want to vomit. They take my handcuffs off and escort me to the bathroom. I sit down on the toilet. It's so pleasant to sit all alone in this little room aloft in a DC-9. It's also nice to be using a toilet. I feel as if I could sleep right here, on the can with my pants down. I take my time, just relax and enjoy this moment of freedom.

After a while there's a knock on the door. "Come on out, Gringo," the voice orders.

"I'll be out in a minute," I answer. I take care of all the paperwork and wash and dry my hands with clean soap and water for the first time in the past few days. I come out smiling and move back to my seat as slowly as possible. They exchange looks while they're cuffing me. My guess is that they're wondering what I'm so happy about.

I am happy. I'm happy to be in flight, suspended in the heavens between one hell and another. My little secret. The stewardess comes by and asks what we would like to drink. I answer before either of my companions. "A double Canadian whisky on the rocks." My companions laugh; the gringo is so funny. They tell her to get me a glass of water.

TIME

As we approach the new base on the outskirts of Maracaibo, I see Mario getting out of the back of a truck. He's still wearing his flashy pants, but with his hands cuffed and his head slumped over his chest, he no longer looks like he's about to embark on the Miami disco circuit. Still, when I meet him a little later in the captain's office, I note that beyond his scowl, he looks good, healthy. And so, when I extend my hand and ask him how he's doing, I'm surprised when he answers, "Not good. They've been beating the shit out of me every day."

"Really," I say. "You don't look like you're hurt."

He opens his mouth to protest, but his eyes widen as he takes in my appearance. "What happened to you?" he asks.

"I'll tell you later."

We do some paperwork at the base and then we're taken to the PTJ (the Policía Técnica Judicial) to spend the night in a cell with eight other prisoners who are waiting to be photographed and fingerprinted. Of course the Guardia Nacional already has our photos and prints on record, but now we'll be in the custody of the police department and they want their own records.

The cell we're placed in is about eight by ten and features a corner toilet, or, more accurately, a hole in the ground with two rippled areas shaped like feet engraved into the concrete. The water in the sink beside it runs continuously, and there's a small bucket beneath it for flushing. There is one barred window, and since the air is stifling, a few of the other prisoners have perched themselves on its ledge to facilitate breathing.

One of our cellmates steps forward and introduces himself as Capitán. He explains that we'll be called for one at a time during the course of the night and the next morning and that we may or may not be beaten. "It's best to tell them what they want to know," he says, "and if they think you're lying, you will pay." He proceeds to give us a little background information on himself. He was once in the Guardia Nacional, a captain, but then somehow he became the head of an organization that devotes itself to car theft. I find myself a place to sit and half listen while he tells Mario how he's afraid that he'll be killed if he's returned to the big prison. When he's finished with his story, Mario confirms that we're the gringos from the airplane, the big drug smugglers. "Don't go overboard," I tell Mario in English.

"Why?" he responds. "This way they'll respect us. They'll treat us good."

The two men on the ledge slide down and press closer, anxious to introduce themselves and tell their stories. But as I'm content to believe that Mario has already impressed them sufficiently to keep them from molesting me in my sleep, I curl up and close my eyes.

I sleep fitfully in the cramped, airless cell, and when I awaken just before dawn, I step over the bodies of the others and make my way to the bars to get some fresh air. A young guard comes by and tells me to put my head down. Mindlessly, I do as I'm told. The guard grabs my hair and bangs my head against the bars three or four times before I'm able to pull away. Laughing, he holds his hand out and shows me the patch of hair he managed to yank from my scalp. I congratulate him and turn to see if the others have awakened and are equally amused. They're all awake or in the process thereof, but no one, I'm pleased to see, is laughing. One of them whispers, "Stay away from the bars, Gringo, and don't look at the guards. They're easily offended."

A short time later my name is called and I leave the cell with a guard. First I stand in line to be photographed and then fingerprint-ed, and then I'm directed to a third line. I stretch my neck and see at its head a man in a white smock. There's a rack of tubes on the table beside him. He's taking blood samples, changing the tubes of course, but using the same syringe. I can't believe my eyes. When it's my turn, I'm adamant. "I want a clean needle," I say. Two guards move forward instantly, and while one lectures me, the other takes hold of my arm. I'm still objecting when the needle punctures my vein.

I'm escorted to the office of the director of the PTJ. The guard pushes me in and shuts the door. For a moment I'm too busy staring at the .45 automatic on the desk to look up. Even though I realize this must be another in their series of tests, I feel my fingers twitching for the trigger. And when I finally do look at the director, his calm expression confirms there are no bullets in the gun; its presence is merely experimental. He motions for me to come and sit beside him. "How was it in Caracas?" he asks, sounding genuinely concerned.

His voice is so soft and compassionate that I don't bother telling him that I have probably just acquired AIDS, Hepatitis or who knows what. I raise my sleeve instead and show him the black and blue and red bruises on my right shoulder. "Not good," I say.

His eyes travel from my shoulder to the top of my head. I lower it so that he can take in the scabs, at least one of which is still oozing from the cell guard's little prank. "Is there any money?" he asks.

I look him in the eye. "If there was, I would have told the people in Caracas. Believe me, I would have talked."

He smiles sympathetically. "Listen, Alan. If you take me to the money, the $900,000, I'll put you and Mario on an airplane and get you out of the country myself." He lifts his chin ceiling-ward, calculating. "In fact, I'll give you $10,000."

Nine hundred thousand dollars. A nice round sum. And ten grand for me. I could take a little vacation with that. The only problem is, there is no money. "There's no money," I tell him sadly.

He nods as he stares at me. "You know, I believe you." He presses the button on his intercom and calls for the guard.

Later, after everyone has had a turn upstairs, Mario and I are cuffed to the other prisoners and put in the back of a van. The majority of the guards stay to watch us while a few go back in to get our paperwork. When they return, some two miserably hot hours later, the plain-clothes man in their company reads off our names one at a time. As we answer, our names are checked off and our files are placed in the van. When we're all accounted for, we pull away from the PTJ and drive to the retén, the hold or prison, in Maracaibo.

It's late afternoon when Mario and I are finally unchained from the other prisoners. We watch them move off toward the gates from between the heads of the group of guards who remain with us. Then we're brought to the gates ourselves. When they swing open, we see beyond them a second set of gates, and when we reach them, a third. The building itself is about 20 feet high, cement, and as long as a city block. Inside and out it's teeming with guards. Some of them approach us and exclaim, "You're the men from the airplane. Well, well, how incredible." We hear this all too often and it's starting to bug me.

In the office, our bags are emptied. The officials there pick through what's left of our belongings carefully, as if they're choosing some token to remember us by. One man comes across a tube of Preparation H. When he looks up at me quizzically, I say in English, "For hemor-rhoids." He recognizes the word, and when he opens it, a broad smile appears on his face. "Can I have it?" he asks politely.

I lean toward him. "If you do something for me," I whisper.

"What?" he asks.

"Let me go."

He laughs heartily. "I'll make it as nice here for you as I can," he assures me as he pockets the only source of relief left to me.

The corridors are noisy, and even with only one operative ear, I can distinguish the voices of women from the rest of the din. They grow more distinct as we move toward our destination, a section of the prison which resembles a wheel. The hub is a large courtyard, open to the air, with nine long cells extending from it like spokes. Four of these cells are occupied by the women whose voices I heard. In the exposed spaces between their cells, vegetables are growing. The spaces between the empty cells are littered with trash, trash bags, and discarded articles of very used clothing.

The cells themselves consist of an open area and two sleeping areas, one behind the other, running parallel to it. As we pass through the open area of our cell, I note there are shower stalls in a small room to the rear. I'm just thinking this may not be too bad after all when the officials accompanying us push us out of the open area and into the sleeping sections. Mario is locked in the front section and I'm locked in the rear. Since the bars in the sleeping sections face the open area, we can't see the other prisoners. Nor can we see each other. But as soon as the officials have gone, some of the guards from the courtyard come into the open area of our cell. "Gringos, Gringos!" they exclaim. "You guys are from the airplane!"

"Yes, yes, that's us," Mario answers. He sounds bored.

"Why are you here?" the young, skinny one with the mustache wants to know.

"What do you mean, why are we here?" I counter.

"Why didn't you just pay someone? You have money, yes?"

He looks genuinely bewildered. "We're trying," I tell him. "How do we do this? Who do we pay?"

"You have lawyers," he says. I turn my good ear toward him to be sure I'm hearing him correctly. "Your lawyers have been here looking for you."

"Who are our lawyers?" Mario asks.

"Nelson Rodrigo and Vicente Lopez."

"Did you speak to them? What did they say?"

"They said for you to keep your mouths shut. Don't talk anymore."

"Easier said than done. But what will happen to us now?"

The guard lowers his voice. "You're here for at least seven days. That's how long the Guardia Nacional has to complete their investigation. And if things go well, you could be released soon. But you won't be, because after the Guardia Nacional's seven days, the PTJ has seven days for their investigation. And the DAS get seven for theirs."

Twenty-one days. I don't know whether this means 21 days in all or 21 working days, but as I prefer to believe the former, I don't bother to ask.

The guard backs away to let some of his fellow guards gain access. Mario engages them in a conversation about food. They tell him there's a small restaurant right beside the prison and they'll bring us food if we'll provide them with a little money. "Yeah, go ahead," I tell Mario.

One of the guards returns later with four sandwiches, two for each of us. They are formed with a bread substitute made of cornmeal and water mixed together and fried in grease and filled, sparingly, with cold cuts. They look bad, and they taste worse. I try to swallow without chewing, but I gag anyway, amazed that I'm hungry enough to eat this shit. I start to gag again and have to ask for water. The water tastes okay, but all the time I'm drinking it I'm picturing the amoebas, the fantastic assortment of bacteria swimming in it.

The young, skinny guard with the mustache comes by with his female companion and four of her friends. I recognize the women as prisoners from the cells across from us. The guard explains that his companion would like to touch the gringo. In my effort to be social, to make the best of a bad situation, I extend my arm for her. She runs her fingertips up to my shoulder. "Ojos azul," she whispers. While she's still studying them, Mario sets about flirting with her friends, impressing them with his perfect Miami street Spanish. I don't get everything he says, but I can tell by his tone that some of it's lewd. When I see the women giggling into their cupped hands, I imagine he's giving them his best Miami disco line.

A tall, well-spoken man in his early thirties appears in the morning and tells us to put our shirts on because the warden, who is female, is coming to see us. We put on our shirts and wait for what we imagine will be a fierce-looking, broad-shouldered, cold-hearted bully of a woman. But when she materializes, we find our imaginations have failed us badly. The warden is a small package of gentle curves. Her face is round and ageless, and though her subtle makeup succeeds in enhancing her large eyes and pretty mouth, it falls short of concealing the scar above her lip. On her otherwise flawless face, the scar seems more an adornment than an imperfection, and I find myself staring at it as she introduces herself to us in her impeccable, upper-class Spanish.

I'm afraid Mario will speak to the warden the way he spoke to the female prisoners, but when I hear his voice radiating from his section of the cell, introducing us, I find he's all manners and humility now. The warden and I are both duly impressed. She explains to us that she has placed us in the women's section because she's concerned our friends will come to help us break out. We interrupt each other with promises. We wouldn't do that to her, we say. And anyway, we have no friends. No one is coming to rescue us. And we can't possibly break out on our own. We have no tools. We're not magicians.

When she smiles, Mario dares to ask if we can be let out into the main section of our cell so we can at least talk to each other. She looks from him to me and considers. Then she smiles again. "All right," she says in her soft voice.

We have more visitors later, and we're brought up to the conference room to meet them. Nelson Rodrigo is about 45, balding, poker-faced, very well-dressed, and with a very professional demeanor. Vicente Lopez is younger, a pretty boy like Mario, with thick black hair. He's neatly dressed, but his clothes are less expensive than his partner's.

After the introductions, Lopez says, "We were hired by Manolo."

I want this to be true, but as everyone in Venezuela has lied to us, I remain suspect. "How do I know that?" I ask.

Rodrigo has apparently primed himself to deal with my skepticism. "Your fiancée's name is Jenny. You bought her a Cadillac," he answers. "An '85 Eldorado. Manolo changed the water pump when it broke."

"Great," I whisper. "Great."

Rodrigo adds, "This is going to cost you $20,000. If Manolo can come up with the money, we can have you out in 15 days."

"Manolo will come up with the money," Mario insists. "Tell him to contact my family. My mother will get the money."

"And my family too," I offer. "Tell Manolo to contact Jenny."

Rodrigo and Lopez look at each other. One side of Lopez's mouth twists into a smile. Rodrigo nods. "We had no doubt you could come up with the money."

I'm puzzled for a moment. Then I figure it out. Like everyone else, our lawyers think we're big drug smugglers. Twenty grand is nothing to a successful drug smuggler. "We're not drug smugglers," I say, laughing. "I'll tell you the whole story, exactly what happened."

Rodrigo waves his jeweled hand before my face as if to brush away a fly. "It's not important. We'll work out the story later. In the meantime, speak to no one. Don't go to interviews. And ask that we be present during any interrogations."

I laugh again and begin to explain about the interrogations they've already missed out on. But Rodrigo doesn't let me finish. "This is Venezuela," he informs me. "They do as they please. Now it's our turn. We'll start the process and get you out as soon as possible."

Now that the future is taken care of, Mario turns the conversation to the present. He tells the lawyers we need mattresses, pillows, decent food, deodorant, toothpaste. On and on he goes, so that I begin to suspect that he has been working on this list for some time. His tone is demanding, arrogant. I keep waiting for the lawyers to laugh in his face. But when he's finally done, Rodrigo nods and Lopez says, "No problem, no problem," and produces a bag from under the table we're sitting around. "Food, real food," he says, "and we'll bring more when we come tomorrow." The words are no sooner out of his mouth than the bag is in Mario's hands.

Back in our cell, in the open area, Mario opens the bag, takes out the two cartons and hands me the smaller one. Then he turns his back to me and begins to eat. I peer over his shoulder and see that his carton is filled with rice. I calmly wait until he's done before opening my carton, which contains the meat and vegetables that were intended to be mixed with it. I turn it sideways and shove it into Mario's face. While I'm eating, I make lots of guttural sounds to let him know how much I'm enjoying it. Midway through I get to feeling guilty though, and I give him the rest of it.

The next day the warden sees fit to tell us a little about herself. She's an attorney who's trying to run the prison as conscientiously as possible. It's not always easy, but she has some help. The tall man who announced her arrival the day before is her number one man. We tell her a little about ourselves, about how we've been beaten since we arrived in Venezuela. We pull up our shirts and show her our wounds. Her beautiful eyes feel like a cooling ointment flowing over my chest. She assures us that no one will hurt us in her prison, that she will protect us. We believe her.

Our attorneys show up like clockwork with our lunch, two foam-covered bed rolls, plus a stick of deodorant for Mario. They announce that they've paid off someone in the office so we can use the telephone to make one call. We follow them in and phone Manolo in Miami. When he hears my voice, he sighs. "You ratted me out," he says wearily.

"What do you mean?" I ask. "You haven't done anything. How could I have ratted you out?"

"You gave my name to the general."

My heart sinks. "Manolo, trust me," I plead. "I didn't incriminate you, I only said that I know you. Please trust me."

The silence that follows is long enough to allow me to contemplate what might happen if Manolo turns his back on us. I'm on my third and most gruesome possibility when I hear his voice again. "You're my friend," he says softly, almost reluctantly. "I trust you. I'll get you out."

I'm overwhelmed with relief. "Hurry, Manolo," I whisper. "I'm hurt. And please get in touch with Jenny. Let her know I'm alive."

When Mario gets the phone, he begins reciting his list of demands, less the mattresses and deodorant, for Manolo. Having rehearsed it yesterday with our lawyers, he's able to run through it quickly this time. I can hardly believe it. It seems to me he should be on his knees begging Manolo not to change his mind. When he gets off the phone, before he can repeat his requests to the lawyers, I barrel in with my own. Since I began drinking the water, I've had diarrhea. I'm already losing weight. They promise to bring some bottled water, but because it's so easy to hide glass in a bottle, they explain, they probably won't be able to bring in more than one liter at a time. I also ask for antibiotics for my ear, which I'm sure is infected. The pain is constant, and at times excruciating.

After talking to Manolo we discuss our situation. Rodrigo informs us that they're still trying for 15 days, but it will be difficult because we're still so popular. There are even articles in today's newspapers. All Venezuela is waiting to see what will happen to the gringos. Twenty days they think is more likely.

Before we can express our disappointment, Rodrigo pulls up his chair and suggests we begin work on our story. Since our original story, the tourist version, was recorded with the DAS, he opts for that. He tells us that he believes Hilda, the woman from the DEA, can be made to testify that our fingerprints were not found in the airplane.

Mario and I return to our cells and go over everything our lawyers said. While we talk, we stand at the bars that look out onto the courtyard and watch the women across the way. Their cells are open now, and one of the guards is explaining to them that since we're here, they must think of the courtyard as having an imaginary line running through its center. They can mill around as they please, but they are not to cross the line. But when the guards get busy discussing some matter of their own, one of the women runs across the line anyway and plants a kiss on Mario's cheek. The other women laugh. The guards, who were only pretending not to notice, laugh too.

The kiss elevates Mario's mood and he decides he doesn't want to discuss our situation for the time being. When he sees a guard go by carrying some empty plastic containers, he asks if he can have a lid. He twirls it toward me. I snatch it in the air and twirl it back. It's a little on the small side, but otherwise it functions just like a Frisbee. We establish some rules. If I miss and the Frisbee hits the wall behind me, Mario gets a point. If my effort hits the bars behind Mario, I do.

With the guards and the women cheering us on, we play all afternoon. And the closer six o'clock comes, which is the time when we'll be locked into our individual sleeping quarters, the harder we play. We play so hard that one of the women asks another if we're trying to kill each other. When we get overheated, we call a time-out and strip and shower. Each time Mario applies fresh deodorant. I laugh so hard that my first few shots are inconsequential when we take up the Frisbee again.

When our fingers begin to bleed, we go to the bars and talk to our cheerleaders. They're as eager to tell us their stories as were our cellmates in the PTJ. The hefty, heavily made-up ones are, as we suspected, prostitutes. The others, for the most part, are thieves. A few of them are shy and it takes some coaxing before they're willing to tell us about the conditions that led them to commit their crimes.

One of the prostitutes tires of these niceties and shouts out something to Mario that I don't get but which makes Mario beam. She bats her lashes at him. Mario shouts back, "Give me a picture, a fotografía." The prostitute lifts her shirt and shows us her sagging breasts. Some of her companions decide to follow suit. They giggle and jiggle while they wait for Mario to judge. Then the largest of the prostitutes waddles up to the imaginary line, and with her eyes fastened on Mario, jerks up her shirt. Her enormous breasts drop out like weights and dangle near her waist. The thieves laugh uncontrollably, but when Mario asks the prettiest among them if she'd like to compete too, she brushes her chin on her shoulder and says, "I don't do that."

Mario deliberates and finally names the big woman the winner. She shouts back that for her prize she wants a photo too. Mario turns around, pulls down his pants, and shows her his big white ass. The girls, even the nice ones, squeal with delight. "Ojos azul," one of them calls, "what about you?" I imitate the shy girl. "I don't do that," I say.

When we're all laughed out, the guards come forward, wanting to know what it's like in the United States. Mario tells them that the streets are paved with gold, and once he's released, he'll find a way to bring them all over to see for themselves. Then he asks what it's like on the other side of the prison, the men's side. They say that it's crowded, but that if we could get the warden to send us over, we would be placed in preferencia. There the prisoners have special privileges. They can leave their cells at will, make phone calls, whatever they like. Then, regrettably, it's six o'clock.

Our elated mood dissipates rapidly once we enter our separate cells. We sit on our mattresses in the corners nearest each other and go back to talking about our problems, about the terrible things they have done to us since we arrived in Venezuela. Mario confesses that he's worried about our lawyers, particularly Lopez. If the man was truly a good lawyer, why doesn't he wear expensive clothes? I remind him that

Rodrigo's clothes look expensive enough for both of them. When there's nothing left to be said about our situation that we haven't said a thousand times before, we talk about our families. I tell Mario all about Jenny. I tell him how she turned down the opportunity to become a concert violinist so that she could teach kids the violin, that she thought that would be a better option for a woman who wants to start a family. Jenny gives kids violin lessons from the house we share. While we never got around to getting married, we did make an attempt to try to start a family. We'd still be trying, if I wasn't in a Venezuelan prison.

Mario tells me about his mother. His father left when he was thirteen, and he and his brother and sister were raised by his mother and his grandparents. Once, when his brother was arrested for auto theft, his mother had to be hospitalized. She has a bad heart. Mario is afraid it may fail her entirely when she learns what's happened to him. We're silent for a while. Then he asks, "Do you think God will save us if we pray?"

I doubt it, but as I can't see any harm in him trying, I tell him to go ahead, just don't do it out loud. I'm in the middle of my own silent meditation when he interrupts me to ask if I know the second part of the Hail Mary. "That's not how you speak to God," I tell him.

"Then how?" he persists.

I tell him to close his eyes and look for a light in the darkness, to inhale slowly through his nose and out through his mouth. For a long time we breathe in unison. Then Mario informs me that he doesn't see the light yet. I tell him to concentrate, that sometimes, if you breathe deeply and concentrate hard enough, you can leave your body. I tried this once when I was a kid, following major surgery for a renal aneurysm. I left my body and went flying through the streets of Paris. I tell Mario about this incident. "How do you know you were in Paris?" he asks.

"The street signs all said Rue."

"What if I leave my body and I can't get back?"

"Then you have a problem."

"How do I know when I've left it?"

"When you look down and see yourself asleep on your mattress."

Mario chews on this for a while. Then he whispers, "I would like to leave my body and fly to Miami, to my mother's house and make sure she's okay. Only thing is, I hope I can get back."

The next day, while the guards are escorting us to the conference room to meet our lawyers, they point out some men in suits going in the other direction with their guards. These men, they tell us, are the ones in preferencia, the ones who have all the special privileges, the ones who would be our cellmates if we could get the warden to let us into the men's side.

After our meeting, which is inconsequential, we play Frisbee again, but it's not as much fun as it was the day before. Nor is the photo contest. We decide that we must find a way to be placed in preferencia. We must have some sort of distraction to make time go faster. And the special privileges wouldn't hurt either.

That night, when we are once again locked up in our individual sections, Mario, who has been subdued since our conversation the night before, asks if I will sing to him. I laugh at first. But when he makes no response to my laughter or my prolonged hesitation, I start feeling bad. Though I can't see him, I imagine his face looks like it did when we got the Chinese food from our lawyers and he took the rice container and I got the meat and vegetables. I begin to sing.

I sing for hours, bits and pieces of every song I can think of. I stop when I hear Mario snoring.

The following day, the women tell me they heard me singing too. They ask me to sing to them. I'm flattered. First I sing verses from *La Bamba*. Then I sing *Unchained Melody*, the only song I know all the words to. It's a great success. I teach them some of the lines and we all sing it together. After a while, even the guards join in. Between one performance and another, we all laugh.

We are laughing when the warden comes down from her office. The guards explain that I have started a chorus. The warden smiles and asks if we're more comfortable now, if we need anything. We tell her that we're doing fine. Then her smile fades and she reminds us once again that it will look very bad for her if we try to escape. We renew our promises to her. She's about to leave when she stops herself. "Would you like to sing for me?" she asks.

I stare at her intriguing scar and sing her *Unchained Melody* as carefully as I can, trying to hit every note just right. When I'm done, she applauds me, tells me that she is very impressed. I ask her if we can go over to the men's side. She promises to think about it. When she leaves, the other women want to sing some more, but my voice is hoarse now and I'm bored with the whole thing. Mario is too. We get down on the floor and do some pushups.

"The Princess of the Guajira is here to see you," one of the guards announces in the morning. While they are bringing us to the confer- ence room to meet her, they tell us she's a lawyer and that she can get anyone off, that all our female friends use her.

I am perfectly content with Rodrigo and Lopez, but I can't see the harm in getting to know a princess. But when we reach the conference room, I find the princess looks more like the prostitutes we've met than the fairy creature I momentarily let myself imagine. While I stare at her face, trying to reckon what she looks like underneath all the make-up, she begins to tell us what a good lawyer she is. Her speech is so fast and her powder is so incredibly thick that I can only half listen. When I glance at Mario, however, I see he's listening intently, bobbing his head in agreement. When she's finished her spiel, he begins to give her the names of the people in Miami who will provide her with the money she needs to get us out. She promises to send her brother up to collect it in person. Mario's whole body is bobbing now. He can hardly contain himself. The princess leans forward so that we're forced to drink in her perfume. It's so strong it makes my throat burn. "I work with money," she says meaningfully. Mario's lips stretch until all his teeth are showing. She grins back at him.

"Wait," I say. Then both turn to look at me. "We know nothing about you. Where's your office?"

She shrugs. "I don't have one. I live with my brother and work out of the house."

I look at Mario for some sign that he's caught this, but he's still beaming.

Later it takes all three of us, Rodrigo and Lopez and me, to convince Mario that the princess is not the lawyer for him, that she's only used to handling petty thieves and prostitutes. Nevertheless, I'm glad to have met her. Between her surprise visit and our lawyers' predictable one, we've shortened the day by at least two hours.

I'm hoping, the next day, that we'll have another surprise visit when the guard comes by and announces that, in fact, we do. And this one must be a queen because Mario and I are told to put on our best clothes. Our best clothes don't look too good anymore, but we get into them and march up to the conference room. Waiting for us is a tall, heavy-set white man. When he introduces himself as Harry Reading, I have to think for a minute. Then I recall that he's the man from the British Consulate I spoke to my second day in Venezuela eons ago. I couldn't be happier if he were the king. "We've been looking all over for you," he tells me while we're still shaking hands. "We've had one hell of a time finding you."

We sit down with Harry and tell him our whole story, the true version, and all about our present situation, our lawyers, and what they're doing to get us out. Harry warns us that we must be careful about the lawyers because almost all Venezuelan attorneys prefer to pay people off to get their clients released rather than pursue more legitimate processes. We ask him to explain "legitimate process." He does: if you can get a judge to release you, the prosecuting attorney can still appeal. Then the case goes to a second or superior judge. And if the superior judge says you're free, the prosecuting attorney can appeal it again. Then it goes to the Supreme Court. If it's dismissed there, that's the end. The whole thing generally takes anywhere from 18 months to three or four years.

When we tell him our lawyers told us we would be released in 15, 20 days, he warns that they're either liars out to steal our money or they're pursuing the less ethical of the two processes. Then he gives us a list of straight lawyers to contact.

The warden is as perceptive as she is beautiful. When she comes to visit us that evening, she can see right away that something is troubling us. We tell her all about our meeting with Harry, that he thinks our lawyers may be crooks. She nods her head slowly. "I didn't want to say so before," she confides, "but I believe your lawyers work with money, that they pay people off."

"This is what I like to hear," Mario whispers to me in English.

I ignore him. The warden tells me about her attorney friends, people who don't work with money, honest people like herself. And although I don't want to hang around Venezuela long enough to meet any of them, I try not to miss a word she says.

In the morning the warden's number one man comes by to tell us that we're going to be moved into the men's section. When we inquire, he says he talked the warden into her decision after our lawyers spoke to him. He also invites us to have breakfast, a meal which has not been offered to us before. And although we turn down his invitation when we learn that breakfast consists of watered-down cornmeal soup, something you need to see to believe, we assume this invitation was likewise inspired by our lawyers and their money. The warden may be as honest as our days in the retén are long, but her number one man, apparently, is not.

The men's section is, like the women's, wheel-shaped, but the spoke-like cells here are full of poor, half-dressed, half-starved Indians. Our cell, the preferencia, is the exception. Our cellmates are all well-dressed, well-educated men. Gordon, who is an embezzler, is the first to introduce himself. In turn, he introduces us to Carlos and Antonio, two young bank robbers, and José and Odeao, brothers who were arrested recently for trying to smuggle cocaine into the U.S. in crab-meat cans. They all want to know if we're the men from the airplane. "That's us," Mario brags. "They've had us in with the women."

Gordon whistles through his teeth. José says, "Wow! What was it like?"

"Lots of beautiful women," Mario assures them.

"Did they bring any to you?" the bank robbers want to know.

Mario's hesitation makes it clear that he's tempted to lie. "We had photo contests," he says at last, and to compensate for his honesty, he describes the contestants and their assets in some detail.

We know that our cellmates are impressed with us when they offer to take us on a tour of the cell and show us their provisions. They have one cooler for ice and one for cold food. They have water bottles and whiskey bottles and bags full of bread and non-perishables. When they invite us to dine with them, Mario elbows me and rolls his eyes to make sure I know how pleased he is. Then he dashes from bag to cool-er to bag, taking what he wants, pretending he's at a smorgasbord. I eat well too, but as I can't help but note the skinny Indians watching us from across the court, I don't enjoy it half as much as I'd like to.

When everyone is full, our new friends ask to hear our story. Since the Spanish these men speak is a cut above my own, I let Mario have the floor. He tells them the version the Guardia Nacional like best.

They are all very impressed—as are Mario and I when six o'clock comes and the guards don't lock us into the inner cells. Our cellmates explain that a collection is taken up every day for the guards. A dollar a man is enough to insure privacy, freedom within limits, use of the telephone for local calls, and decent food. I have nothing left in my wallet except the $400 in the secret compartment, but Odeao assures me he can make change for me. I give him a hundred and peer over his shoulder while he opens his wallet and picks through his stockpile of fives and tens and larger bills. I give half of what he hands me to Mario. José, meanwhile, is running off a list of the items the guards can get for us at the store beside the prison—soap, toothpaste, chocolate bars, etc. Mario asks if they have deodorants and after-shaves.

We spend most of the next day engrossed in Black Jack, making small talk while we play. Gordon asks who I work for and I answer, "Pablo Escobar" without blinking an eye. But Odeao, who professes to be a big time smuggler himself, is suspicious. "If you work for Pablo Escobar," he asks, "then how is it that you're in jail? He should be getting you out any second." I laugh and collect on my hand. "I don't work for Pablo Escobar directly," I explain. "I work for people who work for him. And you're right. They will be getting me out any second."

"Yeah, yeah, yeah," the others chime in. "They'll have you out in no time."

I feel like an actor in a play. I'm playing the part of a big time drug smuggler and my performance is, apparently, convincing. But after a while I get an uneasy feeling, guilty, almost, that I should be enjoying this role. My thoughts are interrupted by one of the guards. "Hey, Gringo," he cries. "Follow me. I want to show you something."

When the other cells are locked, which is most of the day, ours is open, allowing us access to the courtyard. I follow the guard out to a cell beside my own. Because of its proximity and my lack of motivation to wander in the courtyard, I hadn't really noticed it before.

"Look," the guard says. "Look at the beautiful girls, the chicas."

I peer in amazement. There are girls inside. One of them, a tall Latin beauty with long black hair, comes to the front of the cell. Her dress is very expensive looking, silk, and cut to cradle her large, well-shaped breasts. My eyes seize them the way they do the warden's scar. When I manage to look away, I check out the others. A couple look as raunchy as the prostitutes on the women's side. There is one who is downright ugly, not feminine-looking at all. "But why aren't they over with the others?" I ask.

The guard laughs and laughs. He bends so far forward his head nearly slams his knees. When he straightens again, he cries, "Look at the gringo! I fooled the gringo!" The girls in the cell laugh too. I laugh along with them, though I still don't get it. "They're maricóns!" the guard exclaims.

"What are maricóns?" I ask.

His response is preceded by another round of laughter. "They're gays who have had sex transplants or breast enlargements. They wear female clothes and prostitute themselves to other gay men. They're here on the charge of immorality, six months. This one," he says indicating the one with the incredible breasts, "is here for doing this to herself."

I look around the other cells, at the Indians pressed against their bars watching me. They are outside the guard's little joke. Not one of them is laughing. A few are calling out, begging me to get them food or cigarettes. I get the uneasy feeling I'm being treated like nobility because I'm playing the role of a drug smuggler. I justify my conduct by reminding myself of the alternative. I could be in with the Indians, eating cornmeal soup and begging the preferencia for scraps of bread. Instead I'm playing Black Jack, drinking whiskey, cavorting with the guards. I look back at the she-male's breasts. "Are they permanent?" I ask.

The guard shakes his head. "I don't know."

We meet our lawyers in the evening and learn we'll be going to the courthouse the next morning to make the declarations that ultimately will be given to the judge. We've been going over our story all week and the lawyers feel confident that we're ready. Once, a few years ago, I visited Bogota, so I know something about Colombia. But as Mario has never been there and I'm afraid he may forget some of the details we've been working on, I insist on going over them one more time. Before our lawyers leave us, they remind us to wear our best clothes in the morning.

We return to our cell and go through our bags and conclude that our best clothes won't do. Our cellmates overhear our discussion and offer to lend us some of theirs. We spend a good part of the evening sorting through their clothes and trying things on. When I lie down on my mattress, I tell myself I have good clothes, a good story, and that nothing can go wrong. But I sleep fitfully and my dreams are filled with mishaps.

Our guards wake us at dawn, and once we're dressed, they take us to the cafeteria. Having been confined to our cells and then the preferencia, the cafeteria is new to us. The guards offer us breakfast—cornmeal soup and buns. We decline on the soup but accept the buns. Like two small children getting ready for the first day at a new school, we stare at the walls and chew in silence. I notice a stain on the far wall. To keep from thinking about what may happen to me, I concentrate on it. It changes shape, gradually, so that I begin to see that it's not a stain at all. When I squint and drive myself to bring it into focus, I see it's actually a mass of roaches, small roaches, thousands and thousands of them.

We're taken to the holding area where we're to wait for the other prisoners who will be going to the courthouse along with us. The two hours we have to wait seem endless. Although I'm seated, mentally I'm pacing; I'm watching my anxiety march back and forth. With every turn it seems to grow larger, more tangible, like the roaches on the cafeteria wall. When the other prisoners are assembled, we're all cuffed together. I'm the last link in this human chain.

After all the sitting around waiting, all the measured hours I've endured since coming to Venezuela, it's a great relief when we're put in a pickup truck and it finally begins to move. The transportation guards question us about the airplane, but I'm preoccupied with the feel of the wind in my hair and on my face; I let Mario answer.

At the courthouse, Mario and I are uncuffed from the others and brought to a small room to wait. Our lawyers are already there. My anxiety is still with me, but it's more a shadow now than an entity. And it recoils considerably when Harry Reading arrives unexpectedly with another man, David Gleason. Harry asks us how our case is going and I answer, "Very well. We've rehearsed everything. But except for the fact that we're innocent, nothing we will say will be true."

Harry and David look at each other. David says, "This is a sovereign country. There is no extradition between Venezuela and Canada."

I assume his words are meant to assure me that our fabrications are justified. I take a deep breath and nod. Then I incline my head toward Rodrigo and Lopez, who are engaged in their own conversation. "What do you think of our lawyers?" I ask in English.

Harry raises his brows and frowns. He's too polite to respond, even in English. He changes the subject and asks if we need anything. Mario leans forward promptly and jiggles his tie. He says that everything we're wearing is borrowed, that we have nothing of our own. Harry says, "You'll be here for a while. We'll go do some shopping for you."

He nods at David and is about to get up when Mario's palm comes out like a traffic cop's. "Try to get us good stuff," he says, "stylish." We all stare at him. I'm the first to laugh. Then the three of us laugh together. Mario draws his lips together and fits his tie back into his jacket.

The fiscal comes in just as Harry and David are leaving. "Do you have an interpreter for Alan?" Harry asks her. She sighs and rolls her eyes and leaves the room again. "Don't make your declaration without an interpreter," he warns me.

As soon as Mario is called in to make his declaration, my anxiety returns and keeps me company until Harry and David come back. We're just settling in for what we expect will be a long wait when Mario is ushered back into the room. I can see by the look on his face that he's troubled. "What happened?" I ask.

"I gave half of it," he explains. "They told me to come back to finish tomorrow."

We all grunt and groan in disgust. Harry and David accompany us and our guards down to the room where we'll wait for the truck. When it comes, they take a few bucks from their wallets and extract promises from the transportation guards to make sure our new clothes return with us.

Since the fiscal has not yet managed to find an interpreter for me, Mario goes to the courthouse alone the next day to complete his declaration. I spend most of the day going over the embellished version of our tourist story. My cellmates try their damndest to distract me, but it's no use. But then Mario returns, and he's elated. He says he did well, great. I question him to see if he's trying to conceal something. When he sees I'm not likely to give it up, his shoulders slump a little, and his pretense along with them. "The fiscal was expecting to hear the airplane version," he explains. "She was a little disappointed. Other than that, it went great."

Though they don't understand a word of English, our cellmates have noted our exchange. In their eagerness to ease our concerns, they break out the cards and the whiskey. But all the time I'm winning at Black Jack, I'm simultaneously trying to envision how the fiscal's disappointment revealed itself and just how Mario reacted to it.

Meanwhile, Mario begins to sulk. He says he's tired of losing money and goes off to the corner to do pushups. After a while the whiskey kicks in, and one by one we all put aside our cards in favor of watching Mario. The more pushups he does, the louder we count, but as we all started watching him at different times, we are all shouting different numbers. When Mario stops, Gordon says he counted 650. The others make faces. It seems impossible. Odeao shouts "Do ten more!" Mario lies on the floor, puffing and sweating. "He can't do ten more, he's done!" Odeao teases. "Yeah, yeah," we all chime in. "He's finished. He can't do ten more." Mario lifts himself, takes a deep breath, does ten more, and then ten more after that.

An interpreter has been found for me, a woman from the U.S. Consulate. The idea of making my declaration before a neutral party excites me so much that even as I move from the cell to the holding area to the truck to the courthouse, I forget to consider the ridiculous amount of time the whole process takes. I already have my lines down pat, so I use the time to work out my performance, the character I intend to play. I have committed myself to finding a way to impress the interpreter with my credibility and to offset, with the fiscal, any indiscretions Mario might have made the day before.

I'm left uncuffed in the confinement room with only one guard to await the arrival of my attorneys. I'm feeling so sure of myself by now that when my guard nods off, I get out of my chair and tiptoe toward the door. I turn the knob so slowly that I don't even feel the rotation until it clicks. I peek out at the guards chatting in the hall. Beyond them, at the end of the hall, there's another door, and beyond that, freedom.

The guards toss their heads while they laugh and talk. No one seems to notice the crack in the door or my eyeball fixed against it. I get to thinking that maybe I have become invisible, that all my recent hours of intense concentration have resulted in this. I dare myself to open the door a little more, to walk past the guards to the second door. I pull the door open slowly and put one foot down lightly in the hall. "Hey, Gringo, what do you want?" one of the guards calls.

"Bathroom," I say.

Eventually I'm brought into the room where I will make my declaration. The fiscal arrives and nods at me expressionlessly. As she's passing me, I touch her arm. She stops in her tracks, glances behind her at the others filing in. "Don't do that, Alan," she whispers.

Since her tone is something less than heated, I reply, "I like you. Your hair, your eyes, you're the kind of Latin woman I like." I don't mention her figure, but I imply it with a quick maneuver of my eyes.

"I'm married," she scolds. Then she glances around again to make sure no one has overheard us. As she moves away, I see a faint smile at work on her lips.

While I'm greeting my lawyers, I'm simultaneously congratulating myself on my good work with the fiscal. Jenny would be appalled to have witnessed such behavior, but Jenny is home and living in comfort and I have only so many resources I can call on. I'm planning to use my charm on the interpreter as well. An attractive woman enters and returns my smile readily, but then she seats herself in front of the typewriter. A matronly-looking, heavy-set woman comes in and I smile once again. Her jaw shifts, but otherwise her face remains set. "I'm the interpreter," she announces. "And you're the pilot from the airplane."

"That's what you've been told," I blurt out defensively. She grunts, moves to her seat and settles herself smugly.

We're ready to begin. Except for the fiscal, we're all sitting. The typist's fingers are poised above the typewriter keys. The fiscal asks, "How did you get here?" The interpreter, who is sitting across from me, repeats the question in English.

I lean over the table slightly and try to pierce the hard black shields that are her eyes with my innocence. "We came to Colombia on an airliner. We stayed there for six days."

The interpreter translates. The typist clicks away. The fiscal's lip curls a little so that I know the next question will be tricky. "Describe the airport," she demands.

It's all I can do to keep from smiling, from reminding her that airports are my specialty. I describe the layout of the runway, the military airplanes off to the northeast, the large terminal shaped like a hand with its fingers spread. When I see a flash of suspicion disturb the resolve in the interpreter's eyes, I quickly tack on a description of the path down the stairs and into the Immigration and Customs offices.

The fiscal raises her chin and looks down at me sideways, as if she has caught me cheating. "How far is the downtown area from the airport?"

This is so easy that I'm tempted to blurt out the answer. But I remember that the character I'm playing wants so desperately to be accurate that he must sometimes deliberate a moment. "Well," I begin, "it seemed like a long ride. Maybe 15, 20 miles. Maybe a little less. It's hard to say because the traffic was so heavy. We went to the Hilton on Calle Siete, Seventh Street."

I proceed to describe the hotel, the bookstore on the ground floor where an English-speaking tourist can purchase *Time* or the *Miami Herald*. But the fiscal becomes impatient with these details. "How did you get from Bogota to Puerto Limón?" she snaps.

As I will soon be giving her a song and dance, I'm not about to whisk through details that are familiar to me. I stay cool, keep my eyes on the interpreter, and take my time describing the executive bus, its TV, bar, and stewardess. One seat to a customer. Never crowded. The fiscal asks how much the ticket to Cartagena was. I think it was $20, but I'm not certain. I say $20, and then before she can think about that, I throw in the current exchange rate, which I just had Rodrigo find out for me the night before. I glance at him. He nods almost imperceptibly. I say we stayed in Barranquilla, and from there to Maicao, a commercial city, very dirty, garbage in the road, lots of vendors, near the ocean, only 18 to 20 miles from the Venezuela border. She knows the rest.

"Do you know anything about the airplane?" the fiscal asks.

"Nothing at all. We were picked up at Lemon Bridge. We were accused and brought to the airplane."

"What happened at the airplane?"

Finally, I get to tell the truth. I describe the gun at Mario's head, Salinas and his thugs.

"But you told them you were from the airplane," the fiscal insists. "You confessed that to them."

I lift my palms and spread my fingers and say to the interpreter, "They asked me questions. I didn't know the answers. My Spanish is bad, practically non-existent. I said, 'Sí, sí.' And when they hit me, I said, 'No, no.' I would have said anything to stop Salinas from killing Mario."

When the interpreter translates this, I see her eyes are not shields anymore. They're more like curtains or screens through which I can view the conflict going on beyond them. And when the fiscal asks again, "What do you know about the plane?" and the interpreter takes it on herself to answer, "He already told you, he knows nothing," without consulting me, I know the battle is near its end.

The fiscal asks whether I'd like to make a final statement for the judge. I would. "I came on a bus," I say in an irritated voice. "I was stopped at a roadblock. My timing was poor. Someone had landed an airplane. They took me to it. They made me say things that weren't true. I haven't been charged with anything, but still I'm held. I would like you to resolve this as quickly as possible and send me home."

The interpreter's voice echoes my irritation as well as my words.

"What do you think now?" I ask her as we're all filing out.

She nods solemnly and keeps her eyes straight ahead. "It's quite a different picture. I believe you."

I'm optimistic when I leave the courthouse. And when I return to the prison with the lawyers and tell Mario and the others how optimistic I am, they hail me the way a quarterback's teammates do after he throws a winning touchdown. "Hermano! Brother," they shout as they slap me on the back.

Already I'm imagining myself back in Fort Lauderdale, bragging to friends about my imprisonment in Venezuela, about the drug smugglers and the women I taught to sing in English. Caracas, I decide, I will keep to myself, my little secret to be remembered on gloomy days. Rodrigo and Lopez arrive and confirm for Mario how well the gringo handled himself, how in the end he even won the interpreter over. My optimism swells into a feeling of triumph. I'm as good as out. I look at Mario and try to reckon the chances of us being friends back home. After all we've been through, it seems possible. I imagine introducing him to Jenny; I imagine coaxing her to pick up the violin and play something for him; I imagine that she'll do it, shyly, reluctantly, but later she'll scold me for embarrassing her.

"There's only one small problem," Rodrigo says.

"What? What's that?"

He sighs. "Manolo has still not sent the rest of the money. We only have $6,000. I'm sure it's coming, but we don't have it yet. We've paid off many people, but without the rest of the money, we're unable to pay off the judge. We'll have to wait and see how she decides."

"How can this be?" I ask. Since no one answers, I answer my own question internally. My family and Mario's family were unable to get up the money. Or the money arrived, but the lawyers are keeping it for themselves. Neither seems a possibility. "Look," I say. "It's not a big deal. Put up the money for us and get our asses out of here. Please. I'll pay you as soon as I get out."

If these men believe I'm a big drug smuggler, surely they must also believe that I'm capable of coming up with $14,000. But they only look at each other and then at the empty desk between us. "Or hold me hostage," I persist. "Put me up on a ranch somewhere until the money comes in. Just get me out of here."

Lopez smiles condescendingly. "Let's see how the judge decides," he says.

HARD TIME

"This is your fault! You landed the airplane in Venezuela. You got us into this," Mario whines.

I ask him to think about what he's saying.

"We should have gone to Colombia. None of this shit would have happened."

"Look, my crystal ball was broken that night," I say sharply. I'm in no mood to be pushed like this. "Besides no one twisted your arm."

He stays away from me after that. He sits on his mattress in the sleeping area and sulks. I join the others in the open area and try to remain optimistic. I remind myself that my declaration did go well. The judge is likely to release us in spite of the fact she hasn't been paid. She has to! The chicas, the maricóns, the criminals; it wasn't so bad. Some of it even seemed like fun. But I'm only able to view it that way because I believe it's temporary, only 15 or 20 days out of what I hope will be a nice long life.

We play cards, but my mood sours and I'm glad when the others decide to retire early. We are putting away the whiskey bottles and dumping the ashtrays when one of the guards comes by. "Gringo, your billete de libertad is here, in the office. You'll be leaving us in the morning!" he shouts.

We stop what we're doing to stare at him. "Are you sure?" I ask.

Another guard comes up behind him. "It's true," he confirms. "That's what we've heard. One of the guards has seen it. It's really here."

I'm so happy I could cry, but as I'm surrounded by outlaws, I merely turn and repeat the news to their receptive faces. We break out the cards and whiskey all over again. I lose some money, but I couldn't care less. Before we call it quits, Mario comes up to me. "I forgive you for putting me in jail," he says, grimacing to let me know his absolution is a major concession.

We enter the warden's office in the morning and find her standing at the window with her back to us. When she turns and I see her face, I know right away something is very wrong. I refuse to believe it concerns us. "We were told that our billete de libertad is in. We're going home." Her expression doesn't waver. "We were told it was in," I say again.

She moves toward us slowly. "Can you tell me who it was who told you this?" she asks in a voice quivering with rage.

"Who told us? What does it matter?" I answer quickly.

"It matters because it isn't true. Your billete de libertad has not come in. I'm sorry to have to tell you this. Will you tell me who started the rumor?"

"What do you mean, it isn't true? That's impossible!"

"I'm very sorry. You have no idea. I'm very upset."

She continues on in this vein for some time, but I can't listen. There's an abyss between us, a hollow cavity in which the words *It isn't true, your billete de libertad has not come in* is still echoing. When I begin to hear her again, she is saying, "Please get your things. You'll be leaving tonight for the big jail. I'm very sorry. You have no idea how hard I tried." She cuts herself off.

The mood is somber when we return to our cell. Our cellmates' faces reflect the empathy they feel for us. They also reflect fear; this could happen to them as well. While they struggle to form words of encouragement, I pace and rehearse the insults I plan to hurl at our lawyers. But I am constantly interrupted by my recollection of the warden's words. How can it be? I ask myself. How can our billete de libertad be taken away from us like that? When the lawyers finally arrive, I shout at them, "What happened to my testimony? My declaration? You said!"

"The problem is the judge," Rodrigo interrupts. "She won't sign until she's paid. She wants $5,000."

"You have six!"

"We had six. You forget. We had to pay your guards. We had to pay for your food, your special accommodations. There were people at the courthouse, people who work under the judge. We had to pay them."

"And so what happens to us now?" I interrupt.

"Don't worry. It'll all work out. Leave it to us. We'll get you out. It'll just take a little longer."

We stare at each other. Then Lopez says, "Are you carrying any money?"

"Nothing. A few hundred dollars. That's it."

"The place you are going, they'll take it from you. You'd better give it to us. We'll hold it for you."

I've heard about the place we're going to. The bad things that happen in the big jail are one of our cellmates' favorite topics. I take out my wallet and remove the last of my secret compartment money and place it in Lopez's palm. "When you arrive," he says as his fist retreats, "look for a man called Freddy. Freddy is a friend of ours. He'll help you settle yourselves."

We return to our cell for our things. As our cellmates gather around to take turns hugging us, their faces contort with a look of terrified compassion. Gordon even takes out some money and tries to get me to accept it. The magnitude of their concern frightens me more than anything yet.

We're brought to a holding area to wait for our ride. The few times I bother to glance at Mario, I see the accusations flaring in his eyes. There must be something menacing in mine as well because he doesn't verbalize them. We sit in silence, immersed in our own private thoughts, while the time creeps by. It's night by the time the truck finally arrives.

We are on our way to Hell, and when I see the huge brick walls rising up out of their barbed wire net, I know we have arrived. The Guardia Nacional outside are replaced by the Internal Guards, Vigilantes, as we enter. When they part to allow us access to the main hall, the first thing we see is an enormous granite statue of the Blessed Virgin Mary. Our lawyers have deceived us, our guards have deceived us, everyone in Venezuela has deceived us, so it seems perfectly fitting to me that we should find a statue of a saint just inside the gates of Hell.

We turn left after the statue and go down another hall and arrive at the main office where we're met by the guard who will see us to our cell. On the chalkboard over his head I read that the current prison population is 2,810. Below the figure is a breakdown, the number of people in the women's section, the drug section, the habitual crime section, the infirmary, etc. Six hundred, 869, 734, 391; the numbers weaken my already-withering mind. I will be lost here. No one will ever find me. My life, as I know it, is over. Jenny, my family, flying—all of it, gone. How could I be this stupid?

The guards go through our bags and take an inventory of our belongings. Then the one who's in charge of us says, "Follow me." While we're following him, I notice he has a bad limp. He seems friendly enough, and if we were somewhere other than here, I'd ask about his injury. But I don't have the strength for it. Mario, on the other hand, is full of questions. Where are we going? What will happen to us? Will we get special treatment? What will it be like? But he is so frightened that he sputters and falters like a little boy whose tongue has thickened in his mouth. He's so set on being heard in spite of his newly acquired speech impediment that while the guard is still considering one question, Mario is already spitting out the next.

We make a right and go up a flight of stairs. We pause at the top while another guard unlocks the gate. As we begin walking again, uphill, we see in the dim light wings on either side of us. From the cells in these wings, people yell, "Hey, Gringos! You're from the airplane! Welcome, welcome. Nice to see you!" I'm amazed to find that even here in Hell our plight is well known.

We pass through an opening of about 60 feet and then two more wings. We come to a solid steel gate. Our guard opens it and brings us to another stairwell. When the guard at the top pokes his head out of the shadows, our guard yells up, "Carne Nuevo!" New meat. At the top of the stairs there's another gate, this one barred. Once we get through it, we're in an open area about half the size of a football field and barred all around. We reach the end, go through another gate, then into a corridor. At the end of the corridor is another gate, and after that, our new home, our corner in Hell.

The cell itself is dark, but there is a light on somewhere beyond it. While the gate is being unlocked for us, I peer in and see among the shadows cubicles fashioned from sheets draped over bunk-beds. Bodies are strewn everywhere between the sheeted cubicles. We are uncuffed, and as we enter, bodies shift and heads lift. They're all looking at us and they are all Indians. The gate slams closed behind us. The Indians nearest slither out from under their sheets and slouch toward us. Before we know what's happening, our bags and our bed rolls are gone and our assailants have disappeared into the sheeted maze.

We move forward cautiously, stepping over the Indians who seem most likely to have gone back to sleep, looking for a corner in which to hide ourselves. Then a man approaches. He is short, stocky, Latin. He extends his hand and says in perfect English, "You must be Alan."

I'm so startled and relieved to hear someone in the pit of Hell address me in English that my knees buckle. I shake his hand vigorously. He introduces himself as Henny Encina and tells us how happy he is to meet us. Then he cries out a command in Spanish and miraculously our assailants appear from behind cubicles and fling our possessions back at us. Henny indicates the lighted area with a movement of his head and we follow him into what turns out to be a bathroom. There are three holes within, two exposed and one which we view through the partially open door of the stall that surrounds it. In the center of the room is a large sink, ten by four, and filled with water. There are Indians sleeping on the floor in the corner, and there are two men standing at the sink. One of the two looks so much like Henny that I know even before he's introduced that he's Henny's brother, Harold. The other is Freddy. Since it's clear that Freddy doesn't understand English, Mario explains to him in Spanish that our lawyers promised he would help us here. Freddy says he was told nothing about it. But Henny, who's all smiles, assures us he knows about us and we don't have to worry about a thing. When I ask him how he heard of our problems, he tells me he gets the local newspaper every day. "We were so sure you were coming that we made a place for you to sleep," he assures us. "Come. See."

We follow Henny and Harold to their sheeted cubicle, a five by six foot space, defined by their two beds. The railings, which keep the sheets in place, are high and indicate that the beds were formerly bunks, but the upper mattresses are missing. In the area between the two beds, there's a TV, a VCR and a stereo system. Henny says that until they can arrange to get us sleeping quarters of our own, we'll sleep under their beds. He asks if we want anything before we retire. Mario says he needs water. "We don't have water," Henny replies, "but we have some lemonade, fresh-squeezed."

We follow the brothers back out, over the bodies, and into the kitchen area. There are two Styrofoam coolers, both four feet long. Inside the one Henny opens are all sorts of plastic jugs, neatly packed. He removes one and pours us lemonade. While we're drinking, he tells us again how happy he and his brother are to see us. When he sees my puzzled expression, he explains that almost all of the prisoners here are Indians. He waves his hand toward the ones asleep against the wall beyond the coolers. "I am happy to have people to speak English to," he says.

"How did you get here?" I ask.

He pats my shoulder and sighs. "That's a long story, my friend. I'll tell you in the morning. Tonight, just be happy you're safe."

While we're returning to Henny's cubicle, I calculate and conclude that the whole cellblock is no more than 50 by 30. We enter the cubicle and Henny informs me that there are 75 men here, 73 plus Mario and me. To say that it's overcrowded is an understatement. A skinny man with an overly large head sticks his head into the cubicle and says in English, "How are you, Alan? My name is Domingo."

"Yeah, this is Domingo," Henny confirms. "He's a faggot."

Since Domingo can't be much more than a hundred pounds, I assume he's dying of AIDS and I immediately feel sorry for him. "How long have you been here?" I ask as I offer my hand.

"Five years," he answers in near perfect English.

Henny notes my astonishment and says he and his brother have been here nearly that long themselves.

I'm horrified to learn these people have been here so long. But after all the emotions I've experienced in the last 24 hours, my mind lacks the energy to ponder five years into my own future. I lay out my bed roll and slip under Henny's bed with it. Then I close my eyes and dream of nothing.

I awake early and poke out my head. Henny, who is also awake, whispers, "Alan! Good morning. How are you?"

Security is relative. The necessity of establishing rank in the big prison, we were told back in the retén, requires the veteran prisoners to beat the new ones into submission. I'm alive. I haven't been beaten. Other than the aching in my ear, which has become more intense, I'm not in too much pain. I'm looking up into the open face of a man of apparent power. "I'm great," I answer. "Fantastic. I can't believe how good I am."

Henny beams down at me. "Just rest for a while. I'll tell you when to get up."

A half hour later Henny jumps out of bed as suddenly as if he's heard an alarm. He tells me to grab my toothbrush. While we step over the sleepers between his cubicle and the bathroom area, he explains to me that the water only comes on twice a day—if it comes on at all. In the bathroom he shows me the five-gallon buckets where water is stored to be used the rest of the time. I note that all four buckets are marked with his name. He pulls out one of them and pours some of its contents into a one-gallon can. We lubricate our toothbrushes. Harold and Mario come in and follow suit. Others begin to come to life behind us, but Henny goes about his business without paying them any attention. I follow his lead. By the time the Indians begin crowding into the bathroom area, we're already done. We return to the cubicle, and while Henny makes his bed, he confirms what I already suspected, that he's in control of things here. "I've been here nearly five years," he says. "This is the drug area for anyone accused or convicted of a drug crime. In all this time I've only been through the first two stages of the release process. Since the second judge sentenced me to 15 years, my case has not yet gone before the Supreme Court. I have some political enemies here in Venezuela from a long time ago. That's my problem." When I ask him, Why 15 years? What political enemies? he responds, "Slow down. We have lots of time." It's not what I want to hear.

There's a pounding on the gate at the front of the cell. Henny cocks his head to listen. A guard yells, "Número, número." Henny tells me to follow him. We meet up with Mario, Harold, and Domingo. We make a line, all 75 of us. While the guard goes down the line each man calls out his number therein. Uno, dos, tres... I don't go much higher than ten myself, and as I'm number 44, when the guard gets to me I balk. "Cuarenta, cuarenta…" I stammer, but I can't get past it.

The guard chuckles. The whole line does. "Cuarenta y cuatro," Henny says for me. I look down the line in both directions. I'm the only true gringo here. Once the guard is gone, Henny responds to the question I'm forming before I ask it. "If you were Indian," he whispers, "you would be punished for what happened at the count, perhaps severely, maybe even thrown in the hole." I ask about the hole and Henny explains that out in the field there's a barred area where inmates who are to be punished and who are deemed capable are forced to dig their own holes. Once they're in them, the holes are covered over by a cage. And for the duration of their punishment, this is where they eat, sleep, and relieve themselves. "Don't worry," he adds when he sees my expression. "You're the gringo from the airplane. As far as the guards are concerned, you can get away with murder. You saw that today. And as far as any of the others are concerned, well, we'll take care of you—me and Harold and the others. We like you." Here in Hell I have a guardian angel.

The water comes in from two different spigots. One spigot is for Henny and his friends. The other is for everyone else. We all disrobe and line up with our bars of soap, splash ourselves, soap up, and line up again to rinse. As the sink spigot is flowing too, Henny and Harold quickly drain the water from the previous night and plug it up again. Then they take their buckets over to the toilets, the holes in the ground, and pour the water down. "There is nothing worse than a clogged toilet here," Henny explains. When they're done, they rush back to the sink and fill up empty buckets. By the time the water stops flowing, everything is in order again.

We return to the cubicle to get dressed. We're just finishing when the gates are opened. While the Indians are pressing forward with their containers to receive their ration of cornmeal slop, Henny leads us into the kitchen area where he prepares porridge from wheat and condensed milk and makes coffee on the small electric stove. When we finish breakfast, we go into the bath area to take turns doing laundry in one of the five-gallon containers.

The outer area of our cellblock, which is about 100 feet in length and 30 feet wide, is left open during the day. After the laundry is washed and hung, Henny takes us on a tour. It is barred all around and open to the air, and since we are two stories up, we have quite a good view. The prison buildings, I can see now, form a perimeter around a large open area. From the tops of the buildings, guards stand equally spaced in their towers, looking down with machine guns in hand. Out in the field there are several structures, one of which appears to be a sports arena. There are also two water towers. Henny takes us into the corner and shows us some rusty lockers, most of which, he tells us, belong to him and Harold. He asks if we have any money or personal possessions that we'd like to deposit. We explain that we gave the last of our money to our lawyers to hold for us. When we tell him who our lawyers are, he replies, "Bad news. I know them. I know them all. And I don't have any faith in those two."

I go to the bars and peer out while I consider this. But I'm distracted by the two figures I notice up on one of the water towers. Henny comes up behind me. "They've stolen something from someone," he says. "If they come down, the other inmates, the ones they stole from, will kill them. So they're staying up there for as long as they can, hoping the warden will send them to a different prison. There's at least one killing a day here. Sometimes two. There are five different mafias. We're the biggest up here in the drug section. We have people who smuggle in the drugs on visiting day, women who bring them in pouches strapped to their thighs, near the crotch. We sell the drugs. If we aren't paid, people die. That's the way it works. Prison life is very expensive. You have to have a way to get money. You also have to have protection. You can go where you like here; you're free to wander. But if you want to go somewhere, ask one of us to go with you. I can't be responsible if you're off on your own. One thing you should know: don't get involved in anyone else's activities. You have to mind your own business here. Keep your eyes averted, if you know what I mean. On visiting days, Thursdays and Sundays, people bring in all kinds of things—drugs, alcohol, clothes. So on Fridays and Mondays, there are a lot of internal sales going on. Those are the days when you want to stay particularly close. If someone says to you, 'Come in and see my living area,' you stay away. They get you in there, they'll kill you."

None of this seems real to me, but I have no reason to think Henny would lie. I change the subject and ask how he learned to speak English. He tells me he used to live in Fort Lauderdale, but that he and his wife and their little girl were living in Venezuela when he was arrested. His wife, who is American, stayed in Venezuela for a year trying to get him released. They had some money, they got the best lawyers. But as his enemies were political figures, it didn't do any good. Finally his wife gave up on him. She took the child and went back to Fort Lauderdale. She divorced him, and recently he learned she remarried. He explains that he isn't bitter about this, that he's happy to know that his daughter has another man to look after her. But the rigid look that comes over his face is a contradiction to his words, and when he's finished talking, he stares off into space for a very long time.

Later, he tells me about two other pilots who were here for a while. These men, Cubans, were going to Colombia to pick up a load of cocaine for the U.S. market. They were flying over Venezuela when they picked up the Guardia Nacional on their radio. The Guardia Nacional led them to believe they were the people who were supposed to meet them on the ground and gave them directions to their own landing strip. The Cubans, who didn't even realize they were off course, were arrested immediately after landing. They went through the first sentencing and were found not guilty. But the verdict was appealed. The same thing happened with the second sentencing. Finally, after two years and nearly $200,000 in bribes, the case went to the Supreme Court and they were released.

When Henny finishes his story, he gives me a purposeful look. I know what he's trying to tell me, but I don't want to hear it; I don't want to think about it. All I tried to do was deliver an airplane. And so when Harold asks a little later if I smoke marijuana, I'm glad to learn that even here in Hell there are ways to evade the reality of one's circumstances for a short time. "Only when I can get it," I answer, and along with Mario and Henny, I follow him to the cubicle.

Once I'm high, I get the nerve to ask Henny and Harold how they came to be arrested. Henny tells me about his political ambitions and the people who were threatened by them. They set him up, hid a half kilo of cocaine in his apartment and phoned the Guardia Nacional. Since Harold happened to be there visiting when the Guardia Nacional arrived, they were both arrested. Entirely political.

I believe him. A real drug smuggler would have been caught with three, four, maybe five kilos. A half a kilo just isn't the right number. Funny how things work out. Henny tried to be a politician and was arrested for drug smuggling. Now, in jail, he is a drug smuggler.

Though Harold is not as quick to smile as Henny, he's not as apt to brood either. So while Henny is busy staring at the sheets, still stewing over his political enemies, Harold lights up another joint and tells us about some of the other diversions here in Hell. There's a soccer team, a baseball team, and a boxing club. There's a division of the University of Maracaibo, where, once we get permission, we can go to get books and magazines. Sitting in a little sheeted area, high and among what can pass for friends, the picture of my situation repaints itself. It is a picture of the present, and the present is so large right now, so all-consuming, that the bleak prospect of the future all but slips off the page.

The ice cart arrives. I go with Harold down the stairs to pick up the blocks of ice. The stinging sensation on my arms feels great. In the kitchen, Henny is draining the coolers, getting them ready for the new ice. Mario is munching on some buns he came across when the coolers were emptied. Henny, who has perked up again, explains that we don't have to worry about food. His father brings it in once a week. All we have to do is get our lawyers to put up a little money.

When we go down to meet with our lawyers later, we take Henny and Harold along with us. They tell them about the food situation. No problem, our lawyers respond. That makes it easier. If they don't have to feed us, they won't have to come by as often. They're our lawyers after all, not our babysitters. Once that's settled, we explain that we also need fans. The temperature in the cell is incredibly hot, 90 or 100 degrees all the time. Again, no problem. I remind them I'm still waiting for them to bring me some antibiotics for my ear. The infection has now begun to work its way into my sinuses and the pain and the discomfort seem to be increasing by the hour. No problem there either. Henny asks them a few questions concerning our release and they explain about the mishap with the judge. "No problem," Lopez tells him, "we'll get them out in no time." But on the way back to our cell, Henny confesses that he's worried about these guys. He tells us that in the first six months alone after he was put in jail he paid out over $100,000 to lawyers who were saying, "No problem, no problem."

Henny likes to cook the meat, usually steak, himself. But he has a personal chef, a crazy-looking fellow who, for the price of the leftovers, is content to cook the rice and vegetables to go along with it. When he explains this to us, I put my fork down and push my plate away while there are still some scraps left on it. Mario stops chewing long enough to consider what's left on his plate, but in the end he can't restrain himself. When the chef is clearing the table, he looks into Mario's empty plate and mumbles something about leftovers. "We'll have to give him something from the cooler," Henny says.

The water comes on again after dinner. And as Henny has "employees" to do the dishes, we head right for the showers. Then, after the evening count, we enter the cubicle to watch some TV and smoke another joint. Some of Henny's friends come by and we smoke a little more with them.

The next day is identical to the first. We wake up, wait until we get our cue from Henny, then go into the bath area and brush our teeth. Then we line up for the count, return to the bath area to shower, and eat our breakfast. Later, when the ice comes, we clean out the coolers and reorganize our provisions. We talk, brood, get high, laugh, come down, and brood again. By the third day, I have the routine down pat, and I'm absolutely bored with it. Furthermore, the lawyers still haven't brought me the antibiotics and my ear and my sinuses are killing me. I'm beginning to experience some dizziness when I stand or stoop too suddenly. And even though the food tastes good enough, I'm not keeping very much of it down. I spend some part of every long hour at the toilets.

When Thursday comes, I wake up in a better mood. It's visiting day, and Henny has promised me it will be a diversion. After our morning routine, we go down the stairs, through the steel gates and into the open area. People are everywhere. I ask Henny how the guards can tell the visitors from the inmates and he says the visitors have their hands stamped. When visiting hours are over, they will return to the main gate where they've left their photo IDs.

Half the prison population is in sales. They're selling razor blades, sugar, rice, toothpaste, Kool-aid, bubble gum, chocolate bars, dry-mix spaghetti sauce, leather goods, hand-woven baskets, and wood carvings. There's even an area where people are cooking food for the visitors and the other prisoners. And there's a fish stand. Everywhere we go, people stop Henny to say hello and ask how he's doing. He introduces us to everyone, tells them that we're the gringos from the airplane.

Henny treats us to some fresh-fried doughnuts and fresh-squeezed lemonade. Henny has good credit and no money exchanges hands. He says since we're with him, we have credit too, but we must never make the mistake of failing to pay, even if it's just three cents for a doughnut. While we're walking around, Henny says even though we have a fair amount of freedom within the prison, it's virtually impossible to escape. He himself has tried three times. If you cut through the bars in one area, it will only lead you to another barred area, and from there to another. The only possible way is through the infirmary. People pretend to be sick, and once in the infirmary, if they have accomplices and if they're lucky, they may be able to get out.

As we're walking back to the place where Henny's relatives are due to meet him, I see the two men who are still up on the water tower, over 100 feet in the air. I ask Henny how they stay alive. He says that their friends bring them water jugs, which they haul up on ropes. "One way or the other," he adds, "they'll be down soon enough." Then he stops walking and runs his eyes over the walls in the distance up to the guards in their little towers.

"One way or the other," he whispers, "I'll be gone soon. Six months, no more. That's about all I can take."

We begin to walk again. Indians come up to us and beg for money. Henny shoos them away. The conversation turns to the sports arena and then to baseball. Mario has been thinking about baseball since Harold mentioned it a few days before. He wants to get on the team. He tells Henny that he knows José Canseco, that José is a personal friend and once stayed at his house. Were my stomach not feeling so bad, I would laugh. But as I'm full of cramps, I only nod and roll my eyes. "No, it's true, I played with this guy," Mario asserts. "He's the greatest ball player in the world. And I'm not so bad myself."

When we return to our cellblock, we find the place buzzing with outsiders. I've been waiting for all this activity, this distraction, but now that I'm surrounded by it, I find it only makes me feel more alone. Since Harold is with his girlfriend, I can't return to the cubicle. In fact, the moans and groans of lovemaking seem to be emanating from all the cubicles we pass—as well as from the makeshift tents that have been erected in the small spaces between them. There are girls everywhere, and when Mario sees a few who appear to be alone, he goes off to make friends with them. I leave Henny with his youngest brother and a woman who's come to sell him the drugs which he'll sell on the prison market. As I leave, he calls after me, "Remember, don't wander."

I nod, but I do wander. I wander among the conjugal tents, among the mothers, fathers, sisters, brothers, uncles, aunts, cousins, and I consider that there is nothing worse that can happen to a man than to be in a foreign jail. As if they can read my thoughts, a few inmates whom I've come to know through Henny approach and ask me where my visitors are. When I say that I don't have any, they're amazed. "You have no visitors? No one at all from the outside?" In an effort to make me feel better, they take me by the arm and introduce me to their sisters and brothers. "The gringo from the airplane," they exclaim. "Yeah, that's me," I confirm, and after a couple of minutes of chat I wander away again. But there's no place to go.

The heat by noon is staggering, and I begin to feel faint. I find a place to sit on the floor as far away from the tent city as possible. The cramps get going in my gut. I'd like to use the toilets, but there are tents set up even there. My ear is throbbing, and I bang my fist against it until my knuckles are sore. But even my cramps and aches and pains don't dilute my longing for Jenny. I can only hope Manolo is staying in touch with her, and that after all I've put her through in the past she's willing to take on some more. I examine my conscience, attempt to determine how bad a person I really am. In this setting, it's hard to believe I could be worth much to anyone.

Harold finishes his business in the cubicle, waves to me to come over, and asks if I'm okay. I don't want to explain, so I tell him I'm fine and force myself to my feet. "Hey, my woman brought me some vodka," he exclaims. "Do you want some vodka and orange juice?"

"Sure, Harold," I reply. "But go light on the juice."

He takes me to the kitchen and makes me a drink. I pour it down my throat and hope it'll kick in quickly. When his girlfriend leaves the cubicle, he leads me in and tells me to sit down on the bed and rest. Before he disappears again, he promises to find a way to get some books to occupy my mind. Then, he assures me, my psychological problems won't bother me so much. Later, Mario comes in. He tells me about the girl he met. She's the sister of one of the prisoners, an Indian from the city. She's coming to see him again on Sunday. She's clean and he's in love. I try to look happy for him. Either I'm successful or he's too fired up to notice, because he goes on to tell me everything they did together.

Except for visiting days, when I'm forced to leave the cubicle, I stay close to home, close to the toilets, which I need constantly now. But on the day Mario is to play in his first prison baseball game, I make an exception and go down to the sports arena with Henny and Harold and some of their mafia friends from the other cellblocks. Mario has been so effective in convincing us that he's good, that he and José Canseco are best friends, that we're all astonished when he strikes out his first time up. "The pitchers are so good. They throw the ball hard," Henny and Harold say by way of explanation. And it's true, but as Mario has been reminding me again of late that it's my fault that he's here, I don't feel the need myself to justify his blunder.

When the teams switch and he goes out into right field, he fouls up again; by running in the wrong direction, he misses a ball that's coming right at him. I'm amazed and somewhat embarrassed. Even in my present state, I could have caught that ball. I expect Mario to be embarrassed too, but when I ask what happened to him a little later, he shrugs and says he was too busy looking at the walls, trying to plan his escape, to play his best.

The day after the baseball game, I'm on my way down to help Harold with the ice when I hear gunfire, several shots in rapid succession, and then Henny calling my name. I run back up the stairs and arrive at the bars just in time to see one of the young Indians tumbling down from the water tower. When he hits the ground head first, I feel the impact with my own body. The other Indian is running around the edge, trying to hide himself from the ten or so Guardia Nacional who are taking aim at him from below. There's more firing. The Indian grabs his shoulder and spins around. For a moment he teeters on the edge with his free hand stretched and groping for a hold. But then he too tumbles. He lands on his back. Amazingly, he rolls over and lifts himself on his hands. I find myself rooting for him, hoping with all my heart that he'll make it to his feet. But of course the Guardia Nacional is gathering around him. He hasn't quite made it to his knees when they begin butting him, his head, his shoulders, and his back, with their rifles. When he's motionless, two of the Guardia Nacional grab his feet and begin to drag him away. Although he is surely dead, the others, who are walking alongside, continue to kick him and hit him with their guns. "How can this be?" I ask myself. Then I turn to Henny. "They murdered them. How can it be?"

Henny shrugs. "They wouldn't come down," he says. "The Guardia Nacional will tell their families they were shot trying to escape. It happens all the time. People just disappear. If someone wants you dead, you're dead."

I begin to wonder if anyone wants me dead. Manolo, maybe. Or the general in Caracas. Henny tells me how one of his political enemies once paid the Guardia Nacional to take him out in the field where they could say he'd tried to escape. But he began making deals out there, telling the Guardia Nacional the whereabouts of his warehouse, his car, his boat. And in the end his offerings exceeded the ones his enemies had pledged.

Odeao shows up one night, one of the drug smugglers from the retén who got caught trying to smuggle cocaine in crabmeat cans. Since Odeao is a true smuggler, and therefore rich, Mario and I are very surprised to see him. He's pleased as hell to see us, and after we get the Indians to give him back the things they swiped from him when he first entered, we set about finding him a bed. Since he has lots of money, this isn't a problem. There are plenty of Indians who are willing to sleep on the floor for the right sum. He buys a bed in a fourplex, a cubicle containing four bunks. He also purchases a fan. He'll need it; he's a big boy, short, but probably close to 300 pounds. Once he's all set up, we take him around, show him the bathroom and the kitchen area. He sits down at the table and opens his bag. It's filled with cans of crabmeat—which really do contain crabmeat.

In my subsequent visits with Odeao, I get to know the young Colombian who is bunking just above him. Edgar was caught bringing some coke from Colombia into Venezuela and sentenced to 15 years. In his poor English, he tells me he's only done two years so far. His family lives in Bogota, a long hard trip from here. They don't get down much. He's lucky to receive a letter now and then. Edgar has been abandoned by the people he loves, abandoned in Hell. He's no longer an asset to his family; the more time that passes, the more of a disgrace and burden he becomes.

I know exactly how he feels. So when visiting day comes around again, Edgar and I get together. I tell him we must be like the spigots in the bathroom area. We can talk about our loved ones, but only for a short time. Then we have to shut it off, shut it out, because emptiness is preferable to the hurting that follows too much release.

A prisoner leaves from one of the other cubicles and I too manage to get a bed of my own. My roommates, my tent mates, are three Indians from the Guajira. Since I can't pronounce their names, I call them George, Tom, and Tony. They're pleasant enough, but for the most part they keep to themselves. That's fine with me. I'm feeling worse and I don't have too much to say to anyone. The diarrhea seems to worsen daily. My clothes hang on me. The throbbing in my ear subsides only long enough to allow a stabbing pain to start. People still acknowledge me as the gringo from the airplane, but there's more sympathy in their faces than pleasure. I spend a good part of my time trying to decide which of my three enemies—the ear infection, the diarrhea, or the boredom—is the greatest.

Mario has taken to criticizing me. "You don't do enough work," he tells me. "Harold and Henny are complaining." It's true I don't do as much as the others. My equilibrium has been going on me, and there are plenty of times when I have to sit down to keep from passing out. And since I spend the nights tossing and turning in resistance to my cramps, I'm tired almost all of the time. But as Henny and Harold have been nothing but kind to me, especially when I'm feeling poorly, I assume that Mario is making things up. To punish him, I criticize him when I'm up to it. Since he continues to thrive and has even become a celebrity, my opportunities to berate him come mostly at the dinner table where he's still eating more than his share and without any regard for the needs of the cook.

"Leave something for the man. He'll starve without our leftovers," I say. I try not to think about our nights in the retén, the songs and conversations about God.

One day, while I'm standing at the bars looking out, Henny comes by and tells me he and one of his friends from another cellblock are planning an escape. They're going to have guns brought in and shoot their way out. When I tell him that I don't think it'll work, he tells me that his friend already did it once. "Then why is he back here?" I ask.

He laughs. "Because he didn't follow through. Instead of getting out of the area, he went right to his girlfriend's apartment. He was there, making love to her, when the police showed up."

All this stirs me to think about my own escape in greater detail. Mine, I decide, will be more orderly than Henny's. Instead of guns, it will only require nerve. Since I arrived, I have written Jenny two letters and Henny has smuggled them out for me. Now I sit down and compose a third. I tell her that it's unlikely that I'll live much longer, that I have all but stopped eating in my effort to thwart the diarrhea, that the cramps I get double me over, that I don't sleep at night, that my ear infection is spreading upward toward my brain, and that she should forget about me—and here I wonder if she'll laugh—and pick up the pieces of her own life. I also tell her it looks like the lawyers are ripping us off and that she shouldn't bother sending any more money, that I'm in the same boat as men I've met who have been paying out money for years and are still here, that there is no escape, that unless you know someone on the outside, there's nowhere to escape to.

The clothesline near the ceiling is reached by climbing out over the stair railing and standing out on the ledge that extends from it. Harold is there now, about 14 feet up, hanging his underwear out to dry. As I watch him, I think about the first Indian to go down on the water tower, about the way he landed clean on his head and died instantly. When Harold is done, I retrieve my own underwear and use what little energy I have to haul myself over the railing and up onto the ledge. But when my dizziness clears and I'm able to straighten, I think about the second Indian, the one who landed on his back, who managed to push his broken body up on his palms. I wonder if my hands will react instinctively if I take a nose dive. I'm afraid they will; I can feel them twitching just thinking about it.

I get off the ledge and go into the kitchen area. Mario is there stuffing his face full of buns. He doesn't pay any attention to me as I go to the stove and inspect the electrical outlet behind it. As with all the other outlets, the thick, snarled wires are exposed. They look as if they were installed a hundred years ago by someone who had no idea what he was doing. Still, this electrical mess represents a hefty 230 volts. If I grab the wires with both hands, I'm definitely going to fry. If Mario sees me fry right in front of him, I wonder, will he lose his appetite? Or will he just keep eating his buns? I know even as I'm asking myself these questions that I can't do it. The memory of what happened to me in Caracas is still too fresh. Electricity is out of the question.

I'm sitting on the toilet, doubled over with pain, when it hits me. The cleanest way of all—an air embolism. I can't believe I didn't think of it sooner. I finish up in the bathroom and drag myself over to the cubicle of some Indians I've seen using needles to shoot drugs. I realize when I hear the fan running that someone is inside, so I wander towards my own cubicle and wait. I'm just about to enter when a guard shows up to tell me my lawyers are waiting to see me down in the office.

I round up Mario and Henny and Harold and go down. Rodrigo and Lopez go through their spiel. Any day now, not to worry, everything will be fine. They will definitely get us out, but as we've probably already heard from the other prisoners, we may have to serve a short sentence back at the PTJ before we're released for good. "And by the way," Lopez says to me as he reaches into his pocket. "Here's the antibiotic you wanted. See, I told you we'd get it."

"Thank you," I say. "What took you so long?"

The antibiotic is so strong that when Harry Reading shows up a couple of days later I can almost hear him with both ears. He gives me some outdated magazines, cigarettes, and a copy of Stephen King's *Christine*. He tells me that he's been speaking to Jenny and she's not doing much better than I am. She's very upset, very confused. She's also broke. The money she makes teaching violin just doesn't cover the bills for the house we bought together. Her father owns a business up north. If she moves up there, he can give her a job. She can teach on the side, in the evenings. She wants to sell the house, which she could do without me since it's in her name, and go. I agree completely. She should think of herself. Harry promises to let her know my feelings. The reality of her is just distant enough so that I hardly feel my heart as it rips apart.

The boxing club attempts to recruit Mario. At first Mario is reluctant, but when Henny says that if he doesn't agree to an organized fight with these guys, he could end up in an unorganized fight, Mario relents and begins preparing. A few days before his big fight, he confides to Henny, Harold, and me that his jaw is all wired up, the result of a fight he was in years ago. If he gets hit there, it will break and he'll pass out. The last time he got into a fight, he says, the guy only hit him once and knocked him out cold. Henny and I exchange a look. So, the Incredible Hulk has a glass jaw. If it's true, then it was a miracle that it didn't shatter back when we first arrived. He could be lying, but I don't say a word. "You have to fight!" Henny says. "The challenge has been made. You have to go through with it."

Mario nods and lowers his head. The guys in the boxing club are the toughest in the prison; he can't possibly back out. Yet, except for his jaw, he is a match for any of them. He's been working out daily, pumping makeshift weights—steel bars with cement-filled flowerpots on the ends—and beating the hell out of the punching bag in the warm-up area beside the ring. His real strength is in his legs, his feet. We've seen him warming up, spin-kicking, and we all know he has tremendous foot action. We figure the best way to compensate for his jaw is to get him permission to use his feet. We need this to be a kick-boxing match.

We form a delegation of six and go down to speak to the heads of the boxing club. They in turn go into the next room to confer with the challenger. Amazingly, they return and tell us he has no objection. "Hey, if Mario wants to use his feet," the spokesman says, "let him—as long as the challenger can use his too."

Even though it's not a Thursday or a Sunday, there are 700 or 800 people assembled in the arena when the big day comes, half of them guards. I slump beside Henny and try to hold myself together during the two fights ahead of ours. My ear feels great, but the other problem seems to have grown worse proportionally. While Henny is helping Mario with his gloves, Mario says he's never fought with proper boxing gloves before. He's worn the leather kind, but never bulky 16 ouncers. "No problem," Henny assures him. "Just walk up to him and kick him in the head." Then he gives him a shove into the ring, which is actually a human ring. The applause is incredible. You can't even hear the introductions over the screaming and yelling. When it finally dies down, Henny says to me, "I hope he's a lot better at fighting than he is at baseball." I take a deep breath. I was thinking the same thing.

The bell sounds and Mario walks toward the challenger, a mean-looking ugly guy who looks as much like a brick as Mario does. Mario spins around, lifts his leg, and almost takes the poor guy's head off. A perfect spin kick! The guy didn't even see it coming. A true boxer, he has probably never used his feet before. It came out of nowhere, like a rock falling out of the air, and he was totally unprepared for it. He plops down so hard I think he must be dead. When his people jump in to try to rouse him, I see his eyes are swimming from side to side and he's smiling a little. He's conscious, but what he's conscious of is hard to say. They call the fight. Mario thrusts his gloved hand up in the air and turns slowly in the center of the ring to give everybody the opportunity to get a good look at the victor. The audience is duly amazed. Mario is the greatest now, the toughest hombre ever to set foot in the prison.

The only other reading matter I've come across besides *Christine* has been a couple of religious books whose effort to inspire me had the opposite effect. I put off reading *Christine* for as long as possible because starting it means finishing it, and finishing it means having nothing to read again, nothing to do. But now that the big boxing match is over, I've reached a new level of boredom, and I have no choice but to begin. Back in the days when I was a free man, I was inclined to skim. Now I savor every word. Between paragraphs, I compose a letter to Steve telling him how much it means to me when the conflicts in his book blow out those in my gut. Despite my effort to stall, I finish the book in a couple of days. Then I'm bored again, and more aware than ever of how bad I feel.

The university, which I finally have permission to visit, has no books. It consists of eight rooms, and except for the people who hang out in them, they're empty. Still, every now and then when I'm having a good day, I drag myself out there to talk to the other would-be readers. Since they believe I'll be here for a long time if I don't die first, they decide to ask for permission to have me as their English instructor. I like this idea. In addition to their learning English, I'm sure to improve my Spanish. And it'll help pass the time. I'm in the process of discussing my course plans with a few of these guys when a bell goes off. We rush outside and see the Guardia Nacional running toward the maximum security area. By the time we get there, there are five dead and maybe 20 wounded.

The Guardia Nacional shows up again the next day to investigate the murder. The event happened in the cellblock right next to ours, so we see everything. First they have the inmates strip, all 90 or so of them. Then they have them line up with their faces to the wall and their hands behind their heads. Instead of asking questions, the Guardia Nacional beat them, with their rifle butts and with machetes that have had their blades filed blunt. By the time they're done with their "investigation," the cellblock floor is a lake of scarlet sprinkled with white specks where teeth are floating in it, and the unconscious prisoners are being dragged out, one by one, to the hole.

I feel like vomiting, but there's nothing to heave. Still, I go to a stall in the bathroom just to be alone. Staring at the spigots, I remind myself that survival here means shutting things out. But I can't shut out what I've just seen, and I don't want to survive anyway.

With two such incidents back to back, I figure things should be quiet now for a day or two. I'm mistaken. I'm sitting at the table in the kitchen area flipping through a magazine whose articles I know by heart when I see a group of Indians moving forward stealthily. The man they're approaching is a 300-pounder who keeps to himself. He used to be Henny's cook before Henny caught him stealing some food from his cooler. When the Indians reach him, they pull knives out of their pants and begin stabbing him. His friend appears. A few of the Indians let go of the big guy to beat on his friend.

I yell for Henny. He's there in a flash. He sees what's happening and hollers for some of his cronies. Together they pull the Indians off the two men. When the Indians have vanished into the maze of cubicles, I see the big guy is full of holes and that his friend, though not stabbed, is badly beaten.

Henny and his men go right to work. One of the men, a fellow who makes his money sewing leather goods and selling them on visiting days, runs off for a needle and thread. The others help to hold the big guy's wounds closed while the leather goods guy stitches them up. Amazingly, the bleeding stops.

That night at dinner Henny explains that the big guy stole a pair of slippers from one of the Indians. He shakes his head. "They don't seem to realize that a murder here will be bad for all of us." I think about the blood on the floor of the cellblock next door and pray the big guy doesn't die.

That evening, when the guard comes to do the count before locking us in for the night, the big guy and his buddy, both of whom are wearing shirts to cover their wounds, line up with the rest of us. We all hold our breath when the guard stops in front of the big guy's friend and asks about his facial bruises. "I fell down the stairs," he answers.

"Did someone push you?" the guard asks.

"No, I fell all by myself."

The guard moves in front of the big guy. He looks him up and down. I look him up and down myself and am pleased to note that all but one of his wounds is concealed by his shirt, and that the one that isn't is on the back of his arm where the guard isn't likely to see it. "And you?" the guard asks.

"I don't feel so good, that's all."

When the guard is gone, the big guy's friends help him back to his mattress. He lies there with his hand on his heart, breathing heavily.

I go into Henny's cubicle and ask Harold, who is the only one there, to please roll a joint. While he's doing so, I explain that I can't take it anymore, that I've lost everything, including my will to live. I have even considered suicide but lack the nerve to act. I ask him for advice. He pats my shoulder and passes me the joint. "Alan," he says, "be patient. You never know what's going to happen tomorrow. When I look at your face, I say to myself, Harold, this is a lucky man. You have the face of a lucky man, Alan. That's good. Don't be so upset."

His words and the second joint that he provides again in the morning give me a shred of hope. I start thinking of an escape plan. A few weeks ago, a truck backed into one of the walls of the main visiting area, revealing that some of them are made of cinder blocks which are not filled with cement. If I could get hold of a pick and hammer, I could try to dig out the cement between them. Since I have no idea how to acquire these tools and don't have the strength to do the digging myself, I tell Henny about my idea. He doesn't like it, and when I persist, he decides he doesn't want to talk to me for a while.

Soon after I'm called to the warden's office, for the first time. I put on my best shirt and go down. The people in the office are so friendly I begin to fantasize they're going to release me for good behavior. After they've all introduced themselves, they tell me to stand over by the phone, that I'll be getting a phone call. The phone rings and I pick it up and say hello. The man on the other end, Jacques or Jean somebody, says in his heavy French accent that he's the Canadian ambassador in Caracas. He wants to know if I am okay. "Of course I'm not okay," I cry. "I'm in a Venezuelan jail. Do you know of my family in Canada? Some of them are very important politically. Get me out."

"Yes, yes, yes," he says. "We've been in contact with your family in Canada. We're doing all we can."

"Can't you get me on a prisoner exchange program? Can't you extradite me?"

"There's no extradition between Venezuela and Canada except for terrorists."

"I'm a terrorist," I tell him. "I put a bomb down by one of the dams near my home town. Tell that to these people here. Talk to the RCMP, the Royal Canadian Mounted Police, and have them tell them. If you don't get me out, I'll blow up the dam."

He chuckles. "It's good to see you haven't lost your sense of humor."

"I'm not joking. Do this. Please do this. Tell me you'll do this for me."

"I can't."

"Yes you can."

He changes the subject. "I called to make sure that you're in good health."

"I'm great. The food and water don't agree with me. I have diarrhea almost constantly. I'm down from 170 to about 130 pounds. I add a hole a week to the belt I wear to keep my shorts up. The end of the belt reaches my knees. There are about nine million people here who want me dead. Other than these little problems, I'm just great."

"Well, we're doing all we can."

"Yeah, right."

The next day I get a message that a doctor has come to see me, sent by the British Embassy. Since the infirmary has no real doctors, the rumor gets around, and by the time I get down there, 20 or so others have lined up to see him too. He has agreed to see them, but since he came to see me, I'm told to move to the front of the line. I get to feeling bad about all the bitching I did on the phone to the ambassador. I'm wearing clothes; they don't fit very well anymore, but they're clothes nonetheless. The people lined up ahead of me are wearing rags. And they're so emaciated that by comparison I look like Odeao or the guy who Henny's man stitched up. One fellow in particular can't weigh more than 60 pounds and has to be supported by his two companions. But even he greets me and smiles as I pass by. The doctor gives me something for my diarrhea and sends me on my way. As I'm leaving, I wish the dying guy good luck. He wishes it back to me. We shake hands for 20 or 30 seconds. He tells me how pleased he is to meet the gringo, how he's heard about me, but since he doesn't travel too much, he never believed he would actually get to see me. I'm amazed to see how genuine this sick man's pleasure is. Where is God in this place? I wonder as I leave him.

That afternoon a guard comes to tell Mario and me that our lawyers have arrived. We round up Henny and Harold and go down to see them. Since I haven't been eating anything, no one except the poor cook has minded that Mario eats enough for two. But now that I have some medicine for my diarrhea, Henny anticipates a problem. He's eager to talk to Rodrigo about increasing Mario's food allowance. But when he opens his mouth to get started, Rodrigo spreads his fingers into the space between them. Then he turns to Mario and me. "Look, you've got to keep this quiet, very, very quiet," he says. "Go back and get your things. We're leaving."

"Holy shit!" I say. "This can't be happening."

"Go now," Rodrigo urges.

I have lots of questions, but I can see by the look on Rodrigo's face that now is not the time to ask them. With Mario and Henny and Harold on my heels, I turn and set off for our cellblocks. I remember what Rodrigo and Lopez said about us having to satisfy a minimal sentence at the PTJ and I assume that's where we're going. If there's some problem over there, I know, we could be back in a week. I've seen it happen to others. I've also seen people return from a conference with their lawyers and announce they're on their way out only to find, when they've collected their belongings and returned to the conference room, that their release has been called off.

Mario and I play it out anyway, and it only takes about three minutes for the rumor to circulate through our cellblock. Everyone, except for the 300-pounder who is semi-conscious and swelling up on his mattress, comes forward. The Indians, the good guys, the bad guys, they all gather around us. Odeao gives us his phone number and address so we can look him up if he ever gets out. We already have Henny's and Harold's. Some of our cellmates hug us. Others kiss us on both cheeks. Everyone wishes us well. The Indians in my cubicle promise to hold my bed for a few days so I won't have to sleep on the floor if I return.

I find myself choking up, not with the joy of leaving but with the horror of leaving these people behind and the knowledge that there's nothing I will ever be able to do to help them. They are victims. We've all been victims together, and the bond is stronger than I would have ever imagined. I feel as if we've all been stranded on an island, and that now that the boat has finally come in, it only has room for two.

Within 25 minutes we're back with our lawyers. The guard who's standing with them has a questionnaire we have to answer in order to confirm our identities. He starts with me first, asks my name, my birth date, my parents' names. Arthur and Harriet. He tries to repeat it back to me but the pronunciations are too difficult for him. He begins to giggle. He waves his hand in the air and says, "Yeah, you're the gringos."

"Thank you for treating us so well," I say. "We're glad you were the people to take care of us."

We all laugh. "Buenos suerte," he says. Good luck. And he walks away.

We go down the long hall to the gate. Rodrigo extends his hand and holds out some papers and an envelope to the guard there. Rodrigo always looks a little nervous, but today he looks really nervous, and when I see Lopez looking the same, my own anxiety doubles. The guard slides the envelope out of Rodrigo's hand and leaves him holding the papers. Over Rodrigo's shoulder I read, Indocumentado, Held for Investigation. When the guard has tucked the envelope into his shirt, he accepts the papers, looks them over quickly, and stamps them. There is a calendar on his desk beside the ink pad. It is July 31. I have been in the big jail for 45 days, in prison for 60.

We walk to the next gate and encounter the next guard, a colonel. This one tells us to sit down and wait; he has to make a phone call before he can stamp our papers. We sit in a row on the bench near the gate. Rodrigo and Lopez, whose heads are swiveling like ornaments in the back window of a car, tell us to keep quiet, to say nothing no matter what happens. Two men appear. I recognize their uniforms immediately. They are from the PTJ, and they're carrying handcuffs and shackles. I'm in such a hurry to leave Hell, even if it means returning to the PTJ, that I actually begin to lift myself. But Rodrigo shoves his palm in my face and goes forward alone. Some words are exchanged.

Then Rodrigo reaches into his breast pocket and produces another envelope. While he's wiping the sweat from his brow, one of the PTJ men inspects its contents. Then the two step away from Rodrigo to confer. They both begin to smile. They turn their grins on Rodrigo. A few more words are exchanged. Then they head out the way they came.

Rodrigo, who is panting with anxiety now, returns and collapses on the bench. He bolts up again a moment later when he sees the colonel coming back with our papers. As soon as the colonel has stamped them, he whispers, "Let's go."

We move along to the next gate. The guard there inspects our papers and looks down the hall to where the colonel is still watching. The colonel signals with his hand for him to let us by. In turn, the guard signals to the ten or so Guardia Nacional who surround us. They make a path. We pass through it and go out.

Out! I can't believe it. I want to jump and shout, but I note that our lawyers are still behaving as if they're expecting to be accosted at any moment. Lopez rushes over to his Mustang and opens the trunk. Mario and I toss in our stuff and slide into the back seat. It's only after we've pulled away, gone around the block and out of sight of the prison that Lopez cries, "We did it, we did it! It's fantastic!" He extends his free hand to Rodrigo, who shakes it heartily. Mario and I go wild in the back. We scream and shout and punch each other. "We're out!" we cry. "How can this be? How did this happen? This is too much!"

When we've all calmed down awhile later, Rodrigo explains that the two guys from the PTJ agreed to say we were already gone when they arrived. The envelope he gave them contained $1,000. "What about tomorrow?" I ask. "What will happen at the PTJ tomorrow?"

"Tomorrow the director of the PTJ will inform the press that his men failed to pick you up at the designated time. It'll be like a bomb going off."

I punch the back of the seat. "Ah, shit! What have you done? Everyone will be looking for us."

Rodrigo turns his head so that I can see his self-satisfied smile. "It will be a mock hunt. The director has been paid."

"So this is for real?"

Rodrigo grins. Lopez's eyes appear in the rearview mirror. "Where do you boys want to go for dinner?" he asks.

FREEDOM (?)

Would Rodrigo and Lopez take us out to dinner, I wonder, if someone were searching for us? No: I'm confused about a lot of things, but I'm quite certain of that. And so I'm surprised a little later when Lopez turns to Rodrigo in the Chinese restaurant and asks, "Where do you think is the safest place to put them for the night?"

The problem, Rodrigo says, is that we have no papers. We might have been given papers if we'd gone to the PTJ and been released. In order to prevent political uprisings, the Guardia Nacional monitors activities in almost all the hotels. If they find us staying in one without papers, the whole imprisonment process is apt to begin all over again. Our situation is this: the PTJ is pretending to be hunting for us but will arrest us only if they accidentally find us; and our right to stay in Venezuela without papers will be accepted by the Guardia Nacional as long as they don't notice us doing so. So when we leave the restaurant, Rodrigo and Lopez take us to a sex hotel, the kind of place where you pay by the hour to stay in an air-conditioned room with pornographic movies and a double bed. They pay the manager for 14 hours and promise to be back for us the next morning at ten.

Maybe the manager is hoping we'll conclude our business in less than 14 hours and he'll be able to get someone else into the room and double his profit. Or maybe he's just nosy. In either case, every two or three hours he appears at our door asking if we need whiskey or towels or anything else. Between his unannounced entries and Mario's continual hoarding of our solitary sheet in the frigid room—the air-conditioning is ducted in from a central system—it's impossible to sleep. The shower in the morning, on the other hand, is hot, and the water pressure is great. If it were not for the fact that our checkout time arrives before our lawyers, things would be close to perfect.

"Does this remind you of anything?" I ask Mario as we plod down the street with our bags, hiding our faces and clinging to the shadows of buildings.

"Yeah, it does," he answers. "But at least we had money back then. We can't even get something to eat."

I shake my head and marvel that his main concern continues to be his stomach. But now that we're relatively free men, it doesn't annoy me the way it did in prison. We phone our lawyers from a booth. Then we wait in an alley until Lopez picks us up and brings us to another Chinese restaurant for lunch. As Lopez has other business to attend to, he assures us that we'll be safe and leaves us there, promising to return in a short time.

With my dysentery medicine hard at work and my shrunken stomach stretched a little from the meal the night before, I'm as eager to chow down as Mario. I order one dish, and when I find I don't feel sick afterward, I follow Mario's example and order another. I also order beer. I had my first one last night with our lawyers. Now I have four or five more of them. The stuff is great, ice cold. I never expected to enjoy the pleasure of drinking it again. I begin to get a little buzz going. I rave about the beer and the food and take my time consuming them, but by about four, I'm stuffed and bored and the people who work the restaurant are giving us looks and whispering to one another. We phone Lopez again.

The hotel Rodrigo and Lopez take us to now is even sleazier than the last one. But there are two beds and no one bothers us, and in the morning our lawyers arrive without us having to call them.

They take us to their offices. The rooms are large and clean, and there are enough secretaries, receptionists, and researchers running around to convince us that these guys may be semi-legitimate after all. Before we can tell them how impressed we are, Rodrigo sits us down and says that they've done us a big favor by getting us out when they did, because Manolo still hasn't paid all the money. He hopes we understand that they can't take us out of the country until the remainder, $8,000, has been paid.

"What is Manolo doing to us?" Mario exclaims. "Give me the phone. I'll get the $8,000 myself. I'll call my mother."

"You can use the phone, but you've got to be careful what you say on it," Rodrigo warns. "Make it short and don't say you need the money to get out of the country. You can never tell who's listening."

Mario makes his call. He swivels in his chair and whispers into the receiver like a lover, ignoring Rodrigo when he urges him to hurry up. When Mario is done, he slams his palm down on the desk and says his mother has already given what little she had to Manolo. Then he looks at me and smiles. "But she's okay, she's not doing badly," he adds.

I am glad to hear it, and I smile back. Then I remember the $8,000 and suggest we phone Manolo to see how much longer it's going to take. Rodrigo dials for me. "The money is coming, my friend," the old man says once we finish with the niceties. "But I can't risk getting you out of Venezuela. I want you to go to Colombia. From there I can get you out."

"I don't want to go to Colombia," I say, but Manolo goes on as if he hasn't heard me.

"Remember Jota? The man you were supposed to deliver the airplane to in Cartagena?"

"Yes, but—"

"Well, he has a camp in the Guajira. It's very private. You can stay out there with him until I can make the arrangements to get you out safely."

This is so unbelievable I have to laugh. "This man has a camp in Guajira? In the Red Zone? And you want me to go there to wait? No way. I'm not going to Colombia. And I sure as hell am not going to the Guajira."

"Watch what you say!" Rodrigo shouts.

"You have no choice," Manolo continues. "I can't get you out from Venezuela. Jota is the only one—"

"What exactly does he do in Guajira?"

"Not what you're thinking. But we'll talk about that another time. You can't stay in Venezuela. It's not safe."

"But our lawyers said—"

"Your lawyers will take you to the Colombian border. It's all arranged. Jota will meet you there. He'll take good care of you until I can get you out. Trust me."

"I trust you, old man. You got me out of jail, but—"

"Good. I'll speak to you again soon."

"I can't believe this," I say to Mario when I hang up. "Manolo wants us to wait for him in Colombia, in the Guajira. I don't want to go to Colombia. I want to get out of here."

"We're not going to Colombia," Mario informs Rodrigo.

"Now, boys—" Rodrigo begins.

I interrupt. "Give me the phone again," I insist. "You want your $8,000 fast? I can get it for you, no problem."

I dial Jenny in Florida. I'm so anxious to get the money and get out that I don't even consider that she may not want to talk to me after all this time. When the recording tells me the phone there has been disconnected, I dial her father in Connecticut. She's there, sure enough, but she isn't in. I explain that I really can't talk to him about my situation and promise to try her again tomorrow.

Back in our hotel room, Mario and I spend the rest of the day and half of the night agreeing that there's no way we're going to Colombia. In the morning, when Lopez picks us up and takes us back to the law offices, I'm more adamant than ever. "Look," I say, "we don't want to go to Colombia. We want to leave the country. There must be something else that you can do to get us out."

Rodrigo and Lopez exchange a look. Then Rodrigo says, "I'll tell you what. You get up $2,000 each and I'll get you passports with new pictures, papers, everything. We'll still need the eight, but we can work that out with Manolo. But it's not going to be quick. We know someone who might be willing to take you to Aruba in four or five days. From there you can take an airliner home."

"Four thousand dollars, that's nothing. Call the guy now," I urge. "Make sure he'll take us."

"We can't call him. It's not a good idea," Rodrigo states. "See if you can get the money up. Four grand for the paperwork and at least another two to offer this guy for the ride to Aruba. If you can get that much, we'll take you over and see what he has to say. I can't promise anything."

Six thousand dollars. I figure Jenny has to have that much now that she's sold the house. "We're out," I tell Mario. "It's a done deal." And to Rodrigo, "Give me the phone. I'll try my fiancée again now."

"You can't call now. Go back to your hotel and you can call tomorrow. We have some people coming in. You have to get out of here."

That afternoon, before we settle in at the hotel with the bottle of whiskey we persuaded Lopez to buy for us, I risk going down the street to the phone booth to call Harry Reading at the British Embassy. He's happy to hear my voice. He knew I was out and had been waiting for my call. I tell him Manolo is still short a few thousand, but that our lawyers appear to be willing to help us get out of the country anyway. When he asks how, I tell him about the passports and the trip to Aruba. Harry grunts suspiciously. "They're milking this," he mumbles. Then he explains that he can get us passports for nothing, and with these passports we can get to the Canadian Embassy in Caracas. There they'll give us enough money to get out safely. He promises to get right on it and tells me to call the next day to find out when to pick up the papers.

I'm greatly relieved. Even though Rodrigo and Lopez got us released, I still don't fully trust them. I get to thinking Harry is right, that the Aruba thing is just a scam to put a few more dollars in their pockets. I find it hard to believe that with Manolo still owing them money, they would do anything other than what he wants. I should have realized that sooner, when Rodrigo threw us out of the office before I could make my call.

We get up early the next morning and hurry down the road to the phone booth well before Lopez is due to come for us. We have our bags and are prepared to do whatever Harry says. But as soon as he hears my voice, Harry's changes to a whisper. "Don't come by," he warns. "They've got people here watching out for you. Get out of the country any way you can and don't look back."

When I hang up I'm in a state of shock. There was a time when I saw myself as a lucky man. Now, every time I pull a straight, Fate, or whoever it is who is dealing, comes up with a flush. So it's back to the hotel and plan B. And since B is the only one left on the list, I try to put some faith in it, to convince myself that our lawyers might be willing to forego Manolo's promise of eight for a guarantee of less than that.

Lopez picks us up and takes us to the offices. I sit down immediately and dial Jenny's father's number. Jenny answers the phone. She laughs and cries and curses alternately and uncontrollably when she hears my voice. Then she gets some control and tells me over and over again how happy she is to hear from me. In between endearments she is still calling me bad names, some of which I'm hearing from her mouth for the first time. The last she heard of me was weeks ago, from Harry, who told her it could be two or three years before she heard from me directly.

She's still exclaiming when Rodrigo starts in. "Don't dally," he says. "Get to the point and be careful what you say. You can't stay on."

I tune back in and find her enumerating all the details concerning her selling of the house and her move up north. But she stops herself mid-sentence. "Listen to me," she says. "Tell me how you are, where you are! I want to know about you."

I glance at Rodrigo. "I need $6,000. Do you have it?" I whisper into the receiver.

"Watch what you say!" Rodrigo shrieks. "Don't say anything. Remember, someone's listening."

For a moment she doesn't answer. I can imagine her holding the phone up with her shoulder so that she can wring her hands. I can see her long white fingers, and her elbows, not at her side but out at angles. Her expression, I know, is hurt and somewhat stunned—like it was when I first said I would work for Manolo. "You don't have to do this," she said at the time. "Think of us first just once."

When she begins to speak again, her voice is softer than before, and tentative, so that I know she's holding back emotion. "They handled the house as a distress sale," she says. "I took the first offer; I had no choice. I paid off the mortgage and used the rest to move up here. That man, Mr. Reading, said it would be a long time, that you wanted me to take care of myself. At least up here, with my family, I have a support system. I'm staying with my father now, but there's really not enough room. I found a place to rent." She hesitates. "Alan, are you okay? You don't even sound happy to…"

I can see that six is out of the question. It occurs to me that Mario and I can skip the passports. I'm reasonably certain you can get out of Aruba with a birth certificate. I already have one, and we can work out Mario's once we're there. I can't think why I didn't see it before. "I need two then, right away," I say, speaking over her.

"I'm telling you I don't have anything. I gave Manolo seven, our entire savings plus some. He said it was enough."

"But I've got to get out of the country," I plead.

"Don't say that!" Rodrigo cries. "You've got to get off the phone. You can't say that over the phone."

"I'm sorry," she says. "If I hadn't moved up here… But… Your letters…"

She goes on, but I stop listening; I get the point. She forgot me. She wrote me off. I want to tell her about everything that happened to me in Caracas, how I was forced to give Manolo's name, that Manolo may have it in for me—and now he wants me to go to Colombia. But I figure she won't care anyway. And Rodrigo is pacing and mumbling to himself; I know if I get started he'll only rip the phone out of my hand.

I find myself swallowing hard, holding back my feelings. I want to ask her questions, determine how she is really doing, talk about how much I've missed her, but I can't seem to formulate a single sentence that doesn't have to do with me getting money and getting out of the country. I am a desperate man, and I cannot talk of love and devotion in this state. The best I can do is to whisper that I'll be home as soon as I can. I hang up realizing that we have no home together now, that I may never see her again.

I look at their probing faces, Rodrigo's and Lopez's and Mario's, and find I have nothing to say to them. I feel as defeated as I did after the electric shock treatments in Caracas. I feel like I'm sinking into another reality, only this time without the physical pain to legitimize it. I look over to where the secretaries are clicking away at their typewriters and try to remember where I am, what I was doing before I took the plunge.

"So what now?" Mario asks.

"Now we'll take you back to the hotel," Lopez answers. He plants his palms on his desk as if he is about to lift himself. Then he reconsiders, sinks back into his chair. "I can only think of one other alternative." He hesitates, to make sure I'm paying attention. Then he lowers his voice. "I know a man here in town who's looking for a pilot. If you agreed to do him a favor…"

I can hardly believe what's coming out of his mouth. "Are you saying you want me to do some kind of a mission? That you just got me out of jail and now you want me to do something that would get me thrown back in again? You think I'm a smuggler too, don't you? This I can't believe! I really can't believe this!"

Lopez stands. "Forget it," he says. "You're right. It was a bad idea. Come on. Let's get going."

Mario spreads his arm out on the desk and taps his fingers on its surface. "I need to make a call," he says.

"Who to?"

"Don't worry. It's not long distance," Mario scowls.

I listen long enough to hear that he's inviting the girl he met in the prison to come to the hotel, and I sink a little deeper.

Three grueling days later, we learn that Frank is in town, the man who is supposed to pay our lawyers the rest of the money on Manolo's behalf. Rodrigo and Lopez pick us up and drive us over to meet with him. As soon as Mario gets a glimpse of Frank's hotel, his face changes. Once we are inside, he starts bitching. "Why does this guy get to stay in a place like this while we're in a dive?" he asks. Rodrigo and Lopez continue down the hall in front of us and don't pay any attention to him. I begin to think maybe it's better that we're in a Mickey Mouse hotel. In a five star, Mario would be strutting around just as he is now, making a spectacle of himself. It would take no time at all before we'd be picked up.

Frank is a short heavy fellow with a thick beard. "This guy is definitely Cuban," Mario whispers to me in English. And Frank, who, as it happens, speaks pretty good English, looks up from the bottle of whiskey he's opening and confirms that he is Cuban. He tells us to sit, and when he has passed out the glasses, he delivers a little speech about how Manolo considers Mario and me his best friends.

He doesn't smile. His manner is businesslike. I get the feeling he's saying exactly what he was told to say. Mario and I look at each other and roll our eyes, but Frank doesn't notice. "He really wants you to go to Colombia," he continues. "You would be doing him a favor. You have no papers. If Manolo is caught getting you papers here in Venezuela where he has a residence, it could be big trouble for him. But in Colombia, he can get you out, no problem."

We're at Manolo's mercy, we realize that now. We've been through it a hundred times and the bottom line is, we have no papers and we have no money. Manolo got us out. We have to trust him. We don't have a choice. As for myself, since my conversation with Jenny I feel as suicidal as I did when my bowels were leaking and my ear was a battleground for bacteria. I'm still drifting in my own little world, and since I can't get out, the direction I take doesn't much matter. In Colombia, I figure, I'll probably be killed, and since I've already proven I lack the guts to do it myself, it seems for the best.

Frank opens his briefcase and gives the money to Rodrigo. Rodrigo hands it to Lopez and Lopez counts it quickly. A puzzled look comes over his face and he counts it again more slowly. Rodrigo takes it from him and counts it himself. "Short $400," he mutters

Frank sighs. He looks around the room as if he expects to find the solution to this small problem written on one of the walls. Then he reaches into his pocket and pulls out his own wad. He counts out four one-hundred dollar bills and hands them over to Rodrigo. Rodrigo, who seldom smiles, does now. Frank stands; the meeting is adjourned. We put down our glasses, none of which is empty, and leave.

From Frank's we go to see a man who has a gasoline tanker. Rodrigo's idea is that one of us, under the pretext of being this guy's helper, can travel with him to the border. But when the driver says he can't do it for nothing, Rodrigo and Lopez decide to save themselves a few bucks and take the risk themselves. They phone Manolo and tell him to have his man at the border at noon the next day.

Rodrigo and Lopez are nervous now. Instead of taking us back to the hotel, they decide to bring us to Rodrigo's father-in-law's house to spend our last day. Once they're gone, I strike up a conversation with the old man. We talk about kids. He tells me Rodrigo had one once, a little boy who was four when he was hit by a car and killed. That was over ten years ago. This at least explains something about his behavior, his lack of concern and his rotten sense of humor.

Rodrigo and Lopez bring us clothes, white shirts, black ties, and sunglasses, put us into the back seat, and remind us to keep our cool when we go through the roadblocks. We set off, and in no time I see Puerto Limón looming before us like an image from a nightmare. As we roll to a stop, I lower my head so as not to meet the gaze of any familiar faces. I realize I'm holding my breath and force myself to exhale. Lopez sticks his head out the window and greets one of the DAS boys. While they chitchat about the weather, I relax a little and think about how easy it would have been if we had had Lopez with us the first time around. All we had to do, I realize now, was to ask one of the peasants we met to point us to a phone book, call a lawyer, have him pick us up, and give him whatever he wanted to drive us to the embassy in Maracaibo. How did I fail to think of it?

I'm still imagining the possible results from the path I failed to take when we arrive at the second roadblock. This one is in Sinamoica, not far from where we landed the airplane. Lopez knows someone here too, and we're through in no time. It occurs to me now that Lopez and Rodrigo weren't looking for more money when they mentioned the passports and Aruba; they were just stalling for time, trying to tide us over until they could complete their arrangements with Manolo. If Mario got the eight grand from his mother or me the six from Jenny, we would still be on our way to Colombia right now. This deal with Manolo, I feel certain, was worked out a long time ago. And if Manolo wants us in Colombia so badly, there can only be one reason. I gave his name to the general. He bled my people and Mario's people dry, gave our lawyers their cut, and now he's going to pay his man to execute us.

We drive through a third roadblock, and again it's the same situation, except this time it's Rodrigo who happens to know one of the guards. I'm beginning to get bored with the whole thing when we arrive at the fourth, just before the border, and we get a little surprise. A fellow from the Guardia Nacional steps up to the window. Instead of "Good morning, nice day, isn't it?" he says, "Everybody out of the car" in an arrogant tone. Lopez tells him we're in a hurry. But the guard only reiterates his command.

I look down at my knees and try to imagine returning to the big prison. It is unimaginable. Compared to that, Colombia is fine, no problem at all. When I look up again, I see Lopez and Rodrigo have cracked their doors but are still looking around for a familiar face. "Don't you know anyone?" Lopez is whispering. The guard, meanwhile, is just getting really nasty when all at once a soldier emerges from the guard booth. The guard backs away from Lopez's door at once. Lopez's friend exchanges a few words with him and waves us through. I take a deep breath and ask Lopez how he knows so many of these people. He says that he has a cousin in Maicao, that he visits there often. We proceed a few miles to the border and are waved through again.

The Colombian side of the border, which is littered with sales shacks and trash bags, looks exactly the way I described it to the fiscal. In fact, the entire route we've taken from Puerto Limón to the border is the same, only in reverse. Lopez, who is hungry after all the hard work at the roadblocks, stops the car in front of one of the shacks and asks if anyone wants a milk shake. As we're close enough to the shack to see the flies and bees diving into the blender along with the rotten fruit, even Mario declines. "Suit yourself," Lopez says.

The shack alongside the one with the shakes is selling beer, and when we point it out, Rodrigo offers to get us some. Then we stand outside the car, Rodrigo and Mario and me, drinking warm but tasty beer and Lopez slurping his shake, and wait for Jota to arrive.

Forty minutes later, a Toyota Land Cruiser pulls up alongside us and a pleasant-faced Colombian with a terribly hunched back gets out from the passenger seat crying, "Alan, Alan, Alan! What have you done? What's happened? Why didn't you land in Colombia?"

So here he is, the man who Manolo promised would take care of me. But what exactly did Manolo mean by that?

To keep from letting on that I know what he might be up to, I put my questions aside and answer his. I say I was afraid of the Colombian military, of landing in Cartagena with a burning airplane. "But if you had radioed, I could have gotten you to my strip, in the Guajira," Jota says.

I shrug. He laughs it off like it's nothing and strikes up a conversation with our lawyers.

"I don't know what's going to happen," I whisper to Mario as I lean forward to look at Jota's driver and the little black guy in the back of the Land Cruiser, "but I'd say there's some chance Jota and his men are going to take us down the road, out into the desert, and kill us for ruining the airplane." I don't see the point in reminding him that my giving Manolo's name to the general in Caracas might be another motivation; after all we've been through together, I don't want to die with him angry at me.

"He looks pretty happy to see you," Mario responds.

"Yeah, that's the problem. I'd feel a hell of a lot better if he'd make some crack about the airplane or something. These people here have no time for mishaps. The burning airplane was a mishap. They kill people for stuff like that. It happens all the time."

When the lawyers and Jota have said what they want to say,

Rodrigo and Lopez extend their hands for a farewell shake. Lopez says, "When you guys get back to the States, do us a favor. Send us a bonus for all the good work we did for you—a couple of Rolex watches."

What a sense of humor these guys have.

Mario and I climb into the Land Cruiser. Jota introduces his driver, Gordo. With his large head, protruding jaw and all the extra teeth, Gordo has a Neanderthal look about him. Jota doesn't bother to introduce the little black guy in the back. I feel relatively certain if there is going to be any killing, Gordo is very capable of doing it.

As we drive off, Jota, who is still looking friendly, asks us about the airplane. I tell him the short version of the true story. But when he asks for details, I find I'm too depressed to put forth my best Spanish and let Mario take over.

We arrive in Maicao. If Jota were going to kill us he could have done it out in the desert before we got this far. I remain unconvinced nevertheless. I look out at the city's shacks and the street sewage and construction sites and am struck once again by how well the real thing approximates the description I rendered in my declaration.

We stop at what Jota says is the best restaurant in town. It looks okay on the outside, but once we enter, I see it's a pig sty—dirt and roaches everywhere. But the steak I order is only slightly tough, and the cold Colombian beer is excellent. I can't get enough of it. We keep things light, talk about airplanes generally for a while. Then Mario begins a monologue on the interesting women he met in prison. Eventually he exhausts his list and Jota is able to tell us that Manolo is going to send an airplane down for us, that in the meantime, he's working with some very good people who are going to take care of us. I look him over good; his calm round face and curly graying hair and poor posture do nothing to help me figure out how much truth there is in his words. I look at Gordo. He's still hard at work on his steak, grunting his way through it. Some juices have run down his chin, but he doesn't notice. I keep waiting for Jota to ask me about the things I said in Caracas, but the subject doesn't come up. I'm tempted to bring it up myself just to get it behind us.

After the restaurant, Jota explains that there are some serious roadblocks ahead and that he doesn't want to pass through them with us. He brings us to a bus depot, tells us the express bus won't be stopped at any of the roadblocks, and gives the little black guy—Cesar—money to buy the tickets and to make the bribes, should it become necessary. Then the three of us, Mario, Cesar and I, board one of the nice executive buses with stewardesses serving drinks and videos on color television. We go about 35 miles, with Jota and Gordo staying close behind in the Toyota. Then we stop at the bus depot in Riohacha. Cesar tells us that we're not to get off. Since there are plenty of military people outside, I don't have to ask why. Two of them scare the shit out of Mario and me by getting on the bus. Mario immediately slouches against the window and pretends he's sleeping. With his mouth hanging open and his breathing heavy and regular, I have to admit he does a pretty good job. But it's a wasted effort; the two military men are only passengers like the rest of us.

We go a little farther and Cesar gets up to talk with the driver. I study the back of the driver's head for some indication that he has agreed to accept the bribe. When I see something pass from Cesar's hand to his, I shoot a look over my shoulder at the two military men. They're chatting, but looking ahead rather than at each other. I can't tell whether they've noticed or not. I elbow Mario as the driver pulls up to the curb. We get up quickly and follow Cesar out. As the bus pulls away, Jota and Gordo pull up in the Toyota. Then we all set off together for a cheap hotel near the ocean in Riohacha.

They set us up in a room and leave us to do some business of their own. About eight, Cesar comes knocking and tells us to follow him down to the Toyota. Then Jota and Gordo drive us to Gordo's farm.

We hang around the table, eat and drink, talk and listen to Gordo grunt and order his wife around until about ten. Then Jota announces that he has to get up to the Guajira to meet an airplane coming in for refueling. That's his business, he explains. He refuels the airplanes that come in from the interior. Gordo and Cesar drive us back to our hotel to spend the night. They tell us not to leave under any circumstances and promise to send someone in the morning with food and whiskey.

We wind up spending several nights. The manager, a young woman with three kids, brings us the food and whiskey Gordo has paid for with Jota's money. Except for our room, we have access to only the roof and the landing that looks down over the street. We divide our time between them equally. During the days we drag chairs out onto the landing and watch the traffic go by. There are lots of Toyotas, the preferred vehicle of drug smugglers. There is a military base down the road. Riohacha, I know, is a drug town. The military provides protection for the smugglers, sometimes even transportation. Although we're well hidden, we duck when soldiers pass by in their trucks.

On the roof in the evenings we attempt to learn the layout of the city. Jets land to the southeast, indicating the airport. Every now and then we see a helicopter take off heading in the direction of the Guajira. When we aren't talking or drinking or sunbathing, we exercise. I'm still very light and a little weak, but it pleases me to find I'm able to do pushups again. Other than this small pleasure, I'm going crazy. Mario is too. We vacillate between being scared out of our minds and bored out of them. We're more restricted than we were in prison. And with the military base so nearby, we can't even bring ourselves to fantasize an escape.

On the fifth day, Jota shows up. "We've got this big deal going on," he explains when Mario confronts him. "Don't worry. Manolo hasn't forgotten about you. It's just that there's something we have to take care of."

August 19 is my birthday. I spend the entire day sitting in the room sipping whiskey and brooding over the circumstances that have forced me to turn 39 in Colombia, South America, all alone—except for Mario—and with no gift in sight, unless I consider life a gift, which is hard to do under the circumstances. By the time night falls, I resolve to have a birthday party in spite of the situation, and I begin drinking more heavily. What happens between my making that decision and Mario's lifting me out of a puddle of puke down in the lobby in the middle of the night, I have no idea.

I open one eye and see daylight and a man in the room talking with Mario. When Mario sees me stir, he introduces me to Mano and explains that our eviction is the result of my conduct the night before. My head is so thick that it takes me a while to understand that Mano, who is a partner of Jota's, is there to take us to his mother's house until other arrangements can be made. I force myself out of bed, dress, and follow them down to the car. On the way over, Mario tells me that I was yelling in English, calling all our South American friends bad names, accusing Jenny of abandoning me to sleep with a succession of men, and, in between, puking my guts out. I ask Mario to be more specific about the name-calling, but then Mano, who can't restrain himself anymore, starts screaming at me. He screams all the way over to his mother's, the whole time we're there, and right until Gordo arrives to bring us back to the farm.

Gordo is angry too, but except for a couple of unmistakably disgusted snorts, his anger is expressed by silence, a blessing for my throbbing head. He sets up two hammocks outside with the turkeys and chickens and tells us, reluctantly, that we can come in to get something to eat. I groan. Eating is out of the question. While I watch Mario eat enough for both of us, I promise myself I will never drink scotch again.

Jota laughs heartily when he appears the next evening and hears the story of our eviction. I assume his good humor indicates that he's managed to put his deal together. We have a round of drinks to celebrate my turning 39 and he says he's going to take us one at a time by boat to the Guajira where Manolo will be coming to pick us up. Mario leaves with him in the morning and I stay at the farm and, for the most part, sleep in the hammock until Mano shows up with Cesar a few days later to take me to the port. I sleep some more on the way, and in my dreams I tell myself that all of this sleeping is preparing me for whatever it is that's going to happen to me next. Mano and Cesar have to shake me hard to get me to wake up. "What the hell is going on?" I scream at them as I descend from the safety of my dream.

"We're here," Cesar tells me. He looks amused.

"We went through all the roadblocks with you snoring," Mano explains. "No one asked to see any papers."

I follow them to an open boat about 25 feet long and with two Johnson outboards aft. There to meet us are the boat's captain, a young woman of about 22 or 23, and the woman's daughter. Although the young woman's Spanish is decent, I have met enough Guajirans in prison to know she is Indian—they are all Indians—and since I also know there is a serious caste system in South America, I don't believe her when she tells me she's Jota's wife. I shake hands with Mano and Cesar and climb into the outboard. I find myself a place to sit among the crates of water bottles, soda cans, and other supplies.

The sea is calm, but we are slowed by some fishing nets that get fouled up in our propellers as we pull away from the port. The fishermen come alongside and one of them jumps in to help with the unraveling. It's about 8:30 in the morning and both these guys are clearly drunk. When we start moving along again, I find myself staring at the little girl. There is something about the way she stands with her knees curved back that inflames my longing for home, for my life as it once was, for the family Jenny and I talked about so many nights lying together in the dark too sleepy to reach any conclusions, and too in love to give in to sleep.

We round the point at Cabo de la Aguja, pick up speed, and head out into the open water. The scenery is incredible. The granite cliffs along the coast rise some 400 feet into the air and level off into the plateaus. They are red and black and brown, quartz-veined in places. When the surf recedes, I see how smooth the beaches are.

The boat starts getting some air off the waves and the going gets rough. The little girl's mother orders her to sit down. I slide over immediately and invite the child, wordlessly, to squeeze in beside me. She pulls her hair away from her face to stare at the space I've made for her. Then she steps over a crate and nestles into it. We hit a good size swell and are suddenly airborne. Instinctively, I wrap my arms around her to keep her from flying out. Since she doesn't flinch, I continue to cling to her; I close my eyes and lift my face to the ocean spray. Beyond the hum of the motor, I can hear Jenny's voice, whispering children's names, asking me which ones I like, which ones I don't.

When we approach land and throttle down, I let go of the child and she gives me the smile I've been craving, that coy, closed-lipped, dimple-tinged grin that only little girls have. I turn from it and force myself to concentrate on the cliff coming up ahead of us. It's about 150 feet high and scored with winding footpaths. At the top there are three men standing against the cloudless sky. The one in the middle, I can tell by his build, is Mario. The other two look to be Indians. I pick up the largest crate and step out onto the dock.

I had to fly, I think as I climb the steep path. Jenny asked me not to, but I had to do it anyway.

It's a long way up the hill, and by the time I reach the top I'm sober again. I'm also winded. I put down the crate and extend my hand to Mario. He shakes it heartily. "What's going on?" I ask him.

"There's a boat coming," he informs me excitedly. "From the U.S.

They're coming to pick up a load. Jota has it buried here, waiting for them. If they get here before Manolo does, I think we should plan how to get on board and go back with them. What do you think?"

"Dalé, dalé, dalé," I say to him. "Give me a chance to catch my breath."

I turn around and see a small camp of shacks built of plywood, canvas, metal, and a host of other materials. Indians, sheep, goats, burros, pigs, dogs, and a hell of a lot of chickens are moving among them. Off to the right about 100 yards stands a larger shack. This one is made of brick and has a cement slab roof with a high antenna rising out of it. "That's Jota's," Mario says.

We turn and head for it, walking through fields of wood chips and empty soda and beer bottles and lots of broken glass. Mario says the wood chips are packing from the ice that's brought in regularly. He asks me about my last few days at Gordo's farm. I'm in the process of answering when we enter the shack and I see the two men inside look up from the machine guns they're oiling. I stop talking abruptly. My sense of alertness goes up a notch. Jota enters from a back room. His slouch is so prominent that he has to lift his head to show me his smile. "Good to see you, Alan!" he cries. And when he sees my gaze shift back to the guns, he adds, "Don't worry about these fellows. They're here to protect us."

The two men nod at me. I nod back. Mario tells me in English that they're both from Medellin, that they're not very friendly, but otherwise they seem to be okay, and that Jota has them accompany him most everywhere—for protection, of course. I look them over. The light-haired one can't be more than 100 pounds. He's also very young. If not for the machine gun, which he's rubbing as gently as if it were a baby, the notion of him protecting anyone would be laughable. The other, who has a European look about him, is only slightly bigger and older looking. I glance beyond them, at the radio on the shelf against the wall and the car battery it's hooked up to. When Jota sits down at the table, I slide into the chair beside him. "What's going on, Jota?" I ask.

Jota is evasive. "We're waiting for a boat to come in," he tells me. "It should be here already. I'm beginning to think someone's lying to me."

Yes, I know the feeling well enough. "What about Manolo?" I ask.

"The problem is that the frequencies I'm using to communicate with the people on the boat are long-range. If the boat were 50 or 60 miles off shore like it's supposed to be, I should be using short-range, right?"

"And Manolo?"

Jota laughs. "Be patient, my friend. I told you, Manolo is sending an airplane for you. You'll be out of here in no time. In the meantime, relax, enjoy yourself."

Later, Mario takes me on a tour of the camp. The two Colombians with the machine guns accompany us. At close range I see that the metal the buildings are made of is airplane metal. And all around the camp there are airplane parts. The shacks' doors, which are open to catch the sea breeze, reveal the airplane seats used in lieu of chairs. The center shack, Mario explains when we reach it, is actually an outpost for the surrounding area. The young woman from the boat is there. She and her mother run the outpost. They sell cookies, beer, soda, and water when they can get it. Mario points to the old, discolored refrigerator that leans against the shack's outer wall. "The soda is cold," he tells me happily. "We can charge whatever we like. Jota picks up the tab."

Nearby there is a restaurant, or rather a shack with a table set up inside and another outdoors. "What do they serve?" I ask Mario skeptically.

"Chicken, goat, rice. Do you think Jota will really get us out?"

"I wish I could answer that," I reply. "I don't know the man. I know nothing about him."

"He acts like he's your best friend."

"So has everyone else. And look what good it's done us."

In addition to the radio room in the front, there are two back rooms to Jota's shack. The larger of the two is where Jota sleeps with the Indian, the one who claims to be his wife. At night, hammocks are suspended in the other two rooms. The first night Mario sleeps alone in the back room and I sleep in the radio room with the two Colombians and their iron appendages. With the windows open and the sea breeze blowing, it's more comfortable than any other place I have slept recently. But as I like to sleep on my stomach, the hammock is a problem. One of the Colombians hears me shifting around and tells me not to worry, I'll get used to it. I go to sleep hoping I won't be here long enough to get used to anything.

I wake up to the sound of Jota's voice. He's on the radio, talking, to my astonishment, about dresses and shoes and women's legs. When Mario walks in a moment later and sees my puzzled expression, he says, "He's talking in code. He's talking to the boat that's coming in for the coke. The cartel sent it here on a truck. Jota's job is to load it on the boat. The cartel's last several flights arrived at Puerto Rico with half the Pacific fleet behind them. Most returned with the load and a tail. The ones that did drop had the load seized by a huge interdiction force. That's why they're using a boat this time."

"I don't like this. These are bad people," I tell him in English, "And if they get busted—"

"Don't worry," he says. His words are distorted by the yawn he speaks through. "They hide the cocaine in the sand on the beach at the foot of the cliff. They dig holes. Only Jota and a few of the Indians know where. And there's a guard with a radio about ten miles away on the road. If anyone comes, Jota will get plenty of warning. The road is bad. I'll show you later. It's really a donkey path. Jota says it's impassable in the rain. The biggest concern is helicopters. If we hear them, we're supposed to hit the caves. I'll show you. But even that's not much of a problem. The military is paid off. They know he's here, and they avoid him. He's on the radio with Mano in Riohacha all the time anyway. Mano keeps an eye on things from his end."

The hammock remains an obstacle, but otherwise I adapt to the routine in spite of my desire not to. Jota spends most days at the radio communicating with the boat or with his connections in Medellin or Barranquilla, changing the frequencies accordingly at specified times. Sometimes women come in on the radio. These, I learn from Mario, are Jota's other wives. Two live in Barranquilla and one in Maicao. Sleeping with the young Indian occupies Jota's nights. His only other activity, besides eating, is snorting cocaine, and he snorts enough of it to make up for the fact that nobody else has an interest in it. Our protectors, Carlos and José, in fact, look at him with disdain whenever he starts. I have no problem keeping my aversion to myself, but I can feel it, in my gut. On the third day, Jota tells us he has someone coming to see him on business and that we should disappear for a while. In the middle of the next night, he wakes us up and tells us to go find an empty shack to sleep in. But except for these instances, our time is our own, we are free to come and go as we please.

During the hottest part of each day, Mario and I go down to the beach with the two Colombians. They sit with their guns on the white sand and wait for us to tire of the water, which is as clear and as blue as any I have seen. Sometimes they take a dip themselves, but they stay too close to where they have left their guns to really enjoy it. When we're not swimming, we compete at throwing stones at airborne soda bottles, explore the area, or wander through the camp. The Indians, a few of whom appear to be quite sick, don't say much to us. There is one little girl among them whose skin is light and whose eyes are the same color as mine. Mario got it from Jota that she's the result of an American pilot who stayed at the camp for a few months three years ago. There is also a girl of about 18 whom Mario has taken an interest in. She's ugly as hell and smells considerably worse, but Mario doesn't notice. He spends a good part of each day trying to coax her to tour the caves with him. She returns his invitations with a shy smile but refuses him anything more than that. There is no great abundance of food, but often enough there's ham, and always plenty of fish and fruit. The Indians who prepare our meals bring them to us when we don't feel like eating in the restaurant. A man named Toyota shows up almost daily with a large airplane gas tank filled with water for showers. The sea breeze is refreshing. Except for the fact that we remain prisoners, we live decently enough.

On the fifth day after my arrival, Manolo comes in on the radio, calling us from the U.S. When he asks how we're being treated, I tell him the truth, that I can't complain. "Who's your friend, huh?" he urges. "Who's your buddy?"

"You're my friend, old man," I answer. "You got us out. I'll do anything for you. But now you've got to do one thing for me." I resist the urge to be precise because I know the DEA is listening in somewhere. The radio has to be monitored. As long ago as the end of the second world war, the allies were monitoring all of Germany's long-range communications. The technology isn't a secret. And anyone using long-range from here is clearly guilty of drug trafficking.

"Don't worry. No problem. Here. Talk to my friend Leonard. He'll tell you," Manolo responds to my unstated question.

There is some static and then some mumbling and then Leonard's voice. In perfect English with only a slight Spanish accent, he says, "The old man wants to tell you we've got a Cessna Conquest. How do you like that?"

I don't like that at all. A Cessna Conquest is a million dollar airplane. I know Manolo well enough to know he doesn't have these kinds of connections. If such a craft is really coming, it isn't coming just for us. "I'll be watching for you," I tell them. Then I give the mike to Jota and go out.

The airplane, of course, doesn't materialize. But every three or four days Manolo radios to confirm that operation rescue is still in progress. Mario and I are feeling increasingly impatient, but me more so because his interest in the Indian girl is becoming an obsession. His attraction, I decide, must be because of her resistance. He spends a lot of time inventing new approaches he might try. It's hard for me to really get into it because I can't imagine being attracted to her myself. But it gives us something to talk about when we tire of discussing our situation, our boredom, and our rotten luck.

The American boat coming in for the coke reports it's getting closer all the time, and although Jota remains skeptical, he's in almost constant communication with them. Since the person he's been communicating with speaks my brand of Spanish, he often gets Mario to interpret. I hate to see Mario involved in this. I wonder if the DEA is matching his voice imprints to the tapes they already have. I've cautioned him on several occasions, but he doesn't seem to care. He continues to believe that when the boat makes it in, he'll be able to persuade its captain to take him back with them. I've already informed him that that's one trip he'll have to do alone. I would rather stay and take my chances with Manolo than get on a boat carrying 1,000 kilos of cocaine. Given our recent pasts, no one would believe we weren't part of the operation. We would go to jail forever.

When the boat appears to be no more than half a day out from the camp, Mario volunteers to go down to the beach with Jota and help dig up the cocaine and load it onto the outboard. Jota, who is, of course, ignorant of Mario's plan, can't refuse the offer because Mario is stronger than any three Indians he has. With Jota standing right there, Mario can't say much of a goodbye. I wish him luck and make him promise to get on Manolo's case as soon as he gets home. Then I remind him that I think he's crazy and settle into my hammock to wait. To keep from thinking about what's happening down at the boat, I try to remember all the annoying things Mario has done since we left Miami.

Carlos, the light-haired Colombian, has been left behind to protect me. I glance over at him every so often and wonder if the day will come when I will consider him a friend. The operation must be causing him some anxiety too because he's pacing, and even though we're not expecting to hear from anyone—Jota has a radio on the boat—his eye is fixed on the shack's radio. Even if he could be made to say a few words now and then, I decide, he could never replace Mario. He could never be made to understand what I've been through and what it's done to me, that I'm living another man's life, that I can affect pleasure, but that I've lost my capacity to feel it genuinely.

A few hours later the door opens and Jota slouches in. When I see his expression, I suppose that Mario has escaped and is on his way home. I'm just wondering whether Mario will really bother to hunt down Manolo and try to get me out when he comes marching in behind Jota, looking as lost as I felt until now. The boat, they interrupt each other to tell me, picked up a couple of Coast Guard helicopters and had to turn around. The coke is back in the sand.

I'm making an effort to keep from smiling when my eye falls on the flashlight Mario is carrying. It's mine! Other than some underwear, it's the only thing that hasn't been stolen from me since we left Miami, until now. A flashlight is an absolute necessity here. The bathroom, or rather the designated relief area some 50 feet downwind and down the hill from the shack, is a favorite hangout for snakes. Since the Indians insist on cooking our fish in the same oil day after day, occasionally my diarrhea problem returns and I have to go down there at night. We don't dig holes; that would be like having an open septic tank. It's better to let it air and then have the rain take care of it when it comes. I would prefer to make my way amid the snakes and the toilet paper and the crap with a flashlight. I can't believe Mario would deprive me of that small privilege. I jump out of the hammock and reach for the thing. Mario whacks it into my palm. "You only think of yourself," I say in English. "You would have taken it back with you and left me here in the dark. You are the most self-centered son of a bitch I've ever met in my life."

"Hey," he says, his bottom lip swinging, "It's every man for himself out here. I've got to do what I've got to do. If you don't like it…" He shrugs and lowers his voice. "You have to like it because you're my only friend here." He grins. I think about it for a minute. Then I grin back at him.

That week we get up a soccer team and keep an eye out for helicopters, but the camp's monotony persists anyway. I'm still about 30 pounds shy of my regular weight and so dark from all the time I spend outdoors that I can almost pass for an Indian. But I'm not an Indian. I'm a Canadian in love with a woman living in the U.S., and enough is enough; I want to go home so badly that I can't be bothered to help Mario think of new ways to entice his 18-year-old anymore. When we go up to the camp so that he can flirt with her, I look at the little girl, Jota's woman's daughter, and try to remember what it was about her that reminded me of my conversations with Jenny about starting a family. The child is only irritating now. I've seen her making lewd gestures with her hips. I've seen her fondling the dogs' genitals. She has spent too many nights watching Jota and her mother having sex. Her smiles, which I no longer return, do nothing to help me conjure up an image of the children Jenny and I planned to have. I am disconnected, passionless now. When I laugh, I'm only emitting the sound that I know to be appropriate to the circumstances; when I reminisce, my memories are rendered shapeless by the venom they must first be filtered through. Lately, I've begun to get belligerent with Manolo on the radio. "Come on, my friend," I say in a voice that's anything but friendly. "Get us out of here now. This place is dangerous. I don't want to be here."

Just how dangerous it really is hits home one night when Jota is over at the camp with his wife and Mario and I are left alone with our two Colombian protectors. In the beginning these guys were clearly reluctant to talk to us, and given the machine guns they always carry, we felt pretty much the same way about them. But we've been living with them for over a month now. Their machine guns are no more disconcerting than an umbrella would be in the hands of a Brit. The more bored Mario and I grow with each other, the more curious we become about them. And although when Jota is away they spend plenty of time talking on the radio to their friends from Medellin, I guess they must be pretty bored themselves because when Mario sits down at the table and asks, "Who do you guys work for anyway?" they open up like clams in steam.

They work, they tell us, for two men, Mickey and Toro. These men were two of Rodriquez Gacha's men before the CIA took him down. I remind them that the Colombian Defense Forces were in on the kill too and the light-haired one, Carlos, says, "No, no, no. Everyone in Colombia has family in the Defense Forces. And no one wants anyone in their family killed. The CIA did it. It's as simple as that."

I'm not about to argue. I pull up a chair beside Mario and listen while they tell us how Gacha and Escobar and a man named Ochoa were all in it together in the beginning. Gacha was in charge of manufacturing the cocaine and Escobar was in charge of smuggling it to the American market and taking care of the money. When Gacha got himself killed, the other two went their separate ways. So Gacha's lieutenants were left with the manufacturing facilities and tons of cocaine, but no way to move it. They had to be satisfied dispatching it to small-time smugglers. The small-time smugglers can't move that much, but as there are a lot of them, it's better than nothing.

A lot of the coke comes from refineries as far as 400 miles away. So if a piston airplane, which is the kind you need for low flying, were to start off with both the coke and the gas needed to make a trip to, say, Puerto Rico, it would be far too heavy. Jota's is the perfect place to load and top off the tanks. It's a favorite in the area because he's right on the coast with the caves and lots of hiding spots for boats. The only one better is nearby Puerto Australia, where Carlos and José have also done work. But there is more activity going on there, and with all of the recent attention focused on the drug trade, the volume is quickly becoming a disadvantage. Smaller is safer now. The airplanes come in, load the coke which is already waiting for them, refuel, and set out over the ocean. If they pick up a tail and have to come back, they can stop at Jota's to unload and refuel again before going back into the interior. There's only one catch. There are three different agencies whose task it is to bust Colombian drug smugglers. Gacha's lieutenants pay two of them; the most the local police and the military will do is put on a show now and then. But the third, the Secret Police...well, they're the real McCoy. Jota is terrified of them. Everyone is. You can't intimidate them. They come in with machine guns, Carlos says, and start shooting; they shoot everybody.

"Great," I say to Mario, and then to the Colombians in my best Spanish, "What would happen to us if the Secret Police come down on Jota?"

José snickers good-naturedly at my naivete. "Two gringos in the Guajira? They'd throw you in jail and torture you until you talked."

"But we couldn't talk even if we wanted to. We don't know that much. Jota doesn't tell us."

Now he laughs outright. "Then they'd torture you to death, wouldn't they?"

Yes, I suppose they would. And so, since there is nothing to lose,

Mario and I begin to make a habit of sitting down with our Colombian protectors daily, as apt to get lost in their stories of life among drug smugglers as I once was in the bedtime stories my mother told me as a kid. We learn all about the operation, all the details. Each kilo is packed in a plaster wrapper similar to the kind used to support broken limbs. Then the wrappers, 30 or 40 of them, are placed in cardboard boxes or gas or milk containers, whatever is available. The containers are wrapped in burlap and held together with duct tape. Once the coke has been packaged and buried, Jota tells the cartel to send their pilots in for it. The landing strip is about eight miles away. The job of our protectors is to oversee the operation, to protect Jota, and to kill anyone they're told to kill. Mario asks them if we can go with them sometime when an airplane comes in and see for ourselves, but Carlos responds, "You stay the hell away. None of these people are coming here to see you. Gringos scare them off. If they see a gringo, they might get pissed off and start shooting." His fingertips rattle on the barrel of his gun.

Maybe the Colombians tell Jota about the questions we've begun to ask, because one evening Jota offers to take us on a tour of the outskirts of the camp in his Toyota. We bounce along at about five mph, circumventing wild mules as we go. Other than the dust we stir up, it feels great to get out in a truck and really see the place. The scenery continues to be magnificent. Sunken ships protrude from the waters along the coast, reminders of the dangers of the area. In the other three directions, the barren desert rolls out to merge with the horizon.

Jota drives to the airstrip that runs four miles into the desert. He points out the spots where airplanes have crashed while trying to land at night without lights. "The problem," he says, "is that most of these pilots didn't have more than 100 hours total flight experience."

One hundred hours is nothing. It doesn't even get you past beginner status. I tell Jota this. Then Mario chirps up, bragging to him about my training, "real" training, he tells Jota. Jota nods encouragingly, so Mario continues, telling him how my flight instruction began when I was 12, about all the hours that I put into it to learn what I learned—all information Mario knows by heart from our long conversations throughout our imprisonment. Meanwhile, I drift off and think of the second world war and how when the shortage of pilots hit, would-be pilots were given some quick training and thrown into missions. Plenty of them crashed too. The only difference is that here, instead of defending lives, Jota's pilots are in it for the money—a far stronger motivator, the strongest motivator of all.

Along the runway are airplane parts which I recognize as belonging to a four-engine Douglas DC6. Jota confirms my observation and tells us seven people died in that one. We drive down the runway for another mile or so and Jota points out more parts of the same airplane. He says they dragged the parts behind jeeps so it wouldn't look like a crash site from the air. Halfway down the old runway there is a graveyard where the seven people from the DC6 and several others from other crashes have been laid to rest. Jota says the area where our shack is was once an airport. That was during the good old days when smuggling was an easy living and no more dangerous than fishing. "We should try working together sometime," he states when we reach the end of the runway and see the lighthouse on the coast blinking in the distance. "You're experienced. You could land an airplane at night, no problem."

I study his profile and try to think how to answer. I'm not quite sure what he's getting at. Jota is an independent. As far as I have been able to tell, he helps out the cartel with storing and loading and fueling and gets a cut of the action for his services. His business is not smuggling but aiding smugglers. As if he's reading my mind, he adds, "These crashes over the years...I took a few kilos here and there. They add up. I have over 1,000. Just sitting there in the sand. Three months ago there was an airplane, a Piper Malibu, coming in, full of coke. A military jet came along and put its landing gear down. But the Piper didn't respond, didn't make a move to follow him. So the jet shot it down." Jota laughs and holds up his pinky. "The biggest part we found of the guy was his little finger. But we recovered 200 keys of coke. When his people sent in another airplane to pick it up, I dug up some of my old coke and gave them that. I like to keep my supply fresh. What do you think?"

I get to thinking that maybe I can use this conversation to my advantage. "Yeah, Jota, someday. I could land an airplane in the dark, that's for sure. These pilots you know, I don't know about them. But I'd have to get out of here first."

"And you'd want a lot of money of course."

"Oh yeah, of course, that too. I couldn't do it for less than a couple hundred grand. One hundred minimum. I'll give it some thought, and someday, if you ever get me out of here, we can talk about doing some work. But you'd have to get me home first. That's my first priority."

"Yeah, well. You're right. The airplane will be coming for you and you'll be leaving us before long. But it was a good idea, huh?"

As it turns out, Jota is the one who leaves, and for the next four days, Mario and I are left alone with the Colombians. It's very quiet. No one calls on the radio, not even Manolo. When Jota returns, he has with him a case of beer, a big fresh ham, fresh bread, buns, fruit, after-shave, soap, and what he considers to be good news. He visited with the military commanders, paid some money, went to Medellin and met the heads of the cartel, and he had a meeting with Manolo. Jota doesn't offer to provide any details.

The next day a boat shows up with about 800 gallons of aviation gas in 55-gallon containers. While we're helping Jota's Indians to unload it, Jota says to me, "I think I may have some work for you, my friend."

Mario, who is bent over one of the barrels, stops short of lifting it to stare at us. I can see his wheels turning. He's indignant because Jota has work for me and not for him. "What work?" I say to Jota. "What do you mean, work? I'm not doing any work. I want to leave."

"We'll talk about it later," he responds.

That's fine with me. And to punish him for even suggesting it, I put down the container I was carrying and go up the cliff path empty-handed.

The following morning Jota drives off in his Toyota and returns a little later with three men. Since Jota always asks us to leave when he's having company, I figure this is an oversight and head out the door with my swimming towel in hand. But Jota puts his palm out to stop me. Then he brings one of the men, a smallish, good-looking guy with a bit of a limp, right up to me. "Henry," he says, "this is the pilot." I shake Henry's hand and look beyond his broad smile to the other two. One strikes me as being exceptionally delinquent-looking. He has a drooping mustache, thin lips and a protruding chin. His dark eyes are rigid and sunken, and he looks like he never cracked a smile in his life. The other looks a little like Jota, but without the slouch. "Let's go in," Jota says. I realize he means me too, and feeling increasingly uncomfortable, I follow the others in.

Jota sits down at the radio and his three friends gather around him. I sit at the table with Mario and our protectors and play with the handle of one of the coffee mugs that's been left on it. Jota gets Toro on the radio and tells him the airplane has arrived, and that everyone, including the gringo, is present. Then his Spanish gets soft and rapid so that I get the feeling he's still talking about me but doesn't want me to know what he's saying. "Tell me what's going on," I say to Mario.

He holds his hand up. "Wait, wait. I can't hear you both at once." And a moment later, "They're going to make a run. They're talking about you being the pilot."

I snicker. "Mario, I'm not flying."

"Shut up. How can I hear anything?"

Now I don't care what else is being said. "No one told me anything about flying," I say again.

"You told Jota you would fly. Remember?"

"We were speaking hypothetically. He knows that! I said someday, once I get home, that I might come back and fly his stuff, not the cartel's, and I was only bullshitting him anyway. The key phrase here was 'When you get me home.'"

Jota turns from the radio suddenly and looks at me. "They want to know if you'll fly to Puerto Rico," he says. "They want you to be the pilot."

"No," I say bluntly.

Jota laughs. "Okay, then. You can be the copilot."

"No, you're not getting it, Jota. I don't want to be either. I don't want to fly to Puerto Rico."

"Why not?"

I look at Mario. His brows are lifted so high they almost meet his hairline. He is motionless. I look back at Jota. "I don't want to fly to Puerto Rico, that's why."

Jota looks puzzled. "But didn't we already talk about this? I seem to remember telling you about it."

I begin to get flustered. I can't think how to tell him in Spanish that we spoke hypothetically. I tell Mario to explain it to him. It takes awhile because I have first to explain the meaning of the word to Mario. Then Mario says to Jota, "You should have asked him outright."

Henry is staring at me good-naturedly. Since everyone else looks angry, I say to him, "Look, I'm sorry. I really don't want to go to Puerto Rico."

Henry cocks his head. "Come here," he says softly.

I get up and go to him. We turn our backs to the others and put our heads together. "It's an easy job," he whispers. "We're going to drop the coke, come back empty, and land. That's all there is to it. We're not even going to stop. My people are doing it all the time. Only problem is, they keep getting a tail. We've heard that you're the best."

"I'd like to help you out, but I can't. There's no possible way you're going to get in and out without a tail. And then a night landing? No way," I say, and I return to the table in time to hear Jota telling Toro the same thing on the radio, the gringo pilot doesn't want to do it.

Toro doesn't respond right away. I figure his silence is a sign that he's busy deciding who else he can get to do the job. But I'm wrong. "Kill him," he tells Jota. "Kill the pilot."

My body jerks with nervous laughter. I glance at our protectors. They're not exactly aiming their machine guns at me, but they've lifted the barrels so that they rest on the table, and their arms are tensed as if they mean to be ready to take aim on short notice.

In the course of our recent conversations, our protectors have spoken ardently of their loyalty to the cartel. In Medellin, people are taken into the cartel when they're very young. These are people whose families have nothing. The cartel takes them from their cardboard shacks and sets them up in houses. Pablo Escobar built whole villages in Medellin. The whole town was built on drug money. He built subdivisions and gave them away to the families of the people who worked for him. When someone is told to do something, he does it. If these guys are told to kill me and don't, they'll be killed. There is no doubt about it. I know it, and so do they.

I turn around and see that Henry has moved off a few yards, as if to get out of the line of fire. I turn back and look at Mario. Even he's leaning away from me. "Did Toro say what I think he said?" I ask him.

Mario lowers his head and shakes it slowly. When he lifts it again a moment later, he's almost smiling. "You told him you'd need a lot of money," he reminds me.

"So what? I didn't mean it. I was just talking." But then I see his point. If Jota is going to take our hypothetical conversation as a contract, then I can too. I become immediately indignant. "Hey, Jota," I say in a voice loud enough for Toro to hear over the radio. "I told you I'd fly for $100,000 minimum. These people show up here empty-handed and expect me to do a mission? Where's the money, Jota? You're supposed to be responsible for me. You're supposed to respond for me. You're supposed to be protecting me."

I glance at Mario. He gives me a congratulatory nod. If Toro thinks Jota promised me that kind of money, then the blame falls on him, on Jota. How can they justify killing me now?

Jota stares at me for what seems like a long time and without any expression. Then he turns around to the radio. "We've got to give the gringo some money," he says slowly and clearly so that I can understand every word. Then he reverts back to the soft, rapid Spanish he was using before.

"Maybe it's not a bad idea," Mario says. "You could get Henry to land the airplane. You could get away. You could find a way to come back for me."

I start thinking along these lines, but it's hard to concentrate. In the meantime, Jota says something to Henry and Henry produces an envelope and hands it to Jota. Jota tells me that it contains $8,000 in U.S. bills. He holds it out to me. "You'll get the rest when the job is done," he says.

"How much?"

"Ninety-two, what you asked for."

I let him sit with his hands extended and turn back to Mario. "If I could get him to land… He's small, I might be able to overpower him, but he's going to have a gun."

"They'll need a kicker, someone to drop the coke. Take the money. Then tell them you want me to be the kicker. If we go together, maybe we can disarm him while we're still in the air."

I turn around. Jota is still pointing the envelope at me. And my two protectors have shifted their guns so they are a little closer to being pointed at me. "You have to do it," Mario is saying. "I believe them. They will kill you. These guys from Medellin don't like gringos to start with. Look at our two buddies here. They'll do it man, I'm telling you."

I reach over to Jota and take the envelope from his hand. There is immediately a collective sigh of relief. Jota whispers something more into the radio and shuts it down. Our protectors lower their machine guns and try to look like they never had them aimed. It's clear now that this mission was Jota's intent all along. I begin to put the pieces together. Maybe Manolo couldn't come up with the money, the $20,000 our lawyers needed to release us. Maybe he called his buddy Jota, and said, "Look, I can get you a pilot cheap, but I need some money to get him out of jail." That would explain all his stalling, all the lies, Jota's setting me up with our little hypothetical conversation out on the air strip. I'm his. Jota owns me. I am so pissed I feel like I am going to rupture. To keep from saying anything that will get me killed, I bite down hard on my bottom lip. I think about the night in Riohacha when I got drunk and, according to Mario, called a lot of people a lot of bad names. I imagine I felt the same way then. The others don't even seem to realize how pissed I am; when I scan their faces, I find them all looking the same, all looking like they have got all bloody day to hang around and see what I'm going to say next. I take the stack of bills out of the envelope and cut it like a card deck. I hand half to Mario, for safe-keeping and in case I don't get back. Then I pocket my half and sweep the coffee mugs aside with my arm. "Do you have any maps?" I ask Henry. He nods. "Get them," I say.

Variations on Smuggling

Henry admits he's never been to Puerto Rico before. He hands me the maps and shows me on the largest of them the valley where we're supposed to drop the stuff. It looks pretty tight, and already I'm thinking that if this guy is as poor a pilot as some of the others I've heard about, I can probably fix it so we never find the place. I'm no angel; I'll be the first to admit that ferrying airplanes for Manolo was not entirely legal. One DEA agent looking aside for his own reasons doesn't make it all that much less so. But flying cocaine into American markets is south of the line that separates the things I'll do to earn a living from the things I won't.

I map out the distance and figure our destination is about 500 miles away. Another 500 back is 1,000 total. Not a long trip. The airplane, Henry tells me, is a Seneca 2, a model I'm not at all familiar with. If I were home and had my books, I could look up the best power and range settings for the engines. But I'm not home and I haven't seen a book since *Christine*, so I have to take Henry's estimates as gospel.

I ask him how much we're delivering and he says 300 kilos. He tells me he intends to carry 300 gallons of gas as well. According to my calculations, 300 is excessive, 200 should be plenty. I ask him if he has flown this airplane with this much weight. "The airplane will fly," he says. "Fuel is safety. If there's a problem, we'll have other options." I have to agree with him there.

As casually as possible, so that it coasts right in with the mileage and the weight talk, I mention that I would like to take Mario along to be the kicker. Henry responds at once. "No," he says. "No way."

"Look," I say, turning to Jota, "I need someone who can speak English. How am I going to give the kicker orders if he can't speak English?"

Jota shrugs. "Your Spanish isn't so bad when you need it."

"No," Henry reiterates. He shakes his head emphatically. "We'll take Carlos instead."

I turn to look at Carlos. He isn't saying anything, but his eyes are twice the size they were the last time I bothered to notice, and his chin is tilted upward so he looks like he's tuned in to some diabolic voice the rest of us can't hear. He wants to be the kicker just about as much as I want to be the copilot. I look at Mario apologetically. "Go for it, man," he tells me. "If you can get out, get out. I know you'll come back for me. I trust you."

"You have my word," I promise him. "If I get out, I'll get an airplane and come back for you."

Our conversation in English, which Jota is used to, makes Henry nervous. He's fidgeting in his seat and watching us intently. As I want him to trust me, I go back to the maps, but Mario keeps talking anyway. "You've got money now. If you get to Puerto Rico, try to land somewhere; try to talk the pilot into letting you out. It's a long shot, but you've got to take it."

We leave in two trucks, with some of Jota's Indians. It takes us about 20 minutes to go the eight miles to the runway because of the goats and the burros and the ditches in the road. Mario and I spend the entire time saying our goodbyes and confirming plans and promises. I tell him over and over again that I won't let him down, that no matter what the risk, I'll come back for him.

I insist that Jota drive down the runway. I remember it being in bad shape, but the last time I was on it I was too busy listening to him describe its victims to make an evaluation. Now I see it's worse than I thought. It's full of ruts and dried-up mud holes that are easily capable of knocking off the landing gear. I tell Jota to take Henry and me to the airplane and then to get the Indians to work repairing the worst of the ruts.

Three-hundred gallons of gasoline weighs about 1,800 pounds, the maximum load for a craft the size of the one we're approaching. And we have yet to add the 300 kilos and the people. The way I figure it, we'll be about 1,400 pounds overweight at takeoff. Before I get out of the truck, I stretch my hand out to Mario, but somehow I wind up giving him a quick hug instead of a handshake.

I ask Henry how many hours are on the airplane. He says a lot, but that it's been well maintained. We go in and begin to check things out. A while later Jota returns with the load and his assurance that the runway has been adequately repaired. I know the Indians can't have done a very good job in the amount of time that's passed.

We load up and stick Carlos in the back. He looks lost back there without his machine gun. Henry shows me the door. He has it rigged so it can be opened inward and used to drop the cargo. I look out from it and find Jota staring up at me. "Look," he says, "you fly to Puerto Rico, locate the valley, and drop the load in the field. It's very easy, practically a direct course. If you get a tail, you turn around and come back. They'll still pay you all your money. What could be easier? They won't shoot you down. They'll just chase you around until you leave."

Thanks Jota, but I have already considered all that, I think, but I say nothing. I've considered too that if we get a tail, they'll probably follow us all the way back and circle for a few hours. Then the military will feel compelled to get in on the act, to send out some helicopters and put on a show. As I'm heading up to the cockpit, I hear Jota say to Henry, "If he screws up, shoot him. Those are our orders."

I ignore this. My concerns are more immediate. There are eight drums of gasoline right behind our seats and the load is right behind that. If we hit a rut on the runway, the load will come forward and crush us even before the fire begins—a nasty way to die. Then the airplane will burn for a week.

To rid myself of these images, I look over the maps once more. I decide to take a heading for Santo Domingo on Espanola Island 100 miles northwest of Puerto Rico. There's an automatic direction-finding station there, a beacon that we can use our ADF to get to. Navigation should be easy. Henry goes through a preflight check on the engines, running them up to 1,700 RPM. He checks the mags, the fuel flow, and tells me to wait to set the flaps until we're moving down the runway. I don't have to ask him why. With the weight we're carrying, we can't afford to tamper with the airspeed. The flaps in this airplane are Johnson Bar Flaps. That is, there is a bar between the seats that you pull up like an emergency brake handle. The clicks it makes coming up indicate the amount of flap descent.

Henry applies full power, checks the fuel flow and the RPM and releases the emergency brake. As we begin to move down the runway, I hold my breath and wait to see what will happen. I tell Henry to lift the nose a little to get some of the weight off of the nose gear, the weakest point in the landing-gear system. Then I pull the lever up one notch, giving it ten degrees of flap.

We reach about 80 mph and literally waddle into the air. I can't believe we're actually airborne! Henry pulls up the landing gear immediately, demonstrating that he knows what he's doing after all. He tells me to bring the bar up another notch. "No," I say. "Twenty degrees of flap is asking for trouble. We'll be inducing more drag than lift and besides we're climbing." As he doesn't respond, I leave the bar where it is. Out of the corner of my eye I watch to see if he'll pull it up himself. He doesn't. He lowers the nose, builds some more airspeed in ground effect. We're flying level over the ground at about ten feet. When we reach 110 knots indicated, I decide it's safe to raise the flaps and push the bar down to the floor.

We're cruising at full power and gaining altitude. The airplane is stable, flying well. I realize I'm still holding my breath and exhale deeply. I'm amazed and a lot more confident than I was before.

Henry flies the first ten minutes and then tells me to take over. Now, I figure, I'll have the chance to punish him for not objecting to Jota's order. I lower the nose immediately and bring it down to about 80 feet above the water. When I level it out, I glance at him to see if I've given him the scare I intended, but he doesn't look the least bit concerned. I'm astonished, impressed, and disappointed simultaneously.

After about 15 minutes of hand-flying the craft, I turn it over to Henry again. He keeps it between 80 and 100 feet. Fifteen minutes later, he turns it back over to me. When the main tanks have burned down a bit, about an hour and a half into the flight, I show Carlos how to use the hose and pump to transfer fuel into the tanks from the gas containers we're carrying. He works quietly, with jerky movements and a tautness around his mouth that confirms his discomfort. When I return to my seat, Henry points out how stable the airplane is flying in spite of all the weight. I have to hand it to him; she really is doing quite well, flying perfectly, in fact. And Henry seems to know what he's doing. I forgive him, somewhat—for the fact he's carrying a gun and is prepared to use it—and start a conversation concerning prison life.

He tells me he spent nine months in jail himself. He went down to Venezuela to look at a King Air and someone paid somebody to arrest him and stick him in jail in Caracas. We compare horror stories and conclude that the prison in Caracas is worse than the one in Maracaibo. Then I tell him about Jenny, about how long it's been since I've seen her. I'm hoping for some sympathy, some indication that he won't object when the time comes for me to insist he land the airplane. But he only offers me a sidelong glance and continues to handle the plane.

When I see that we're nearing the Dominican Republic, I stop talking so I can concentrate on my navigation. I remember reading once in *Playboy* about a Dominican Republic Air Force pilot who shot down a drug plane over the water. The pilot managed to get out and was floating around, worrying, no doubt, about drowning and sharks, when the jet came in to make two or three more striking runs on him. This horror story sticks in my brain. I definitely don't want to accidentally enter their air space.

I have Henry turn the airplane a full 90 degrees. I can only guess the distance from here to Puerto Rico. We're supposed to be there at six and it is now 5:25. I tell Henry to bring her down to about 50 feet. After ten minutes, we spot La Mona, an island off of Puerto Rico. I realize we can't be more than ten or 15 miles away. It looks like we'll be on time after all—a fluke since we would have left an hour earlier if I hadn't challenged Jota and insisted on the runway repair. Now I wish I hadn't done either. The ground crew will all be waiting. Even if I get Henry to land the airplane, I doubt it'll be easy for me to walk away from it.

Just after La Mona, I get the surprise of my life in the form of an American destroyer no more than 250 yards straight ahead of us. Since Henry is busy with the instruments and hasn't noticed it, I immediately take over the controls, gain some altitude, and turn to the right. Henry jerks his head up and realizes what's happening. I tell him I'm sure they've spotted us. Even if no one is on deck with binoculars, which is unlikely, they have to have us on their radar. "If they don't shoot us down, you can be sure we'll have a tail in no time," I shout. "There's no way we can drop this load! We have to turn back."

Henry continues to stare at the destroyer. He looks astonished, but also somewhat amused. "Well," he says casually, "we don't have a tail at the moment. Let's see what happens. If we get a tail, we'll turn around."

"We will get a tail," I insist. "They have to have seen us. We've got to turn back."

He opens his mouth to respond but just then Carlos starts shouting from the back. "You see," I say sharply. "We have a tail."

"That's not what he's yelling," Henry shouts. "Be quiet. I can't hear him over you and the engines."

The yelling continues and is rising in pitch. Henry and I both turn around at the same time. When I turn back, I realize I must have relaxed pressure on the column for an instant because we're heading straight for the water. I can't believe I let such a thing happen! I yank it back immediately and just in the nick of time. Carlos is yelling louder than ever. "Tell him to shut the hell up!" I shout.

Henry, who missed the thrill of seeing us nearly crash, turns forward in his seat. "We don't have a tail," he tells me. "You see, you were wrong. Carlos's hands are cold. That's all."

"Holy shit! We've got an American destroyer out there and Puerto Rico dead ahead and he's yelling that his hands are cold!" I take a few deep breaths to calm myself. Carlos's hands, I realize, are probably cold from fright, from anticipation of the moment, which won't be far off if we don't get a tail, when he'll have to use them.

We pick up the coast and I gain another 2,500 feet of altitude. The whole world should be able to see us on their radar now, the Coast Guard, the DEA, the CIA, the military, everybody. Henry tells me where to turn to find the valley. Before I can consider turning too much or too little so as to miss it, it appears before us. Henry tunes the radio to the frequency of the people on the ground and hands me the mike. "Hola, hola," I say to them, but when they all respond at once, I turn the radio back over to Henry. He and the ground people are in the process of exchanging passwords to identify themselves when Carlos shouts, "There's an airplane behind us!"

"There's an airplane behind us," Henry repeats into the mike. "We're heading back to Colombia."

I am greatly relieved and not at all surprised. Of course there's an airplane behind us. How could there not be? I tell Henry to take over and put the spare T-shirt I brought along over my head Ninja-style so only my eyes are exposed. When Henry looks at me quizzically, I say, "I don't want to be photographed." This is what they do in movies, but I guess he hasn't seen the same ones I have. He thinks it over and decides to follow my example nonetheless. As we're turning, we see an American Airlines airliner going by. "That was the tail?" Henry shouts back to Carlos. "That's an airliner! It's nothing to worry about, you idiot. Look for military or civilian airplanes, or turbo-props or jets or Coast Guard. Look for the big orange stripe." Then he gets back on the radio and tells the people on the ground that the tail wasn't a tail after all, that we're going to fly over the valley once and they should look to see if there's anyone behind us because it might be difficult for our man in the back to see. The people on the ground say they can't even see us. Henry turns on flashing lights, landing lights, all the lights the airplane has. "Can you see us now?" he asks. "Do we have a tail?"

"How do we know you're not the tail?" one of them shouts.

"This is nuts," I say to Henry. "This is chaos. This is not going to work."

"Drop it!" the voices on the ground shout. "Drop it now! Drop it! Drop it!"

The valley is nothing more than a creek with mountains rising up steeply on either side. It's far too narrow to turn an airplane around. And the field, if you can call it that, doesn't look large enough for a game of soccer let alone to land an airplane. And now that we've seen the destroyer, I don't want to land anymore anyway. I'm expecting the helicopters to come raining out of the sky at any moment and I don't want to spend the rest of my life in prison for smuggling cocaine. I just want to drop the load and get out.

So much for heroism.

We pass out of the valley and get ready to turn. I yell back to Carlos to open the door. The last thing I see before I turn back is a look of terror spreading across his face. I'm just thinking that he won't be able to do it when I hear the wind rush in and I know he's managed in spite of his nervous state. Henry, who looks a little frightened himself now, prepares to come in over the field. "I've never done this before," he admits.

"What?"

"I'm not going to be able to get too low."

I look him over good. If the man doesn't want to get low, that's fine with me. Altitude is safety. If you get too low in an airplane like this one and lose an engine in a valley this steep, it's over. It's highly unlikely you'd be able to climb out. It will take us no more than 20 seconds to pass over the field. We'll have to be exceptionally precise, or the coke will wind up all over the valley from this high up. But hey, I don't have the controls. It's not my problem.

"You're too high, you're too high," the people on the ground are all yelling at once. At 1,000 feet not only are we too high, but at 120 mph, we're also moving too fast. I turn around to Carlos and tell him to start throwing. But the noise between us is incredible, and by the time he figures out what I'm saying and gets the first bale out, we're already over the far end of the field. He gets the second bale ready to go and starts in yelling again. I know he must be asking whether he should drop it or not, but I pretend not to understand. I realize all at once that I'm smiling and make some attempt to alter my expression. Out goes the second bale. By the time he gets the third out, we're a good mile beyond the field flying over a gorge with no access road in sight. He's ready to toss the fourth when Henry turns around and shouts for him to hold it up until he can turn the airplane around.

Our instructions were to make only two passes over the field. We made the first just checking things out, the second dropping, and now this will be the third. The people on the radio are yelling, "Get down lower, slow down the airplane, the bales are going everywhere." There are some houses on the mountainside; with us putting the power up to the maximum and then pulling it back and turning, someone must have noticed us by now. I can't imagine why we don't have a tail. "Drop it now," the people on the ground yell. I turn back to Carlos to see if he's heard. He looks confused. He doesn't know what I want. I hesitate for a moment before confirming the order. Enough time elapses to ensure another misfire. He throws out the next bale right after it. We are about three miles away from the field and turning when he is poised to throw the next. I wait until he has it halfway out the door and shout, "No, don't throw it yet!" But of course it's too late. The bale goes tumbling. Carlos trembles from head to toe as he closes the door. I turn to Henry. "I told him to wait," I grumble.

Henry, who is concentrating on flying the airplane, nods his head to let me know he knows I did my best. Then he gets on the radio, interrupts the chaos there to tell them we're going home.

I tell Henry to put the power to it and get it up to about 6,000 feet. I am still wearing my T-shirt Ninja style because I'm expecting at the very least that someone will come by to take pictures. But there's no one out there at all.

At 10,000 feet we take a heading for Aruba and put it on auto-pilot. I look back and find Carlos curled up on the floor with his hands between his knees. Except for the fact he's still quivering violently, he looks like a fetus. Henry and I settle in for the inevitable discussion about what went wrong. I would like to feel that I'm responsible for all the mishaps, but the truth is I couldn't have done it without Carlos's incompetence and Henry's reluctance to swoop down into the valley. But as I'm not about to criticize Henry, I agree with him that the valley was too narrow, that the person who picked the location can't have been a pilot—and I add that you have to have someone who can throw. "You see," I say, "we should have taken Mario. He's big, he's strong, he could have thrown out the bales with one hand."

"Well, we did the best we could with what we had to work with,"

Henry acknowledges. "It's their problem now. Let them worry about it."

We take turns flying and dozing alternately and get to Aruba in three hours. I keep going over the whole ordeal, wondering how we could have got in and flown at those altitudes without being detected. An airliner just about ran over us. He must have seen us. And then the ship; it's incredible.

We've burned over 150 gallons of gas, and, with the load gone, we're finally down to about the maximum allowable takeoff weight. From the Aruba VOR, we turn outbound on the 275-degree radial. I check the DME, the Distance Measuring Equipment, and get our ground speed. From that and the distance from the station, I calculate how many more miles we have to go on this course, and by using my ground speed, dividing that into miles, I determine the minutes. Then, using my stop watch, minutes and seconds, I start the navigation. It must be impeccable. If I'm lucky, the lighthouse I'm looking for will be nothing but a dot in a big black hole. But it may be even less than that; there are plenty of nights when a dense cloud cover forms over the Guajira at about 300 feet. I recall Henry insisting that we carry the extra gas. Now I'm glad we did. If it's overcast and I can't find the light-house, we can circle for five or six hours, until morning if necessary, at reduced power.

My efforts pay off; we find the lighthouse at Punta Gallina without any problem. But as I anticipated, it's nothing but a speck of light in the darkness. I think I remember the heading I need to get from it to the airstrip, but I can't be certain. When we were leaving, I was so sure that one way or the other I wouldn't be coming back that I didn't bother to commit it to memory. Jota is supposed to have the airstrip lit up with candles, or, rather, kerosene-drenched rags burning in buckets. But without even some indication of where the horizon might be, I can only guess at the direction in which I should look for them. There are no visual clues to help me figure out what's up, down, left, or right. It's just the lighthouse and the darkness surrounding it.

We get Jota on the radio. He confirms that the runway is lit and that the trucks are there with their headlights on. We get a little lower and see a few lights scattered here and there, but nothing that looks like a runway. Using the lighthouse as our reference point, we fly to the west. We tell Jota to point the trucks in the direction we'll be approaching from. Henry turns and slows her down to about 85 mph for the approach. He puts down the landing gear and I lower the flaps two notches. We still can't pick up any definite lights other than the slow blinking of the lighthouse. I take over the column and Henry the other controls. I tell him to get it down to 80 mph. He gets it right on the nose and holds it fast. When I begin my gradual descent, I finally make out the faint line of lights that mark the runway. Amazingly, I find I only need to make a slight correction to align the airplane with it. But I overcorrect just slightly in the process, and Henry, who notices before I do, touches the column to compensate before going back to his own work.

As we get closer to the strip, I see the trucks. Everything looks good. We're down to about 150 feet and the airspeed is still right on. We get closer and lower until the runway is right before us. It's no wonder I didn't see the light from the buckets at first, with the force of the wind flattening the flames out. And besides that, Jota has the buckets spread out about 300 feet apart.

We come down smoothly and stop well before the end of the runway. "We got in and out without a tail," Henry declares as we turn to taxi back.

I glance at him and see that he's smiling. "I guess that means you won't be shooting me," I say in English for my own amusement.

Mario and José and the other two Colombians are there with Jota when we stop. "You did it!" the Colombians exclaim as we climb out.

"It's fantastic." Mario alone is not smiling.

"We received radio confirmation," Jota begins. "They're still searching for a couple of bales, but more than half has been picked up."

I step toward Mario and try to hide my astonishment. "Who's saying that?" I ask him. "We dropped the coke all over the valley!"

"Why didn't you land? I thought you were going to try to land?"

"I couldn't. It was impossible. What about this confirmation? Who did it come from?"

"Why was it impossible?"

Back at the shack Jota gets on the radio with the people in Medellin and Puerto Rico at the same time. Everyone seems to be happy. I can't understand what they are so happy about. The report has to be a mistake. I figure when the truth is learned, it may look as if this is my fault. I decide it's in my best interest to prepare Jota ahead of time. I pull him aside as soon as I'm able and tell Mario to translate so that what I say will be as clear as day. I explain that he shouldn't be excited, that the coke went up and down the valley. His smile collapses. "What happened?" he asks.

"Carlos," I say. "He's too small. He can't throw. The bales were too heavy for him and the field was too short. A pilot has to pick these spots."

Jota places his finger beneath his nose and nods contemplatively. I'm contemplating myself. When Henry and I were landing the airplane, it occurred to me I might be forced to do this all over again. If I am, I want to make sure it will be the last time. "I would have liked to make sure that the whole load was accounted for, Jota. Come down low and land is the key. If you don't have a tail, you can just come in and land. And then you can hand the load over from the airplane to the cars. We could have done that if it hadn't been for the location. A pilot has to pick the site. If they recovered 100 keys, I'll be surprised. I don't know where this other information is coming from."

"And," Mario adds as part of his translation on my behalf, "what about his pay schedule? Where's the rest of the money?"

Jota nods and walks off to where the others are celebrating with a bottle of whiskey. He joins them, saying nothing about the mishap.

The next morning, Jota wakes all of us to announce that he has the cartel on the radio and they're saying the entire ground crew is in jail. They were supposed to pick the stuff up and bury it immediately. But since they didn't see any helicopters, they brought what they found, some 200 kilos, to a shack about five miles from the drop site. But the local police had already been notified because one of the missing bales actually hit a house. The ground crew was arrested with the goods.

Henry and the other Colombians stare at Jota with their mouths open. "What's going to happen to me?" I ask Jota. "Will I be blamed for this?"

Jota keeps his eyes on Carlos as he answers. "No way. You did your job perfectly. Your job was to be the navigator and get the pilot to the valley and help with the flying. You did all that." He picks up the mike and speaks his rapid Spanish into it. I understand enough to know that he's telling the cartel the same thing. I don't hear them disagreeing. When he's done, he turns to me again. "But don't expect any more money for this," he adds. "They're not going to pay you."

Before I have time to respond, Henry, who is just about ready to leave for Medellin, interrupts to ask if I want to come along with him. "My people want to meet you," he says.

We both turn toward Jota. His arms are folded and he's shaking his head. "No," he says softly.

When Henry steps forward to confer with Jota privately, I step back to where Mario is standing. "Jota won't let you go," Mario says.

"But if he does...if Henry gets him to—"

"Then go for it. Same as before. Nothing's happening here. It's our only chance. If you get out—"

"No," we hear Jota saying emphatically to Henry. "Absolutely not." Then he turns toward José. "Henry needs a ride to the strip," he says. "Take the truck."

The other two Colombians are staying behind to keep an eye on the next shipment of coke that's coming in. They stand around with Mario and Carlos and me and watch Jota set out the mound of coke he will have for breakfast. When Jota turns around and sees us all watching him, he cocks his head toward the doorway, his way of saying he wants to be alone. We move outside, but we linger near the shack, discussing the mission amongst ourselves. Beyond our discussion, I can hear Jota busy on the radio again through the open door. I'm close enough to listen, but I'm too busy watching Carlos to bother. He's standing somewhat apart from our little circle, staring down at his feet with his machine gun dangling at his side as if it's suddenly far too heavy for him. I can't help but feel bad for the kid. His only objective in life has been to please the cartel, and he's failed miserably.

Carlos turns and takes a few steps toward the cliffs. While he's standing there with his back to us, Jota emerges, sniffing in response to the coke. I notice he's carrying a gun, the .357 Magnum he usually keeps in his room. Before I know what's happening, there's a shot, a piercing explosion that hangs in the air like a fog.

Time gets sluggish when these things happen. I see Jota sniffing, turning, the gun smoking at his side. But I'm still thinking he's come out to test the gun. It doesn't penetrate that he's come out to kill a man until I turn my head and see Carlos down on the ground, up on one elbow, looking over his shoulder, his right arm raised in an appeal. His eyes are enormous, shining with terror. His mouth is open, coughing, gasping, gushing blood. There is a hole in the middle of his back, small, precise, encircled with red.

I find myself stepping toward Carlos, but when I see that the others are doing the same, I turn toward the shack. Jota is facing the radio.

His gun is now on the shelf beside it. "It's done," I hear him saying into the mike.

My rage is concentrated in my hands, my fingers, and its object is Jota's neck. But I am unable to act, even when Jota turns and looks at me expressionlessly. I'm caught between two forces, a weak but persistent survival instinct and a killer instinct I may be acknowledging for the first time.

I turn in time to see José coming back in the truck. He's out the second it stops, his eyes bulging and his mouth quivering. Mario and the other two Colombians, who are bent over Carlos, shake their heads; Carlos is dead.

I insist on carrying the body from the truck to the graveyard beside the airstrip myself. It's so light he could be a child. I never look at it, at Carlos's face. My state is one of disbelief. If I want to survive, I have to get out; I have to cling to that.

Later, when we get out of the truck in front of the shack, José bends down to retrieve Carlos's machine gun. The sand surrounding it has already absorbed most of the blood and is now only tinged with pink. As I pass it, I use the side of my foot to cover it over completely. The kid is gone. It's done.

Since I no longer believe that Manolo is going to send an airplane for Mario and me, I start working out a new plan. I don't say anything to Jota about the rage that surges in me every time he comes into my sight. Instead, I continue to tell him the cartel made a mistake in setting up the drop. "Let me work with you," I tell him. "Just you and me and Mario. Get us on an airplane to the States. Then Mario and I will go to Puerto Rico and find a field where you can land an airplane. Mario will stay there to receive and I'll come back to fly. Just me and you and Mario."

"Yeah, that's a good idea," Jota says. "We'll work together, just the three of us."

Is he buying it? I can't say. On the one hand, he doesn't make an attempt to get us out and put the plan to work. But on the other, he rewards us by presenting Mario and me with machine guns of our own. They're accompanied by a long lecture. He trusts us, he says. We're his brothers now. He'll have to go to Medellin in a few days to explain to the cartel in person about the mishap in Puerto Rico. If the Indians from the neighboring villages get drunk, which they do often, and decide to come by and dig up his coke, we'll be able to help the others hold them off. But if we shoot, it better be for a good reason.

My father was a hunter; I have been around guns all my life. And when I was an Air Cadet, I spent a lot of time at the range learning to use all kinds of guns. Mario surprises me by confessing he doesn't know a thing about them. I have to show him how to take his apart to clean it. Because of the humidity and the dust, they have to be cleaned every day. I also have to teach him how to load it. He's an enthusiastic student. In fact, he's too enthusiastic. "It's not a toy," I keep reminding him. For all that I like the idea that we're now able to protect ourselves, it makes me nervous to see Mario walking around with a gun. If a military helicopter were to fly over and see two tanned gringos strolling around, that would be bad enough. But two gringos with machine guns is another matter entirely. I talk to Mario, try to get him to understand that we don't always need to carry the guns, that we don't need to carry them at all except when Jota is away. We can keep them up near the roof, accessible, loaded, and ready to go.

While Jota is gone, we eat the ham he left behind and hang out on the beach with José and the two new guys. Sometimes we discuss Carlos, but the consensus among the Colombians is that what happened was business. Mario and I nod in agreement and avoid the subject until we're alone. Then we go over the details, over and over again. A man dead… The way things work here… We have to get out.

We now have guns and money. Anything seems possible. Mario

proves that. He changes a hundred dollar bill at the outpost and approaches his 18-year-old with a ten in his outstretched hand. She steps forward to peer at it. Then she takes it from him and turns it over to study the back of the bill. For the hundredth time he invites her to explore the caves with him. She slips the ten in her pocket and nods shyly. He takes her hand and off they go.

His success causes me to reconsider my own obsession. Since Jota didn't jump for my delivery idea, I fashion a new one and take it down to the Indians, the fishermen. One of them agrees to take us to Aruba for $2,000. "When?" I ask.

He looks up toward the top of the cliff. "As soon as Jota says it's okay," he answers. "If Jota says okay, I'll take you. *Only* if Jota says it's okay."

"You better not say anything to Jota just yet," I tell him, and I go off to see if Mario is back.

"You shouldn't have done that," Mario exclaims when I tell him. "They'll tell Jota. Jota will be mad. We'll have trouble."

"I put an idea in his head. I could see he was thinking about it. All I have to do now is offer him more money."

I wait a day and go talk to the same Indian again. I offer him four times the amount he asked for. His eyebrows shoot up. "Aruba is only 75 miles away," he says. He looks out at the horizon and bites his lip. "We have orders from Jota not to take you anywhere while he's gone," he confesses at last. "I can't do it."

When I tell Mario, he gets pissed all over again. I assume he'll brood all day, but as it happens, that's not the case. We're sitting in the shack with José and the other two when a man comes walking in, smiling lopsidedly, an Indian we've never seen before. He's very tall, about 6'7", and the ridge at his brow and the size of his nose give him a primitive look. His hair is straggly, his knees are huge, and his toes are pointed in unnatural directions. The two new Colombians go for their guns, but José tells them to put them down, the guy is harmless, he's retarded and can't even talk.

"Look how dirty his shirt is," Mario marvels. And then to José, "Where did he come from? What's his name?"

"I don't know his name. He lives in one of the nearby villages with his family. He herds their sheep and goats. Sometimes he comes by to visit. He likes Jota. Sometimes Jota gives him money for his family," José answers. Then he turns toward our visitor. "Jota's not here. Get out of here. Go away."

The poor guy's lips tremble. He's clearly about to cry. Mario leaps out of his chair. "Hold it," he says to José. "Let's clean him up, send him home looking like a new man. Fred, let's call him that. Everyone's got to have a name. Come on in, Fred. Sit down. I'm going to give you a haircut."

Fred comes in and takes a seat. He's smiling again, but his eyes are registering suspicion. Mario gets out the scissors and goes to work on him. He takes his time, really gives him a decent cut. When he's done, he stands back to admire his work. Then he makes a decision and gets out the razor. Fred doesn't move an inch. Mario hums while he's shaving him. Then he goes into the back room and reappears with one of his shirts and a pair of his sandals. The shirt fits, but Fred's unruly and tremendous toes cannot be made to adapt to the shape of the sandals. Mario returns them to the back room and comes out this time with a pair of sunglasses. He puts them on Fred and leads him to the mirror, which, like everything else in camp, once belonged to an airplane. We all get up and gather behind the two to better observe Fred's response. His smile expands slowly, but it doesn't stop. It keeps getting bigger and bigger until his back teeth are exposed, until the corners of his mouth are tucked deep into his cheekbones. I've never seen anyone look so happy in my life. "Cute, Mario," I say. "Very cute."

Mario smiles. I go through our provisions and make Fred a nice fat ham sandwich. He eats it smiling and with his sunglasses on. I have the feeling he's never going to take the glasses off. When he's done eating, he goes to open the top button on the shirt. "No, no," Mario says. "You keep it. It's yours."

And out he goes. We assume he'll head right back to the village, but he must go to the camp first because we hear a lot of laughter coming from that direction.

We're on our way back from the beach the same day, carrying our guns, when we see Jota coming down the path to meet us. "Look," he says softly when he gets to us, "you're my responsibility. You're my friends. What would happen if you went off to Aruba and got arrested and were thrown back in jail?"

"I told you they'd tell him," Mario says to me in English.

"Am I supposed to get you out if you get thrown into jail?" Jota asks, his voice rising in pitch.

"He doesn't seem all that mad," I say to Mario.

"It's coming," Mario responds through his teeth.

And he's right; it comes. Jota's voice gets louder and louder and his Spanish faster and faster so that after a minute I can't understand a word. He goes on and on and on, shouting so loud that eventually some of the Indians appear at the top of the cliff to see what's happening. "We could shoot him," Mario says.

"Yeah, we could," I answer. "But what do you think would happen to us then? If Indians are too loyal to accept $8,000 in exchange for a ride to Aruba, what do you think they'll do if we kill him?"

"I really want to kill him though," Mario says. "I really do."

"Go ahead," I dare him. "See what happens." There's a part of me that's hoping he will.

Jota's finale is nice and slow and emphatic and I get every word of it. "You can suck my dick if you think you're going to get out of here without my permission," he yells. His chest is heaving, and he's blowing air out through his nostrils. His gaze falls from our faces to our guns. It stays there for a long time. Then he lifts his head to look at Mario. "And the girl! She told her family she bled. She was a virgin. There are obligations. You must have realized. You're going to have to marry her now. Otherwise her family will come and string you up."

"I don't care," Mario shouts. "Let them come over and try. What do I care?"

"News travels fast here, doesn't it?" I say to Mario, but he doesn't answer. His chin is lifted indignantly and he's strumming his fingers on his gun as if it were a guitar. I can see that he's still thinking about using it. It's his friend now; the more he learns about it, the worse his attitude gets. I realize a little encouragement from me would do the trick. "How did it go in Medellin?" I force myself to ask Jota.

He cocks his head and looks seaward. When he finally looks back, he's somewhat composed. "I explained everything. No one thinks it's your fault. They're happy with the pilot, the gringo. Henry told them how well you flew. They want you to make another trip."

"I haven't been paid in full for the last one, Jota."

Jota's expression changes again. "You forget! You dropped it from too high. You did everything wrong. Everybody's in jail over there. They'll have to get them all lawyers."

"Jota, you just said—"

He puts his palm up to stop me and looks away again, contemplating. When he looks back, his voice is softer. "It was the first trip. They understand. The next one will be better."

"But Jota, I don't want to work for these people. I want to do my own thing. They didn't even pay me."

I see Jota's upper lip quiver as if he's repressing a smile. Mario sees it too. "They paid," Mario whispers through his teeth. "Jota wouldn't be in such a good mood if they hadn't. He'd have killed us already for talking to the fisherman. He's got the rest of the money. That's probably why he went up there. But he's not going to give it to you."

"They'll pay you next time," Jota says. "Next time they'll give you the whole thing."

Jota has brought back a gift from Medellin for his wife—a small boombox and a tape to play in it. She's delighted, and when she sees that Mario and I covet the thing, she makes a spectacle of turning up the volume whenever she walks past us with it. I figure out this much: when you go too long without any intellectual stimulation, your intelligence level drops a few notches. Like two ill-behaved boys, Mario and I put in a lot of time trying to figure out how to get it away from her.

Eventually we get the chance. As her fellow Indians want the thing too, she leaves it behind one morning when she goes to work at the outpost. We sneak it out from the back room and set it up on the table. We're listening to the tape, which features old Latin songs, for the third time when her little girl comes in and catches us. We quickly return the box to the back room and wait for Jota's wife to come storming in. She makes her appearance at the door within minutes. Her mouth is wide open and her tongue is poised to lash, but then she realizes the box isn't there with us. She goes into the back room, ascertains that it's there, and leaves again, smiling. As soon as she's gone, we get it out again. But when I press Play, nothing happens. I press Eject and find that Jota's wife has taken the tape away with her. The Colombians laugh their heads off. While I'm calling her bad names in Spanish for the amusement of the others, Mario fools with the radio dial and comes across a station broadcasting in English. I cease raving immediately. They're giving the news in English! I haven't had any news of the world in so long that I've forgotten there was a world beyond the Guajira. UN member nations have been asked to detain Iraqi ships that may be used to break the naval embargo. Desert Shield is heating up. It occurs to me that maybe the indifference of the destroyer off the coast of Puerto Rico had something to do with this operation. I hear too that the World Series is about to begin. The news ends and a religious program begins in Spanish. I turn the dial back and forth, but no one else is broadcasting in English. I shut the thing down and return it to the back room. But I can't seem to shut myself down; I need an outlet for the emotions stirring in me. I go on and on about the World Series and baseball generally in my best Spanish. The delinquent-looking Colombian asks me if I want to make a bet on the game. Yeah, I want to make a bet! I bet him $40 that Cincinnati will win the first game. "Why do you want Cincinnati?" Mario asks.

"I want to bet but I don't want to win the bet," I explain. "This guy is too nasty looking." But the real reason is that Cincinnati is the underdog—and I can only relate to that.

The next morning the Colombians are as eager as I am to listen to the boombox. We tune in just in time to hear that Cincinnati won the first game. I can't believe it! The Colombian pays me, but he looks disgusted as hell, especially when his buddies begin to ridicule him for losing to the gringo. I don't want this guy to be angry with me, but I can't resist this quick fix for my boredom either. "Double or nothing next game," I tell him.

Cincinnati wins the second one too! What are these people trying to do to me? I explain to the Colombian that Cincinnati is the underdog, but I'm still willing to double the bet again for the third game. He looks to his buddies. They're tossing their heads and making suppressed laughing sounds in their throats. He turns back to me and growls through his teeth. "Okay."

Mario and I spend half the night talking baseball. We start off with the Series, but after a while it becomes a one-way conversation with Mario telling me about his experiences with José Canseco and other famous players he's known. I've heard it all countless times before, but I let him go on and on anyway because there isn't anything else to talk about. We wake up when it's still dark and listen for some sign that

Jota's wife is getting ready to leave for the outpost. She's hardly out the door before we have the boombox set up on the table. The Colombians get so close to it and their expressions are so intense you'd think they could understand everything that's being said. But they understand enough to know even before we report it that Cincinnati has won the third! The Colombian I have been betting against is mad as hell. His fist comes up from his side, but he only strikes the speaker. "You don't think they'd go and win the next one, do you?" I ask Mario.

He shrugs. "You're in big trouble if they do."

But I am betting they can't. "Double again on the next game," I tell the Colombian.

"How can this be?" he screams the morning we hear that Cincinnati has won the Series. "You told me they were the underdogs!"

"They are, they were," I stammer. His buddies are laughing so hard that I have to repeat myself. But he still can't hear me. He yells at the other Colombians. Then they all yell at me. The one I bet tells everyone to shut up and then demands that Mario translates so I get it all. "He says you lied to him," Mario reports. "He says you're trying to make a fool out of him. He's really pissed. You'd better do something."

"Hey, the game was bought off!"

"What?" Mario asks.

"Tell him that. Tell him I'll give him back his money because the game was bought off."

"Are you kidding?"

"They buy off the soccer games here all the time! Don't you know that? They kill the referees if they don't go along with it. It's business, Mario, business. We're in Colombia, Mario. These guys are from the cartel. These aren't some guys we've come across in one of your Miami discos. We're in Colombia, in the Guajira, where a dumb kid can get killed because some dumb voice on the radio says so!"

When I calm down enough to note the startled expressions on the faces of the Colombians, I realize that I was shouting, and that sometime during my tirade, I rose to my feet. As Mario explains about the buy off, I sit back down again and fumble in my pockets for the bills. The Colombians smile. They're satisfied. As for myself, I'm miserable as hell. I see now that I am as far removed from the World Series as a man can possibly be. Beneath my ability to be amiable under even the worst of circumstances, I am clearly falling apart.

One night there is some screaming going on over at the camp, and Jota and Mario and I go running out to see what's happening. We find six or seven of the Indians, Jota's wife among them, throwing pails of water on the small Spanish woman they're holding down on the ground. "It's only Lucy," Jota says.

I move to help Lucy, but Jota stops me saying Lucy is dirty, very dirty, so dirty that even the Indians get offended. "How is that possible?" I ask. "The Indians don't bathe themselves."

Jota laughs. "But the Indians don't smear themselves with shit."

The Indians release Lucy, and when I see that she isn't hurt—just very wet—I follow the others back to the shack. Jota fashions a mound of coke for himself and tells us Lucy's story between snorts. Lucy is from the city, from Barranquilla. She had a baby a long time ago, but it died. How, he doesn't know. Ever since then, Lucy has been mad, bonkers. She walks. That's all she does. She goes from one village to another begging for food. She appears here every few months, sometimes more often. The Indians clean her up and put her to work to pay for the food they give her.

The next morning, at dawn, I wake up with the feeling that someone is watching me. Sure enough, Lucy's nose is pressed to the window. I get up and go out and introduce myself. She's wearing shorts, but her shirt is in her hand. I look her over. Her breasts sag, but the rest of her is solid muscle. Her feet are red and ragged and torn. They look terribly painful. When she lifts one up to scratch at it, I see how callused her heels are. "How are you doing?" I ask.

She glances at the rim of sun ascending at the horizon. "Look, the moon is full," she says. "That's bad, very bad."

"I hear you walked all the way from Barranquilla."

She smiles. "Oh, that's the goats. They eat a lot."

I tell her to wait and I hurry in to wake up Mario. He comes back out with me and I introduce the two of them. We have a nice chat, Mario and me making comments about the weather and the surroundings, and Lucy responding senselessly. We try not to chuckle, but it's impossible. Our chuckles, however, don't disturb her. She seems to enjoy our company. And we enjoy hers too; after all the manipulation we've been subjected to, her innocence is refreshing. But in the middle of our conversation, she turns suddenly, as if she's heard someone calling to her, and wanders away.

When the Indians bring us our food in the evening, they say they will send Lucy by to gather the pots and pans when we're done. Lucy shows up wearing her shirt this time, but her shorts are on her head like a hat. Jota cracks up laughing. He swings so far back in his chair that he almost tips over. Lucy remains utterly serious. She doesn't seem to notice that there's anyone else in the room. She doesn't realize that her head is the wrong place to wear her pants.

That night, when I'm in my hammock on the verge of sleep, I hear Lucy screaming again. José takes his gun and goes out. Before I can decide whether to join him, the screaming stops. I assume Lucy smeared herself with shit again and the Indians felt compelled to wash her. But in the morning, José tells me she was raped, that some Indians from a neighboring village came by and got her. I bolt up in my hammock and give him a look of disgust. He shrugs. "They were all drunk," he tells me. "They were looking for trouble. Who knows what would have happened if they didn't find her. She didn't offer much resistance. I couldn't do anything. You can't just jump in and start shooting. I didn't like it happening either, but I didn't want to start killing people, and that's the only way it would have stopped. She's gone now; she went away. She'll be okay."

Lucy's rape stays with me. I can't get it out of my mind no matter how hard I try. Innocence is a thing to be ravaged here in the Guajira, I conclude. It has no other value. And as much as I would like to think I would have risked my life to try to save Lucy had I known what was happening to her, I can't be certain. After all, I helped fly a load of cocaine to Puerto Rico, and then I stood by and watched a man being murdered because he wasn't strong enough to move a couple of bales around, because I reported that he wasn't strong enough. If I don't get out of here soon, I realize, I will cease to value innocence too. So this is how it happens, I muse. This is how evil filters into a life.

The idea I've been dangling in front of Jota, I understand now, has been elusive, insubstantial. If I want his mouth to water—if I'm ever going to get out of here—I'm going to have to find a way to make my plan more appetizing.

Jota leaves for Medellin again, and that evening we sit outside the shack with the Colombians and watch the sunset. The sunsets here are almost always spectacular. Plenty of days go by when the sight of that orange orb merging with the horizon is the most interesting thing that happens. Sometimes I can lose myself, forget I'm in the Guajira for a time. Tonight's sunset is especially awesome because the moon is simultaneously on the rise. It's an amazing sight.

Once the sun sinks, we take to rocking. Rocking, I've concluded, is what people all over the world must do when they're bored. Here it's a ritual. We rock and look at one another to see whether anyone has anything to say. The Colombians go in after a while to play with the radio, and Mario and I are left alone. We already know we have nothing to say, so we don't even bother to exchange glances. Mario takes a matchbook out of his pocket and begins striking matches. The fact that he uses far more force to light each match than is necessary tells me he's in one of his less indulgent moods. He gathers up some of the wood chips that are everywhere and fashions them into a little hill. He strikes another match and holds it at the bottom of the hill until it catches. Then he gets on his hands and knees and begins pushing more wood chips toward the fire.

Mario stops what he's doing to stare at the old broken table leaning against Jota's shack. The look of determination I see on his face keeps me from reminding him that Jota would go wild if he knew someone was making a fire near the camp. But what's the difference? The whole area is covered with soda bottles and beer bottles and there are always a couple of Toyotas out front—none of which are present in front of the shacks of the Indians that Mario and I have seen during our explorations of the area. And of course there's the radio antenna sticking up out of the roof. We might as well have a billboard facing skyward, reading, Smuggling Activities Take Place Here.

Mario gets to his feet and heads for the table. It's been outside so long that it doesn't take much effort for him to break it into pieces. Once it's burning, I pitch in and add some more wood chips to the fire. Mario rushes inside and returns a moment later with a quart can of kerosene. The flames leap up to seize it. There's a cement wall nearby and all along it piles of wood chips. I find an old pail and begin to scoop them up. The dogs have been pissing on them and they smell like hell. When the pail is full, I dump it onto the flames. The fire is burning really well now, a nice orange color like the setting sun. Mario runs in once more and returns with two empty aerosol cans and some old flashlight batteries. He puts the cans down by his feet and leans into the fire to read the little print on the batteries. "Warning. Do not dispose of in fire," he reads aloud.

The firelight on his face gives him a demonic look. He's all teeth and arched eyebrows. "You'd better not throw them in," I tell him. "I don't know what will happen."

He tosses the batteries in gleefully, and then after them, the aerosol cans. "Way to go, Mario," I say as I back away. But nothing happens.

José appears at the door of the shack. "What's happening?" he asks.

Mario laughs wickedly and scoops up more wood chips. "We're just burning off our frustrations. Nothing to worry about," I shout in English. He waves his hand in disgust and makes the same sound the goats do when we get in their way.

The next morning, while Mario and I are standing at the scene of the crime, marveling that the batteries look exactly the same as they did before Mario threw them into the fire, some of the Indians leave in Jota's Toyota. They return a while later with four men. A tall one, who appears to be half black and half Latin, introduces himself as Armando and says that they've come in by boat to wait for their load to arrive and then for an airplane coming in from the States to get it. He's very impressed with the area, with what he saw from the boat. The scenery was fantastic and the ride was smooth. We go over to the truck to help them unload their things. They don't say when the airplane is coming, but I suppose it won't be anytime soon because they've brought an awful lot of provisions along with them. When Armando sees Mario peering into the bag of groceries he's carrying in, he says, "Help yourself, friend. Take whatever you like."

The other three guys, one of whom speaks a little English, are as friendly as Armando, and before long we have them swimming and playing soccer with us. They're amazed at Mario's leg action. When he goes to kick a goal, they all run out of the way. When we question them, they open right up, tell us everything. The man they work for is called Giovanni. Giovanni isn't part of the cartel. He gets his coke from everybody, 50 kilos here, 100 there, until he has enough to make a drop. Then if the drop goes bad, no one is out too much. And he himself has only lost expenses, in this case, the money he is paying Jota to find him the airplane.

"You can't trust these people," I warn Armando. "They lie. You should work with me. Get me back to the States and I'll make the arrangements for your airplane."

Armando shrugs. "I like that idea," he says. "But you belong to Jota. We'd have to kill Jota."

"I don't work for anyone," I insist. "I'm an independent, like Giovanni."

He tosses his head back to laugh. "Giovanni works for his brother, a lawyer. There's no such thing as an independent in this business. Everyone works for someone."

"But Jota doesn't even pay me."

"It doesn't matter. He owns you. You can't go to someone else and say, I want to work with you. It doesn't work like that. We'd have to kill Jota."

I laugh hard so that what I am about to say will sound only half serious. "So kill Jota."

Armando roars with laughter. "Did you hear him?" he asks his companions. Then to me, "We like Jota. Jota is our friend. Now, if we were in a neutral zone, out in the city maybe, we could talk about this. But we're not. This is Jota's camp. He owns everyone here."

We get some more visitors—Jota's sister-in-law and the doctor she travels with. They were over at the camp, the doctor tells us, trading clothes from the city for shrimp. They heard there were some gringos and they wanted to meet us. The doctor, a big guy, half black and half Spanish like Armando, is very friendly. I get to thinking maybe he can find a way to get us out. I ask him if he wants to play some Black Jack. He does. So do Armando and his boys. Mario is the only one who doesn't want to play. He takes his gun and goes out.

I deal, and of course I rake it in. No one seems to realize I have an unfair advantage in representing the house. The doctor explains he isn't really a doctor, that he wasn't able to finish medical school. I figure his reason was financial; otherwise he wouldn't be making his living bartering for shrimp with the Indians. When we finish our game, he asks if I want to give him some money to buy medicine for some of the sick people at the camp.

I look him over carefully. I'm thinking he may not be a man of medicine after all, that he may be a hustler like everyone else around here. I'm used to being hustled. I probably wouldn't mind so much if I didn't like the guy. My mind jumps to Raul Hernandez, the Cuban in Miami who hustled me for 50 grand. I liked him too. If he'd paid me, I wouldn't be here now. I'd have bought my plane and returned to work and instead of sleeping in a hammock in a room full of outlaws at night, I'd be in a queen-sized bed with Jenny in my arms.

I try to shake it off. Whenever Jenny pops into my head, I try to dismiss her swiftly. I figure by now she's met someone else, another musician maybe, someone more suited to her temperament. Most women are pretty impressed when you tell them you have an airplane. On the day I met Jenny, she only raised one eyebrow and stared at me, waiting for me to say something more.

The doctor is still waiting patiently for my response. His woman friend, Jota's sister-in-law, strolls in with Mario. I wonder if they were out together. The doctor smiles at her. She smiles back. They seem to genuinely care for each other. I push my winnings, about $100, across the table. "Here," I say. "Buy the Indians some medicine."

Jota returns, but before I can get him alone and describe the crispness, the succulence, the striking orange color of the carrot I've been cultivating for him in the otherwise fruitless garden of my mind, Henry shows up again too. "I'm flying to an island off the coast of Puerto Rico today, to drop near some boats. I'd like you to come with me," he says.

I turn immediately to Jota. "I wasn't paid for the last trip. You can't do this to me."

Jota sits down at the table with Henry and me and we have a little discussion about payment policies. Henry finds $2,000 in his pocket and holds it out to me. "I can give you this much now and guarantee you that you'll get the rest after the flight. You have my word. And then I'll take you back with me. My people in Medellin want to meet you."

Jota jumps out of his seat immediately. Someone, apparently, failed to relate this part of the plan to him. "You can't come here with $2,000 and expect my pilot to fly," he shouts. "You've got to come with all the up-front money. I'm responsible for him."

Henry's still smiling. "Okay, sure, I understand," he says.

I can't believe it. He's not even mad. And no one wants to kill me either. To show my appreciation, I accompany Henry and his buddies back to the airplane in Jota's Toyota.

Some hours later, we hear that Henry is on his way in. Jota goes out to meet him on the runway and leaves Mario and me to watch the landing from outside the shack. My stomach tightens when I see how the wind has picked up and how the low clouds are swarming in over the area. My dislike of Henry the drug smuggler is immediately overcome by my empathy for Henry the pilot. We hear the airplane descending over the runway and then the increase in power, and we know it's a missed approach. Henry will have to pull her up and try again. "This is bad," I say to Mario. "This weather is shit, a pilot's nightmare." Then I think about all the fuel Henry has on board; he can circle for hours if he needs to.

The radio is on in the shack and we can hear him talking to Jota. He's going to try again. He sounds calm enough, but the clouds are still racing in. We can see the glow of his lights intermittently as he goes in and out of them, flying down towards the coal port. He turns and comes back in again, flying beautifully, perfect instrument flying.

The clouds must be moving at 50 mph, and they can't be more than 40 or 50 feet from the ground.

Henry gets lower. He's almost there. I can imagine him watching for some small break in the cloud cover for a glimpse of the runway. Then all at once we hear the engines go to full power. Shit! I think. What this poor guy is going through! I go through it with him, the procedures, in my mind and in my gut. Raise the gear, build some airspeed, begin a positive rate of climb, raise the flaps slowly, keep watching for that magic number, 100 feet above sea level, take a deep breath and watch for the next one, 200 feet, then 300, then 400, then break out of the cloud cover and start all over again.

He flies back down towards the port and circles for a while. Conditions don't improve. They might not; he might be stuck. I hear his voice on the radio and realize he's still cool, still composed. Jota sounds cool too. Henry comes in again, right down on the water. All he needs is a little opening for a couple of seconds and he'll plant that thing right on the runway. Perfect speed control. The flaps are out, the gear down. He can't be moving at much more than 30 mph forward speed with these headwinds. He looks almost like a helicopter coming in. His approach is flawless. "No problem," I whisper to Mario. "He's got it made." But then there is a silence—it lasts forever—and then the sound of the engine power coming back on again, taking off again. Another perfect missed approach.

I'm back in the plane with him, more nervous than he is. He climbs again, circles again, comes in again—again, a beautifully-controlled approach, barely moving. He disappears from our sight. We listen again to the silence. We stand watching, transfixed, wondering if the next thing we see will be the flaming yellow ball, if the next sound we hear will be that of an explosion. It would be huge with all that gas on board. Then we hear Jota's voice on the radio. He made it! Henry made it!

When Henry returns to the shack, I disregard the fact that he's a drug smuggler and we embrace like brothers. I tell him I knew what he was going through up there and he tells me that I wasn't far from his mind either, that he was trying to imagine me advising him, telling him what to do. I know what he means. There have been times when it's brought me some comfort to imagine my oldest brother, who is also a pilot, sitting in the seat beside me giving me instructions.

When we're finally done exclaiming over the landing, Henry tells us the details of the drop. He's very proud; he did it all on his own, without a copilot. The boys in Medellin promised him an apartment in Barranquilla if this went well. After he refuels, he tells me he will take me back with him if I want. Before I can weigh my chances for freedom, he says I would then have to work for his people. Jota spares me from having to make a decision. "No," he says. "He appreciates your offer, but he can't accept."

A few days later a huge boat, maybe 150 feet long, comes in. The Indians run down the cliff and start unloading it. When we see them coming up carrying crates of cigarettes, cookies, clothes, and scotch, my personal favorite now that my birthday is long past, Mario and I decide to volunteer our services too. Jota comes down the cliff to buy a few cases of whiskey. His wife purchases several cases of cigarettes to sell in the outpost. The rest of the stuff, Jota says, will go on the trucks. I look up and see them arriving at the top of the cliff, ten or more semi-trailers. When Jota's transactions are completed, I begin to make small talk with the captain, just tell him as nicely as I can that my buddy and I wouldn't mind riding with him, wherever he happens to be going. "Sure," he says, but then he shields his eyes and sweeps them up the cliff face until he pinpoints Jota at the halfway point. The Indians, I note, are now coming back down the cliff with merchandise from the trucks. I get a whiff of the crates they're carrying as they pass me. Marijuana. "Well, forget that idea," I say to Mario.

The captain goes down on one knee to open and inspect one of the crates. Inside are several highly-compressed round discs. I figure each one weighs a pound. The captain looks up at me and Mario. "Take what you want," he says, grinning. I can't help but grin back at him. This is the stuff that kept me sane in prison, that made me feel like I was sitting in the back seat while someone else, someone competent, was driving. I take one disc and tuck it into my T-shirt. But it occurs to me that I may have to spend the rest of my life here in the Guajira, and I don't want to tamper with my sanity for that long. I take another eight or nine discs and stuff them in with the first. The captain laughs like hell. "What are you going to do with all that?" he asks.

"I'm going to smoke it."

He laughs again. "No, no," he says. "Take one."

I give him back his discs one at a time, hoping his hand will retreat before I am down to one. He laughs the whole time, but his hand keeps coming back for more. I climb the cliff with the one disc bulging at the front of my shirt.

The doctor returns, with medicine for the sick people, and my faith in humanity is temporarily restored. I seek him out at the camp and let him know I'm ready for another game of Black Jack when he's concluded his business. Later, while we're playing, I ask him if he can get us IDs and help us get out. Very casually, without even looking up from his cards, he tells me he wouldn't cross Jota on a bet, and he flips an ace up beside his queen. I give him his money and don't say anything more about needing his help. I respect the man too much to press him. But Mario apparently doesn't feel the same. When he sees Jota's wife's sister appear at the door looking for the doctor, he abandons his hand and goes out to talk to her. The smile she gives him assures me that she likes him too. I look to the doctor to see what he has to say on the subject. Since they travel together, I assume they're sleeping together. But the doctor keeps his eyes on his cards and doesn't say anything for a moment. When we finish the hand he says, "The girl is crazy. You'd better tell your friend Mario that. She shot a man from an affluent family, her ex-lover. She found him with another woman. He's paralyzed now from the waist down. His family put out a contract on her. You'd better tell Mario not to get too intimate. She's my business partner. Things are good between us. But I can't be responsible for what she does to anyone else." This time I don't win much, so I have to give the doctor medicine money from my own pocket.

The doctor could be lying to me, trying to scare Mario away from his girl. But I decide I can't take that chance and confront Mario with the news. "But she loves me," he moans in response.

"Your amorous ways, your indiscretions, are going to get you into a heap of trouble," I tell him. "If she's really as unstable as the doctor says, even finding out about your 18-year-old might set her off."

He shrugs. He says he isn't involved with the woman anyway, that he kissed her a few times, nothing more. "You're always looking to criticize me," he challenges.

I would like to respond to that, but his liaisons start me thinking about Jenny. Suddenly I feel particularly low, and I realize that any further confrontation might be dangerous. I decide I need a distraction, and I go over to the camp, to spend some time with the Indians. But Mario, who must be looking for a fight, follows me.

A few of the women at the camp are complaining because the fishermen have been so busy lately and there's no one around to slaughter the goats. Mario offers his assistance. We have watched the process plenty of times and he thinks he has it down. He takes the chosen goat and ties it up to a limb on one of the scrubby trees. Then, holding its mouth with one hand so that it won't cry, he jabs a knife up its throat toward the back of its head. He turns and gives me a look which I take to mean that this is what he would like to do to me.

The idea is to get the knife into its skull and put the animal out of its misery quickly. Mario must not get it that far because the poor thing is still kicking for all it's worth. "Jeez, Mario," I say. "Would you kill the poor thing already?"

He gives me another look. I find myself clenching my fist. I back off a bit, take one of the huge joints I've gotten into the habit of carrying around all day out from my pocket, and light it up. I take a few puffs and put it out again to save for later. In the meantime, one of the women slips a filthy bowl under the goat's neck to catch the blood. Nothing gets wasted here. The blood will be used for soup. Mario gives the knife another jab and the goat's eyes finally stop looking around for help. Its pupils dilate; it's dead. Now it's time to gut and skin the thing. Mario looks at me uncertainly. Now that the killing's over, he doesn't know what to do. But I'm nice and high now and not inclined to offer my participation. I sit down on a rock and give him step-by-step instructions instead.

He finally gets it gutted. The goats have a double stomach, full of green from the plants they eat. The Indians boil the green stuff. A woman rushes over to collect it as soon as it's discernible. The stuff stinks. The woman does too. Mario is all smiles. His problem, I decide, is that he needs work.

Manolo comes in on the radio the next day. It seems like ages since we last heard from him. He apologizes for his disappearance and explains that he was in a car accident. Mario and I roll our eyes. We shouldn't worry, he says. He's okay now, back in business again, though it was touch and go for a while. He's sending down an airplane for us. A one-engine long-range 210. Should be down tomorrow. I ask him if he's been in touch with Jenny. He answers me evasively, saying circumstances have made contact impossible. I assume that means that she won't talk to him anymore, that she doesn't care to know how I am or what I'm doing. I'm actually happy for her, happy that she's getting on okay without me.

Another call comes in on the radio. I don't recognize the voice, but it must concern something important because Jota lifts his palm to Mario and me—the signal for us to retreat. We head out to the camp to see how Mario's 18-year-old is doing. His interest in her is waning lately, but her interest in his money is just reaching its peak. He gives her a few bucks and she goes to the outpost to buy us a couple of sodas. When enough time has passed, we return to the shack.

Jota is all smiles when we enter. "You boys are getting out of here," he tells us.

"Yeah, yeah, Jota," I respond. "Manolo already told us. He's sending an airplane tomorrow. You see me packing?"

"No, no, Alan. This is another airplane, for some people in Barranquilla. We're going to load it up and you're going to take it to the Bahamas. Mario can go too. There'll be a boat there to take you to the States."

"We've got to go," Mario says. "This is our ticket out."

I slump into a chair. The Bahamas: the chance I've been waiting for is a suicide mission. I'm speechless.

The airplane from Barranquilla comes in, sure enough, a Piper Navajo with a Panther conversion which gives it bigger engines and some L-tips on the wings—in other words, more speed, stability, and weight tolerance. As soon as we get back to the shack with the pilot and his friends, I begin hounding them with questions. For some reason, the pilot has trouble understanding my Spanish and I have to get Mario to translate. His plan is this: we're going to fly over Cuba to Mores Island in the Bahamas, drop the stuff along the beach, and then land on a strip so that Mario and I can get off.

I get out the map and locate Mores Island. It's 1,000 miles away and right up there by Nassau. I can't see how we can help pulling a tail flying into that area. "I'm not going," I inform Jota.

"You're going as a copilot," he responds calmly.

"I'm not."

"Yes, you are. The guy has $10,000 up-front money for you and Mario."

"I'm not going."

His face is still calm. "They'll kill you," he says. "They spent too much money getting this arranged." He spreads his arms out to show me that it's a no-win situation, absolutely out of his control.

"Let's do it, Alan," Mario says. His eyes are burning with determination. "You hear the man. They spent too much money. They'll kill us."

"Frankly, Mario, I'd rather die here and save myself the trouble, because you know it isn't possible to carry enough gasoline on that airplane to make it there and back. And if we pull a tail, we'll be coming back. And that's assuming that we can even get off the ground to begin with with all the weight. Think it out, Mario. It's a suicide mission. It's just not possible." I do some figures in my head. "Between the gas he's planning to carry and the load, you're talking a good 2,000 pounds overweight."

"If you don't make it," one of the pilot's buddies says, "you won't be held accountable."

I have to laugh. "Great! If we die, no one will be pissed at us," I tell Mario in English. "Isn't that good news?"

Jota gets on the radio with the pilot's boss, the same voice I heard the day before. I know what's coming. It's twist-the-gringo's-arm time again. "The gringo doesn't want to fly," he says. This time I don't even bother to listen to the response.

The pilot yells, "I'm not going alone. If the gringo won't fly, I'm not flying either."

Jota throws his hands up in the air. "Did you hear that?" he says to the voice. The response is muttered. Jota swivels around to face the pilot fully. "Repeat that," he says into the mike. The voice says, "Then kill the pilot too."

"That's a lot of blood," I say to Armando. He grins half sympathetically. Then something occurs to me. "I want to confer with Mario privately," I explain. No one objects. Mario and I head out the door where Armando's English-speaking buddy won't hear us. "I've got a plan," I whisper. "Will you go along with me?"

"I don't know. What's your plan?"

"We'll go, but we'll pick up a tail early into the flight and turn around and come back. That way they won't kill us here and we won't have to fall into the sea either when the airplane runs out of gas."

"How are we going to pick up a tail?"

"We're going to pretend we have a tail. You're going to say we have a tail."

"I'll do it," he says, and he turns to go back in.

"Wait. They'll want to know what we were talking about."

"I'll tell them Cuba."

"Cuba?"

"Yeah, that you don't want to fly over Cuba."

"Alan won't fly over Cuba," Mario announces as we enter. "He had a bad experience there once. He's afraid we'll be shot down. He says if you're going to make him fly over Cuba, you might as well shoot him now and get it over with."

"The gringo won't fly over Cuba," Jota reports into the radio. "He'll go around."

"Anything he wants."

Jota shuts down the radio and gives me the $10,000.

Out on the airstrip, where container upon container of gas is being loaded, I check the engines and find that the left one is low on oil. "How much oil did you have when you left?" I ask the pilot.

"It was full. It's full right now."

"No, it's not. It's down three quarts. How many hours did you fly?"

"Three."

A quart an hour. According to my calculations, the engine won't do more than eight hours. When the oil is gone, it will melt. And the flight, if we were really going to do it, would be between 14 to16 hours. "This motor won't go," I tell Mario. Then I ask the pilot how many hours are on the motor.

"It's brand new! Only 200 hours," he shouts.

It's clear to me that my questions are making him testy. I don't take it any further. The engines might be brand new, but a lousy pilot can ruin a piston engine in ten minutes. Mario and I look and find a lot of oil under the wing. He agrees with me that the engine won't last much longer. The airplane is so heavy that it's hard to imagine it getting off the ground. Mario and I push the bales and the gas containers as far forward as possible so the greatest weight will be over the wings and not the tail. Then Mario takes his place on top of the gas containers just behind the pilot and me, where he can see everything that's going on.

The pilot starts the engines, floods them, revs the shit out of them. It's clear already that we're in big trouble. He does his mag checks and applies full power. An airplane this size should push you back in your seat taking off, but with all the weight we don't feel the shove at all. We move down the runway with, fortunately, a good wind on our nose. When we get to the end, the thing lifts into the air like an overweight duck trying to get off a short pond. We retract the landing gear immediately to reduce drag. Still, the airplane feels like it's falling. The pilot, who doesn't seem to notice, pulls back on the column. I push it forward, to allow the airplane to descend a little and gain some airspeed. When we're about ten feet over the ocean and have the airspeed I'd hoped for, I pull it up again, get it to about 60 feet. It begins to fall again. You have to let it go down. The pilot, who doesn't understand this concept of ground effect, begins arguing with me, adding to the tension. I try my best to ignore him and wait until we're about 20 feet over the waves this time to pull it back up.

We continue to porpoise. Now we get up to 100 feet and go back down to 50. I glance back and see that Mario is holding his breath. The airplane is close to being out of control. It's simply too heavy; it doesn't want to fly. Any mistake made in recovering from each stall—which is in essence what it's doing—could be devastating.

The right engine temperature indicators, I note when I finally get the chance to look, are running normally, just a little on the hot side because of the high power settings and low airspeeds. But the left engine indicators are all in the red, the oil temp, the cylinder-head temp, the exhaust—everything. I ask the pilot if this is how the airplane always runs and he says, "Yeah, it's okay, this is the way it's supposed to be."

"This man is very smart," I report to Mario. "The temps for the left engine are all in the red, the engine is about to melt, and he thinks it's normal. It could quit at any time. If it does, I'll give you a signal and you'll have to open the door and get everything out real fast."

"What will happen if I don't?" Mario asks childishly.

"We'll probably go into a flat spin or flip upside down and go into an inverted spin which we won't get out of at this altitude. So either you open the door and get everything out very quickly or we die. You got it, Mario?"

He nods, trying to look cool, but I can tell by the way his teeth are clamped that he's as nervous as I am.

We've gained some altitude, but the airplane is still porpoising. I begin to think the porpoising will never stop—but after about an hour and a half, it does. By that time it's dark and we're closing in on Haiti. We can see a large lightning storm off in the distance. I turn to Mario. "Five minutes, that's it," I say. "Go in the back and then come up here again and tell this guy in Spanish and me in English that we have a tail, an airplane on our tail, and that you can see him very plainly, that he flashed his lights a couple of times and that you think it must be the American military or the DEA."

I know I have to do things right. Flying with the anticipation of something going wrong at any second is taking its toll on me. The pilot is too ignorant to be anxious. The responsibility is all on my shoulders. I want to get this tail business over with as soon as possible. I tell the pilot in my best Spanish that I think I see some airplanes on our right going by in the opposite direction. "Look over there," I say. "Do you see them?"

He looks toward Haiti. She is a band of lights with stars in the foreground and lightning beyond. I point out one particularly bright star. "There! Do you see it?"

He shakes his head, annoyed. "No, I don't see anything." He yells to Mario to change the gas. We're burning an incredible 60 gallons an hour. It's time to change the internal fuel line to another tank.

Mario is busy carrying out the pilot's order when the left engine quits. It feels like a parachute just opened at the back of the airplane. I glance at the fuel gauges and see there's no fuel flow into the left engine. I realize that Mario has pulled the fuel line out of one tank and that it sucked in a lot of air before he got it to the other. The idiot pilot advances the propeller and mixture controls full forward to try to restart. In a piston engine, when the fuel is taken away, the wind will keep the propeller rotating. All you have to do is get the gas flowing again, hit the boost pump and force the air out of the lines so that the fuel can begin to flow. But thanks to the pilot, the motor must now be recalibrated, the RPMs reset, the mixture reset, everything. In the meantime, we are flying sideways, working the rudder to compensate, and trying to deal with everything else at the same time. It takes close to two minutes before we have control again. It's only then that I realize how fast my heart is racing. I turn around and give Mario a look. He has to do it now.

Mario comes forward. "We've got an airplane on the right," he shouts.

His expression is sufficiently alarmed.

"What?" the pilot cries.

Mario tells him in Spanish.

We both look to the right but can't see anything because the cabin is full of light. "I can't see anything," I say to Mario.

"It's there, it's there," he cries.

The pilot doesn't look entirely convinced. I've had the radio tuned to 121.5, the emergency frequency, with the volume down. Now I turn it up. I tell Mario to tell the pilot that the loud static noise we're hearing means they have locked onto us electronically. When he's translated this, I tell him to go back again and then come forward in a couple of minutes and say we have an airplane on the left too.

"Do you think it's a tail?" the pilot is saying to me.

"I told you before that I saw something. Those were airplanes. Two, I'm pretty sure, going in the other direction. We're in the middle of the Caribbean, off the airways. We shouldn't be seeing anything at this altitude. If they're airliners, they would be much higher, 30,000, 35,000 feet. Only two kinds of people fly at this altitude—smugglers and people looking for them. We're off the airways in a Panther Navajo. They definitely think we're a drug plane. They probably picked us up on radar from Guantanamo Bay." I show him on the map. "Guantanamo Bay is only about 120 miles away." He doesn't look impressed. "It's a U.S. military base!"

His face registers surprise. I quickly get out my spare T-shirt and put it over my head with the sleeves tied in the back. The pilot looks at me like I'm crazy and continues flying the airplane. Then Mario comes forward again. "We've got another one on the left! We've got two. One on the right, one on the left. I saw them both at the same time and then one turned its lights off!"

"He's probably coming forward to take pictures of us," I tell Mario, and I readjust my headdress.

The pilot looks at me and then at Mario, then pulls off his T-shirt and covers his face. I sigh deeply into my own shirt. The lightning in the distance cooperates too, transmitting more static over the radio. "What do we do? What do we do?" the pilot shrieks.

"What are your instructions?" I shout at him in English. "Take the tail to the boats? Drop to the boats so that they all get busted?"

Mario interprets. The pilot tells Mario his instructions are to turn around and go back with the load.

"Then turn it around!" I shout. "Turn it around now. Take a heading of 180 and let's start heading back!"

We pick up the VOR coming out of Santo Domingo and start heading toward Aruba. But I'm no less anxious than I was when the engine quit because now I'll have to explain to Jota why the tail hasn't followed us back to his strip. I could say they had a fuel problem if it had just been one. But two? A mistake, but there is nothing to be done for it now.

As we get closer to Aruba, we pick up our navigational aides and begin our course to Jota's strip. For all the gas that we've burned, we still remain tremendously overweight. I see an airliner at about 6,000 feet, very well lit and heading toward the northern end of the island where the airport is located. I point it out to the pilot immediately. "There's our tail. Looks like they're going to Aruba. Maybe they're not going to follow us all the way back after all. We're in luck."

I call Mario forward and explain the problem in English. I tell him to tell the pilot that our tail is probably going to the big DEA base in Aruba to refuel, that they know we're headed back to Colombia because our last heading change put us on direct course to the Guajira.

The pilot starts the descent from about 45 miles out. The left engine indicators are all still in the red. I plead with him to pull some of the power back and let that engine cool in case we need it later on. He squints at me confusedly. He has no idea what I'm talking about.

As we begin circling, we get Jota on the radio and tell him about the tail. He explains that he's not going out to the strip right away because the tail will have followed us back. His voice is soft, but I can hear the repressed anger. He tells us to turn out some lights. He can't see anyone following us, but that doesn't mean a thing. The DEA wouldn't necessarily have their lights on; and if they didn't, you wouldn't know another airplane was up there until yours had landed and you heard the other.

The pilot wants to land. I tell him that we have to keep circling for now. But he's in a panic; he isn't into flying anymore. He begins to argue with Jota over the radio. There is no air-conditioning in the airplane, and we're low now, about 2,000 feet, and in much warmer air. The pilot is sweating bullets. He's through with this circling, he tells Jota. He wants to land. He wants to get out of the airplane.

Jota finally lights up the strip. We find ourselves almost directly over it. The pilot starts turning the airplane toward it. I tell him that we have to get out a little further and then turn into it, that our descent will be too steep from here. He wipes the sweat from his brow with his wrist and continues turning. His lips are drawn back. The guy is crazed now. He can think of nothing but getting down. I look at the left engine indicators and see that for the first time they are slightly out of the red. I call Mario forward to help me convince the pilot to go out a little further. He veers off, finally, and heads down toward the big coal strip at Puerto Bolivar and turns around. Jota turns on the truck lights. The pilot yells into the radio for Jota to turn them off. He's afraid the lights will blind him coming in. I try to explain, through Mario, that this won't happen, but he has his mind made up.

We begin our approach with an airspeed that's much too high. We are down to 1,000 feet and moving at 150 mph indicated with the nose tipped down. The pilot puts down the landing gear and the flaps and heads for the strip. He won't let me assist him at all. But I hold fast to the controls anyway, pull back to compensate for his pushing forward. I tell him to put on the boost pumps and check to make sure the cowl flaps are open. We get down to about 100 feet and fly over the beginning of the runway. We can't possibly land. "We're too fast and too high!" I shout at Mario. "We have to go around again," Mario and I both yell.

"No, no, no. I've got it! I've got it!"

"We can't do this!" I tell Mario.

We've overshot half the landing strip. We're 50 feet up and moving at 140 mph. There's no way we'll be able to stop. Mario and the pilot are shouting at each other. I shout over them. "I'm taking over," I tell Mario. "If he fights me, grab him out of his seat."

I apply full power to the engines and pull the nose up. If the left engine quits now, it's all over. The pilot is still trying to counter my actions. "Grab him!" I shout.

Mario grabs him around the neck with one arm and pulls him back far enough to keep him from reaching the column. I get the landing gear up and lift the nose. Everything is black. I need the instruments to tell me what to do, but the instruments are on his side and it's difficult for me to see them. I see that the altimeter indicator is reading minus 20 feet, the result of the barometric pressure change. Jota is yelling, "What happened? You were too high! Alan, you've got to do this right!" I glance at the left engine temps and find them all back in the red again. We are ascending, but with all the weight, not quickly enough. The pilot is yelling, "Let me go! Let me go!"

"I'll let you down," Mario shrieks, "but he's in charge. Can you understand that? You screwed up. You almost killed us. It's his turn."

Mario lets him down. I remember that the pilot has a gun and I'm about to remind Mario when I see he's still up on the fuel barrels, leaning over him. He looks as alert as any predator I've ever seen. All the pilot has to do is look wrong and Mario will take his head off. The pilot is shouting that he was in control, that he could have landed it if we'd left him alone. Spittle is flying from his mouth. "Yeah," I tell Mario in English, "we'd be burning at the end of the runway by now." "What do you think we are, stupid?" Mario shouts. "There's no possible way you could have done it at that speed and altitude." He's right in the pilot's face, screaming right into it. "Now stop acting like a stupid child and watch how we do this!"

I get it up to about 600 feet and take it around and head back again. The night is black. No moon, no horizon. I might as well be flying a simulator. The pilot calms down and agrees to help me get her in. I tell him to turn on all the rest of the lights as we are approaching Jota's strip. I get to about 300 feet with the airspeed under control. The cowl flaps are open, the landing gear is down. At about 200 feet and half a mile back from the strip, the pilot tells Jota again to turn off his truck lights because they're bothering him. I tell Jota to leave them on. We get down to about 50 feet with everything looking good when the pilot suddenly pulls the nose up. "Take him out of his seat!" I scream.

Mario grabs him by the throat. He's screaming like hell. Now I have to make adjustments for what he's done. I lower the nose some, feeling for the runway. The airplane descends, almost flat. I am flying by the seat of my pants.

We touch down. I have to use maximum breaking power while trying not to lock the wheels. I just barely stop before we run out of runway. Mario lets go of the pilot. He slumps into his seat. Mario is screaming at him in such rapid Spanish that I can't understand a word. "I'm the pilot," he's screaming back. "I'm the captain. You shouldn't have done that to me."

"You're an idiot," Mario tells him. "You tried to kill us. Twice! You're incompetent. You'll never be able to do this, you idiot!"

While they're still screaming in each other's faces, I turn and taxi back. I realize the nose wheel light was never turned on. No wonder I couldn't see well. Using just the wing-tip lights leaves a big black spot in front of the airplane, the equivalent of a shadow. I can't believe I pulled it off. I feel like the luckiest man in the world. But also the angriest. "Why didn't he have the nose wheel light on?" I shout to Mario. "He's over there. I can't reach those switches. He didn't even turn all the lights on in the airplane. No wonder I couldn't see."

Mario doesn't hear me. They're still at it, still screaming at the top of their lungs. I have the feeling Mario is hoping the pilot will go for his gun so he can get it away from him and do what he wants to do. As soon as the motor is shut down, the pilot kicks out the door and leaps down. Mario is right behind him screaming, "I'm going to kill you!"

I shut the pumps, turn off the radios and the master switch, the main for the electric. As I climb out, I realize that my whole body is shaking. Jota is standing there. "Holy shit!" he says. "I thought you were gone. I've never seen one so close. I thought you were gone. What happened? What's going on?"

I look beyond him and see the pilot's people holding Mario back. Mario is shouting and kicking, trying to get free. His eye is fixed on the pilot. "It's this pilot," I tell Jota. "He's no good. He's a lunatic."

Jota looks off and then upward. "Where's your tail, Alan?"

"We saw them going into Aruba. Maybe they were low on fuel…whatever, but we definitely had a tail. I saw two airplanes go by us and Mario saw them behind us and we picked them up on the radio too."

"You were lucky, Alan, really lucky."

Mario is still yelling at the pilot but no longer trying to break free from the people who are holding him back.

Back at the shack the shouting continues. Jota gets on the radio to tell the pilot's people about the tail. There's so much yelling going on that he has to shout. The people on the radio want to know what the shouting is about. Jota explains about the pilot. Their pilot screwed up? They can't believe it. They ask a lot of questions about him. Jota tries to answer them. The issue of the tail recedes in importance.

Mario and I go to another shed for the night. I have to smoke a big one to calm myself down enough to even consider sleep. When Mario finally gets over what happened with the pilot, he begins praising me for my flying and for saving his life. "We're never doing this again," I tell him. "They can shoot me first. I don't care anymore."

In the morning, when the pilot and his people have gone, I tell Jota the same thing. "We'll buy an Aztec, $50,000, a disposable plane," I declare. "An Aztec can carry enough fuel to get to Puerto Rico and back. Mario and I will go to Puerto Rico and pick out the landing sight ourselves. We'll have Mario on the ground. We'll take your coke and land the plane over a nice big field. Mario knows how to watch for a tail. We'll only need a minimal ground crew, two people. It's the only way. If you have me and Mario do any more of these missions, you're going to lose us. We won't do you any good if we're dead. And think of how much money you're going to make if we're running your coke, Jota."

"Yeah, you're right," Jota concedes.

"Of course I'm right. Except for Henry, these Colombian pilots are lunatics." I hesitate for a moment to think about how incredible a pilot Henry really is. "It's too easy to die," I continue. "I'm on your team, Jota. I could have gotten away with Henry if I'd really wanted to. If I pushed it, his people would have forced you to let me go. But I didn't, did I? You're my friend, Jota. You want to refuel airplanes for the rest of your life, fine. But we can make three, four million dollars doing it my way. What are you making now, 30, 40 grand? And that's when the flight's successful." I stop to determine whether I have covered everything. It occurs to me if I haven't gotten paid for my work, then Jota probably doesn't always get paid either. "And that's when you get paid!" I add.

Jota looks off pensively. It must seem plausible to him; it's a good plan. It makes perfect sense. "You're right," he says at last. "No more missions. Last night was the last. The next time you fly, it will be for me. We'll talk to Manolo again; see when he can get an airplane down for you."

"Manolo has been sending down an airplane for three months now. How can you believe him?"

"Well, if he doesn't turn up soon, I'll see if I can make some arrangements myself."

Jota is more friendly after this. He tells his radio buddies we won't be flying for a while. He takes to calling us Socios, partners. We spend a lot of time talking about the plan, fine tuning it, reflecting on what we are going to do with the money we make. Sometimes it gets to sounding so good that I'm actually tempted to go through with it. I figure I have no life anymore anyway.

We hear some drumming start up one night from the camp and we all go out to have a look. Mario and I are amazed to see that the Indians have cleared a large area and decked themselves out in their best clothes, which is to say frayed skirts for the women and fly-less pants held together with rope for the men. Some of them are unfamiliar, Indians from the neighboring camps. They are standing in two circles, the women in the outer one and the men in the inner. They seem to be waiting for some cue. "We're really seeing something," I say to Mario. "This must be some kind of primitive celebration that's about to begin. Maybe a fertility rite."

We get a little closer. No one seems to mind. I elbow Mario and point out the drummer as soon as I recognize him.

It's Fred, the Indian whose feet couldn't be made to fit into Mario's sandals. He's pounding away on his drum, smiling like hell in Mario's shirt and sunglasses. I notice there's a lot of pure alcohol around, which is what the Indians like to drink.

Someone gives a signal and the festivities begin. As the men skip forward with their hands behind their backs, the women skip back as if trying to get away from them. Whenever a man comes within reach of a woman he's pursuing, his hands come out from behind him and he grabs for her. If she's fast, she darts away just in time and the man goes tumbling. If not, they tumble together. Then they get up and begin again. Everyone is laughing, howling with joy and intoxication. Fred is pounding away rhythmlessly—pa pum, pa pum, pa pum.

In the morning, there's no sun. It's been blocked out entirely by the low black clouds that are moving toward us over the sea. I'm enchanted by their progression. I can't help but wonder if what went on the night before was actually some kind of rain dance.

I think of Raul Hernandez again, the son of a bitch. I've been thinking about him a lot lately. After what he did to me, he seems a fitting target for my repressed anger. Had I known then what I know now about myself, maybe I could have killed him back in the States, when I had my chance. Some nights I dream I hear his laughter. Fifty thousand dollars—the price of his friendship.

When I knew him, he was into voodoo, into believing that forces could be called upon, consolidated, made to work in one's interests. He even took me to meet one of his voodoo guides once, ostensibly to get me to become a believer. But the real reason was to find out whether he could trust me. The guide made a prediction: "The two of you will die together, that's how close you will be." So much for prophecy.

The sea begins to swell. The waves invade our little strip of beach and smash themselves against the rocks. It's an incredibly beautiful sight. I've just decided that I'm going to spend the entire day watching it when the rain begins, not the occasional drizzle we're used to, but big fat drops that bounce on the parched earth before they settle.

It rains and rains and rains; three days worth of the stuff. And there's so much lightning to go along with it that no one dares to go outside and see how the seas are doing. Sitting in the shack with nothing to do but listen to the waves break brings my boredom level to an all-time high. I can tell by Mario's expression that his is up there too. I resolve to ignore him if he gets testy.

When it finally stops raining, we all go out to take a look. The transformation is incredible. Shrubs that were brown since my arrival are a glistening green. Puddles are everywhere. Flowers are in blossom. The earth is saturated. The air smells like perfume.

No one wants to go back indoors. Even when it gets dark, we stay on outside looking at our new world. Jota, who is in a particularly good mood, begins to tell us how in the early '70s he used to see things in the sky, weird things that made right hand turns and then darted away and disappeared: UFOs.

Jota isn't much of a storyteller. He doesn't have the imagination for it. In fact, the only true fabrication I've ever heard him come up with is the one about getting us out. While we question him about these sightings, we all stare up at the stars. And incredibly enough, what do we see but two satellites going by at tremendous speeds, crossing right over us, right over each other! When we get over our amazement, Jota tells us that some of the Indians say the aliens came one night and touched them. At first I can't imagine why aliens would waste their time in the Guajira. But then I get to thinking they were probably trying to make some sense out of the smuggling activities. Who knows? Maybe they stole a little coke themselves, took it back with them. It seems as plausible as a mostly honest pilot being imprisoned in Venezuela and then sold to a drug smuggler/murderer in the Red Zone.

Henry shows up again, with gifts—fruit, deodorant, T-shirts, ham, sandwiches, even pastries. "You're still here," he says, shaking his head with wonder. "You still haven't left?" He has come, of course, to do a mission, but this time he doesn't even bother to ask me to go with him. Now that he's been successful on his own, his confidence level is off the scale. He no longer believes it's possible for him to pull a tail.

Jota and his Indians load him up and off he goes to meet some boats off the coast of Puerto Rico. When he gets back to the shack, Jota gets his frequency on the radio. Mario and I cut short our afternoon swim and go back to the shack to sit with Jota and listen. I'm thinking that Henry's luck is bound to run out when it comes in over the radio that Henry has a tail, a royal one, a Coast Guard Falcon flying right alongside him over the boats he was supposed to drop to. We speculate with Jota. Maybe there's an agent on one of the boats. Maybe they got him on the radar and decided to bust him this time. I can't imagine why it didn't happen sooner.

Henry's in a panic. Now he sees a four-engine P3 Orion and some helicopters. He seems to think he's going to be shot down. He's screaming a lot of things in that rapid Spanish that continues to befuddle me. I ask Mario what he's saying exactly, but Mario is listening too intently to bother answering. Jota asks me what Henry should do. I'm the authority on these matters since my phantom tail. I ask Jota to tell Henry to just climb normally and fly back straight and level. Jota says into the radio, "Alan says…" And Henry answers, "I'll do whatever Alan wants." And I'm thinking, great, let's talk about Alan a little more on this frequency that's definitely being monitored so that the whole world can figure out there is a gringo pilot in the Guajira.

Henry's in such a panic that he keeps Jota on the radio the whole way home. Jota actually talks him home. Jota tells him to come right in, not to worry about whether his tail is following.

We go out to the strip with Jota and watch Henry land. He gets out of the airplane looking like he's about to cry. He's so shaken up that he ignores our outstretched hands and walks right by us. Mierda, I hear the Indians who are unloading the bails say, Shit.

"Hey, Henry, beautiful landing," I offer. "And they didn't shoot you out of the sky. What the hell! Don't be so choked up. Everything's okay."

He turns from me, looks up where his tail is circling at some distance, and hangs his head as if he's really embarrassed about botching this up.

You would think Henry had been in a World War II dogfight the way he goes on to his people on the radio back at the shack. I can't help but chuckle. The way I see it, this should have happened with every one of his flights.

And for all that I like Henry, I can't help but feel proud that the Americans are finally doing something.

Henry leaves that night, and the next day, as we're expecting company, we get up very early and take down the radio antenna and head for the caves. Sure enough, a couple of hours later some helicopters go buzzing by. But they don't land. Jota takes the credit for it. "We paid the general," he says. "With 17 different landing strips in the area it's not so hard to convince the DEA that the one a half mile away is the actual strip."

We linger on in the caves anyway. "Henry sure was bad," I say to Mario, "really choked up."

"Yeah," he says. "He shit himself."

"Yeah," I respond, "I guess I would have shit too in a situation like that."

Mario begins to grin. "No, he really shit himself."

I'm grinning too now. "You mean he shit his pants?"

"Yeah. Didn't you hear the Indians talking about it? He wiped it all over the bales."

"No!"

"Yeah! He shit all over himself and he put the shit on top of the bales so he wouldn't have to fly home with it in his pants and when the Indians were unloading them, they got shit all over themselves. That was Henry's shit!"

Mario and I laugh like crazy. The longer we think about it, the funnier it gets. Jota and the other Colombians don't think it's so funny. They pretend they don't hear us laughing. But when we finally calm down, we hear a few grunts among them too.

When we're all serious again, I discuss the situation with Jota. I suggest maybe the agencies in Puerto Rico are using P3 Orions rather than AWACS now. A P3 Orion, I tell him, is a sub-chaser that can pick up a periscope in the water. If it can do that, you know it can pick up an airplane, no problem. I tell him some research has to be done. Someone has to go to Puerto Rico and find out what kind of airplanes are being used and when they're in the air and when they're not. Jota agrees emphatically. When there's nothing more to say on the matter, I turn to Mario again. "You mean he really shit himself?" I ask. And we crack up all over again.

The antenna goes back up and Jota radios his people in Barranquilla to let them know he's coming to see them. Before he leaves, I remind him of our plan, about how willing I am to work for him. While he's gone, I remind Armando, who's still waiting for his airplane to show up, that I'll work for his people, if only they'll get me the hell out of here.

Things go back to normal; the hopelessness sets in again. Mario and I feel certain we're never going to leave the Guajira. We also feel certain that someone will get to Jota in Barranquilla and that he'll come back trying to convince us to do just one more mission.

We hear some gunshots the second day after Jota's departure and run out with our machine guns to see what's happening. We find Jota's wife's mother standing with her gun in hand before the bodies of four dead dogs. When she sees our bewilderment, she says that the dogs killed three goats in one of the neighboring camps, that once they get the taste, you can't stop them. "It's going to cost me $20 a goat," she says.

The next morning there's another shooting. I'm in my hammock, not quite fully awake, when I hear machine gun fire very, very close. I whip out of my hammock and onto the floor and scramble over into the corner where my machine gun is. I grab it and get it into position.

The firing is hitting the roof of the shack. I can hear stuff flying. So this is how it will end, I say to myself. I will never even get to tell a single soul back home what's happened to me. I realize I never cocked my gun. I cock it quickly and yell for Mario at the top of my lungs.

The door to the back room flies open and I see him with his machine gun. With the blood pounding in my head as it is, it takes me a moment to realize that he's grinning and that his gun is smoking. "You stupid shit!" I scream. "What did you do?"

His smile broadens. "The iguana was right at the end of my hammock, Alan," he declares excitedly. "It was about to eat me."

I take a few deep breaths and step past him, into his room. My sense of relief floods over me and I find myself laughing. "Did you get it?" I ask.

"I don't know."

There are holes all over the place and concrete chips all over the floor. Some are as big as my hand. Dust particles are swirling. We laugh for a long time. "Please don't ever do that again," I say when I gain some control. "You don't know how scared I was. I thought it was the military or someone else coming to rob us. I thought we were dead."

Mario's eyes get very round, very serious. I see there's some moisture in them, but I can't tell whether it's a teardrop forming or just a reaction to the dust. Then his features contort. "Alan," he says, "we've been here so damn long; it's time to leave."

THE GAMBIT

Jota only laughs when he sees what Mario has done to his roof. "Don't worry about it," he says. "The Indians will patch it up while we're gone."

Mario rises slowly from his hammock. "Gone?"

"December is a bad month for business. The military gets greedy. They claim they need extra money for Christmas presents."

Mario and I nod to encourage him. We're hanging onto his every word. He smiles cunningly and lets a long moment pass. "I can't afford to pay them. I'm shutting things down. Tomorrow one of the fishermen will take you up to the port, to Puerto Bolivar. From there another boat will bring you to Riohacha. At Riohacha, Mano will meet you and find a place for you to stay until I can make arrangements to get you to Barranquilla. We're getting you out."

Armando has been standing in the doorway listening. He steps forward now with his hand extended. He is, he says, so happy for us. We're happy for ourselves. We're ecstatic. We can't stop laughing and slapping each other's shoulders. Neither of us dares ruin the moment by asking Jota what will happen to us once we get to Barranquilla.

But of course that's an issue. So when we go down to the beach in the afternoon for our final swim and learn that Armando and his friends are leaving tomorrow for Barranquilla too (their airplane never came in), I remind Armando once again that I'm willing to work for his people if they'll only get us to the States. Armando was out on the runway the night I saved the Piper Navajo from crashing. And he's heard Henry rave about my flying on several occasions. If Jota doesn't make an effort to get us out, I want something to fall back on. Armando says yes, we'll get together, definitely do some business. He gives me his phone number in Barranquilla.

When the fisherman comes for us in the morning, we're all packed and ready to go. Jota is already gone. He wanted to get there first, he said, to arrange everything for us. Armando will be leaving a little later in the day, after the truck comes to cart his coke away. We take one last look at the place, at the blue blue waters, the Indians and their animals just beginning to stir in the camp, the endless expanse of sky. The dangers here, it seems now as we consider the tranquility of the landscape, were negligible, and we admit to each other that we're uneasy about leaving. We knew what to expect here, and now we're venturing back into the world of the unexpected. Jesus stayed in the desert for 40 days, some 50 less than our own sojourn, according to my calculations. I wonder whether He too left apprehensive about the future.

The fisherman drops us off at a dock at Puerto Bolivar at noon. Since we don't find anyone waiting for us, Mario and I go off to a bar on the water, where we can keep an eye on things. While we eat, we look out at the freighters. Coal from the nearby mine is being loaded into them along incredibly long conveyor belts. We go out to have a better look. Then we return to the bar and have a drink. We agree we should keep from speculating on the possibility that no one may be coming for us, but after our third drink we do just that. We walk around a little more, slowly, to encourage time to pass. We stand on the edge of the dock we were dropped at and check out all the incoming boats. From a distance, any one of them might be our ride. But as each gets closer the possibility diminishes. This lack of organization is typical of Jota. We alternate between laughing at his predictability and cursing him. We watch the sun prepare to go down over the horizon. We make out a motorized canoe at a distance but agree it's not seaworthy enough to be our ride. But as it approaches the dock, the little black man in the front begins waving. "That can't be for us," Mario says. I look behind us. There's no one there.

The little black man is the same one who arrived with Jota and

Gordo to take us from the border to Riohacha almost four months ago, Jota's employee, Cesar. In the boat with him are two young, long-haired Colombians, wearing earrings. I've been around Jota long enough to know their jerky movements indicate they're both whacked out on coke. "No," Mario says. "No way am I going in that canoe."

"I don't think we have a choice."

While one of the long-haired guys is cutting the motor, a 20 horse-power job, Cesar jumps onto the dock and secures the boat. Then he stretches his hand to greet us. I shake it feebly. When it swings toward Mario, he only looks down at it. "No way am I going on that boat," he reiterates.

"It's the best we could do," Cesar says. "We have a spare motor."

The two guys in the back of the boat point out the spare. It is a 40 horsepower. "Why don't you put on that one and use the smaller for the spare?" I ask.

Cesar smiles apologetically. "It's broken. We're on the emergency motor now."

Mario and I look at each other. "I'm not going," he grumbles again.

We're wasting time. I want to get out so badly that I'm prepared to water ski to Riohacha if I have to. "Do you see any other form of trans-portation?" I ask, raising my voice. "There's no other way. It's either we get into this canoe or we don't go, because Jota and Mano aren't going to send anything else."

Mario continues to argue. He tells Cesar to go to a phone and call Jota and tell him to bring a truck. "There's not going to be a truck, Mario," I tell him. "Nobody's going to send a truck. We don't have papers. This is the only way."

I go on in this vein for some minutes while Cesar listens anxiously. The other two look amused. Finally I toss my bag into the boat and tell Cesar to prepare to cast off. "I'll only go if we stay close to the shore," Mario calls out.

Cesar nods rapidly. "Anything you want, no problem. We'll hug the coast. Get in."

There's not a lot of room. In addition to the broken motor, the boat is jammed full of gasoline containers. There's a small plastic windscreen up in the front, so Mario seats himself just behind that. I sit down in the middle, in front of the broken motor. Cesar hands me a plastic garbage bag.

We're not too far out and moving at a snail's pace when I see a fin ahead of us. I've seen plenty of them at Jota's, but never this close up. I figure it's best not to point it out to Mario. A little further out we get the propeller caught on some nets that are attached to nearby buoys. While the two long-haired guys are unsnarling them, they tell Mario this is going to keep on happening if we don't get out into open waters. Mario doesn't care. The long-haired guys say okay, but they gradually head out into the ocean anyway. Mario screams at them to get in. They scream back. We get going a little faster and all the screaming gets blown overboard.

When it's totally dark and Mario can't see the shoreline anymore, he stops screaming. The two long-haired guys don't even have a compass. We can't see a thing anywhere except for the storm in the distance, which we seem to be heading into. I have no idea how these people are navigating. The waves are getting higher. Many break over the bow. I make a hole in the end of my garbage bag and put it over my head like a hooded shirt. The rain begins. It only takes a few minutes before I'm thoroughly soaked in spite of the plastic. Now it's my turn to start in. I scream at the guys in the back to stop. We can't see what we're doing and the waves are getting higher all the time. After everything I've been through, I don't want to die in the ocean when I'm on my way out. "Take us to shore," I yell. Nobody answers. I figure maybe the guys in the back are having trouble with my Spanish.

"You're an idiot," Mario screams. "I told you I didn't want to go in this canoe. It's your fault, again. You keep getting me into this shit!"

"Tell them to take us to shore," I yell to him.

"Take us to shore. We want to go to shore," Mario shouts.

"Don't worry, Gringo, we're okay," one of the guys in the back declares. "We've been in worse than this. We know what we're doing."

"Yeah, we have a bilge pump from the U.S." the other adds. "It's automatic. When the water gets so high, it comes on." They both laugh hysterically.

The thunder bellows all around us. The guys in the back laugh like lunatics and shout incomprehensibly up at the sky. I get the feeling they're encouraging the storm, defying it to worsen. A bolt of lightning lights up the place where I last saw shore. There's nothing there.

We're humming along at about six or seven mph. The rain is cold and I'm freezing. My teeth are chattering. My feet are submerged in two inches of water. The guys in the back have a raincoat. Every so often they slow down and pull it over their heads so that they can do a line or two of coke. Actually it's not a line. They just grab the stuff between their fingers and snort whatever's still there by the time they get their hands from the bag to their noses.

The storm ends and the sea calms somewhat. The stars begin to twinkle overhead. I close my eyes and let the steady hum of the motor lull me into something approaching sleep. When I open them, I see Mario looking back at me.

He still looks nervous. His expression reminds me of Carlos's in the airplane. I laugh. I'm just drifting toward sleep again when something slaps me hard across the face. I come to life with a start and see tiny winged fish flying all around the boat. I turn on my flashlight and examine the one that hit me before throwing it overboard. A beautiful little fish. Mario must get hit with one too because all of a sudden he starts screaming again. He finds the culprit and throws it away disgustedly. But then he stiffens and starts screaming once more. "Sharks,

sharks," he yells. "Oh my God, the water's full of sharks!"

I see the fins too. They're all around us and very close. But they're not sharks. I don't bother telling Mario because I'm still a little pissed about his accusations earlier. When the dolphins begin leaping, he figures it out for himself and settles down.

The spirited mammals are a beautiful sight. I saw them this close once before, when I was in Bolivia. A friend and I had been boating through the headwaters of the Amazon when all at once we saw a school of smallish, white dolphins. We cut the engines immediately, and they came in pairs to play at the side of the boat. Suddenly I feel everything is going to be okay in Barranquilla after all, that the dolphins would not have come again like this otherwise. They seem to be asking us to jump into the water and join them. Damned if I'm not tempted. I'm soaked to the bone anyway.

The sun begins to come up just as we're approaching Riohacha. Cesar, who's been quiet all night, gets anxious. "We were supposed to arrive at night," he tells us. "Things could be bad."

"Great," Mario responds in English. "Another well organized plan. Jota pulls another one."

We begin to see small communities and boats at anchor. We crawl along between the fishing nets. When we clear them, we come to a stretch of water filled with dead fish, a result of industrial waste in the water. We pull into a small river that winds around behind the hotel where I had my birthday party back in August. I didn't think much of the place at the time, but after Jota's shack, it looks almost appealing now. We round another bend and see Gordo leaning on his green Toyota. We beach the canoe and get out. "What happened?" Gordo asks. "I've been waiting for you guys for hours."

We tell him the story on the way over to his turkey farm. I think of it as a grim story with a few comic details here and there, but Gordo seems to find the entire thing humorous. This disturbs me. I sit back in my seat and ponder the few humorous events that took place in the Guajira and in prison in Venezuela. I wonder whether Gordo would laugh if he knew about them too. I wonder whether he would understand about the rest of it—the boredom, the frustration, the fear—or if the humorous parts would always get in the way. Maybe, I get to thinking, boredom and frustration and fear are things that don't stand up too well to the telling of them. You can say I was so frustrated, but what does that mean? People get frustrated every day. On the airliner going to Caracas I was frustrated. So were the young American vacationers I found myself watching. We were all frustrated. How will anyone know how much greater, how much more genuine my frustration was?

At Gordo's we take showers and get into fresh clothes. Even these are damp when we put them on, but the heat is staggering and it doesn't take long for them to dry out. When Mano pulls up, I decide he's not going to get the chance to laugh at our story and I charge out to the gate to meet him. "What kind of a boat was that?" I shout. "We want to be your friends, but how can we when you do shit like this?"

His expression, which was eager a moment ago, sours. What am I doing? I ask myself. Mano and I are not friends—we both know that—but I need him just now. "We did the best we could," he says tightly. "We had a nice boat for you, but it broke down. We had to get you out quick. We did our best."

"Okay, okay. I understand." I stretch my arm toward him. We shake hands and go in.

The kitchen table is covered with the hundred dollar bills Mario and I have been drying out. "You'd better give some to the girls," Mano says when he sees them. He tilts his head toward Gordo's wife and her sister, both of whom are busy at the stove. I give them each a hundred and gather up the rest before Mano can give the money much more thought.

Later, I happen to be standing near the window when a police car pulls up in front of the house. "It's over," I whisper. Mario gets out of his chair to see what I'm referring to. He turns around at once, his mouth hanging open and his eyes darting about as he searches for the best means of escape. Mano, who has seen the car from another room, steps in and tells us calmly to go and hide in the bedroom.

We hightail for the door and collide when we reach it. We bounce off of each other, banging our shoulders on either side of the frame. Mario blocks me with his elbow and manages to scramble under the bed before me.

We say nothing; we don't even look at each other. I strain my ears to hear what's going on, but I can't hear anything beyond the sound of my own rushing blood. Fifteen minutes pass. Then the bedroom door flies open. I see Gordo's wife's swollen feet appear in their leather sandals. "It's okay now," she says. "You can come out now. They're gone."

I emerge slowly, half expecting to see the police standing just behind her, smirking at her little joke. She laughs heartily when she sees my face. She wipes her hands on her apron and bends to get a look at Mario, who's just sliding out. She laughs again. "You didn't have to worry so much," she says. "They come by once a week to pick up their pay."

Two hundred dollars seems excessive for a meal and a couple of nights at a turkey farm where there's no escape route, where the closest thing to safety is the space beneath a bed. So in the evening, when Jota shows up, I ask him if he can get us into a hotel until we leave for Barranquilla. Much to my delight, he tells me he has it all arranged for us to leave early in the morning. There's no reason to go to a hotel. His eyes flash furtively. "You'll be traveling with a man from the DAS," he says. "In his personal truck with all the right stickers and a license plate. But this kind of protection isn't cheap. It's going to cost you $2,000." His hand comes out from his pocket and spreads itself flat.

His smile is so self-composed that I feel the urge to jab my fist into it. But instead I hand over the money. He puts it into his pocket and slumps away.

The DAS guy, an area manager from Colombian Immigration, appears in the morning, very early, right on time. Since he's all smiles, I assume whatever Jota gave him satisfied him and that he won't ask for more along the way. Mario and I get into the back of his jeep and put our sunglasses on. "If we hit a bad roadblock," he tells us, "the story is that you're my prisoners and you're without papers and I'm taking you to the head office in Barranquilla."

"Wonderful," I say to Mario, but he only shrugs.

The DAS guy likes to talk; he wants to know all about us. But when he sees we're not going to give his questions much in the way of a response, he begins pointing out the scenery instead. I have to admit it's beautiful once we're out of Riohacha. In fact, much of it is breath-taking. The road we're on goes right along the coast. Many of the cliffs on the other side feature waterfalls. I get to feeling like we're tourists and our driver is our guide, especially when we arrive at the road-blocks. He waves his hand and someone waves back and we go right through. "Well worth $2,000," I say to Mario.

"Yeah, cheap," he responds.

We stop for gas and head on toward Santa Marta. The beauty of the landscape continues to be amazing. The waters of the rivers that run down from the mountains are crystal clear. I've seen rivers with such clear waters before only in my country, in Canada. Likewise, the road-blocks continue to be a joke. I get to thinking that maybe it would have been better if Mario and I had gone with the Colombians when we first landed the airplane. With a few dollars you can do anything here it seems. And I would guess those Colombians had more than just a few dollars on them.

Coming up on the bridge that spans the Magdalena River there's another roadblock, a military one. The uniforms the soldiers are wearing are similar to the uniforms of the Guardia Nacional in Venezuela. As we roll to a stop, a man comes up to the truck with a rifle, a 7.62mm, in hand. The soldiers behind him are also armed and ready to take aim. This doesn't really surprise me. The military in Colombia are well known for their animosity. Everyone has it in for them, the cartel, the M19 guerilla groups, everyone. I adjust my sunglasses and try to look unconcerned. "Everyone out of the car," the soldier says. "I want to see papers for everyone."

"Don't you know who I am?" our driver asks as he hands his papers over.

The soldier inspects them carefully, but after he's handed them back, he only repeats his demand. Some of his buddies gather in closer behind him. Our driver says, "Look, we're not getting out of the car. I have two prisoners here. You'll have to bring me your boss."

They continue to argue for a few minutes. Then the soldier relents and goes off, but not until after he's fixed our driver with an incredibly hateful stare. He returns a moment later with a colonel. I can see by the colonel's expression that he recognizes our driver. They shake hands. "How are you doing, friend?" our driver asks. "I've got these two prisoners here. They lost their passports. I'm taking them to the embassy. I'm going to dump them off and then I'll be back."

Mario and I look at each other. We take this to mean that our driver will be back with a few bucks, to pay off the colonel. The colonel nods. Off we go again. I whisper to Mario, "I don't know how many more of these close calls I can take."

Barranquilla is large, maybe four or five million people, and with lots of highrises. Our driver weaves through its streets familiarly. He has a slip of paper in his hand, Jota's address. Every once in a while he lifts it up and looks at it. After about 30 minutes we reach our destination, a beautiful apartment building on a heavily trafficked street.

Our driver goes in to announce our arrival and a moment later Jota is bounding down the front entrance. "Oh, Hermanos, you made it! Come in, come in."

His apartment is on the second floor. It's large, beautifully furnished, and has marble tile floors throughout. It's strange to be seeing Jota in these surroundings. And it's stranger yet to hear him introduce the attractive woman who appears at his side as his wife. Maria looks to be part Indian. She's a little older than the Guajiran, and very short, but well-shaped. Her teeth are chalky white and her skin is the color of hazelnuts. "You must be Alan," she says in perfect English as she reaches for my hand. "And you're Mario," she says turning to him. "You must both make yourselves at home."

We venture further into the living room and are introduced to Jota's aunt and uncle and their little boy, all of whom have black stumps for teeth. We're also introduced to Jota's son, a young man of about two who, except for his flawless posture, looks just like his father. We shake hands with everyone and sit down. When Jota and Maria go into the kitchen to fix us drinks, Mario snarls in English, "So this is what he was coming to while we were out in the desert." I assume he means the apartment, but when Maria returns and I see the once-over he gives her, I realize I'm mistaken.

"So, Socios," Jota says. "Tell me how was your trip."

With everybody looking so happy I find myself reluctant to say anything negative. "Well," I begin, "it was pretty amazing the way your DAS friend got us through. It was only the last roadblock—"

"Yeah, yeah," Jota interrupts. "It's those damn M19s. They're in town. They've been blowing up cars and hotels. You'll have to be very careful about going out into the streets. Two weeks ago there was a car bombing a block away. Whatever you do, don't go out at night. Don't take rides at night, no taxis, nothing. Oh, and I should tell you, Manolo is coming by in a few days to see you."

"Oh good," I hear myself comment, but really I'm thinking, oh shit—because I'm still worried that there may be repercussions from my giving his name to the general.

"Is there anything I can get you in the meantime?" Jota asks.

I look him over. I'm still having a hard time associating this pleasant man with the beautiful wife and child with the bastard who killed a kid and threatened to kill me in the Guajira. The only thing they seem to have in common is the slump. "Yeah, there's one thing. I have to call Jenny. I'd like to do it right way."

"No problem, no problem at all. Phone your woman, phone your friends in America. Tell them to get ready for us."

Jota's uncle, Xavier, jumps up from the table and offers to take us right out.

Down the street there is a cambista, a house of change, where Mario and I each exchange about $700 for pesos. Right next to it is the Entel, the public telephone center. The Entel is divided into two areas, one for national calls and one for international. There are a lot of people waiting, but I tip the girl at the counter a few bucks and get a booth right away.

Since I don't know Jenny's new number, I dial her father's, the hardware store that he owns in Ridgefield, Connecticut. I'm prepared for a confrontation, or worse, to have him hang up on me. But amazingly enough, it's Jenny who answers. She has to say hello three times before I can speak. And then the only thing I can muster is her name. I whisper it several times before I catch myself and stop.

I take the silence that follows to mean that she hates me, that she's found someone to replace me, a man who likes to stay at home at night, a man who has never known the seduction of the skies. But then I realize she's sobbing quietly. "Where are you?" she whispers.

"I thought you forgot me," I dare to say.

She makes a noise, something between a gasp and a hiccup. A

moment passes. "I thought you were dead. I didn't know if…" She clears her throat. "I didn't forget you," she says in a voice that cracks with every word. Then she laughs. "I would like to forget you. That would be a healthy thing for me. But I haven't."

Suddenly I want to tell her everything that's happened to me, but I can't imagine that it's safe to talk on these phones. I tell her a little in a kind of code and she catches on and refrains from asking any incriminating questions. I promise her that it won't be much longer until I'm home and that I'll call her back tomorrow. She gives me the number.

When I hang up, I'm exhilarated. I feel like the luckiest man in the world. I turn to Mario, to let him know I haven't been abandoned after all, but he's preoccupied asking Xavier to take him shopping. I decide to keep my feelings to myself and suggest to Mario that maybe Xavier wants to get back to the apartment. But Xavier insists that it would give him pleasure to show us around.

He brings us to a drug store that sells lots of American products. They're very expensive, but we stock up anyway on shaving cream and shampoo. Then we set off for the shops to purchase underwear, socks, pants, and shirts. In my celebratory mood, I wind up buying almost as much as Mario.

We settle down later with Jota and his relatives for a home-cooked dinner of T-bone steaks with plenty of trimmings. We're just finishing when Henry shows up. He has, he says, an apartment right upstairs, on the fourth floor. He invites us up to have a couple of drinks with him and some friends he has over. I feel like I'm dreaming. How else can it be that my surroundings have changed so drastically while the cast of characters remains the same? I have talked to Jenny, ascertained that she still cares for me; I have new clothes, my stomach is full, and everyone is treating me like they're genuinely happy to see me. I suspect I'll wake up and find myself back in my hammock in the Guajira.

That night Jota takes us over to the apartment where we'll be staying until he can get us out. It's not as large or nicely furnished as his, but it has everything we could need including a small, well-stocked kitchen. He says that he'll be out of town for a few days. Henry and his people want to do another mission and they're making it worth his while to return to the Guajira to help them out. In the meantime, he says, we should make ourselves at home. If we find ourselves needing anything at all, we have only to tell Xavier.

I still haven't figured out whether Xavier and his family actually live at Jota's place or just visit an awful lot, but it's clear that they live on Jota's money; nobody seems to have anything to do but sit around all day. Hence Xavier is more than happy to drive us anywhere we want to go. He takes us to get haircuts, and then to have our nails filed, as is the custom for men in South America. When we're all groomed and looking good, I ask him to take me to the Entel again so that I can phone Jenny. But once I'm alone in the booth, I dial Armando's number first and tell him Jota is out of town for a few days. He promises to come by. He says his boss, Giovanni, has agreed to meet me.

I call Jenny. As if only a little time has passed since we were together, she tells me about the things she's done in the last few days. Then she describes the terrible things she's going to do to me if I don't get home for the holidays. I'm glad she's doing all the talking; I don't want her to realize how choked up I am. It's early December. I feel confident that I will be back in the States by Christmas. Again, I have the sense that I'm the luckiest man in the world. Either that or I'm dreaming.

That night we go to an elegant Chinese restaurant with Maria and Xavier and Claribel, Jota's aunt. Mario, who insists that's he's paying for everything, orders a bottle of champagne and the most expensive entrees on the menu. When we finish our incredible meal, we slide into a booth in the lounge to listen to the three guitar players. They had been going from table to table, but after Mario hands them a twenty they stay at ours. We order more champagne. Xavier's jokes, which weren't all that funny when the evening began, are getting funnier by the minute. So when Maria's hand falls on my thigh, I assume it's only a gesture to accompany her laughter. But it doesn't move—or rather, it does, but not away.

I'm shocked. I look at Jota's aunt and uncle. Their faces are red from laughing. I excuse myself and head for the men's room. When I return, I sit down on the other end of the booth by Xavier and start talking to him about Colombian politics. Claribel, the aunt, joins us. This leaves Mario and Maria to converse on their own. As our conversation gets louder and louder, theirs, I note, gets softer and more intimate. With the corner of my eye, I see Mario's knuckles brush Maria's cheek. One of her hands is around the stem of her champagne glass. I can't see the other, but I think I know where it is. I try to listen to what they're saying while I'm nodding at Xavier, but I'm too drunk to concentrate on two conversations at once. I get the feeling Xavier and Claribel are trying to listen to them too.

When Xavier gets up to use the men's room, I say to Mario in English, "The aunt and uncle are watching you. What are you doing?"

"Nothing , don't worry," he responds, and turns his attention back to Maria.

We're invited back to the apartment for a nightcap. Maria brings rum and fruit juice drinks out to us in the living room and then returns to the kitchen to fix us a little snack. Mario decides to go in and help her. Xavier and Claribel, who have given up pretending to ignore what's going on, continue to talk to me about Colombian politics, but with their eyes continuously returning to the kitchen door.

Giovanni and his boys appear at our apartment first thing in the morning. While Giovanni is introducing himself, his boys wander toward the doors to the other rooms and look behind them. I can't imagine who they expect to find lurking there. Once they're satisfied we're alone, they become very friendly. Mario doesn't return their small talk. I didn't bother to tell him about this meeting beforehand. He's fuming, but he keeps his mouth shut.

Giovanni is a tall, heavy-set guy. Like all the people in the business, he is impeccably dressed. He says he's very, very happy to meet us. What he wants to know is how Jota treated us. I figure if I can convince him that Jota treated us badly, he'll be able to justify crossing the line and "employing" us. I tell him Jota lied to me on a number of occasions and that he didn't pay me all of the money he promised. "If I do a job," I say, "I expect to get paid."

He nods. "Yes, if you don't get paid, then you have a good reason to change camps."

I go on to remind him that his people had all that coke sitting there and that Jota never managed to get the airplane to come for it. Giovanni's grimace confirms that he still remembers the incident very well himself. "I want to work with you, Giovanni," I say. "Mario and I can handle the whole operation. I'll fly it and Mario will receive it. We have all the connections. Remember Mario is Cuban."

Giovanni smiles broadly. "We might be able to work something out," he says.

"Great, but one thing. This has got to be top secret because—"

His hand comes up reassuringly. "I understand. Don't worry. You can trust me."

As soon as they're gone, Mario goes wild. "What's wrong with you?" he screams. "What are you doing? What if he tells Jota? I warned you about this before. You don't know what his relationship with Jota really is."

"Calm down, Mario," I say. "I'm taking the chance that he won't tell Jota. I don't think he will."

"The chance? You can't take chances now. We're here. We're too close."

I'm taking a chance because I can't stand this shit anymore. And I don't believe it's much of a chance anyway. Anyone can load gas into an airplane. But a pilot who can organize and run a mission from start to finish doesn't come out of the woods every day. Don't you understand?"

We go over to Jota's apartment and sit around for a while with Maria, her son, Xavier and Claribel. Mario is happy enough to be in Maria's company, but I'm bored silly in no time. Maria suggests I go out with Xavier and pick up some videos while she prepares lunch. When Mario hears that the video shop is only down at the corner, he decides to join us.

We return with several action/adventure films. Xavier inserts Jean-Claude Van Damme's *The Kick-Boxer* into the machine. The film features an English soundtrack and what even I can tell is a lousy Spanish translation at the bottom of the screen. Mario sits at the edge of his seat watching Van Damme's every move. He's probably thinking he's just as good. He's probably right. Maria's little boy looks up from the plastic contraption he's playing with and stares at the screen too. Then he abandons his toy and joins Mario and me on the sofa. Xavier and Claribel announce that they're going to go pick up their kid from the sitter and then do some shopping. As soon as they're gone, Mario mumbles something about being thirsty and shoots up from the sofa. In a moment I hear laughter coming from the kitchen.

Mario and Maria come out into the living room and perch themselves on either end of the sofa, on the arms. Maria asks if her son and I are enjoying the film. The little boy is so enthralled he doesn't bother to answer. I pretend to be equally enthralled. Maria gets up as quietly as a cat and moves toward the hallway. A minute later Mario gets up and follows. Later, when I go to use the bathroom, I find the door locked.

"Did you?" I ask Mario that evening when we return to our apartment.

His features dissolve into one colossal grin. "She's fantastic," he confirms.

"Oh, no, Mario. You can't do this! This is really bad."

His grin vanishes and suddenly he's his arrogant self again. "Why can't I do it? Jota's a son of a bitch. He's got all these wives. Maria is just one of them. He beats her. She's an attorney, and he beats her."

"She's an attorney?"

"Yes, she's an attorney. She met him when she was twelve. He basically bought her. He sent her through school. He helped her get a degree in law. She didn't even want to study law. She wanted to study something else. But he wanted her on the inside, where she would have the right connections if he got into trouble. He never lets her forget what he did for her. A beautiful girl like that and he treats her like shit. He leaves her alone for months at a time. He's got his uncle and aunt watching her every move. They make sure she doesn't have any friends."

Maria telephones in the morning to speak to Mario. I don't like this at all. The calls here go through a switchboard and we've been warned by everyone to do all our telephoning from the Entel. Mario is still whispering sweet nothings into the receiver when Giovanni shows up with Armando and a few others. "I love you, I want you forever, I want to marry you," I hear him say. I can't believe my ears. "My little baby, my little girl, I'll take you anywhere, I'll save you, I'll be your savior." On and on he goes, shit like I never heard before. I greet Giovanni boisterously and hope that he won't notice Mario in the corner making love to the phone. I move toward the entrance to the kitchen and ask them if they want something to drink. They don't. When Mario replaces the receiver, they all turn to look at him. He's smiling inanely and his eyes are glazed over like a man on drugs. He's in love!

"I can get you to Costa Rica," Giovanni says, turning back. "We'll have to pay a few people. We figure we can cover it with $6,000."

When I reach in my pocket for the money, Mario becomes alert. "To Costa Rica?" he asks, crossing the room.

Armando makes a circle with one hand and jabs the middle finger from the other hand into it. "Making love, Mario?" he asks.

Mario forgets Costa Rica immediately and smiles from ear to ear. Everyone laughs. "Go ahead, set it up," I tell Giovanni.

When they leave, it's the same shit again. "I can't believe you're doing this! I know they're going to tell Jota. They're setting you up!"

"Oh, yes, Mario. Have you given any thought to what will happen when Jota finds out that you're jumping into bed with his wife? We're in big trouble. You and me."

We spend the day shopping with Maria. Every time she says she likes something, Mario purchases it. By noon he's bought her three dresses and about $2,000 worth of gold jewelry. When she goes off to the ladies' room during lunch, I remind him that we're not out of the country yet, that he should try to hang onto his money. He tells me he doesn't care about the money, that he's in love. I have no comment, but the shit, I know, is soon to hit the fan.

Maria tells us that Xavier and Claribel have agreed to baby-sit so the three of us can go out to the discotheque in the building right next door to their apartment. When I look at her questioningly, she adds that Jota's aunt and uncle understand that we're all just friends and want to go out. I gather she's trying to tell us we don't need to worry, that she trusts them not to betray her to Jota. I've noticed some tension between Jota and his aunt and uncle. But he's still the man with the paycheck. I can only hope that I'm wrong and Maria is right.

It makes me a little edgy to find myself in such a crowded place, but after a couple of drinks I get over it and take Maria out onto the dance floor. There's a large screen against one wall and a Madonna video is playing on it. Back at our booth I can see Mario watching us very carefully. And beyond him, at another booth, there's another man watching us too. I point him out and Maria tells me he was once a friend of hers. I can tell by the set of her mouth that their friendship was more than platonic. The music gets slow. Mario reaches his limit. He strides across the room and cuts in. I go back to the table to watch them.

In South America you order a bottle instead of a drink and the waitresses bring you mixers. Since I don't see a waitress around, I pour some whiskey and drink it straight. Every now and then I turn and glance at the guy in the booth behind ours. He's sitting quietly, drinking his drink and watching Maria. I don't like the look in his eye. And I don't like the mindless way he's brushing his stirrer against his bottom lip.

I get up to go to the men's room. The fact that I have trouble bringing my face into focus in the mirror makes me realize I'm more than a little drunk. I conclude my business and am just returning to the booth as Maria and Mario are coming back from the dance floor. As they're about to pass Maria's friend's booth, he rises slowly and puts down his drink. He's staring at Mario, but Mario, who is laughing at something Maria is saying, doesn't notice him. Maybe that's why he brushes past Mario and shifts his hateful gaze to me.

I don't take the time to figure out his intentions. When we're face to face, I simply step down hard on his foot and push him over the back of his booth. The next thing I know his three companions are climbing over the booth. Mario spins and kicks and the first topples onto the table behind him, spilling drinks and breaking glass. Mario kicks again, and the second falls to the floor. The third is perched on the top of the booth and about to jump on Mario's back, but just as he leaps, Mario turns and catches him in flight and swings him into the wall. The thud is incredible.

Maria is crying, "Let's go. Now! We have to get out of here."

We race behind her to the door. The bouncers there are military men. Maria opens her bag and shows them her attorney's license and some other ID, something with her photograph on it. It seems to impress them. She tells them that there are people coming after her. I turn around and see a group of men helping Mario's victims to their feet. Some of the group are already breaking away and heading toward us. The military men hand Maria her papers and go in as we're going out. I start to run to Jota's building but then Maria grabs my arm and turns me toward the street. There's a line of taxis waiting there. We jump into one and tell the driver to get moving. As soon as we're off, Maria begins to laugh. Mario and I join her. We're laughing so hard even the driver begins to chuckle. But then I stop suddenly and consider what might have happened if Maria hadn't had the right papers to show to the men at the door. Mario and Maria stop laughing too. When I turn to look at them, I see that they're at it again. "What the hell are you two doing?" I shout. "Maria, what are you doing? You can't do this."

"I can't stay with Jota anymore," she whispers harshly. "I can't stand him. He beats me. He—"

"Hey," I interrupt. "If it isn't good, leave. But don't do this. This can get you killed. Jota's not a nice man."

Jota returns from the Guajira and shows up at our apartment with Mano and Manolo and Carlos, a Cuban. Carlos, it turns out, is someone Mario knows from Miami, a friend of José, the man who brought Mario to the airport on that fateful day in May. While I'm greeting Manolo, I note that Mario and Carlos are shaking hands, slapping each other's backs like long lost brothers. With all the exclaiming going on, it's a minute before I remember that Jota is there too, and that Mario and I have crossed him in his absence. But when I glance at him, I see that he's smiling like everybody else.

We all sit down and Mario begins telling Manolo and the Cuban how bad it was in the Guajira. I can't believe he's doing this! Jota is on the edge of his seat listening with his mouth open. "Yeah," Mario is saying, "the food was lousy, the beds were lousy, we had to bathe with a bucket of water…"

"I did my best," Jota interjects. He looks genuinely hurt.

Manolo, who doesn't appear to be the least bit ruffled by Mario's confrontation, looks at me. "And what about you, Alan? What do you have to say about all this?"

Everyone turns to hear my response. "Well, it wasn't the Hilton," I say. "But I don't want to talk about the accommodations."

Manolo and Jota nod for me to go on. "The problem," I begin, "is that I never got paid for what I did. It wasn't my fault that the ground crew in Puerto Rico screwed up."

The main point of my complaint is to keep Mario from advancing his, but I'm also thinking about the future. Should Jota learn that I promised to work for Giovanni, I want him to see that I was justified. I figure if the justification is adequate, maybe no one will kill me. Jota says, "Well, we haven't got all the money yet."

"How much money do you have?" Manolo asks me.

"I have some five or six grand."

Jota laughs all at once. "Why are we talking about this? There's no problem. You'll be paid. And in the meantime, we'll make our plans to get you out and back to the States so that we can concentrate on the future."

We talk a little about the missions I'm going to fly for Jota and then the four of them get up and move toward the door. Manolo tells me where his hotel is and insists that I come by. His words are polite, but I can tell by the glare in his eyes that this is more of a demand than an invitation. When the other three start down the hall, Manolo pops his head back in. "Alan, my friend," he says, "lend me $2,000 for a few days. My situation isn't good. I didn't earn anything for your flying. I just sell airplanes."

He looks like he could go on. I don't want him to get to the point where he reminds me about the money he paid to get me out of prison. I give him $2,000 and shut the door.

I run into the kitchen and watch out the window for their heads to appear below. When they get into their car and pull away, I go back into the living room to confront Mario. "What are you doing, Mario?" I shout. "You have to pretend to be Jota's friend until we get out of here. You can't be running him down about the food and hammocks and that kind of shit. That was crazy what you did. And all because you're jumping into bed with his wife."

"Okay, okay, okay."

"The man is a murderer. You know that."

"Okay, okay. I'll be nicer to Jota."

The next day we stop by Jota's so Mario can show him some appreciation, but Xavier tells us that Jota and Maria are still in bed. He invites us to wait, but Mario is so enraged by this information that I have to usher him right out. As soon as the door is closed behind us, he says, "I'm going to kill that son of a bitch! He's with my girl! He's with my girl! I'm going to kill him!"

I grab his arm to keep him moving but he pulls away from me and continues to mutter about what he's going to do to Jota. "Hold it, hold it," I say. "Calm down. Let's go and see Manolo. Your friend Carlos will be there. Let's go and find them." Down in the street I hail a cab and push Mario into it.

Manolo's hotel does nothing to cool Mario's anger. It's a five-star job with swimming pools and lots of beautiful women working the desks. "I can't believe Manolo's in a place like this while we're in a dive," Mario grumbles as we climb the stairs.

Manolo's room features a color TV with cable. We find him and Carlos watching CNN's updates on events in the Gulf. I say hello and sit down to watch too. I'm amazed at what I'm hearing. It sounds as if there's really going to be a war. I'm amazed this has happened without me knowing about it. Manolo gets up and brings some beers from the kitchen area. Mario, who's still standing, says he's going down to check out the pool and weight room. Carlos offers to go with him.

With his eyes still on the TV screen, Manolo says, "So, you talked about me to the general."

I reach for my beer. "I didn't say anything about you. How could I have? You haven't done anything wrong."

"You gave him my name."

"He already knew your name."

Manolo turns to look at me. Behind his glasses his eyes are reproachful. "The general took me to his house."

"What?"

"He lives in a big mansion on a hill with lots of guards. He told me he had a tape recording with my name on it."

"What did he say it said?" I ask tentatively. I remember only giving the general his name. But I wasn't with it the whole time in Caracas. I might have said anything.

"He said that you said I had radios."

"Radios? I don't remember—"

"In Venezuela, Alan, radios are enough to get you into big trouble. Do you understand that?"

"But—"

"Because once they think you're involved in…things…they come and ask you for money. The general asked me for money. A lot of money. He said to me, 'If you want to stay in Venezuela, you'll have to give me money.'"

"But, Manolo—"

"I'm going to give myself a new name. These people, they do their homework before they blackmail you. They—"

"Manolo, will you listen? They tortured me. I don't remember saying anything about radios, but what they did to me… there were times when I wasn't fully conscious." He squints his eyes like he doesn't believe me. "They used electricity," I protest. "They hit me in the balls…twice, three times, I can't remember anymore."

He stares at me a moment longer. Then he says softly, "Let me see."

I put down my beer and stand up and drop my pants and show him the welts on my flesh. "They were larger six months ago."

Manolo adjusts his glasses. "Oh, my friend," he mutters.

I pull up my pants and sit down again. Manolo's look of reproach is gone, replaced by a somewhat sympathetic one. "Let's talk about Jota," he says. "Are you going to work with Jota? Or are you going to work with me selling airplanes? Because I've got a long line of people who want to buy airplanes and I did get you out of jail. I think I've proven I'm your friend."

"Yeah, you got me out of jail, but I'm still not out of the country. And I don't like to say this to you, old man, but Jenny… I thought you'd stay in touch with her, reassure her. All that time in the Guajira she thought I was dead."

"Now hold it a minute, Alan. I tried to stay in touch with her. But every time I called she got hysterical, demanding. 'I want him here, now,' she'd say. She started threatening me. She's going to give my name to this one, to that one…to the police. Like everything was my fault. You forget Alan, I'm an alien. I don't have papers to live in the U.S. I don't need that kind of abuse. You understand?"

I drop the topic. I don't want to get him going again about giving out names. "I don't have a passport, Manolo. I'm probably wanted by everybody in the damn world. I want to get to Costa Rica, to San José. If I can get there, I can get out. Then we can do business again."

"Good. But if you change your mind and decide to go to work with Jota…"

"This is between you and me, isn't it?"

"Yes, of course."

"I'm not going to work for Jota. I'm no drug smuggler. You know that, don't you?"

"I won't have anything to do with that. If you want to, that's your business. But I don't do that kind of work. My job is selling airplanes."

"Yeah, that's what I'm saying to you. We're on the same page."

"Okay, because I won't get involved in that."

"Okay, yes, I hear you. That's what I'm saying too."

We look at the TV screen again. "But from now on," I add, "no more passengers. If it wasn't for them, none of this shit would have happened."

He chuckles. "I'm sorry, Alan. That will never happen again."

People in love are supposed to walk on air, but when Mario comes back to the apartment that night he sounds like he's wearing work boots and stomping on metal. He wakes me up, which, I'm certain, is his intention. "Everything's okay, Alan," he says. "He didn't touch her. He was tired. He went right to sleep. He's leaving again tomorrow to finish things up in the Guajira. She's got my number in Miami. I'm going to bring her over. I'm going to marry her. You want to hear the story she told him to get out tonight?"

I turn over and go back to sleep, but I dream that he's telling me anyway.

Giovanni and Armando show up in the morning. "It's all set, Giovanni says. "Get your stuff together. Wear your suits."

On the way over to the airport they rehearse with Mario and me what we should say if anyone questions us. I'm so intoxicated with the prospect of getting out that I can hardly follow them. They give me a list of phone numbers to call when we get back to the States. "If we're not at one of the numbers," Giovanni says, "try another. You make sure you call us as soon as you're in so we can make our plans."

We shake hands with Giovanni and go into the airport with Armando. He tells us to have a seat while he walks our tickets through.

His first destination is the counter where the tax is collected on the tickets. The little man there looks at our paperwork and says, "These aren't stamped. These people can't get on the airplane."

I hold my breath and watch while Armando looks around for help. There are all sorts of people watching him, military men, plainclothes men. They're all nodding and tilting their heads to show Armando that the coast is clear. "He didn't pay this one guy," I say to Mario. "I bet that's what happened."

Armando argues with the guy, but he doesn't give an inch. I'm tempted to get out of my seat, jump the counter, and wrestle the bastard to the floor. His voice is getting louder. I can hear him telling Armando he'll have to talk to the airport manager. Armando comes over and tells us to stay put and not to worry because the airport manager has been paid. Then he goes off to find him.

A man in plain clothes notices us and wanders over. He isn't one of the ones I saw nodding at Armando. I assume he's from the secret police. "Did you enjoy your time in Colombia?" he asks in perfect English.

I assure him that we did, even though we were here on business. While I'm talking, I try to relax my face, to look friendly. He inquires about my business. Mario turns his head as far in the other direction as it will go. I can see he's not going to help me out at all with this one. I tell the man that Mario and I are in the coal business, that we're mining engineers from Canada.

"Oh, what part of Canada?"

"We're from Vancouver," I say.

"Oh, really? I'm from Calgary."

"Did you go to the tower?"

"Yeah, yeah, I went there."

"Cold, huh?"

"Yeah, not like here at all."

"No, nothing like it."

He wanders away. Mario turns back to me. "How long they going to leave us sitting here like this?" he says through his teeth.

"Armando will be back in a minute. You'll see," I answer in an effort to keep him calm.

In fact, we sit for an hour and a half before Armando returns and admits that he's failed to find the airport manager. "He probably got scared after we paid him and took the afternoon off," he says. It doesn't matter anyway. The airplane is already long gone.

Mario is so pissed about the mishap at the airport that as soon as he sets his bag down in our apartment, he leaves again to find Carlos to tell him all about it. Since he doesn't come back, I assume he went to meet with Maria afterward. In the morning he's still not back. So when the phone rings, I expect it to be him. But it's only Manolo asking me to come over and have breakfast with him. I tell him I want to sleep a little longer, but he insists.

When he opens the door for me and I see his reddened face and the way his eyes are bulging, I surmise the old man is having a heart attack. I lead him over to a chair. "What do you want me to do?" I ask.

He puts his hand over his chest. "Tell me one thing, Alan. And please tell the truth. Is Mario sleeping with Jota's wife?"

I slap my hands over my eyes and shake my head. "Oh, no, this is terrible!"

Manolo slaps his hands over his ears and rolls his head from side to side in anguish. "Oh, no, it's true." He gets to his feet and moves around the room with his hands still in place over his head. "Oh, no, I can't believe this!" he cries over and over.

"How the hell did you find out?" I cry.

"Everybody knows! The whole world knows!"

"You've got to get us out of the country, Manolo."

"I can't get you out. There's nothing I can do."

"But Jota's going to kill Mario."

"You've got to get away. If you can get to Bogota, you can go to the British Embassy there and get a passport."

"But I can't get there. I need a passport to get there!"

When I return to my room, I phone Giovanni and ask him in my best code how long it's going to take to get us out. He says he was just about to phone me because his brother the lawyer is in town. His brother, he says, is going to take care of everything now.

Mario returns from his night with Maria just as I'm getting ready to go down to wait for Giovanni's car. He tells me that he's disgusted with Giovanni and his people and that he's dead tired too. But when I tell him that even the old man knows what's going on, he gets a second wind and puts on some fresh clothes and comes down with me.

Giovanni takes us to what he says is the best restaurant in Barranquilla. His brother, Eddy, a trimmer version of himself, is already there waiting for us when we arrive. When Eddy sees Mario looking around like he's expecting to be apprehended any minute, he says in perfect English, "Don't worry about anything. I own Colombia. You can do anything. What do you want to do?"

"We want to leave the country," I say hastily.

He laughs. "I hear we blew it at the airport for you yesterday. My brother doesn't really know how to handle these things." He gives Giovanni a sidelong glance. "But I'll tell you what. I want you to go to Cartagena in a day or two. It's only an hour and a half drive from here. I own the airport there. I'll put you on an airplane and bring you up to Bogota. You'll stay in my apartment there until I arrange to get you to Mexico City."

"That sounds good," I say. In fact it sounds great. Once we get to Bogota, I figure we can find a way to get over to the embassy and get out on our own. But Mario is rolling his head and mumbling to himself. "Carlos knows a lot of people here in Colombia," he says to me.

"What? And they're going to get you out?" I ask him.

He shrugs.

"I'm a fair man," Eddy says, "If you don't like the deal I'm offering, I'll give you back the money, the $6,000 you gave Giovanni."

"Yeah, take the money back," Mario says.

"Go ahead and make the arrangements," I tell Eddy. "But in the meantime, you've got to get us another place to stay, a safe place. There's too much going on. Everyone knows our business." I glance at Mario to see if he appreciates the precautions I'm taking for him, but he only shakes his head in disgust.

After lunch Eddy takes us back to the apartment to collect our things and move to a hotel a few blocks away. His friend at the desk checks us in. The place is beautiful and very modern. It even has elevators. I'm expecting Mario to be impressed, but as soon as we're alone in our room, he begins berating me for not taking the money back when Eddy offered it. I don't give him much of a fight. He was out all night; I figure he'll run out of steam in no time. But instead of going to bed when he's done with his lecture, he goes out again, to talk to Carlos.

During the next few days Mario appears in our room only when he needs a shower and a change of clothes. Jota is still away, so he's spending most of his time with Maria. When he isn't with her, he's with Carlos, making plans, he says. He insists he's not coming with me to Bogota. I don't say anything. I assume that when the time comes, he'll come along like he always does, like he did on the boat. In the meantime, I sit in the hotel room watching CNN and waiting for Eddy to call. I'm so afraid of missing him that I take most of my meals through room service. But after a while my craving for companionship overcomes me, and I call Manolo and ask him to meet me for lunch.

When I see him coming into the restaurant, I know right away that something is wrong. He sits down and picks up the menu and sighs.

"Jota knows about Mario," he says.

"But how? He isn't back yet!"

"The aunt. She told a friend of hers, a woman who knows Mano's wife. Mano's wife told Mano and Mano got Jota on the radio. He's coming back tomorrow. I don't know what's going to happen, but it isn't good."

"What are we going to do?"

Manolo runs his finger down the list of entrees. "You've got to leave town, or at least get away from Mario. If Mario won't go, you have to leave without him."

I return to the hotel and find Mario there polishing his shoes. "The whole world knows," I tell him.

"The whole world knows what?"

"About you and Jota's wife. Jota is coming back tomorrow."

"Jota knows?"

"Yeah. I got it from the old man."

Mario puts down the shoes and goes right to the phone and dials. "You got to get me out of here right away," he says into the receiver. "Jota knows. He's coming to kill me."

"Mario, you dumb shit," I yell. "You can't say that over the phone! And you're not going anywhere with Carlos. He can't get you out. Trust me. I know my plan will work."

Mario hangs up the phone. Then he turns his head away and breathes heavily through his mouth. When he turns back to me, he speaks through his teeth. "I couldn't even hear him over your big mouth."

I throw my hands out in resignation. I can see there's no point in arguing with him just now.

A little later, Giovanni calls to say he's coming tomorrow at noon to pick us up and take us to Cartagena. When I hang up and tell Mario to get his stuff together, he reiterates that he's not going, that Carlos is going to get him out, that Maria is already out of the apartment and that she'll be coming to the States to live with him in his apartment on the ocean. I nod. I still feel certain that he'll come with me when the time comes. There's no sense in bickering with him about it. I don't even remind him that he doesn't own an apartment on the ocean...though it's tempting.

Carlos and his Colombian friends show up early the next morning. In spite of everything Mario's threatened, I'm amazed to see him getting ready to leave with them. I follow him around like a dog, from the dresser to the closet to the bathroom, while he packs. "You're crazy, Mario," I say. "My plan is going to work. In Bogota there is an embassy. These people can't get you to Bogota. They don't have the connections. You have to come with me!"

He ignores me and speaks only to Carlos and the others. They tell him to hurry up, that they still have to stop at Carlos's hotel room before they go to wherever they're going. "And even if we can't get to the embassy," I continue, "I still believe we will get out. They tried to put us on an airliner the other day! That proves something."

Carlos tells Mario that I'm making him nervous. Mario makes a face which I don't see but which makes the others laugh. I back off after that.

Our parting is unceremonious, a contradiction to everything we've been through together. We don't even shake hands.

Mario is gone about 20 minutes when a Colombian I've never seen before knocks on the door and hands me an envelope with Mario's name on it. I open it up and find a passport inside. The photo in it looks nothing like Mario. Still, I race to the phone and call Carlos at his hotel. I tell him something just came for Mario, that he had better get Mario over right away to pick it up.

I pace while I'm waiting and rehearse the words I'll use to convince Mario that he can't use this passport, that he has to do it my way.

When I think I have them down, I curse Carlos for showing up in Colombia and then Mario for falling under his spell. The phone rings. "I'm in the lobby," Mario says. "Is anybody with you?"

"What do you mean, is anybody with me?"

"You know. Is anybody there? Have they come to kill me?"

"Get your ass up here right now!"

I pace more furiously. The door opens and two of Carlos's friends come in with their guns drawn and cocked. Mario enters behind them. "Do you think I'd set you up?" I shout.

He nods rapidly. "If you had a gun to your head you might."

"Bullshit, Mario. Here. Take your passport. But you can't use it. It's not usable." I fling the thing out at him. His fingers snap it up.

I expect him to turn and go, but he stands there, staring at me. "You got any money?" he asks.

I laugh in his face. "I've got very little left. We spent the rest like water, remember?"

His eyes flash. At first I think they're gleaming with hostility, but then I realize it's fear. I take out my wallet and extract a few hundred dollar bills and hold them out to him. He wraps his thumb around them and leaves the other four fingers out for me to grasp. "You can't use that passport," I say. "It doesn't even look like you. It won't work."

"I'm using it. Don't waste your breath."

I can see he means it. "Well, then, good luck," I mutter.

"Yeah, good luck to you."

The Colombians back to the door. Mario's features contort. "Stay with me," he pleads. "Come with us. They'll find a way to get us out."

"Shit, it doesn't look good to me, Mario. Nobody's going to help us here. At least Giovanni's people made an effort."

"Some effort."

"Look," I urge. "Get rid of these guys for a few minutes and let's sit down and talk about it."

"I can't. We have to hurry. There's no time."

"Dalé, dalé, dalé. Come on, Mario. Think about it."

He shoves the bills in his pockets and clasps my hand once more. Then he turns and rushes out.

To keep from brooding, I go to Manolo's and say goodbye to him. The solemn look he gives me as we shake hands assures me that he knows as well as I do that our relationship is over, that I don't want to work with him any more than I want to work with the smugglers.

Giovanni shows up and we take an uneventful ride to Cartagena. He sees I'm in a foul mood and attempts to cheer me up by reminding me of how rich I will be once I start working for him and his brother. His brother meets us at the hotel, not the lawyer but a younger brother, Louis, a quiet guy of about 26 or so, Mario's age. Another man comes by a while later, a well-dressed Latin who addresses me in English and then speaks to Giovanni at the door. I have no idea who he is, but he must be somebody important because he's carrying a portable phone, a rarity in these parts. Before he leaves he calls to me, "I'll be back tomorrow to put you on the airplane to Bogota." Then he and Giovanni and Louis all go out together.

The moment they leave, I try to recall all the times I've seen Jota angry so as to be able to figure out whether he's really capable of killing Mario. He killed the young Colombian, Carlos, but in his screwed up mind, that was business, something the cartel demanded that he do. This is personal. I switch on the TV but I can't concentrate on it. I leave it on anyway just to hear other voices in the room.

Giovanni returns in the evening and reports that one of his people saw Jota. "He's back," he says. "My friend went to his apartment and found him sitting in bed with a gun in his hand raving about Mario and his wife. He said there were empty whiskey bottles all around and a mountain of coke. You don't have to worry so much. According to my friend, he was in no shape to kill anybody."

In the morning the man with the portable phone arrives. He tells me his name is Julio. We go down to his car, a chauffeur-driven Mercedes, and he takes me to the airport. He explains on the way that the security is very tight at the airport. He says the cartel has been planting bombs on airplanes. So far, they've only been successful with one, a 727 with over 100 people, but there's no reason to believe they'll stop trying. We enter the airport and a soldier comes right up to us and takes my bag. As we follow behind him, people all over nod at Julio. He points out the Secret Service people to me. After a while, I can point them out to him. They're all wearing Ray-Ban sunglasses and very expensive clothes. He leads me to the VIP lounge and tells me to sit down. Except for the waitress, we're the only ones there. We have a drink and wait.

The waitress tells us that the airplane has arrived. From the doorway we can see the people lining up to go through the various security checks. Julio tells me that we'll be going straight to the ramp. Every few minutes he looks at his watch. When the time is right, he gives the waitress a handsome tip and leads me out.

I notice a line of suitcases near the ramp. Julio explains that as the people board, they must identify their suitcases and hand them over to the attendant to be put on the airplane. The hope is that no one with a bomb will get on the same airplane with it. He points out my bag and tells a soldier to place it on the conveyor belt. The man at the ramp hands it back to me. A blinking sign informs me that another flight is getting ready to take off for Costa Rica. It seems to me that it would be just as easy for them to put me on that one. But I'm in no position to ask questions or make demands. I thank Julio and board.

The skies are clear and I get a good look at the Andes and the Magdalena Valley. The part of the valley I'm seeing is all swamp. The waters that run through it are brown where they meet the sea.

Since this is a national flight, there are no Customs to clear an hour and 20 minutes later when we land at Bogota. Nor do I see anyone waiting for me. I collect my bag and am about to walk out the doors and try my luck getting a cab to the embassy when a little guy appears and whispers, "I work with Eddy. Please follow me." He takes my bag and leads me outdoors.

Eddy is leaning against his Mercedes. He's wearing a very expensive-looking suit and a large diamond on the hand that reaches to shake mine. "My friend, how are you? I'm so happy you made it," he exclaims. "Any problems?"

I try to smile. "None at all. I'm very impressed. You weren't kidding when you said you own the airport."

He laughs. "I can do anything in this country. This country is mine." When he sweeps his arm out to take it all in, I see that he's got a .357 Magnum sitting in his shoulder holster.

"So then why do you wear a gun?"

"Kidnappers. That's the one thing you have to be careful about. When you run around in a car like this one, the guerilla groups and the other bad people try to grab you. You have to be ready to fight your way out of a situation."

"Did that ever happen to you?"

"Only once."

He takes me to the apartment where I'll be staying. "It will take a couple of days," he says. "I have to get your paperwork organized. In the meantime, don't use the phone."

"I have to call my fiancée."

"That's fine. You can go down to the Entel. I'll send Louis over to take you."

He waits with me until Louis arrives. They exchange a few whispered words, then Louis drives me to the Entel. It's damp and raining out, and after all my time in the tropics, the air feels very cold. Louis stands behind me while I dial. I glance back and see him concentrating. He is memorizing the number. As soon as I get Jenny on the phone he drifts away.

I whisper nevertheless. I tell her that one way or another, I'm on my way home. We keep it short. It's enough to know the distance between us is closing, that we'll have all the time in the world to say the other stuff we have to say before very long. Louis stops to get me an American newspaper at the Hilton, the same hotel I said I stayed at when I made my declaration in Venezuela. I can't help but think what an incredible coincidence it is that I'm back in Bogota where, according to my story, the whole thing began. I'm so intrigued that I tell Louis all about it.

I'm back at the apartment reading about the Gulf and wondering whether I'll get the chance to sneak off to the embassy in the morning when Eddy shows up with two of his friends, both of whom speak English. They sit down and begin discussing business. I put the paper aside and join them. "Are you going to work with us?" one asks.

"Oh, yeah," I say. "I'll be working with you. You're definitely organized, not like Jota."

"Yeah, Jota and his connections are all idiots, real losers, costaneros, coastal people. The hot air makes them lazy. We're winners. You see how we live. We keep this apartment for people like you who come and visit."

"I lived in New York for a while," Eddy chimes in. "I have a lot of connections there. But I won't be going back anytime soon."

I wait for him to say why but he doesn't. I look around and find that everyone is looking at me. "Well," I begin, "I'm looking forward to working with all of you."

Eddy sits forward in his seat and folds his hands. "Would you consider doing some work before you go?"

I lean back and rest my arm on the back of the sofa. "Well, you know I'd like to, but there's no possible way. Christmas is coming. And it's been over six months since I've seen my girlfriend. We're going to get married. It's serious. I can't put her off any longer."

My remark is met by silence. Then one of Eddy's friends asks how I came to be in Colombia. I'm eager to take up another topic, so I begin at the beginning, with the Colombians starting the fire on the airplane. When I tell them about how I got in and out of Puerto Rico without a tail, Eddy exclaims, "We've got a winner here. We've got a llave, a key."

It's late by then, so they don't bother asking me again about doing missions before I leave. But the next morning they all show up very early to tell me the specifics of the job they had in mind. They want me to fly from Panama to Saint Martin the next day. Then they'll fly me to Puerto Rico and let me go home. I decline with as much courtesy as I can muster. "I can't do it. There's no way. I've got to get home to see Jenny and then I've got to make arrangements to have my people on the ground, my own crew. I'll do everything you want, I'll fly your stuff. But I have to use my people. I've seen too much shit since I've been here."

They spend another couple of hours trying to get me to change my mind. It takes all the resources I have to keep from getting angry. Then Eddy promises to come back and take me to dinner, and the three go out. Ten minutes later, his two friends return without him and insist on taking me for lunch. I leave Eddy a note just in case he gets back before me.

The restaurant they take me to is incredible, one of the most beautiful places I've ever seen. Our waiter, whose job is to serve our table alone, professes to have everything we could possibly want. After the salads, he brings over dishes of vegetables and potatoes and a spear with three beef roasts on it, one rare, one medium and one well done. He cuts what we want and returns again with a pork roast. After that there is chicken—legs, breasts, hearts, gizzards—and then lamb. "We really want you to do some work for us," one of my companions says as he pushes his plate aside.

"I already told you and Eddy—"

"Us," he says. He rubs his paunch and smiles.

"Hold it. You guys work with Eddy. I don't understand. What are you talking about?"

He is about to explain when we spot Eddy rushing toward our table. He opens his mouth and his rapid Spanish comes pouring out even before he arrives. For a few minutes he yells at me. "What are you doing here with these people? What did you come here with them for?"

"Hold it, Eddy. Why don't you sit down. Everyone's looking at you."

He takes a look around. Then he pulls out a chair and plops into it. "You fools. You would try to take my pilot!" he growls.

I'm not your pilot, you son of a bitch, I think. But I only say, "Look Eddy, let's straighten this out. First of all, I'm not going to do anything with anybody without you. These two men, who I thought were your associates, came by to take me to lunch. Now, if I were intending to conspire with them, do you think I would leave you a note? I left you a note, Eddy. That's why you're here. I told you where I was going. Think about it. There's nothing going on behind your back and there never will be. Okay? Do you understand what I'm talking about?"

"Okay, okay, okay," he says, but he still looks pissed.

"Okay. Calm down then. Have a drink. We don't have a problem here."

He takes a deep breath and makes the effort and orders a drink. But after a few sips he shakes his head. "Let's go," he says.

For the rest of the day he insists on taking me with him everywhere he goes. I spend most of my time sitting in his car while he's at someone's door doing business. I don't mind the boredom nearly as much as I mind our conversations when he returns: he still wants me to do a job before I go. "I'll do it as soon as I get home," I promise him 50, 100, 200 times. We work out all the specifics of his new idea. Now he wants me to take his stuff to the States, to New York, and sell it to the Colombians he knows from when he used to live there. And in the meantime, while I'm making the arrangements with my ground crew, he wants me to find him an airplane for a smaller mission that one of his pilots intends to fly. I agree to everything.

He leaves me alone to sleep but shows up again first thing in the morning. "How much money do you have?" he asks while I'm still rubbing the sleep from my eyes.

"I don't know. A couple of hundred dollars."

His hand unfolds and he passes me some hundreds, maybe ten of them, and tells me to get dressed and get my things together.

I don't ask any questions. I assume we're going to the airport, but I'm afraid to ask and find out we're not. I take a quick shower and put on a suit. When I come out into the living room, he's stuffing a pad into his breast pocket. Then we go down to his Mercedes and head for the airport.

He tells me on the way there will be a man waiting for me who will put me on an airplane to Mexico City. But the man isn't there when we arrive. We wait at the curb for him a while. Then Eddy tells me to go inside, that when the guy shows, he'll come and find me. In the meantime, he has business to attend to. "I'm so glad that we'll be doing business together," he says as he shakes my hand. He reminds me about the airplane I promised to find for him. He says he needs it immediately.

I'm on my own. But before I can consider the possible repercussions of making a run for it, the guy who met me when I arrived in Bogota appears and takes my bag. I follow him toward the first of several security checks. There's a line there, but we bypass it and go right to the counter. The man there says, "No, no, no, you can't come through here. You have to go to the end of the line." My escort moves down along the counter toward the man who appears to be the supervisor. I can't hear what they say, but the nodding and pointing they do make me feel a little less uneasy. Then the little guy turns toward me and jerks his head to indicate that I should follow him. We go to the next security check and the man there goes through my bag. "Go on and board," he says.

Another man appears out of nowhere and begins walking at my side. He doesn't say a word to me, but he gives orders to the other officials we pass as we go. He takes me right to my seat.

It seems to take forever until they shut the door and start the engines. And even then I'm expecting the door to open again and some military people to come running up the aisle with their guns drawn. Once we begin to taxi down the runway, I start to believe I'm really on my way out.

I look out the window and smile for the next five hours. Surges of bliss wash over me and bring me to the verge of tears. Between them I brood over Mario and wonder what will happen to him, what may already have happened. When we arrive in Mexico City, I go through Customs without any problem. I have my bag checked, fill out some forms, and get my visa. As I'm walking toward Immigration, I extract a hundred dollar bill from my wallet and slip it in between my driver's license and birth certificate. "Passport," the man there says in Spanish.

"I don't have my passport," I say softly and matter-of-factly. "I lost it. But I do have my birth certificate and driver's license." I hand them over. He finds the bill and slips it into his pocket without any alteration in his expression. He stamps a piece of paper and hands it to me. "Welcome to Mexico," he says.

I float out of the terminal area and go to the ticket counter. The woman there informs me that there's only one flight to Tijuana that's not already booked, but it doesn't leave until eight in the evening. When I try to imagine sitting in the airport for another five hours, I begin to realize how tired I am, how much pressure I've been under for the last few days…for the last several months! Well, the pressure is off now. I can get to the States from here even if I have to walk. I make a reservation for the morning and go to the swank hotel right beside the airport.

They want $200 a night, but I'm happy to hand it over, to indulge myself; I figure I deserve it. My room has a bar and a hot tub. I fill up the tub and make myself a drink to take in with me. If Mario were with me, he would insist on using the tub first. He would stay in it for hours. By the time he emerged, I would be fast asleep. In the morning he would tell me how great it was, ask me why I didn't try it out. I try not to think about him; even the negative thoughts lead me back to the question, Is he still alive?

This was so easy, I say to him in my head. This Eddy guy had such unbelievable connections. Why aren't you here?

I have a friend in San Diego, Jack MacIntyre. When I arrive in Tijuana, I call him. "It's Alan," I say. "I need a ride."

He doesn't respond right away. Then he whispers, "I heard Alan was dead. Who is this? What's going on?"

This strikes me as being incredibly funny and I begin to laugh. I can't stop myself. He recognizes my laughter and begins to laugh too. Then he promises to come right down and pick me up.

When we get through exclaiming about how happy we are to see each other, I explain to Jack that I'm a little anxious about going through Customs at the border. He asks me why while we are driving, and by the time I've finished answering, we're there. The woman at the booth we pull up to asks, "Where have you guys been?"

Jack replies cheerfully. "Oh, we just went for a couple of beers. We went to a Mexican church to see what it was like, and then we had ourselves a couple of beers."

"Are you both American?"

"No. I am. He's a good Canadian. He's down visiting me."

"Okay, go ahead."

"How easy was that?" Jack asks as we pull away.

I nod and turn my head to the window to look at America, the home of the free. "Mario, you dumb dumb shit!" I mutter against the glass.

THE ART OF DECEPTION

I get out of the cab on the corner, walk past the lumber yard and down the dark, tree-lined street. I stop before the house, a duplex with side by side apartments, and try to figure out which of the two front doors will lead me to Jenny. The moment is monumental; I don't want to make a mistake. Framed in the front window of each apartment is a Christmas tree. From the sidewalk they both look the same, but as I make my way up the walk to the entrance, I see the angel on the top of the tree in the window on the left. I take a deep breath and ring the bell.

I've rehearsed this moment, the things I'll say to Jenny before I let her escape from our first embrace, but her scent and her warmth—the reality of her—render me speechless. When we finally release each other, I tear my eyes from her beautiful face and sweep them over the furniture, the lamps, the pictures hanging on the walls, and all the other familiar objects that marked me as her partner, an integral part of a romantic unit, in the days before the fateful flight.

Jenny and I go into the kitchen to talk. She sits with her fingers spread over her eyes weeping and waving me on when I come to the parts that are too painful for her to hear. When I get to the last days in Barranquilla, she nods her head rapidly. She knows all about Eddy. He's already called the house a few times looking for me.

Things haven't been easy for her either. She found a position teaching the rudiments of violin to pre-schoolers, but her small salary doesn't quite cover the bills. She's putting in 20 hours a week at her father's hardware store to supplement it. When we get around to talking about some of the things she did to collect the money for Manolo while she was still in Florida, I learn that she got $5,000 from our joint savings account, and $2,000 more by selling the car I bought for her.

Manolo seemed satisfied. She assumed that Mario's family put up the rest.

"Two for the car!" I exclaim. "It was worth a hell of a lot more than that. How could you let it go so cheaply?"

I realize I've raised my voice and apologize immediately. But Jenny only sits back and folds her arms. "Okay," she says softly. "I understand you went through an ordeal. I expect there to be some repercussions. But I went through an ordeal too. I love you, but I've been angry. I asked you not to go..."

"You know why I went."

She gets up and puts on a pot of coffee. Beyond her, I can see the first light of dawn at the window. "You could have satisfied your commitment from home, Alan. You know that as well as I do. You went because you had to fly, because you had to satisfy your obsession...this hunger you've got that I can't quite understand...this need to create adventures for yourself at all costs... But I've forgiven you on that account."

I snort a little laugh. "Forgiven me for flying? How is that possible?"

She laughs a little too. Then she slides back into her chair and looks aside. "I fell down the stairs and sprained my wrist."

"What?"

"My bow hand. This was when I was still at my father's. I had boxes all over the place. Some were on the stairs. I tripped. I couldn't use my hand for a good three weeks. I was miserable. That piece of wood was my only solace after you left. You know, I've always believed the trouble with you is that you have no appreciation for ordinary life. Well, playing the violin may not be extraordinary, but when I couldn't do it anymore, I felt cheated, frustrated. The days were too long. I tossed and turned at night. I felt that hunger...the one that you must feel, that makes you do such crazy things."

I can only stare at her. She smiles and sweeps her long dark hair behind one ear. I grab her hand as it's descending. "I guess what happened is that I began to have an inkling as to how you felt when they took your airplane away. And I began to feel badly because… Well, frankly, I'd abandoned you…mentally, emotionally. But the last letter you sent, back when you were in Venezuela…and then the thing with my wrist, well… Then I got a call from you, from your lawyers' office. You sounded so desperate, so let down. But there was nothing I could do; I didn't have any more money. Still, after we got off the phone, I decided I would find some way to get it, the whole thing, $6,000. It was going to be my way of making it up to you…for abandoning you. I made some calls…your brothers, some other people we know. Nobody wanted to get involved. And that's when I thought of Hernandez."

"You called Raul Hernandez?"

"I went to see him."

"Are you crazy?"

"I left that very day, not an hour after our conversation. I borrowed my father's car, which I've since bought from him, and drove to Miami, then called him, had him meet me in a bowling alley parking lot."

"You met with Raul Hernandez in a bowling alley parking lot?"

"I told him I wanted the money he owed you." She stops to laugh, a giggle that she conceals with the back of her hand. "I drove straight through, 25 hours from here. I didn't want to spend the money for a hotel…or the time. So by the time I hooked up with him, I was a maniac. I screamed and yelled and threatened him. You wouldn't believe the things that came out of my mouth. I think I actually scared him. But he gave me the same story he gave you, that the money was stolen. Then he promised to help me out all the same."

"Jenny," I whisper.

"He took me to his apartment."

"Jenny, do you realize…"

"I gave him your lawyers' number and he called them. He spoke to them in Spanish, so I got only very little of the conversation. When he got off the phone, he said the lawyers said you were already out, that you didn't need the money anymore because Manolo had come up with the entire sum. So, in a sense, I made the drive for nothing. But in another sense, I learned something about myself, about how strongly I felt about our commitment. Hernandez gave me $100 so I could get a room that night before driving back."

Jenny is the least impulsive person I know. Generally, she will weigh the pros and cons of a situation for days before she acts on it. It takes me a long time to get beyond the recklessness she displayed here, beyond the incredible risk she took. Once I do, I realize that there is one thing wrong with this picture. The day after I spoke to Jenny from the law offices, the day she would have arrived in Miami, the lawyers had still not been paid the entire sum. And even if they had, they would have jumped at an offer of more. Hernandez never called them, or if he did, but he spoke about the weather. The phone call was a sham, more of his bullshit.

We have four cups of coffee each and reach an agreement concerning the future. Since Jenny has heard nothing from Justin Kane, the DEA agent, we can assume, for the time being, it will be okay for me to go on with my life. But my life will be here in Connecticut. She's not going to move again. She wants to be near her family.

I tell her to go to bed but to please try to stay awake until I come up and join her. She gives me a kiss and promises that she will. I find the bathroom, take a quick shower, and go up the stairs with a vitality that's unnatural in a man who has been awake all night. But when I reach Jenny's bedroom, I remember the needle in the prison in Maracaibo and realize I'll need an HIV test before I can end my celibacy. I go back downstairs and drink more coffee.

I'm a free man now, I remind myself continuously in the days that follow. I have a few loose ends to take care of, but for the most part, my life is pretty much my own again. But these acknowledgements, and the sense of relief that accompanies them, are increasingly fleeting, and more often than not I find myself feeling angry again and the same frustration I felt when I was in South America. I can't drive my mind from the past. This thing with Hernandez begins to take on new dimensions now that I know how he hustled Jenny. I can't stop thinking that if he'd only paid me the money he owed me, I might never have got myself into this situation in the first place. His betrayal is the crux, the focal point of my anger. At the periphery are Jota's lies, Manolo's procrastinations and Mario's abandonment. And it doesn't stop there. I curse and slam drawers and closet doors, frustrated that I can't find my possessions without assistance, suspicious that Jenny may have ditched some of them along the way.

Jenny is late one day when I appear at the hardware store to pick her up and I have to send one of the clerks to the back to get her. When she appears, smiling like I've just come home to her all over again, I scream, "What the hell were you doing? Don't you realize how important timing is?" I call her names. I mock her for living her middleclass life while all over the world there are people living in strife. I know I'm wrong to be saying these things even as they are pouring out of my mouth, but I can't stop myself; I'm out of control. Her efforts to calm me only increase my anger. I realize that I'm going crazy, now, after the fact; it makes no sense, but I don't know what to do about it.

I have Mario's sister's number in Miami. I ask Jenny to call her to see whether there's any news on Mario. I figure a woman talking to a woman will be more fruitful than me calling. Jenny's not comfortable with it; she would rather I called.

I insist. She complies.

She gets hold of Mario's sister and identifies herself. Before she can say anything more, his sister screams into the phone, "You bitch, you whore, how dare you call me when your lover abandoned my brother?" Jenny opens her mouth to reply, but the woman hangs up on her.

Eddy calls. He's very upset that I haven't been in touch. He understands, he says, that I need time to get my people ready for the mission he wants me to do, but in the meantime, he needs the airplane I promised to find for him. There's a woman called Delia down in Miami. He wants me to meet her. She'll help me set it up. In spite of my irrational behavior, Jenny pleads with me to stay, to resolve the matter from home. I tell her I'm sorry and reserve a ticket for Miami.

I don't have a plan. I only know three things for certain: I want to find out what happened to Mario, I want to find a nice way to get Eddy off my back (he was, after all, the one who finally got me out), and I want my money from Hernandez.

I get a room in a dive and buy an old Chevy for a couple of hundred bucks from a friend of mine and set out for the warehouse where Mario's friend José works. There's no one there when I arrive, but I wait, and later, José pulls up in his Honda. As soon as he sees me, he goes into reverse and shoots out again. It's clear that he doesn't want to have anything to do with me.

On the way over to the hotel where I've arranged to meet Delia, I wonder if I'm walking into a trap, if Eddy's group might have been infiltrated. I resolve to be careful, but I'm surprised to find I'm not much more concerned about what happens to me than I was when I was imprisoned in Venezuela.

Delia is a young attractive Cuban. She's also very careless. In the course of our conversation in the lobby she uses words like "coke" and "money" as freely as if she were talking about the weather. She tells me about the airplane that Eddy wants me to find. Once I've found it, he'll send the money to pay for it and a pilot to fly it back. I tell Delia I have an airplane ready to go right now, but that I don't know how much longer it will be available, that Eddy has to send up the money now. She promises to get right on it. I figure I'll wait a week or so and then tell her the airplane is no longer available. I'm betting Eddy can't put the money together in that amount of time.

In the meantime I borrow a gun, a .38 revolver, from a friend, and make a few purchases at the local army/navy store. Then I drive over to Pedro's, the barbershop owned by Hernandez's uncle, where Hernandez is known to spend his free time. Sure enough, Hernandez's truck is there in the lot. I park behind it and remove the chamber bullet from the gun. The others I leave in place so that the gun looks fully loaded. I stick the gun into the waistband of my shorts and pull my baggy shirt down over it. Then I wait.

Hernandez comes out eventually and heads for his truck. But before he reaches it, he turns on his heel and goes back into the barbershop. Damn, I think, He's seen me. But a moment later he returns and I know he simply forgot something. I slide out of the Chevy as he's sliding into his Explorer. I cock the trigger and put it to his side.

He starts and turns. "Oh, Alan! It's you! I'm so happy to see you!" he exclaims. Then he sees the gun.

"I'm not happy to see you," I say. "Move over. We have to talk."

In the pocket of his door I see his gun, a 9-mm. I step in front of it so that he can't go for it. He looks up from it and into my face. "What's the gun for, Alan?" he asks.

He doesn't look quite as nervous as I would like him to look. "Move over," I demand. "We have to talk."

He shakes his head. "You've got to put the gun down first, Alan. You've got to put it down."

"No, Hernandez. This is serious. We have to talk."

"I can see this is serious," he says, his voice rising in pitch. "Just put the gun down and we'll talk about it."

I'm about to reiterate my demand when a big arm flings itself around my neck and yanks me back. I pull the trigger. Since the chamber is empty, the click it makes is absurd. Hernandez grabs it, but I withdraw it just in time. He jumps out of his truck and goes for the gun again. I struggle to hang onto it while the powerful arm tightens around my neck. "Let go of the gun," Hernandez screams into my face.

"No, you'll kill me with it."

"No, I won't kill you. Let go of the gun."

I kick and buck and swing and try like hell to hang onto the gun, but I don't have a chance with the big guy choking me. After a moment Hernandez gets it away from me. He holds it up in the air. "You stupid son of a bitch!" he shouts.

"Go ahead and shoot me," I shout. "I don't care. I tried, I lost, go ahead and kill me."

"You stupid idiot! Why did you do this? Why do you have an empty gun?" he shouts. "You are one stupid Canadian!"

I stop struggling against the big guy's grip. Hernandez swings the barrel open. "You had the chamber on me empty, you idiot."

"I had to impress you, you son of a bitch. You stole money from me."

"You never come to a man with a gun and no bullet. If I'm going to come to you with a gun, you can bet there will be a bullet in the chamber."

Hernandez talks with his hands. While he's screaming at me, I watch the gun swing through the air. "What the hell were you doing fighting with a man who has a gun at your head?" I snarl back at him.

"Alan, when a man comes to you with a gun, you have to fight for it, because it's over. He's come to kill you. So it's better to fight than just to wait until he shoots you. See my logic?" Hernandez asks.

I do, but I don't say so. It's street logic; no discussion, just go for the gun.

"Let him go, Miguel," Hernandez snaps at the big guy. "You shouldn't have grabbed him anyway. You don't grab a guy from behind when he's got a gun in his hand." Then to me, "Alan, you're my brother. What are you doing? You've gone crazy. It must have been too much for you down there."

"Yeah, you're right. I'm crazy. And I'm going after all my enemies and you happen to be number one on my list."

He looks down at his hand. Our struggle with the gun has left him bleeding, a small gash on the side of his thumb. He grabs my arm and steers me toward the barbershop. I turn around to see if I can make a break, but the big guy is right behind me. Beyond him I see the spectators who've gathered to watch the event. They look disappointed to see us leaving, everyone in one piece and no blood to speak of.

Hernandez finds a Band-Aid and wraps it in place. Then he leads me out again. We get into his truck, me in the front with him and the big guy, Miguel, in the back. "I'm your friend," Hernandez whines as we drive off, his hands flying back from the steering wheel to punctuate his conviction. "I'm your buddy. It's that Manolo that put all these crazy ideas in your head about me. He filled your head with shit."

"You stole my money," I insist dryly. "You've got my gun, but I know where to get another one."

He smiles. "You can't talk like that, Alan. You're sick. Your mind isn't working right. Look, have I hurt you?"

I have to think about it for a second. "No, you haven't hurt me. But before you can convince me you're not going to hurt me, take me to the Everglades. And if you still don't shoot me, then I'll believe that you're not going to hurt me."

He laughs. "I'm not going to take you out there."

My mind gets stuck on it. "Yeah, take me out to the Everglades. You want to prove to me that you don't want to shoot me, take me out there and put the gun in your hand and don't shoot me, because then I'll know that you don't want to shoot me."

He laughs again. His amusement exacerbates my anger. I remember the things I bought at the army/navy store, and while we're driving through town, I remove them from the bag one at a time and lay them out on the glove compartment between the seats: a pair of handcuffs, a 50,000-volt electric zapper, and a length of rope. Hernandez glances at them. "Holy shit!" he exclaims. A sense of mania rises up in me and I have to smile. Hernandez doesn't notice. "I've got this lot that no one knows about," he says as he turns into a poor black residential area.

"Take me out to the Everglades."

"I'm going to help you. You need some work. You know I can get you work, good work. You're my family, my brother."

"I really want to go out to the Everglades and get this over with."

We turn again, onto a back road, and after a few miles we come to a high wooden fence set back a couple of hundred feet. Miguel jumps out to open the gate and we pull up to the trailer within. Hernandez stops the truck and tells Miguel to get the bag in the back. Hernandez rummages through it and pulls out ten neat piles of hundred dollar bills. "Ten grand," he says. He slaps it down on top of the handcuffs. "Don't ever do this again, Alan. If you have a problem with me, you come and tell me, you talk to me about it."

I stuff the money into my pocket and go into the trailer with them. Carlos, Hernandez's brother, is inside. Hernandez must assume the ten grand has appeased me sufficiently because he asks me very casually to tell them all about what happened in South America. "It wasn't fun," I say. "It was a lot of shit."

Hernandez laughs. "You're all screwed up in the head." He tells his brother about the incident with the gun.

Carlos laughs like it's the funniest thing he's ever heard. "He's screwed up in the head," he confirms. "He doesn't know who his friends are anymore."

"You're right," I say. "I don't. Everybody I've done business with has stolen from me." I turn to look at Hernandez. "You stole from me because you could get away with it. I had no recourse. I was a lone gringo. I didn't have all these Cuban friends around to find out the truth. There's no way that money got stolen."

"Look, Alan, you want $50,000?"

"Yeah, I want my money."

"I'll give it to you. I'll get it for you. Just be patient. In the meantime, remember I'm your brother. You've got to stop talking to me like I'm a stranger. You're screwed up in the head. Let me be your… What? Your psychologist. That's the word. I'll tell you who's your friend and who isn't. Because you can't tell yourself anymore."

I give them what they want, an account of the worst of the events that occurred in South America, but I keep my tone testy so they'll know I haven't calmed down. When they hear about the mission I flew from the Guajira, they look at one another, signal one another with their eyebrows. "Remember the 210 I had?" Hernandez asks.

The Cessna 210 was the single-engine airplane that he bought back when we were friends so I could teach him how to fly. He was just getting good at it when the thing happened with the money and we parted company. He didn't have a pilot's license or enough confidence in his flying skills to apply for one, so he sold the airplane shortly afterwards to a man named Pete, an employee at the International Flight Center. "Yeah, I remember it."

"Maybe we should buy it back. I hear that Pete is looking to sell. It was a good airplane, Alan. We could load it up, make it ready to do some business."

I'm not surprised to hear that Hernandez is back in the smuggling business. I should have figured it out when he refused to kill me.

Everyone seems to need a pilot these days. But this is one pilot who can no longer be bought, at any price…including his life. "I would really like to go out to the Everglades," I mutter in response.

Hernandez laughs and throws his hands out. "Look, I can kill you here! There's nobody around. I can take your body out without anyone seeing."

"Yeah," I encourage him. "There's nobody around. Pick up the gun and let's see what happens."

He picks it up and hands it to me. "Where you staying, Alan?" he asks.

"A dive, the cheapest hotel I could find."

"As long as you're in town, I want you to stay here. I would like to do that for you."

I don't refuse. Except for the ten grand, which I plan to give Jenny, I'm practically penniless. "You're pretty trusting, aren't you, Raul?" I say.

His grin disappears and he fixes me with a dark gaze. "Alan, you and I will die together," he says. Yes, his voodoo guide's prediction. It seems a possibility now.

Hernandez, Miguel, and Carlos go out and leave me alone. I sit at the table tapping my fingers and trying to figure out my next move. Later, Hernandez's father-in-law pulls up, Sal, who I know from the old days. He comes in laughing. He's seen Hernandez and heard all about the gun and how screwed up I am. "You're family," he exclaims when he sees that I don't share his amusement. "We're going to let you work with us. We have some really good stuff happening here."

If I hadn't figured out on my own that Hernandez is back to smuggling, the sailboat he takes me to the next day would have convinced me. It's an incredibly beautiful 47-footer with more navigational aides than I knew existed and a sub-floor that I figure can hold about 400 keys of coke. "This is my new project," he says. Then he takes me around and introduces me to the crew, tells them all about how I came to him with an empty gun.

His friends are duly amused. One of them, a Chinese-looking Cuban called Roberto, says, "You mean he came to you with a gun without bullets?" Hernandez laughs and tells him about the fight we had over the gun. Then he asks if I'd like to go out for a sail.

"Sure, why not?" I say. "Are you going to shoot me now and dump me overboard?"

He looks genuinely hurt. "Why do you persist?" he whines. "I'm your brother. I could have done that back at the trailer. You're so screwed up, my friend."

While we're sailing, he tells me that Roberto is a Marielito, a Cuban who came on the boat lift from the Port of Mariel about ten years ago, and that he did a lot of business with him when Roberto first came to the U.S. Then they stopped doing business. He doesn't say why, but I suspect he tried to screw the man somehow, like he did me. Later we go to Roberto's house. It's a beautiful place with a good-sized pool in South Miami. The cars outside are new and expensive. He hasn't done bad for an immigrant who can hardly read or write.

I spend a few more days at the trailer. Since it's a hideout where no one actually lives, I'm often alone. Other times I'm joined by Hernandez and his associates. For the most part I sit and stare out the window and concentrate on my plans. My detachment does not alarm anyone. They chalk it up to my imprisonment. I'm still there with them, so as far as they're concerned, I'm coming around.

On the third night Hernandez tells me that he wants to take me for a little drive. We get into his truck and pull up in front of a Chinese restaurant. Then he turns off the ignition. "I want you to see how easy it is to make money," he says. When I ask him what he's up to, he pats the air between us with his palm. "You'll see. Just keep your eyes open and watch." A few minutes later, Miguel pulls up behind us in his

Grand National. And a few minutes after that, Sal pulls up in his big Caprice.

Hernandez takes out his portable phone, looks at his watch, and tells Miguel to get going. "Are there drugs involved with this?" I ask as we pull out into the traffic behind Miguel.

"Just watch. You don't have to do anything. You're just the lookout."

We drive down Route 1 to the airport arrival section, which is underground. The area is hot and humid, full of exhaust fumes. Miguel pulls up to the curb and we drive past him with Sal right behind us. We go around and come back up behind Miguel again. A porter steps out from nowhere and moves toward the parked car. On his hand truck are three blue suitcases. "You just keep your eyes open," Hernandez says. "We're the crash cars, us and Sal. If someone suspicious pulls up, we'll crash into him, make it look like an accident. That will give Miguel enough time to get away." Miguel, meanwhile, gets out of his car, opens the trunk, gives a piece of paper to the porter and collects the suitcases.

We return to the Chinese restaurant. Sal gets out of his car and opens Miguel's trunk with his own key. He takes the suitcases and drives off with them. Miguel and Hernandez and I return to the trailer.

"Did you like it?" Hernandez asks when we're all inside.

"What was I supposed to like?"

He laughs. "Did you see how smooth we were? How good? We just got 100 keys of coke. The Colombians in Barranquilla send it in every 20 days. They have their own people to remove the suitcases from the conveyor belt before they get to Customs. They deliver them to the porter. He brings them right out to us. This is the ninth time we've done it. We're making so much money, it's sick."

Miguel laughs. "I've been here a year and I'm already a millionaire," he says. "All I have to do is open my trunk. Only in America can a man become a millionaire so fast and so easily."

"I'm going to give you another ten grand just for being a lookout," Hernandez states.

The next day Hernandez has a pig brought in and all his drug friends show up at the trailer for a big party. He walks among them with his chest puffed out like he's some kind of superstar. It's clear to me that he thinks of himself as the head of a Cuban Mafia. But the subtle nods and sideways glances his so-called friends give one another once he's walked away from them tells me these people are just like him and will stab him in the back as soon as they get the chance. One of them, a man called Jorge, even comes right out in the midst of the festivities and openly accuses Hernandez of holding back some of the profits on one of their deals. Hernandez waves his hand at him. They'll talk about it later. In the meantime, he wants everyone to know how happy he is to have his pilot back in the family.

His pilot. Fine. Now I know just how to play the game. I've become a master. But now I'm making up the rules. I smile at everyone, the happy hostage. I act like I'm content to be here. I mingle on my own, and I learn that these people are mostly little people, the people who drive Hernandez around, fix his boat, buy his kilos, people who used to be his partners before they were demoted. Miguel is there too, with his brother-in-law. He too bitches when Hernandez's back is turned, a far cry from the attitude he displayed after the airport. Hernandez seems really pleased with himself, happy to be throwing this little party for his friends. I figure he's screwed everyone here in some manner or other. But he isn't going to screw me, not this time. When things wind down, he gives me the additional ten grand he promised, and I tell him the truth, that I'm going home to give the money to Jenny. He reminds me that I have to be back in 20 days if I want to see more action. I promise him I will.

I call the airlines and make a reservation. But before I leave, I phone

Delia. She tells me Eddy has just about got the money together. I tell her they blew it, the airplane is no longer available, but that I'm working on another one. I leave satisfied; things are falling into place.

Jenny is happy to see me, but when I tell her I'm not back for good yet, she gets disgusted and refuses to listen to my plans. "You're a very lucky man," she screams. "You could have died in Venezuela, or in the Guajira, during those flights. Why must you push it? Why can't you just feel lucky to be alive and start enjoying your life?"

I figure it's just as well. My plan is a dangerous one and I don't really want her involved in it. I phone Justin Kane, my friend from the DEA. He heard I was back and was wondering when I was going to get around to calling him. I tell him I know of some action going down. When we get down to the details, I find out that he already knows something about Hernandez but until now had nothing to convict him on. He tells me to get myself back down to Miami so I can stay on top of things and alert him to any changes.

I fly back down and hook up with Hernandez again. He's so nice to me that sometimes I feel like a rat. But then I remember what he did to me, and what he and the other coke-smuggling scum do generally to keep the machine in motion. When we go out to his boat, I make a mental note of the names and license plate numbers. When I'm alone, I phone them in to Kane. I'm a little anxious about the bust itself, but Kane promises I'll be protected. For one, he's planning to bust the lead car leaving the airport. He won't get Hernandez, but when you have an insider, you can afford to wait on the prime agitator. Raul Hernandez isn't going anywhere. He's used to making big money now. He has houses, cars, people who are dependent on him. He's not going to be switching vocations anytime soon. And anyway, there's a chance Miguel will talk. And if he doesn't, well then they'll have seen the porter. They can use him to infiltrate further, to get to the Colombians who are setting things up.

The big day arrives; I sit in the airport underground with Hernandez, behind Miguel's Grand National, breathing in exhaust fumes and waiting for the porter to show. I look around like the last time, but I don't see anything more than I did then. It's incredible to me. I know the DEA agents are all around, but I can't see a suspicious-looking soul. Time passes. No porter comes out. Miguel radios back to us. "It's been five minutes. No one's coming." Hernandez confirms that he can see that for himself. We wait another two or three minutes. Then Hernandez gives the order and we take off like a shot and return to the trailer.

"Nothing!" Miguel exclaims. "What could have gone wrong?"

Hernandez looks pensive for a moment. Then he declares, "Well, maybe it's all for the better."

I swallow hard. I take it from his comment that he's on to me, that he suspected there was going to be a bust. But then I remember how he used to use those words back in the old days, how his voodoo guides told him that when things went wrong, it was for a reason, it was all for the better. And he always went along with that. This time he's right on the money.

I phone Kane in the morning. Before I can say anything, he says, "Yeah, I know, it didn't come in. What happened?"

"I don't know," I say. "The porter never came out. Maybe the stuff never arrived."

"I have a hunch it arrived all right, but someone picked it up before Hernandez got there. Hernandez has a reputation for not paying his bills. I need something concrete, something to lead me to the people in Barranquilla who are setting it up."

I promise to try and find out more. And a few days later I get my chance. I'm sitting in the trailer with Hernandez when a young Cuban pulls up in a late model Corvette. Hernandez doesn't look surprised to see him. When the Cuban knocks at the door, Hernandez goes into the kitchen to talk to him. "How are you? How's your mother? Your father? Your cousin?" I hear. They come into the living room with their arms around each other's shoulders. But as soon as the Cuban sees me, he stiffens. "Who's that?" he asks.

Hernandez gets him moving again. "Don't worry, don't worry. He's one of us. He's my brother. He's my pilot. He's going to do some work for me. Don't worry."

The Cuban sits down, but now he seems reluctant to talk. He keeps glancing at me. Eventually he admits to Hernandez that the people he works for made the delivery to another group, because Hernandez was late in paying his bills. Hernandez nods pensively. "We'll have to work this out," he says.

The Cuban shakes his head enthusiastically. "I told them you would work it out. I trust you. I told them that."

We walk the Cuban to the door. As he pulls out of the driveway, I glance at his plate number. Hernandez starts in grumbling, calling the Cuban and his people lots of bad names. I nod my head in agreement, but I'm too busy repeating the plate numbers to myself to really listen. "You were right," I tell Kane later on the phone. "Hernandez got behind on his bills. They delivered it to someone else. How did you know?" Since he doesn't answer, I go on to explain what I know, all about the Cuban in the Corvette. I give him the plate number. "Is that concrete enough?" I ask.

"Could be," he answers. "I'll let you know."

In the meantime, Hernandez begins to organize for his other plan. He buys back the 210 with travelers checks and leaves an obvious paper trail in the process. He doesn't care because he's put the airplane in my name. He insists this is to show me how much he trusts me, but of course I know that it's to keep himself covered. He begins loading the airplane up with extras, a fuel computer, wing-tip tanks, and a fuselage tank. When the work is done, the airplane will be able to fly approximately 14 hours without stopping to refuel. It's all legal, but some Customs people come out one afternoon anyway, while I'm at the hangar killing some time. They watch me work. They ask me who I work for and since Hernandez isn't around, I say the DEA, if they want to get in on the act, they'll have to check with them. When they leave, Pete, the IFC employee who sold the airplane back to Hernandez, corners me. "You can't talk to those people!" he exclaims.

"Do you know who they are?" I ask. "They're Customs."

He yanks on his collar. "Well, don't tell Hernandez that Customs was here."

I can see I'm not the only boy scout in town.

I'm still in touch with Delia on a regular basis. Eddy still wants his airplane. This business I haven't shared with Kane. I want to work it out on my own. I tell Eddy through Delia I've almost got things worked out with my ground crew, and that in the meantime I have the airplane he wants and he should send his pilot down with the money.

A few days later, I phone Delia at a prearranged time and learn that Eddy's pilots, two of them, have just arrived on an airliner. They've cleared Customs and have gone to their hotel. I'm to go right over and meet them and make the arrangements for the airplane they're taking back to Colombia. I tell her it's all set up.

In fact, it is. I call my friend Sergio and give him the name of the hotel. Then I get myself over there and meet the two goofy-looking Colombians in the lounge. We're having a nice chat about the phantom airplane when Sergio and his cousin appear, both of them all decked out with sunglasses and portable telephones. Real cops in Miami don't dress this way, but my friends are seeking to impersonate the cops the Colombians are used to seeing, TV cops. They sit down at the table near ours. In the meantime, my companions take the conversation from the airplane itself to the things they propose to do with it. "Hey, hey, hey," I say. "You can't talk about that in here. There are all kinds of people around." They follow my example and scan the faces surrounding us. Sergio and his cousin are whispering and pointing in our direction. "Oh, shit," I say. "Have you seen those guys before?" They say they haven't. "Well, maybe we'd better go up to your room."

We pay our tab and get up to go. As we pass Sergio and his cousin, they're asking for their check too. We get off the elevator and begin walking down the long hall. One of the Colombians is struggling to get the key into the lock when the elevator opens again and Sergio and his cousin get out. The Colombian gets the door open and we all rush in. As soon as it's locked behind us, I say, "You've got a tail! You've got feds all over the place. What are we going to do now? Did you pay cash for this room?" They nod. "Ah, jeez, no one pays cash up here. You come up here and put yourselves in the best hotel and pay cash for everything and sit in the lounge and talk about missions! Shit, we'll all wind up in jail! Don't you know that you can be arrested here just for conspiring, just for talking about this shit?"

They look at each other. I know what they're thinking. There's nothing more terrifying to a South American than to be locked in a foreign jail. I understand the reasoning perfectly. I open the door and peek out. "I don't see them," I whisper. "Stay here. I'm going to go and see what I can find out about this. I'll phone you in a little while."

Sergio has his orders. He and his cousin are to introduce themselves as DEA agents to the bellboys and the maids, most of whom are Latin themselves, and ask a lot of questions about the two Colombians. One, if not all, of the hotel staff, we know, will be brave enough to inform the Colombians. Then Sergio and his cousin are to go up to the room and question the Colombians themselves.

I wait a few hours and phone the hotel. The person at the front desk tells me my party has checked out. I phone Sergio. He says he questioned everybody, and that when he got upstairs and knocked on the door, the Colombians didn't answer. We have a good laugh. We figure they're sitting at the airport waiting for the next flight out.

I phone Eddy. "Eddy," I cry, "I got the airplane ready and your guys are gone!"

"I know, I know," he whines. "I heard from them. They had a tail, they had police looking for them. They're coming back."

"It's your fault, Eddy. You can't send people like that. They come up here acting the role of smugglers."

"Yeah, well, pilots have big egos. You can't tell them what to do. You have to kiss their asses to get them to work."

"Yeah, yeah, but that's beside the point. What are we going to do now? They're gone, nobody's going to arrest them for sitting in the airport waiting to get out. But what about me? Now the feds will be watching me! They really screwed things up. I'm going to have to wait and see what happens now up here before I can make any moves."

When I get off the phone with him, I phone Delia and tell her what happened. "Look," I say, "I don't want to go to jail. I don't know if I can work with your people anymore. And if the feds are really onto me like I think, I'm no good to you anymore anyway. I'm really pissed about all this."

She sighs. "I can't blame you."

"Well, I'm glad you understand. And listen, I don't want to hurt your feelings, but you'd better clean up your act too, sweetheart. I mean, the things you said to me…and you didn't even know me."

I return to the trailer satisfied. Except for locating Mario, there's only one loose end remaining. And in he comes a while later, with a woman he introduces as Teresa, his wife. When I knew him last, Hernandez was married to another woman, Maria. As soon as Teresa leaves the room to fix herself a snack in the kitchen, I ask him what he's up to. He explains that he's still married to Maria, that she and their two daughters are doing fine. But Maria had her tubes tied, so he married Teresa too. He and Teresa have a three-month-old baby, a girl.

Hernandez wants a boy; they're going to keep trying. They're using all the modern techniques to ensure the next will be a boy. I ask him how he keeps his two wives from meeting. He says he knows where Maria is all the time, that Teresa knows about Maria, but Maria doesn't know about Teresa. I didn't think she would. Maria once caught him at a downtown intersection with another woman in his car. She had a gun with her. She started shooting. It cost Hernandez $100,000 to shut everyone up and pay for the damage to the car. I tell him I've been out to a discotheque. "Good, good," he says. "I'm glad to see you're beginning to have a little fun."

"I'm having a lot of fun, Hernandez," I answer. It's the first true statement I've made in days.

My enthusiasm stirs his, and he wants to talk about the 210 again. His friend Roberto, he explains, is already on his way to Colombia. He's picking up a load there and bringing it, some 400 kilos, to Puerto Rico on a boat. Then, if he gets in without a tail, we can fly over and pick it up and bring it to Miami.

Hernandez moves to the edge of his seat. "Maybe," he continues, "we should make this the big one, take it all ourselves. You know, I've never ripped anyone off," he tells me earnestly, "but this is the big one." He looks to me for a response, a confirmation. When I don't flinch, his eyes get larger and rounder. I can see his wheels spinning. "How about this? We land in Miami, but not on the strip where they're waiting for us. Then we crash the airplane, set it on fire." His finger soars upwards, highlighting his idea. "We could even kill the pi..." he begins. But he sees his mistake before the word is out and covers himself. "You know, take someone with us, knock him off, put him in the pilot's seat. Make it look like an accident." He reconsiders. "Well, we don't have to go quite so far, do we? Just as long as we can crash the airplane and burn it."

I phone Kane in the morning from a booth and tell him

Hernandez's new plan and how he slipped and let me know that he's considering killing the pilot. "Think he had anyone in particular in mind?" I ask.

"Wow, that's the best I've heard…and I've heard a lot," Kane responds. I figure he has. He's had me give him Hernandez's number at the trailer, so I know he's got it tapped as well as his portable phones. "I think you'd better get out of there," Kane goes on. "Find another place to stay. If Hernandez is caught there with something by another agency, there's not a lot I can do to get you out."

"You trying to tell me something?"

"Yeah, get out."

Exactly what I've been telling myself. I've seen Sal pull up in the car and Hernandez go out to him with a bag in his hand. I know there's plenty of drug activity going on right now from the trailer.

As it turns out, it's not too hard to remove myself. Since the fiasco at the airport, Miguel and Hernandez have been at odds. Hernandez has other plans, other things going on, but Miguel's sole source of income was dependent on this airplane delivering every 20 days. I go down to the bar where Miguel hangs out and find him crying in his double scotch. He bitches about Hernandez sufficiently for me to feel at ease about doing the same. I tell him I don't want to stay here anymore, that Hernandez has too many things going on and I'm afraid there'll be a bust. He chews on this for a minute. Then he says, "Hey, you want to come and stay at my place for a while? It's an apartment complex. It's got a pool and an exercise room and all kinds of good shit."

"Sure," I say.

We go to the hardware store and have a key made and then I follow him to his apartment in North Miami. There's nothing in it, not even a bed. On my way back to Hernandez's to collect my things, I stop at Service Merchandise and pick up a couple of air mattresses.

Hernandez is at the trailer when I arrive. I tell him I'm moving out, that of course I'm still going to work with him, but in the meantime, I need to be someplace where I can get a little exercise, a little swimming. I can see he's upset, but he doesn't say anything. When I return to the apartment, Miguel explains that he's on probation for some trouble he got into awhile back and that he has to be present at eight each morning to answer the phone and let the computer on the other end know he's in. Other than that, no one will disturb us. I figure his place is bugged too and not a lot safer than the trailer.

To celebrate our new status as roommates, Miguel takes me out to dinner at a fast-food Cuban joint. "Is this your idea of a good dinner?" I ask him when I get a look at the steak and fries I ordered. I promise to take him to a real restaurant, and the next night we go to Calico Jack's, a place I used to frequent in the old days. I run into a few people I used to know. I introduce Miguel, whose English is a lot worse than my Spanish, as a singer from Spain. The women in the group suddenly become alert. Had they known he was a Cuban who has only been here a year, they'd never even look at him. But a singer from Spain is another story. Miguel really gets off on our charade. He begins buying everyone drinks. Before we leave, he gets one of the women to give him her phone number.

We climb into his Grand National and set off for his apartment. We're flying down U.S. 1 and getting ready to make the turn by K-Mart onto 104th when a tree jumps out at us. The air gets knocked out of me. When I come to, I find I'm alone in the car. I remove my seatbelt and look at the deep gouge it made in my flesh. My shoulder is sore. I get out of the car and try to remember where I was headed before the accident. I'm a little drunk and very confused, and I can't come up with a thing. Some people pull up to ask if I'm hurt. I ask them what happened. The driver laughs. "Looks like you hit a tree," he says.

I walk across the street and head off into the trees and then into the maze of houses beyond them. I have no idea where I'm going. I climb a ridge and look down and see police cars everywhere. It takes me a moment to realize they're there for the accident. I go back through the trees and head toward K-Mart. I find some change in my pocket and call a cab from the booth there. Just as it arrives, a police car pulls up. The cop gets out and comes over to me saying, "You're from the car that hit the tree, aren't you?"

"I don't know anything," I respond.

I move to get into the cab, but the cop stops me. "You're coming with me," he says. "You're from the car. A security guard from across the street gave us your description."

I look across the street, at the car lot there. "Am I under arrest?"

"No"

"Well, then I don't want to go with you. I want to go in this cab."

"No, you have to come with me."

"Are you going to take me by force?"

"If I have to."

I reconsider. "Okay, fine. I'll go with you." I lean toward the cabby and tell him to follow us back to the scene of the accident. When we arrive, I tell the cop again that I don't know anything about it. But he has a muzzled dog there, and when it rushes over to me and sniffs, the cop tells me that I have just been identified as being from the car. He asks for my driver's license and I show it to him. Every time he asks me a question, I say, "I don't want to talk to you. I want to talk to my lawyer." A man appears and tells the cop I was not the driver, that it was some big fat guy who got out and walked into the bushes. The cop looks to me for confirmation. "I don't know anything," I say. "You'll have to talk to my lawyer."

They tell me to sit down on the curb and then they send the dog into the bushes to find Miguel. I figure he must be hurt pretty badly because he didn't have a seat belt on. But a few moments later I hear the dog whimpering, and I know Miguel must be beating on it. The cops go in and drag Miguel out. They put him in an ambulance and it takes him away. Then they write me up a ticket for not reporting the accident and let me get into the cab.

I go to Miguel's home and phone Hernandez. He appears in no time and reminds me that Miguel has to be back by eight to answer the phone. It is already 4:30. Hernandez gets right to work. I don't think it's so much that he cares about Miguel as it is that he can't afford to have an angry Miguel back in jail where he might be tempted to throw some names around so as to reduce his sentence. I lie down on my air-mattress and listen to Hernandez negotiate on his portable phone. He calls one bondsman after another. He's calling lawyers by the time I fall asleep, promising everyone lots of money. When I wake up in the morning, Miguel is there, bruised but otherwise intact, and Hernandez is gone.

Hernandez stays in touch. The 210 is just about ready and he wants to do this Puerto Rico job as soon as possible. I talk to Kane and let him know what's going on. He says one thing we can do to counter the killing-the-pilot idea is bust the airplane as soon as it lands. He's not happy about it, because in order to make a good bust you really should wait until the merchandise is transferred. I'm not too happy with it myself, because the way I see it, if the airplane is busted as soon as it lands, I'll be arrested along with Hernandez. He tells me not to worry, that with his weight it won't be difficult to extradite me to Canada and take care of it there. That way the Cubans will never learn about my part in it; they're not going to be checking the Canadian jails to see if I've gotten out. When I don't answer, he sighs. "But I should tell you, you don't have to do this. I would like you to, but I'm not going to force it. The plate number you gave me, it turned out to be concrete after all."

"Are you telling me I'm a free man?"

"I'm telling you that if you go ahead and do this, then there will be some money in it for you, a percentage of the value of whatever we confiscate."

The money part I like, but the rest of it remains a concern. In the meantime, the fighting between Miguel and Hernandez gets worse than ever, I suppose because Hernandez is pissed about having to lay out money to save Miguel's hide. And Miguel, who seemed happy enough about his income before the arguing began, begins to confide in me about the times that Hernandez paid him less than he was owed. I remind him that Hernandez did the same thing to me. He thinks it over. He says that maybe we can start our own thing without Hernandez. I tell him I don't see why not. After all, all we need is connections and a pilot. And he has the connections.

I get a call from Hernandez saying the airplane is now sky-worthy. I tell him I'd like to try it out before we take it over all that water to Puerto Rico, that Jenny's birthday is coming up and I'd like to go home. "Okay," he says, "Go ahead and take it up and see her. I'll send Jorge with you for company, and another man, Cid."

For all the work that's been done on it, the airplane isn't flying all that well. The motor isn't humming right and the lights on the dash aren't working at all. About halfway to our destination, I land at a small airport in North Carolina to see if I can get the lights working. I tell Jorge and Cid not to speak Spanish and to keep an eye out for men wearing raincoats. They were brave enough in Miami with all their Cuban friends a phone call away, but the further north we go, the more anxious they become. By the time we get to Connecticut and I set them up in a local hotel, they're already pestering me to make my visit short and get them the hell back.

That suits Jenny just fine. She's had it with my schemes by now. She doesn't understand why I can't just drop it, especially now that Eddy isn't calling the house anymore looking for me. I ask her to be patient, tell her that I have things very nearly wrapped up, that I need some kind of closure after everything that's happened to me.

We fly back down and I tell Hernandez the airplane has to have a new motor before we can risk taking it to Puerto Rico. He's not happy; a new motor will cost $17,000. But Jorge confirms that it was making strange noises and Hernandez promises to get on it. As soon as the motor is installed, I ask permission to use the airplane once more. I tell him Jenny and I parted angrily and that I want to patch things up before we do the Puerto Rico job. He says he understands. He adds that I was so prompt in getting back the last time that he's not even going to send anyone with me. I figure that means Jorge and Cid bitched about having to go along the first time. I take a deep breath and ask him to give me all the documents for the airplane. I'm prepared to explain that we took a risk the last time, that if there had been a ramp check we could have wound up in a lot of trouble. But my explanation is unnecessary. He hands the documents over.

I go to the apartment and tell Miguel I'll be away for a few days, that as soon as I get back, I'll tell Hernandez that I'm going to be working with him instead. Then I call my friend Sergio and ask him to come and pick up the Chevy from the airport once I'm gone. On the way to the airport, I stop again at the warehouse where Mario's friend José works. This time he's in and I catch him off guard. He backs away from me, but there's nowhere for him to run. "Look," I say, spreading out my hands. "I just want to know where Mario is, if he ever got back."

"No. He never came back. No one knows what happened to him. That's all I can tell you. Now get out of here. I don't want you here. You left him there. You're a bad man. You're trouble."

I fly the airplane up to Connecticut and land it at a local airport south of Danbury. When I push it into the parking slot, I feel my hernia breaking loose. It's been a long time since it bothered me.

Generally when it acts up, I ignore it. But now I need a good excuse to be here for a while. All for the better, I say to myself.

I'm no sooner in the door than the phone starts ringing. Miguel calls first, then Hernandez. It seems neither of them was completely certain that I was going where I said I was. I tell them about my hernia and that I think I need an operation. They both insist that I put it off. Hernandez wants me to go back down and get this job over with first. Miguel has talked to some people; he wants me to get right back and meet with them. Their indifference to my health pisses me off. I tell them I'm going to see a doctor and get a second opinion. And sure enough, the doctor I see wants to put me right into the hospital. I'm happy to go.

I spend one day in the hospital working out the final details of my scheme. Then Jenny takes pity on me and agrees to pick me up. On the way home she tells me Hernandez called to say that he was sending someone, Jorge, to see me. She also informs me that she's no longer willing to put up with my running back and forth between home and Miami, that it's over if I can't settle down. "You're lucky I have a heart," she says. "If not for the fact that you just had an operation, I'd probably call it quits right now."

"I'm a lucky man," I agree. I have to laugh at how lucky I am.

Since she doesn't comment, I begin to think about this new complication. If Jorge has been persuaded to come up, it can only be because Hernandez is suspicious. He's had some time now to think about the documents I asked for and to consider that the airplane is in my name. It would be just like him to send a pilot up with Jorge to bring the airplane back until I'm on my feet again. The airplane is parked in the same place where we parked it last time; Jorge would know just where to find it.

Every little bump in the road causes me excruciating pain. It's clear that I won't be able to fly the airplane by myself just yet. But I have a friend in Millbrook, New York, not far away, a man I trust who might be able to help me out. Bruno is an ex-Vietnam pilot who likes to fly low. He claims he gets a nosebleed whenever he goes over 3,000 feet, a result of all the low-level flying he did in Nam. When I get back to the house, I phone him, ask him if he'd like to do me a favor and move an airplane for me. "How famous is this airplane?" he asks.

I assure him he won't have any problem picking it up at the airport as long as he can get on it right away. I tell him where I've hidden the keys in the rear wheel wells. My abstruseness, I can tell, interests him. He says he's not going to tell me over the phone where he plans to take it. That's fine with me. I tell him it has a brand new motor and lots of fuel and that he should use it as much as he wants. I'm pleased with myself for having thought to call him. He's one of the best pilots I know, and other than my oldest brother, the only person I would trust with my airplane.

Jorge shows up at the house the next day. He says he came alone and took a cab from La Guardia. This volunteered information confirms that he's lying, that the pilot he brought with him is already out scouting the local airports. I can't help but think what a smart move it was to have Bruno take the airplane. Jorge relates that Hernandez is frantic about all the time I'm taking up here. I show him my incision. It's swollen and purple and very impressive. He gets Hernandez on the phone. "Yeah, it's true. He can't do anything. He can hardly walk. He's practically dead. Yeah, I saw the scar with my own eyes."

That night, after Jorge leaves for the hotel, the unexpected happens. I wake up in the middle of the night and see a wall of flame outside my window. The lumber yard behind the house is on fire! I wake up Jenny and we go running out into the street. The firemen arrive and stand around trying to determine the best way to proceed. In the meantime, the back garage, which is only 20 feet from the house, is burning and the tiles on the roof of the house are beginning to melt.

People appear, spectators who have come to watch the show. One of them helps me pull the hose out of the fire truck and get to work on the garage. I try to ignore the sensation that my stitches are ripping open. I'm soaked in no time. My feet, which are bare, are burning from the flames that have spread into the grass. When one of the firemen approaches, I hand him the hose and say, "Look, you take over." I'm doubled over in pain, watching the firemen finish up the job, when Hernandez's words come back to me again. All for the better. I begin to see that I might be able to turn this calamity to my advantage. I decide to sleep on it.

I call Jorge at his hotel first thing in the morning. "Who started the fire?" I shout into the phone.

He comes by to have a look. While we survey the damage, I tell him I heard a Molotov cocktail go off in the middle of the night. I act like I'm pissed as hell. "Someone started a fire here," I yell. "Someone assumed by the time I noticed, my house would have gone up. You know Miguel and Hernandez have been at war. Both of them want me to work with them. One of them had someone start this thing so that I wouldn't work with the other."

"I'll be here for the weekend," Jorge informs me. "I plan to visit some friends in the city. I'll stay with them until you're well enough to travel. Then we'll take the airplane back to Miami and talk to Hernandez and Miguel and see…"

"You go find out who did it. You find out who's trying to scare me. I'm not going back until this is cleared up."

"What will you do in the meantime?"

"I'm getting out of here. I have to get out. Jenny is throwing me out. She's sick of this shit! But I'm not going back to Miami until you find out what's going on."

I can see Jorge struggling to come up with some reason why I have to go right back to Miami. But the lumber yard is in cinders now and the garage looks like hell and there isn't much he can say. I sigh and roll my head in disgust and finally tell him what he wants to hear, that I'll stick around for a few days, if Jenny will even let me, and give him some time to find out exactly what happened. I drive him back to his hotel so that he can make his calls, but then instead of going home, I stop at a booth and phone Bruno. Then I phone Jenny to let her know where I'm leaving her car, and that I'll be gone for a few days. She tells me not to bother coming back, that she's had it with me and my disappearing acts and all the bad people I'm hanging around with. I tell her that I love her, that it's almost over, that she has to trust me because I love her and only her and that's forever. She hangs up the phone.

Bruno picks me up. While we're driving, I explain that I have to sell the airplane right away. He seems to understand that now is not the time for questions. He tells me that California is the only place where airplanes are moving lately. I have $1500 in my pocket and friends in San Diego. It seems like a good idea. We arrive at the grassy strip in the middle of nowhere where the airplane is waiting. Bruno tells me how much he enjoyed flying it and wishes me luck.

In San Diego I go through my *Trade-A-Plane*, call all the people in the region who are looking to buy. I find an interested party in Phoenix. When I tell him the price, $45,000, and that the airplane has a new $17,000 motor, he commits himself to the purchase right over the phone. But when I fly over to make the transaction, the cashier's check he gives me is for $42,000. Nice to be doing business with the honest public again. We stand around looking at one another, the guy who wants the airplane, his buddy, and me. The paint is so bad, the interior is bad, they say, and they can see that the airplane has been crashed before. I can only shake my head. The sons of bitches must know the airplane is a gift. Its book value is $65,000. But what the hell. I take the check and fly back to San Diego on an airliner to wait until the check clears.

A few days later, after I've been to the bank and the post office, I take a cab to the airport and phone home.

Jenny informs me that I've had lots of phone calls, from Jorge and Miguel and Hernandez. She says she told them all the same thing, the truth, that she didn't know where I was, that she cared less, and that she was recording their calls and that if they didn't stop bothering her she was going to send the recordings to the CIA and the FBI and the DEA and anyone else she could think of. In the last 24 hours, no one has called at all. It won't be necessary for me to check in with her again.

I wait patiently until she's done screaming. Then I tell her why I called. To the best of my knowledge, I have satisfied my obligation with Kane; I have recovered the rest of the money Hernandez stole from me, plus expenses, the bulk of which I'm sending along to her; and if she'll give me a little more time, a mere two weeks, I'll be home for good.

"I have a life here," she responds angrily. "I've allowed you to disrupt it since you got back from South America. I can't just keep giving you more and more time."

"Just two weeks, Jenny," I plead. "That's all I ask for. Two more weeks. No more."

"Go then. Do what you have to do. When you get back, call me. I'll let you know whether you can come home or not."

Her tone is still angry. "Aren't you even a little curious about what I need the time for?" I ask.

There's silence for a moment. Then she sighs. "I know what you need time for, Alan." Her voice is soft now, nearly loving. "Mario, right? I know you better than you think I do. You're going to go and get a passport and fly to Colombia and try to find him. I wish you luck. I can't see how you'll do it in two weeks. I can't see how you'll do it at all. But go ahead and try. I'll give you two weeks. That's all I can give you. I'm not a saint."

"You are a saint," I whisper. "And I'm a lucky man." And because I'm lucky, and maybe smart too, I know in that moment that I will find Mario.